THE APRIC

Firelight in the Dark is dedicated to every single reader who read through the entire Apricity series.

This book is out of control.

See you on Goodreads.

Book cover photo and character illustrations by Amelia L. Carter
www.meialoue.com

Novel content, book design, cover design, typesetting, and manuscript editing by Mariah L. Stevens
www.starlightwriting.com

This is a work of semi-autobiographical fiction. It was taken from multiple separate experiences in the author's life and compiled into one narrative.

Some characters, places, and incidents are from real pieces of the author's personal life. All names are fictitious. Some characters, places, and incidents either are the product of the author's imagination or are used fictitiously. Some resemblance to actual persons, living or dead, events, or locales is inevitable yet coincidental. Any musical personality mentioned is real.

Novel Copyright © 2021 by Mariah Lynn Stevens
Cover Photo Copyright © 2021 by Amelia Louise Carter

All rights reserved. No part of this book may be reproduced or used in any manner without written permission of the copyright owner except for the use of quotations in a book review. For more information, e-mail:
starlightxwriting@gmail.com

First paperback edition February 2021
ISBN-13: 9798411837803 (paperback)

TRIGGER WARNINGS

If you choose to read this trigger warning page, unfortunately it will spoil a bit! So be mindful and aware before you read the warnings.

This trigger warning is a blanket warning for the entire Apricity series.

If you are a minor reading this book, please understand that it is an 18+ book, as is the entire Apricity series. The characters are age 19-20. They are not minors.

The Apricity series contains trigger warnings for:

Sexual assault/rape *(Book One – Chapter Eighteen: pg. 240-244. Do not skip page 245 and onward unless you want to miss an important plot point.)*

Emotional and mental abuse

Eating disorders *(heavy, graphic ED content throughout Books Three & Four)*

Toxic relationships

Mentions of racism/discussions about race *(extreme trigger warning for excerpt at back of this book).*

Religious themes and absence of faith *(specifically Christianity)*

Mention of suicide *(Book Four – Chapters 11 – 13)*

Adult content warnings:

Marijuana and drug use

Sexual content

Foul language

Things the author ensures:

Author's personal experience with all content

Tasteful descriptions of content

The end goal of recovery *(no matter how toxic the relationship gets, the end goal is recovery. The point of the Apricity series is to show the dark side of trauma and why the only solution is recovery and medical help.)*

THIS BOOK SERIES IS WRITTEN FROM THE MALE CHARACTER'S POV FOR A SPECIFIC REASON

This is to showcase the eating disorder and the way it affects the people who exist outside of the eating disordered individual's experience. It showcases how eating disorders affect those around you, and what happens when someone takes it upon themselves to "fix" something that can only be healed through medical intervention and recovery. It has nothing to do with race or skin color, though those things as well as the "white savior trope" are tackled in this novel.

This is a graphic depiction of struggles that the author has faced, presented in a way that can help others seek the first step towards recovery. The author has written this story according to her personal experiences with rape/sexual assault, a 10-year long battle with Bulimia, and a 4-year long abusive relationship, however the narrative itself is done to tell a story for the characters.

For example, the author's sexual assaults were not under the same circumstances as the main character, however the author has still written completely accurate to physicality, emotional turmoil, trauma, and thoughts.

This novel as well as the Apricity Series is written by a Black author to provide representation and healing for other survivors of both sexual assault and eating disorders. While it does have an overarching plot, this series is meant to encourage taking the first step to recovery to save your life. And while the main character is also a Black woman, it is not a novel meant to exploit Black trauma.

The Apricity Series takes a pro-recovery stance.

There is no sugar-coating and there is no pretending that things like abuse, racism, and trauma do not exist.

If you complete reading of this novel and feel that a trigger warning is missing from the page, e-mail the author at starlightxwriting@gmail.com to notify her, and she will add it to subsequent novels in the series.

AAVE IS NOT GEN Z SPEAK

African-American Vernacular English is not Gen Z speak. It is a cultural dialect spoken by Black people — including the author — and has significant importance to our community.

When you see phrases and words like "no cap," "finna," "ain't," "bruh," "bae," "woke," used in the context that they are in my novels, it is through the usage of AAVE. Calling it "Gen Z speak" or a product of Generation Z is incorrect and disrespectful to the Black community.

It is my culture.

THE APRICITY SERIES

FIRELIGHT
in the Dark

BOOK FOUR

written by MARIAH LYNN STEVENS

illustrations by AMELIA LOUISE CARTER

CHAPTER ONE

The stars had swallowed his sun and now, Ash burned.

Flames devoured, consuming the light within him to heat the landscape of his body to a blazing inferno that could tear itself apart. Raging storms consumed him, eradicating air and filling the space with smoke. What pieces of his soul remained after his mother breathed her last breath were Tayshia's to use for kindling. What embers lay dying after his father betrayed him were hers to ignite so she could incinerate him.

There was no room in his lungs to scream. They were blackened to a crisp, splintered with cracks that scorched his spirit. The only air the cosmos saw fit to grant him was Tayshia's. She breathed in the stars. Fire danced in his exhalation of starlight.

If there was a moon, the smoke of his charred heart was too thick to see it.

Tick tock.

The clock in the probation office had grown to become the bane of his existence since June of the previous year. It was one of those old clocks that elementary school teachers always had hanging high above the whiteboard, and it ticked, and it tocked. So loud that it grated on Ash's nerves.

The door swung shut behind him with a loud *click*. The entry room looked typical for any sort of office building, with eight or so chairs, end tables adorned with bowls of candy, and a front desk complete with a typing secretary.

She sat with her back straight in her swivel chair, acrylic nails tapping at the keys. They flew across the keyboard at a pace that Ash could neither match nor fathom.

"Hello, Ash," she said in the sort of amused tone that a girl might have when she's pretending not to have a crush on the class flirt.

"Kenzie," he replied in the same tone, a smirk playing about his lips that was as much a mask as it was playing the role of who he used to be. "I'm here for my appointment."

"Obviously. Not like you're here to shoot the shit. Hang on a sec. Finishing an e-mail."

Ash stood there with his hands slipped into the back pockets of his skinny jeans while Kenzie tap, tap, tapped the keys. He rolled his neck until it cracked, offering him a tiny amount of stress relief.

That morning, he'd nearly wanted to call a mental hospital and have them wing Tayshia in there.

It was a Saturday—the last one of January—and he'd had two hours of sleep. He'd woken to find her categorizing the fridge. Fruits and vegetables by color, packaged items in alphabetical order, drinks by height. She didn't say anything when he entered, like she didn't care if he saw.

On its own, organizing the fridge wasn't that big of a deal. But when she finished and didn't get up, instead starting to take everything out again, he understood.

She started caring about his presence when he grabbed her by the waist, hauled her to her feet, and dropped her kicking and screaming onto the couch. He'd had to grab her wrists and pin them to get her to stop slapping at him and when he'd looked into her eyes, he saw a measure of terror there that could only be connected to Paris.

No matter how angry he was with her, he would always hate that man more.

The first two times she'd had one of her meltdowns had terrified him. Both were his fault. He could still remember that first time it happened, in the kitchen, when he'd boxed her in after they argued over the dishes. Then the second time, when her parents showed up at the apartment.

And now, here was the third time. He was grabbing her body and lifting her, pinning her down and restraining her. He'd never hurt her like that, but when she had a meltdown, it was like nothing and no one could get through to her. She was no longer in her body, no longer human, no longer Tayshia. The way she'd looked up at him, so animalistic and afraid and furious?

He'd left the house immediately and sat in his car for three hours before his eleven-o-clock appointment.

Tick tock.

Kenzie was a slight little thing, with bleached blonde hair, blue eyes, and arms covered in tattoos. She was just as old as Ash and had the same energy about her—a deadpan air of acceptance that enabled her to hide behind a mask of indifference.

Over the summer, she was one of the girls he matched with on the dating app.

She still liked to give him the flirty eyes and smirk she always had, but neither of them had ever brought up the fact that they could have hooked up. They simply greeted each other at his monthly probation appointments, two passing ferries in the night.

"Did you stop and do your drug test before you came up the stairs?"

Ash nodded.

"You're lucky your judge lets you use recreational marijuana. You know I can smell the weed on you, right?" Kenzie said with her drawn-in eyebrows risen, running her tongue across her teeth. Ash knew she had a smiley piercing and that it bothered her sometimes. "There's a few judges here in Crystal Springs who just *love* putting y'all back in for that."

"Maybe he felt bad for me."

"Why?"

"Because my mom's dead," Ash replied, his tone flat. "Died at my trial."

Silence.

"You are literally one of *the* most asshole guys I've ever met, Ash." She waved a dismissive hand, rolling her eyes and returning to her typing. "Sit down and I'll tell him you're here."

Tick tock.

Ash slouched in his seat, stretching his long legs out. He put one foot flat on the floor so he could bounce his knee anxiously while he waited.

Crossing his arms over his chest, he tipped his head back against the wall and stared at the window. It was blurry with late January frost, crystals of it gathering white on the edges of the windowpanes. If it weren't for that infernal clock, he might find it peaceful, just gazing out at the grey sky and listening to the keys on Kenzie's keyboard clicking away.

His stomach curdled and churned. He hated this. Hated being in an office that was meant for bad people—for criminals and offenders and people who hurt other people intentionally. He didn't want to be thrown together with people like this.

Tick —

"Betrand? Ash Robards is here. He's early."

"Oh, good." Officer Cook's voice wafted out from the unusually loud speaker. "Send him on in. Better early than never."

Kenzie set the phone back in the cradle, offering Ash a smile. "He says he'll see you now."

As much as Ash wanted to snark at her that he was sure that the entire building heard him, he simply returned her smile with a half-one of his own and headed down the hall.

Officer Cook's office was large enough, with bookshelves and accolades hanging on the wall. There were medals and awards and honors from before his retirement, displayed sporadically amongst countless pictures of his wife, kids, and grandchildren. The entire room smelled like apple cinnamon, the scent coming from a wax warmer perched on the windowsill behind his desk.

Officer Cook was a man of short stature, robust nature, and warm disposition. He had the sort of white skin that turned as red as a beet no matter the weather or level of exertion. He liked to wear three-piece suits every time Ash saw him, and he seemed to maintain a smile regardless of the circumstances of the conversation. It lay perpetually hidden behind his frost-white mustache, which reached from one side of his chin to the other like an arch. He possessed the sort of eyes that sunk into his face, peeking out at everything from beneath folds of wrinkled skin. They twinkled when he was *really* in a good mood.

It didn't matter what mood he was in, though, because he was always seated in that same position: with his meaty hands intertwined on his desk amongst a mess of paperwork and stationery.

"Well, well, well," Officer Cook said in the deep, gruff voice of his. "Look what the cat dragged in. Take a seat, young man. And shut the door to my cave — you're lettin' all the light in."

Ash's face relaxed into one of those awkward smiles that one gives when an older person speaks in idioms and closed the door behind him. Once they were shut in with the apple cinnamon aroma and the sound of country music playing faintly on Officer Cook's stereo, Ash took a seat at the soft cushioned chair in front of his desk.

"So, Ash," Officer Cook said, still with that same trademark smile, "Whacha been gettin' into? Stayin' out of trouble?"

Which should he tell him first?

That he was living with a girl he just fucked in the backseat of his car after nearly killing them both by speeding on the freeway a week ago? That he was on the verge of hatred with her, toeing the line between rage and giving up on her entirely with each day that he had to fight to get her to eat? That he cared about her so much more than was healthy? That she'd manipulated him for so long it made him sick?

"Yeah," he said.

"That sounds like a pretty loaded *'yeah.'* You got anything you need to talk about?"

Ash shook his head.

"Well, let's get the crap out of the way," Officer Cook said with a sigh, shifting some papers so he could withdraw Ash's file from beneath them. He opened the manila folder while he wrote the date and Ash's name on the top of an official check-in form. "Do you have your check for this month's payment of your fines?"

Ash ran a hand through his hair, reaching into the pocket of his hoodie and withdrawing the check he'd filled out in the car. He slid it across the desk to the officer.

God, why was he so *nervous*? Officer Cook was nice. He liked him. And this wasn't the first probation appointment.

"You got a ways to go." Officer Cook fixed him with a stern eye. "Don't you go missin' a single one. I don't wanna see them throw you back in jail because you forgot to write a check."

"Right." Ash breathed a laugh to hide the fact that his heart had begun to knock on the wall of his chest.

"All right, let's pull up the warrant check on ya. I ran it before you got here but didn't look at it yet." While still writing with his right hand, the officer used his left hand to move the mouse on his computer. He typed slowly with one hand, talking to himself under his breath. "Okay, here we go. It's loadin'. And here we go… Nothin'. That's good. Just make sure you keep it up. I don't wanna find out you got pulled over for—for drunk drivin' or something stupid."

For a moment, Ash felt panicky over the fact that he'd been pulled over before Christmas, but then he remembered he'd seen Officer Cook right after that and everything was fine.

"All right, crap's over with." Officer Cook crossed a T and dotted and I on the form, and then moved to the large white box on the page. "Time to tell me about how things are going."

Ash grimaced. "My grades are bad."

"I know." Officer Cook frowned while writing it down. "Your school faxed the report over today. Any reason for that?"

Yeah, my life is a fucking mess.

"No, I just have some trouble sleeping. I forget to do my homework, too."

"Well, you got to work on that. All you have to do to follow the rules and stay out of trouble is focus on school. That's it." Officer Cook gesticulated with his hand. "Just focus on school. Get good grades, graduate, stick around until probation is up, and head off into the sun to some college or another."

In the beginning, Ash hadn't been able to understand why the probation office would require his school to send in his monthly progress report, but now that he'd met Officer Cook and heard directly from the judge who set the terms of his probation himself, they both just wanted rehabilitation for him. In their minds, school was the answer. The best chance he had at a future with the hand of cards he'd been dealt.

And he was fucking it up.

"I know," he said, the words coming out in a mumble of shame. "I did good fall term, but I've been…Stressed out recently."

Between Tayshia's problems, getting jumped by Kieran, jumping Kieran back, finding the gun, getting accosted by the two members of Ricky's gang after the concert, and then throwing a weapon into the Pacific Ocean?

Yeah, he was stressed.

"And you did *really* good while you were still in jail. You've only got three terms left, Ash. Then you get to graduate. I'm tellin' ya—do *not* drop the ball."

"I won't. I mean, I'm not. I'll work on it."

"Make sure you do." The officer finished writing everything down and then said, "How are you handling things with your family situation?"

"Uh, well…I reconnected with my godparents for Christmas," Ash said. "That was okay."

"Oh!" Officer Cook said with a large smile and an appreciative tone. "That's great, Ash. So you had a good Christmas?"

Ash nodded, running a hand through his hair again.

"That's *really* great to hear. We had the same Christmas we always have. The entire family heads on over to Lake Michigan. We got a lake house out there. We did the whole shebang: tree, presents, food. Even some ice skating. You know how that lake freezes this time of year."

"I've never been there," Ash said. He could almost see himself there, holding Tayshia's hands as they both stumbled over the ice. Perhaps he'd get to see her smile reach her eyes then. "Maybe someday, though."

"And your father? Have you spoken to him?"

In seconds, Ash's lifting mood crashed back down to Hell.

"No."

"Are his letters not getting to you? I know you said he sends letters. I can make a call and figure out if there's some way to—"

"No, I don't want to speak to him." Ash clenched his jaw for a moment to alleviate the tension in his body. "It's okay."

Officer Cook held his gaze for a moment, one that was so drawn out that Ash started to get antsy. Then, when he thought he might simply keel over and die, the probation office reached over to a pad of small blank papers. He peeled one off, grabbed a pen out of a cup beside his computer monitor, and scrawled something down.

"I know this might be overseppin' a bit, but I wouldn't be able to sit still if I knew I didn't try to do somethin' to help." He held the paper out to Ash, who took it and looked down at the solid, bold handwriting. "That's the number to my family therapist. Me, my wife, my kids, and my grandkids all see her. You've been through a lot, Ash. I wouldn't want to see you fail school and end up back in jail because you needed someone to talk to."

Ash frowned, his brows gathering as he read the phone number over and over.

A therapist?

He didn't *need* a therapist. He needed a miracle. He needed someone to grab Tayshia by the hair and yank the eating disorder out of her throat so she could breathe. Because if she could breathe, then he could finally rest. He hadn't had a full night's sleep all week, his self-imposed vigilance as he listened for the door to her bedroom or the bathroom to open until the darkness faded to early morning, keeping him from knowing peace.

He just wanted to sleep.

"Thanks, Officer Cook."

"Do you promise to call her?"

At this point, he would rather die.

"Yeah."

"Good. Well, I'm gonna let you go now. I'll make sure this check gets to where it needs to go, and I'll finish writing up your monthly report. And we'll see you next month?"

Ash nodded and stood to leave.

"That's a nice necklace, by the way, Ash. You get that from Crystal Springs Caverns? My wife and I went there last summer. Can you believe it? Thirty-five years in this town, and we'd never been to the caverns. I tell ya."

Ash looked down at the necklace, memories of his dreams with Tayshia flashing by as fast and as fleeting as happiness seemed to be for him. What had sometimes felt so beautiful now felt like rot. Like the cracks in the faces of the crystal were filled with poison.

It wasn't like Tayshia wore hers.

"Yeah," he said softly. "I did. But it wasn't a necklace."

"Really?"

He closed his hand around the sharp edges of the amethyst, lowering his gaze to the floor where he imagined he could see the outline of his mother's haunted smile traced in the whorls and lines of the hardwood floor. "My mom turned it into one."

"That's very nice, Ash," Officer Cook said in *that* tone. The one that people used with him whenever they found out his mother was dead. "Anyway, see you next month, Ash." He pointed at him and raised his bushy white eyebrows. "Get those grades up."

CHAPTER TWO

Winter term was underway, with Ash's schedule weighing just as heavily as the previous term. He had classes all day, starting at nine in the morning. He would arrive home after Tayshia, who was repeating her previous term because her final grades for fall were so bad. The classes Ash was taking were all simple: literature, an introductory art history class, another math class, a gender studies class, and a personal elective: nutrition.

The week had passed just as tensely as he figured it would. After what happened in the Gianni's parking lot — after she admitted what she'd done — they'd barely said a word to each other that didn't drip with acid and wrap itself with barbed wire. It was impossible to talk to her without her snapping at him in a curt tone, inciting his own ire so that he snapped back.

Then, they yelled.

They yelled about everything. From the tone of voice she used to the expressions on her face. From the way he put too much food on her plate to the way he crowded her in the kitchen. It was the dishes and the clothes on the floor and the fact that she locked the bathroom door when she took two-hour showers. It was the blinds being too open when she had a headache from dehydration. It was the fact that she kept stacking dishes in her room for her stupid fucking binges and bringing them out days later when he couldn't find a single bowl in the cupboards to eat from.

It was Hell.

Her anger was painful, cutting so deep that he felt like his heart was bleeding out in the cavity of his chest. It drowned him in a sadness that filled every inch of his body with cold. Cold seeped into his veins, dripping icicles from his heart and turning his organs to stone. When he tried to think of their happy moments, he couldn't remember them. He didn't have the energy to make new ones.

He wished she would stop.

On school days, Ash insisted he drive her there in the mornings so he could make sure she didn't try to purge before they left. With the way he hardly slept, he didn't think she'd had much opportunity to do it since that day at Gianni's. And even when they fought and her voice was tipped in venomous barbs, he could sense a fear lingering below the surface. Fear caused by the ominous way he'd said, *"I'm weak. I'm fucking soft for you. For you, Tayshia. But you haven't seen toxic yet."*

She feared him.

The car rides to school were silent save for the music he let blast out of the speakers. It was the only bit of peace they seemed to get from each other during the day. He cherished that peace and wished he could ask her if she felt the same sadness he felt. But she didn't wear her necklace anymore, so he didn't think she missed him at all.

It was the only time he could remember the happiest memory he had with her. The moment they'd shared all those months ago, when they held hands in the store for the first time and he kissed her in front of Kieran and Quinn.

"Come here, sweet girl."

It felt like smoke now, drifting away from a house that burned.

They fell into this somber routine without preamble, as though they'd been on the frozen ice of Lake Michigan just a few weeks too early. Driving in silence to school, going their separate ways for class without so much as a good-bye, her taking the school shuttle, and then him coming home to fight with her for the rest of the night. Ash lying awake with his ear turned to the door, listening.

This exhausting, sad, maddening purgatory would last forever.

Until the last day of the month.

January 31st. A Wednesday. A day so cold that his fingertips had gone numb in his car even with the heat blasting on his way home from school. So cold that a slight exhale of breath would cloud the air and hover there, frozen in space.

That was the day Ash snapped.

He'd just gotten home from stopping at the store, his thoughts quiet for once at the end of a relatively uneventful day. He was looking forward to putting some of the firewood he'd just bought into the fireplace so he could warm the apartment up faster than the heater could. If he was cold, Tayshia had to be hypothermic.

He'd entered the apartment with snow clinging to his hair, a cold nose, and a bit of a sniffle to see that the bathroom door was wide open.

She was there, on her knees before the toilet, with vomit rolling down her fingers, the side of her hand, and the bottom of her forearm. It was smeared on her chin, just like the last time he'd caught her purging. Only this time, he wasn't immobilized by a state of shock. This time, he knew what he'd lost the patience for.

This time, he knew exactly what he was going to do.

He dropped the firewood on the floor in his haste and stormed down the hall, mind racing with conjectures. She had to have rushed in there and fallen to her knees when she realized he wasn't going to be home on time. She must have been trying to take the opportunity as it came. She must have thought that there was no chance he would suddenly return. She'd left the door open.

"Do you have *no* sense of fucking self-preservation, Tayshia?" he said, snarling the words out with a curled upper lip as he came to a stop in front of the open doorway. The smell wasn't as rancid as he thought, showing him she must have scarfed the food down and immediately ran to get rid of it. This was not a planned situation.

Tayshia, looking drawn and almost chagrined, started to stand.

"No, it's okay," Ash said, crossing his arms and leaning against the doorframe. "You can finish."

She stared up at him, face and fingers dripping, a look of pure horror twisting her facial expression. Her voice sounded somewhere between hoarse and a croak. "What?"

"You heard me. Go ahead and finish."

"*No!*" she cried, her hand smearing her vomit along the seat of the toilet as she pushed herself to her feet. She stumbled to the sink, where she reached for the handle on the faucet with her clean hand.

Ash's anger flared, pushing him forward to cover that clean hand with his own.

"I said *finish*."

"I'm not doing it in front of you!" she shrieked, trying to turn the handle beneath his grip. "Are you *insane*? I could be peeing or getting ready to shower, and you want me to just *do it in front of you*?!"

"I don't care," he snarled, squeezing her hand. "This is my home, and I have the right to know what's going on inside it. When you decided to purge, you gave up the right to privacy while you're here. From now on? Door stays open."

She looked him up and down, revolted. "What the *fuck* is wrong with you? You used to—"

"What? I used to *what*, Tayshia?"

He ripped her hand away from the handle and then turned it himself. Glaring at her, he stuck his hand into the water. Before she realized what was happening, his left hand was around the back of her neck, shoving her towards the sink. His right hand, full of cold water, rubbed the vomit off of the lower half of her face. He yanked her hand into the water stream and cleaned it, too. As he did, he continued to rant.

"I used to be your little servant, letting you manipulate me into letting you have free rein to destroy yourself as you please. You had soft, marshmallow, *teddy bear* Ash Robards, and all you had to do was bat your eyelashes and cry a little. Take advantage of him. He'll just let you waste away to *nothing*!"

She looked terrified, but she was Tayshia Cole. She wasn't going to back down. With water dripping from her now-clean face, she whirled on him. She struck his cheek with the full force of her body. It hurt, but he didn't care.

What was left to care about?

"This apartment is *ours*!" she cried. "It's *both* of ours, and I have a right to privacy when I'm using the bathroom."

"Not if you're in here killing yourself." He let out a bitter laugh, shaking his head. "Not if I'm the one who has to clean up your fucking body. No, this apartment is mine. This bathroom is mine. *You* are as good as *mine*. And if I tell you to leave the *fucking* door open, then I mean it."

Her jaw hung agape in the wake of his fiery tirade, any words she might have had left in her arsenal having been eradicated in flame. Eyes wide and terrified, she took a step back, further into the small bathroom.

"So get on your fucking knees and finish," he snarled, somewhat breathless, as he pointed at the toilet. It looked as disgusting as he felt inside.

"This is wrong. This is *wrong*, and I'm not doing it."

"Then you're not doing this ever again. Because that's the thing, little girl. I'm not enabling you anymore. I'm not letting you use me. I'm not letting you manipulate me. So, you can either purge in front of me, or you can stop. For good."

"It doesn't work that way."

"And I don't give a fuck."

An impasse.

Ash knew that all it would take was the shedding of his anger to break down. To gather her up in his arms and apologize. To make it all better. He could kiss her like he used to, until her tears dried and the tension was gone.

But he could see it painted in the lines of her face like unrestored Renaissance art, with cracks running through the breadth of her strong disposition. That burning, molten tension increased, spreading like wildfire that ripped across a California forest. He saw resignation behind the rage in her eyes as she reached up to pull her curls into a tighter bun than the one she'd already pulled them into.

"Fine, Ash. All right. You wanna tell me what to do and take away the only thing that makes me happy? You want all the control? I'll give it to you."

Ash watched as Tayshia turned to face the toilet. She bent at the waist, stuck the three forefingers of her right hand down her throat, and retched. She retched again. And again. The food came up, just as they both knew it would. Her jaw stretched open. Her eyes were flat, as dead as he felt inside. It was messy. The smell was pungent and acrid. It was grotesque.

This was what his mother had done to herself. This was what had killed her.

And he was standing there, watching it happen all over again.

When she was done, she stood up straight. An almost euphoric look passed across her face as she staggered to the side, crashing into the open door. A shudder ran through her body that caused Ash's muscles to tense, his fingers to twitch. If only he could go to her. If only he could find a way to quell the flames of their hatred and bring them back to the field of gardenias in his dreams. Whereas his neck hung heavy with amethyst, her throat was as barren as the tundra.

She swayed forward to the sink and cleaned herself up. The silence felt horrifically thick, blanketing Ash with the realization that they'd crossed a line that there would be no coming back from. He'd wrapped ropes around them, tying them both to a stake. With the image of her porcelain worship burned into his mind, he had ignited the tinder that had gathered at their feet.

They were going to burn.

"If you're going to purge," he said in a soft voice, one that barely contained the flames of his storm, "you do it with *my* bathroom door open."

She glared at him for as long as it took for him to blink three times, and then she shoved her way past him towards her bedroom. Before her door could close, Ash—who still faced the bathroom—looked over his shoulder at her. He narrowed his eyes, his challenging gaze pinning her in place with her hand on the doorknob.

"The rules have changed, Tayshia. Don't like it? Then you can cry about it."

✵✵✵

He made pasta for dinner and told her to sit at the table with him. She sat, stubborn, on the couch through two instances of his stern utterance of her name, and then he came to stand in front of her.

Tayshia, whose arms were folded and feet were on the floor, glared past him at the sliding glass door. She was wearing one of his hoodies over his joggers, trying to keep warm because the apartment heating system and the crackling warmth of the fire in the fireplace weren't enough. The fact that she was wearing his clothes was ironic, given that they'd just argued an hour ago.

"I said, it's time to eat," Ash bit out. "It wasn't rhetorical."

"Make all the requests of me that you want to. I'm not hungry."

He dragged a hand down his face. "I don't have the energy for games, Tayshia. Get up off the couch and come to the table to eat."

"Why don't you drag me over there by the ear, dad?"

"I'm nothing like your fucking father."

"No, you're not." Her eyes glittered as she fixed him with a malicious gaze from beneath the kinky curls of her natural hair. "But you're a lot like yours."

He was quick, in that moment, to remember that she was not someone that he would emotionally survive throttling.

Everything she said hurt him lately—more so than even before. It was like there was a demon living inside of her body, lounging about while it devoured her sanity and heart and left her empty. And with that emptiness came darkness. Darkness that she left trailing in her wake, that she used to spit that vitriol right up at him.

He couldn't remember why he'd ever liked her.

Ash steepled his tattooed fingers together, letting his eyelids fall shut as he regained his composure.

"Tayshia," he said carefully, slowly, and with a voice clear of anger. "Please come eat."

"Nope."

The clarity grew thick with smoke from the fires of rage that had been building within him since that morning's argument.

He moved with a speed so quick, she couldn't possibly have seen it coming. He wrapped his hand around her wrist and dragged her to her feet. Gripping her left ear, he twisted hard enough to make her squeak. Without a word, he dragged her over to the table, ignoring her cry of pain as he did so. His other hand was used to drag the empty chair out, and then he practically threw her into it. He put his right hand on the back to use as a handhold as he leaned down close to her.

"If you get up from this seat, you're fucked. Eat."

It was definitely more Earth-shattering for her than it was for him, with the way she glared at her full plate as though it were the problem. He then took his seat adjacent to her, picked up his fork, and began to spear his pasta noodles. His crystal felt too heavy around his neck.

He really should take it off.

"You're a jerk," Tayshia hissed, her hands in fists on her lap.

"Making sure you eat is a full-time job." He stopped to take a bite.

"This wasn't in the rules. You never said I had to eat on a schedule, with you, or at the table."

"Fuck those rules." His icy gaze snapped to meet hers. "I made some new ones. Start eating."

She didn't move.

"Are you trying to make this more difficult? I'm not kidding. Pick up your fork and eat."

Tayshia did so with shaking, begrudging fingers. They were violent and tremulous as the fork slid into the noodles and meat, picking up enough for a small bite. He wanted to tell her to take more, but he knew she'd dig her heels in even more.

His hawklike gaze remained on her while he chewed his own food, until the fork was placed into her mouth. She chewed, her jaw moving up and down at a speed that was too slow to be considered average. Her brows knitted together in what seemed to be pain, and she whined behind her closed lips, stamping her foot under the table.

"I don't care," Ash said like he'd read her mind, shaking his head. "Let's go. Take another one."

"But I don't want to do this."

"Like I said—I don't *give* a *fuck*." He took another bite of his own food, his eyebrows raised. "Keep going."

Her head tipped back in what he could only describe as anguish.

She picked up another bite and brought it to her mouth.

As they ate — her with a trembling hand and agonizing, slow bites — he mulled over the things he planned on saying to her over this horrible dinner. He'd thought about it all evening and had come to the conclusion that they were both at fault for the broken, mangled state of their situationship.

He'd betrayed her by telling Kieran what happened in Paris, which was not his secret to tell and a violation of her trust, body, and privacy. She'd betrayed him by manipulating his feelings for her to get him to buy her binge food, therefore making him an unwilling accomplice in what was sure to be her eventual death..

He needed to do what he should have done all along.

Put his foot down.

"First new rule is—"

"*New rules?*" she screeched. "I don't want new rules! The other ones are fine, Ash!"

"...First new rule is that you're gonna eat breakfast, lunch, and dinner. You're gonna eat them," he said, his fork loud on the porcelain plate as he speared more pasta with it, "and you're gonna sit with me. Whether we're at home or at school."

"I'm not doing it," she shot back, her tone sing-song. "You can't make me."

"Test me, Tayshia. Go ahead and test me. See what happens. Pick up that fork."

She didn't move.

"Pick up that fucking fork, little girl, or I'm going to shove your dinner down your throat."

The horror mingling with the hatred in her eyes hurt. But he forced himself not to care — to turn his emotions off. He couldn't let himself feel anything when it came to this. Not anymore.

"You wouldn't *dare*," she whispered.

"I would, and I will."

"Ash, force-feeding me? Really? That's *literally* a form of torture. Like, they legitimately use it in war."

"Shut your fucking mouth unless you're opening it to eat."

Her gaze fell to her plate, shoulders rolling forward as though she wanted to curl in on herself.

"Second is — take a bite, Tayshia. Come on. Let's *go*."

She did, a sour expression on her face.

"Second rule," he continued, "is that if you're gonna purge, you can do it in front of me. No more being in the bathroom for forty-five minutes to an hour. No more looking in the mirror before or after. No running the water or the shower or playing music, or whatever it is you think you can do to mask the sound. It's a quick in and out, or it's nothing at all."

"Don't you think that's a little weird?"

"Eating everything in the house and then throwing it up in the toilet? Yeah, it *is* weird."

She clenched her hand around her fork, her jaw clicking as she ground her teeth together. "I don't understand why you'd want to see it, then."

"I don't understand why you'd *want* me to see it. Remember — I'm not the one who's destroying their insides and their life. That's all you. And if it's embarrassing, then maybe that's because you shouldn't be doing it. Now, do I need to repeat myself?"

She pulled another sour face.

"Third — I'm not playing with you." He pointed his fork again. "Eat your fucking dinner."

"And *I'm* not playing with *you*! I've already had like, three bites!"

She had three seconds, is what she had.

"If I have to ask you again..."

"Oh, shut up! What are you going to do? Hit me?!"

He set his fork down on the table and looked at her with an expression as deadly and calm as the sea before a tidal wave. In seconds, she looked much smaller, dwarfed by his clothes and seconds away from crying. The heat drained from her face, leaving her pale and drawn. Defeated.

Afraid.

"You don't know what you're doing to me. What you're ruining," she whispered. "Please. This is going to make me worse, Ash."

"No," he said, glaring at her so hard that he felt like it hurt worse than her being scared of him felt. "Enabling you is what was making you worse. Making those bullshit rules I made before? All that did was make it easier for you to manipulate me. For you to get away with it. Being too nice to you, coddling you, being gentle. Well, not anymore."

"I'll purge it." The fear was gone, replaced by fierce determination that was as foolish as it was embarrassing to see. "It won't stay in my body. None of this will. You're wasting your time."

"Good." He smirked. "Perfect opportunity to test out the second rule, isn't it?"

"That's mortifying."

"Eating your food and throwing it up is mortifying."

"I'm not doing anything you say." She dropped the fork to the table, sending flecks of food spraying away. Some of them attached themselves to the back of the third and fourth chairs. She crossed her arms over her chest. "This is ridiculous. You're not my parent and you're not—"

"Are you ready for the third rule, or are you just gonna sit there being needlessly stubborn?"

"And you're not my boyfriend," she finished, her eyes blazing as bright as stars. "So why pretend to care when what you really wish you could do is hurt me like everyone else?!"

Ash felt it like a physical blow, but he was ready. He was ready for anything she threw his way. She was a cat, cornered and attacked, and she was lashing out to try and fend him off. It wouldn't work this time.

He could dish it out, too.

"Do you wanna die, Tayshia? Do you want to die? Sit there and ask yourself if you want to die."

She said nothing, still staring at him with those bright stars burning there.

"Because that's where you're headed. Right to the *fucking* grave if we don't get a handle on this shit. The fact that you haven't had some sort of health complication is a damn miracle. And if we don't figure this out, you and me, then I'm going to wake up one day and find you on the bathroom floor, and then there'll be nothing I can do to save you. You'll be dead. Do you get that? *You will be dead.*"

The stars flickered for a moment, then blazed back to life.

"As if you care if I die."

"I asked you a question." He reached for her chin, curled his fingers around it, and forced her to look up at him. "Do you want to die?"

"No." Her voice shook, lower lip trembling.

"Then eat. Please."

He let her go and resumed eating. A few seconds later, she picked her fork back up and resumed.

"Third rule is that you're leaving your bedroom door open. While you study, while you sleep, while you read, while you exist—I don't care. No doors will remain shut in this apartment. Got it?"

He could almost hear her desire to protest.

"Fine," she mumbled. "I need some time."

"Time? For what?"

"To clean my room."

He was angry, but he wasn't unreasonable. "How much time do you need?"

"A few days."

"A few days?" Ash gave her an incredulous look. He'd never seen the inside of her room, except for the day he helped her move her furniture in. "Why would you need a few days to clean it?"

"I don't know," she said with a shrug of her shoulders. "It's just really messy."

"Just make sure you do it. You have until Saturday, I guess."

"Okay."

Chapter Three

February 2019

Time passed like a comet, as slow as molasses through the layers of the atmosphere that masked the truth of its speed. Fleeting, with an aching, cold emptiness that burned white-hot and reminded the clock on Tayshia's life was ticking.

She had not cleaned her room, like he'd asked her to. The door remained shut over the weekend and while Ash knew there was no way she was cleaning it, he let it go. He didn't press her. Something at the back of his mind nagged him to let her keep one last bastion of peace. To not take *everything* away from her. Something that told him he was being cruel enough as it was—he didn't want to leave her bereft of safety.

He would give her one last ounce of trust.

Even though he still wore his necklace, she didn't. It was all he needed to see to know that things might be irreparable between them. But there were times she'd taken it off before. She always put it back on.

He would wait for that day.

After school on Monday, after a sickening argument about how much trouble she'd given him at lunch, and how he hadn't been able to tell her off because then everyone would see, he dropped her off at the apartment so he could go buy weed from Andre. He knew it was a risk, but the argument had been so bad that he figured she'd probably spend the thirty minutes or so that he was gone crying.

He felt bad about that.

When he got back, he stopped.

The mail was strewn about the table, like she'd thrown it there without a care. White rectangular papers, tossed and forgotten. But in spite of the envelopes cascading toward the edge, Ash had eyes for only one, and it was in the kitchen, in Tayshia's hands.

An opened letter.

He wouldn't think anything of it if it weren't for the fact that she was staring at him with a look of pity that he recognized. He recognized it so well that he knew exactly what she'd opened and even though he didn't know why she would do this to him, he was scared of what he wanted to do to her at that moment.

"Did you open my mail?" he said, his voice cracking as the panic threatened to tear him limb from limb.

"I was...I don't know why I—" Her brows pulled together and she gulped as though she were nauseous. "I was angry with you."

Ash walked over to her. The first step he took into the kitchen had her scrambling back against the corner between the counter and the dishwasher. She kept her gaze low to the ground and her hands tightened around the letter and the envelope.

He didn't want to see what it said.

With a gentle hand, he took the paper away from her and folded it back up without glancing past the surface of his father's spidery handwriting. His gaze then snapped to meet hers, cold ire meeting hot fear. He'd never seen her look so afraid in front of him, and the last time he was this angry with her was during the volatile weeks after they'd first been assigned to the wrong apartment.

Slowly, he wrapped his hand around her jaw, fingers spanning to dig into the flesh of her cheeks. She fought back a whimper, failing as he dragged her to the tips of her toes. Flashes of pain shimmered in her brown eyes but he couldn't see them, couldn't let them in.

Those letters were off limits.

"Never touch my mail again," he breathed out. "It's mine. Do not touch my things."

"I wasn't—I was just...I'm sorry, okay?"

"Tayshia. Do you understand me?"

"Yes," she gasped out, her fingers prying at his to try and get the ache to stop. "Yes, I understand."

"If you touch my mail again, we're done."

Crestfallen.

That was the only way to describe the look that passed across her face like rain clouds across a quiet prairie. Her fingers stopped clawing, one hand dropping to the counter beside her hip, and the other sliding to wrap around the back of his palm, covering the rose tattooed there.

"Ash, I'm sorry. I won't do it again. But please." Her voice quavered and eyes shone. "Don't leave me."

His heart twisted and clenched, the chains that he'd wrapped around it turning golden and starting to melt. When he dragged his closed eyelids up to look down at her, he felt like it was June 2017 again. Like they were in the cavern pool, the water soaking up to their waists as he held her and kept her safe. He should be keeping her safe right now.

Even from himself.

Like he wished he had that night, he lowered his face to hers and kissed her. He grabbed her hair at the back and devoured her with the mouth of a man starved. And he was starving—starving of her, her kiss, her touch for the last week. It felt like so much longer.

The way she kissed him back, lips parting as easily as though he were pouring sweet water down her dry throat, showed him she felt just the same.

"I miss you," she moaned against his lips, wrapping her arms around his neck so she could scrape her fingers through his hair and hold herself on her toes. "I miss you."

Ash turned his head and dove into her, his tongue laving against hers, caressing it and trying to tell her that he missed her, too. That he didn't know how to get her back without signing her death warrant.

They coexisted like two binary stars, burning apart, spinning, never coming closer. Consuming one another if they ever did.

He slid his hands down to the backs of her thighs and lifted her onto the kitchen counter. The back of her head hit the wooden cupboard, and then they were consuming each other. Tayshia made noises at the back of her throat—needy noises, keens, whines. Audible representations of emotions that neither of them wanted to live in. That neither wanted to open up and embrace. He dropped kisses to her jaw, tracing a path to taste her like a vampire with a yearning for her blood.

His lips cascaded those kisses like falling stars, showering them along the surface of her skin as though it were the night sky. His fingers dug into her hips, pulling them closer to his as her head fell back. The press of his lips and fluttering of her hands along his biceps, neck, and face spun a fragile sphere made of glass around the two of them. Something to keep them ensconced in a world separate from their own. Something only for them, a fraction of his dreams.

And then it shattered.

"Your dad is sick."

He froze, his lips hovering over her pulse point, heart racing to a stop. He squeezed his eyes shut, trying to forget the words she'd just said, trying to pull himself back into that spun glass world. Not only had she read his father's letter—the most recent in a string he'd been receiving and stuffing into a wooden chest for almost an entire year—but she'd memorized the last thing he wanted to hear.

When he looked up at her where she sat on the counter, he could see his own anguish reflected in her eyes.

"You needed to know," she said, still breathless from their kissing. "He wants you to go see him."

"I don't have any desire to see that man."

"Don't be so selfish, Ash," she said, sounding desperate. Like she thought his father was the answer to whatever was wrong with him, with them, with her. With everything. "Go see him. He's *sick*. If it wasn't serious, I doubt he would have written to you about it."

"Then he can die."

Her hands cupped his face. "He's your father."

"He's not my father."

"Yes, he is," she insisted, fingers curling in his hair. "He's your *dad*. You shouldn't let him go without trying your best to forgive him."

Forgive him?

For what? Killing his mother? Beating him into submission? Ruining their family and letting them perish the way he'd let his rose garden die?

"Stop," he whispered, his voice breaking again. His hands came up to curve around her own, caressing them for a moment as he held back the tears that had wanted to burst forth since the last time he cried over his mother in the loneliness of his jail cell. He couldn't look at her. "Please."

She opened and closed her mouth several times, grimacing as the words evaded her.

Ash took advantage of the silence, pulling her hands away from him and pushing them into her lap. He stepped away from the counter and turned from her. There was no coping with this. Not now. Maybe not ever.

"Ash, he's all you've got left."

He stopped, a sadness unlike anything he'd felt in months weighing his heart and pulling his shoulders down. He looked back at her over his shoulder, his entire body feeling as heavy as the center of a black hole.

"No, Tayshia. *You're* all I have left."

She frowned as he started around the corner, toward the hall. "Where are you going? Shouldn't we talk about this?"

"If I don't leave right now, I'm going to punch a hole in the fucking wall."

If the stars died in her eyes, he didn't stay to see it.

☼☼☼

Ash leaned his head against the locker next to Tayshia's, watching her gather her things in silence. It was between their first and second classes on Tuesday. While the students passed by in the hall behind them, he felt like they were once again in their own universe.

Things were subdued. He'd spent his entire evening brooding and alternating between staring at the ceiling and sitting on his bed, smoking out the window it was positioned beneath. He listened for the bathroom door, but fortunately, he never heard anything but the heavier door of Tayshia's bedroom once that night. He was relieved that she didn't purge, but still conflicted about her opening his mail.

He didn't read his father's letters because he wasn't ready. He would *never* be ready. It was an impossible mountain to climb that, once he reached the summit, would erupt beneath him and scorch him. He couldn't fathom it. He didn't *want* it.

But Tayshia had a point.

If his father was truly as sick as she seemed to worry he was, he didn't want to let him go without at least telling him how he'd affected his life. Without showing him how his mistakes had caused Ash to make several of his own. He wanted him to know how much he hated him. He wanted him to die knowing that his son wanted him to.

Ji Hyun strolled up, her arms wrapped around her books and high-heeled boots clicking against the floor. Her black hair contrasted Tayshia's: whereas Tayshia had sewn in a weave made of thick, bushy curls that fell to her waist, Ji Hyun's waist-length hair was as straight as a pin.

"Hey, guys," she said with a bright smile. "Weather's shit, as usual."

"What do you expect in Oregon in February?" Tayshia said with a slight laugh that sounded alien.

Had it been that long since he heard it?

"I expect less snow, that's for sure. Kinda crazy that it snowed at all." Ji Hyun said, wrinkling her nose. "Anyway, I'm glad I caught you guys. I was just thinking during my last class, and I wanted to know what you guys had planned for Valentine's Day."

The spinning Earth screeched to a halt. Valentine's Day was the *last* thing on their minds, with how volatile things were lately. What type of chocolates was he supposed to gift her with if getting her to eat it would be another fight?

"I don't think we had any plans yet," Tayshia said, looking up at him as he pushed away from the locker. She bit her lower lip, studying him carefully. Trying to converse with him through the power of their intuition. "Did we?"

Ji Hyun frowned, her gaze darting from friend to friend. "Why are you looking at her like that, Ash?"

"Like what?"

"So intense. It's super creepy. It's not like she's going to *disappear* if you look away."

"I'm looking at her no differently than I would look at anyone I liked," he said, even though he knew that was a lie. He *was* afraid that Tayshia would disappear. In her case, it didn't matter whether or not his eyes were open.

"You never looked at me like that," Ji Hyun said with a perturbed expression. "I don't know. You guys must just have a different relationship than me and Andre. Whatever. Do you guys want to fuck around and go to Seattle the weekend of?"

"The 16th to the 18th?" Tayshia asked, closing her locker while holding the textbook for her Anatomy class close to her chest. She looked up at Ash, silently begging him with her eyes to just be normal, to not get angry, to say yes. "I would think it should be okay. If we don't have plans. *Right,* Ash?"

Ash knew there was no reason to say no. It was two weeks away, so there was plenty of time. Perhaps things would even settle down between them by then.

"We're down," he said, and then his hand slithered down her arm to grab hers, his fingers wrapping around her palm. When he straightened his back, it pulled her arm up a bit because he was so much taller than her. "What are we going to do?"

"Tattoos and the club. We figured we could just go overnight."

"The club?" Ash pulled a face.

"No, that sounds so fun," Tayshia said, her tone lifting. "The only time I've ever been to a club was a couple of times on my Paris trip."

"You went to Paris?!" Ji Hyun gasped as the bell rang for the high school students. They had a couple extra minutes before the students in the program had to get to their classes. "I'm so jealous. What was that like?"

"It was fun. I went with my youth group. We saw a lot of things and the nightlife was so lively that we wanted to go to a couple clubs and see what it was all about. We got to drink, too."

"Oh, yeah, because the drinking age is lower there, isn't it?"

"Yes, and we just wanted to take advantage of it."

"Well, that sounds amazing. I love traveling. I just went to Seoul this year for Christmas with Andre. We had a lot of fun."

"I bet it was. Did you do a lot of sightseeing, or just see family?"

"Well, I was born there, you know, so…"

As the girls continued to chat, Tayshia squeezed Ash's hand so hard that he wasn't sure she even realized she was doing it. He looked down at her, his hair falling into his eyes, and leaned all the way down to drop a kiss to her shoulder, where the wide neckline of her crewneck exposed her skin. He didn't want her to think he didn't care about her or the things she'd been through. He wanted her to know without him having to say it that he was always going to be there for her when it came to Paris. Despite what they were currently going through, he knew that she was talking about Paris because she wanted to feel normal.

"Aw, so cute," Ji Hyun said with a roll of her eyes. "Don't make me gag. I actually want to *keep* my breakfast."

"Whatever," Ash said. "We better get going. Her class is all the way across campus."

"You're already late," Ji Hyun sang. She wriggled her fingers in a wave and turned to go. "See you guys later!"

When they were alone, Tayshia looked up at him with a troubled expression.

"What?" he asked, fingers smoothing over her soft, fluffy curls.

"I don't think I can pretend like that again. I can't pretend like Paris was a good memory."

He tugged on her hand, bringing her face to his chest, and cupped the back of her head. In the silence that remained in the emptying hallway, he let himself feel something other than anger. She tilted her head back, gazing up at him in that way she did when she felt broken all over again. He lowered his mouth to press a soft kiss to her lips, one that she returned with a ferocity that showed him she needed it.

☼☼☼

Ash had a panic attack in class.

It assaulted him out of nowhere, a volley of bullets slamming into his lungs and bleeding them of oxygen. One moment, he was listening to the lecture, taking shorthand notes, and thinking. Always thinking. Thinking about the letter. Thinking about his father being sick. Thinking about having to look at him through fiberglass with phone receivers held to their ears. Thinking about looking him in the eyes when he was sober.

Then he couldn't breathe.

He tried, but it felt like someone or something was squeezing his chest, keeping him pinned to the surface of the Earth. Wind rushed past his ears.

The chair at his table screeched against the ground as he scrambled to his feet and stumbled out the door. He fell against a locker outside with a hand clutched to his chest, gasping for air as he sank to a crouch.

The professor, Mrs. Alistor, came running out of the room, letting the door swing shut behind her as she came to his side. A rather tall woman, she bent at the waist, placing her hands on her knees so she could look at him with close concern, her box braids swinging in the air as she did so.

"Ash, you've got to breathe. Whatever it is, just close your eyes and take a deep breath."

He closed his eyes tight and tried, the action futile. He gasped several times, unable to get the image of his mother falling to the ground in the courtroom out of his head. Resting his elbows on his knees, he buried his face in his hands, his body shaking. Shaking as though he were cold.

"Breathe in through your nose and out through your mouth," Mrs. Alistor said, brown eyes glittering with worry. She came to crouch beside him, placing a hand on his upper back. The warmth of it grounded him to reality. "There you go. Everything's okay. Breathe in and out."

He did so, using the darkness of his face in his hands to help him focus. He inhaled through his nose, imagining his lungs swelling. He exhaled through his mouth, feeling them constrict the way they were supposed to. And then he could breathe again.

Mrs. Alistor took her hand back but did not yet stand. "What's going on, Ash?"

"Panic attack, I think," he mumbled, lifting his head from his hands and looking at her through bleary eyes. He felt exhausted. Drained. "Just a panic attack."

"Have you seen a counselor?"

"You know, my probation officer recommended the same thing," he said with a short, mirthless laugh.

"Maybe because he thinks you need to," she said, nudging him with her elbow. "It's not good to keep things in. Talking to someone can really help, more than you think. And if money is an issue, there's counselors here at school who are just as qualified."

"I'm sure there are."

She sighed. "Why don't you take some time to collect yourself, then come back inside?"

Ash took the extra time she granted him and sat on the floor with his back to the lockers. He pulled his knees to his chest and buried his face in them, letting his mind wander to something he could handle. Something that wasn't Tayshia, his father, or his mother.

Therapists weren't for people like him. He was well-adjusted, wasn't he? He followed the rules of his probation, had served his time, had learned from his mistakes. He was in school, had a car, and was financially responsible. He paid for their apartment and he took care of food. All of the expenses were handled. And on top of all that, he wasn't depressed. But if this was the second time someone had recommended he get help, then maybe he really *did* need it.

What were people noticing about him that he couldn't see?

☼☼☼

After school, Ash, Andre, Tayshia, and Ji Hyun decided to sit on the stone wall that decorated the front of the school. It surrounded the front of the main building, housing not only the building itself, but the snow-covered, large front lawn. It sat at the foot of the wide entrance steps, with the parking lot on one side and the snow on the other. Several groups of other students mingled along the wall on either side of the steps, too, everyone seeming to want a break to relax in the middle of a relatively normal school year. There were some other friends standing around with them, everyone spilling across the sidewalk and hanging out.

Ash and Andre sat perched on the wall while Tayshia, Ji Hyun, and a few other girls practiced some sort of dance that was popular on social media. Andre snuck drags out of his pipe and made comments on their efforts, while Ash stretched his legs out and crossed his arms over his chest. It was cold, but not as cold as previous days had been. So while everyone was still shivering and wearing scarves and gloves and hats, the sun was out, causing crystals to glitter in the snow.

He felt heavy. Like he didn't have the energy to breathe, let alone watch Tayshia learn a dance. And she did look cute doing it, but he was so exhausted that it was like he couldn't see anything at all. Not even the way she smiled.

What the Hell was he supposed to do with a therapist? Cry? He didn't cry. Not unless he was pushed to the absolute edge, like the time Kieran and his friends jumped him.

As if on cue, the Devil himself came strolling down the stairs, his boisterous voice heard as loud as though he were right in front of them. He was telling something to one of his friends, but when he caught sight of Ash, Tayshia, and their group, his voice seemed to fade into nothing. The expression in his eyes was unreadable when they fell upon Tayshia, who was still dancing and hadn't noticed him.

There was satisfaction, Ash thought, in the sight of the bruises that still littered Kieran's body.

Andre cleared his throat and leaned in, the edge of his Afro brushing Ash's hair. "He'll probably leave you alone from now on."

"I fucking hope so."

"Well, whatever you do, don't be waving that shit around."

"What?" Ash lowered his voice. "The gun? I got rid of it."

"Oh, for real?"

"Yeah. Threw it in the ocean."

"Shit, you went to the coast? When did you do that?"

"Doesn't matter."

"I feel like your life is hella dramatic. Like, you probably got somethin' goin' on every damn day."

"You...Are not wrong."

Andre stopped to smoke again. While he took a drag, Ash watched several more cars pull out of the parking lot, including the shuttle bus.

When he blew the smoke out of the corner of his mouth, waving his hand through the cloud to disperse it so it didn't hang on the frigid air, Andre said, "You seen Elijah?"

"Nah," Ash said, taking the pipe and bringing it to his lips. Andre lit it for him. The marijuana burned in his lungs, smoke smooth on its way out of his throat. "I'm not even gonna lie to you, man, we're not cool."

"You and Elijah?"

"Yep."

The parking lot emptied further. Kieran and his friends had all piled into his car and left. There were only a handful of cars left, most closer to the school with one well-taken care of dark blue Oldsmobile that looked to be from the seventies lingering near the furthest edge.

"Ah, that's a bummer," Andre said. "I figured you guys would talk and figure things out. It's weird seeing you guys be so distant. Speaking of weird…What the Hell's going on with you and Tay?"

Ash's gaze slid to him, sharp and inquisitive. Suspicious.

"What do you mean?"

Andre handed him the pipe, but Ash didn't take it, so he held it in his lap. "I mean, things seem off between you. Even Ji Hyun noticed it. She said you guys were acting bizarre."

"Does Tayshia *look* like she's acting bizarre?"

The two of them glanced at her. She was laughing with Ji Hyun and another girl, the three of them falling against each other as they failed another dance move.

"Not right now," Andre said, then stopped so they could both say goodbye to part of their group of friends that were heading home. He resumed their conversation afterward. "But that doesn't mean somethin' ain't wrong. What's going on?"

"Nothing."

"Nothing means something. What is it?"

"*Nothing*," Ash growled, glaring at him. "Nothing I want to talk about. Give me that."

He snatched the pipe up, taking an agitated drag and thrusting the glass back against Andre's chest. He made an exasperated sound and took the time to praise Ji Hyun for her horrible dancing.

Ash needed to be more careful with how he acted around Tayshia. He needed to lower whatever intensity it was that Ji Hyun seemed to think was there. The last thing he needed was for people to ask questions. He was the best person to deal with Tayshia's disorder. Doctors, parents, teachers…None of them would know how to help her. They'd make her worse than he ever could.

Ash rose from the wall, zeroed in on her, and he crossed the distance between them.

She had just stepped off the sidewalk and onto the asphalt of the parking lot after spinning out of a dance move. Still laughing, still letting out girlish giggles that didn't require the attention of anyone else. Lost in her own thoughts.

And she was still laughing as he wrapped his hand around the back of her neck and swallowed the air from her mouth. She let out a gasp of surprise, passing it into his own lungs as though she wanted him to have it. Wanted him to suffocate her. His tongue found hers, twining with it, stroking it, tasting it. He kissed her with something similar to determination, a possessive desire to prove to everyone that everything was fine.

That she was still his.

It took the span of a heartbeat for her to throw her arms around his neck, that same girlish giggle from earlier coming from her chest as she pushed herself into the kiss with gusto. She danced on her tiptoes as she tried to keep their lips locked together, marrying their mouths and telling him that she was happy with him.

At least, for now.

He ignored the raucous, obnoxious cheering that came from their friends, finishing the spell he wanted to weave with this kiss. And then, when he felt her begin melting against him, when her fingers started to stroke down the back of his neck in a way that told him she wanted to go home, he pulled back.

"What was that for?" she said, voice hoarse.

"Because I like it when you smile."

Tayshia lowered her head with a shy blush on her cheeks. As she lifted it, she looked to the side, at the parking lot for a second. A frown tugged at her lips.

"What?" Ash said, following her line of sight with his hand still holding her neck and her hands flat on his chest.

"That car's got people in it."

"Which car?" There were a few in the lot.

"The blue one at the far side." Her frown deepened. "It's been here since we got out here and I never saw anyone get in."

"Maybe they got in while you were dancing?"

"Maybe. But they look sort of familiar, like…" She narrowed her eyes and stared. Her jaw dropped and she gasped. "Ash. That's the guys."

"What guys?"

"From after the show. The guys. You know, the ones." She held a hand to her temple as she wracked her brain. She snapped her fingers. "Uh...The redhead. He's got that spider tattoo."

He wasn't listening anymore. There was electricity sparking in his body, setting fires.

"Tayshia? That your girl's name? I wonder how many Tayshias live in Crystal Springs."

"Shouldn't be too hard to find out."

Ash felt something turn on in his brain, gears clicking into place as though the rusty machine was coming to life, finally working. Nothing mattered. Not her disorder, not their arguing, not his father.

They were fucked.

"Ay, we're leaving," he called to Andre.

"Already?" Ji Hyun pouted. "We were thinking of going to Gianni's for dinner."

"Yeah, we're tired. But hey, we'll see you tomorrow at school."

"Ash, you good?" Andre said, giving them a strange look from the wall.

"I'm fine. I'll see you tomorrow. Tayshia, get your bag."

She jumped to do as she was told, seeming to grasp that in this, she needed to let him order her around without a fight.

Ash kept his eye on the Oldsmobile, stretching his arms above his head. He knew that they'd see Ricky's guys again. In the back of his head, the knowledge of the threat had lurked in the days since the night they'd gone to the show. He supposed he'd just been a little too hopeful.

Maybe they were bored. He hoped they were. If they were bored, then all Ash and Tayshia had to do was seem as uninteresting as possible. That way, they might be able to fly under the radar.

Tayshia started to say something, but he wrapped his arm around her, slinging it around her neck to signal her to stay silent.

They walked to his car and got in. He glanced over at the Oldsmobile one more time, putting his keys in the ignition. Tayshia tried to speak again, but he held up a finger. Placing his hand on the back of her headrest, he pulled out of his parking spot and turned the car with one hand spinning the wheel. Their eyes met.

"It's okay," he said, for his sake as well as hers. "They're probably just fucking with us."

They drove past the Oldsmobile. Ash kept his gaze trained forward, pretending that the men hadn't turned their car on, too. That they weren't pulling onto the road, driving after Ash's car towards the mountain highway that led back to town.

The first time Ash met Ricky, there were only a few other members of his gang there. The house was a derelict foreclosure on the outskirts of Crystal Springs, borderline condemned. It was merely an outpost of sorts for his unsavory goings-on, not any sort of home to anyone. Ash remembered his father bringing him inside, telling him to keep his mouth shut and head down.

There were a few men there, and a bald man on his knees in front of a blonde man wearing clothes better suited to a teacher than the leader of a gang. Complete with sweater and slacks, he was focused on a book—not the pleading of the man before him. Apparently, Ricky didn't care about the sob story. If a payment was missed, punishment was doled out.

Ash could still remember the way they beat the bald man black-and-blue. He remembered Ricky's piercing blue eyes almost as vividly as he remembered the house and the look his father had given him as if to say, *"Don't make a sound."* And he remembered the redhead with the spider tattoo. The man with the brown hair and the undercut. How they leered.

His past had caught up with him.

"What are you going to do?" Tayshia asked, her voice ringing with fear.

"Drive around for a little while, try to lose them. I don't want them figuring out where we live."

"No, I mean, what are you going to *do?* You got rid of the gun."

Fuck.

Another wrong choice. One that had seemed right at the time.

"I don't know," he said.

"Ash...I'm scared."

A determination flared inside of him like morning sunlight coming over the mountains. His hand slid across the center console, into her lap. She clutched it. He felt how badly she shook, how she quivered with the bone-deep sort of terror he remembered living with all the years he sold for his father.

"You don't have to be afraid. I'll take care of you."

CHAPTER FOUR

"Can I take a shower?"

It took a second for Ash's TV-addled mind to slide back out of the muck and into reality. He'd been trying to drown his fears in an *anime* Tayshia liked about a girl who befriended the members of the zodiac for the last two hours. The show, a huge joint, and a bag of potato chips was all he needed to zone out and forget.

"What the Hell did you just ask me?"

Tayshia was in the process of getting up from her side of the couch. She jabbed a thumb over her shoulder and gave him a confused look. "I asked you if I could take a shower."

What?

"Why would you need to *ask* me if you could take a shower?"

"Well, because of the rules," she said. "I've got to keep the door open."

What if she purged?

What if she passed out and he couldn't get to her in time?

What if it was the last time?

What if she died?

"I can see you freaking out," she said with a grimace. "It's okay, I'll just wait until tomorrow morning."

"Tomorrow—tomorrow morning?" he said, his tone dumbfounded and thoughts stumbling. "Why the morning?"

"The only time I can shower is when you sleep, and that's like the two hours you get. I just wake up early so I can. I mean, I leave the door open, of course, because that's the rule, but—"

"You don't have to leave the door open while you shower," he said, feeling sick. How fucked up was he? Seriously, how fucked was it that he'd set a rule that didn't enable her the privacy to *shower*?

"I mean, it's okay," she said, "it's just that I don't like people—anyone seeing my body, and you haven't seen it yet. So, I—"

"Tayshia," he said, sitting from his slouched position on the couch and fixing her with a serious expression. "You do not have to leave the door open when you shower *or* when you go to the bathroom. I shouldn't have made that rule so restrictive."

"It's okay. Really. We both don't know what we're doing."

He arched an eyebrow at her seeming acceptance. "That means you want to recover?"

"I mean, yes."

The elation that buoyed his heart was short-lived as he remembered what this girl was good at. Manipulation. Lies. He couldn't believe everything so willingly, but he also couldn't bang the gavel without giving her a chance.

"It's not okay, and I'm sorry I made you feel like that. You don't have to leave the door open if you're going to the bathroom or showering. Just promise me I can trust you during the times the door is shut."

Once he was alone, a torrent of thoughts began to pour through his head. Groaning, he leaned forward with his elbows on his thighs and his head draped between his hands.

He was literally a horrible person. Making rules for her like a parent, cursing at her, getting angry with her. Treating her just as bad as Kieran. Othering her and reacting to her mental health as though it were a burden. He was letting his fear control him, letting his fear of losing her tell him to make it as difficult as possible for her to be bulimic.

If it was too hard, maybe she'd stop.

Ash fell back, the back of his head resting on the top of the couch while he stared up at the ceiling with fatigue. His limbs were full of stones. The weight of the past five months was crushing him.

Had it really been five months already?

Over the sounds of the television, Ash heard the shower turn on. The dull thud of hot water hitting the floor of the tub was odd in the way it provided a cicada song backdrop to what he could only describe as depression.

He was fucking *depressed.*

What was he supposed to do about the gang members in the Oldsmobile, the ones from the show? He'd gotten rid of the gun and promised to take care of her, but how could he do that without a weapon? He wasn't going to involve Elijah or Andre. He wasn't going to send his friends to the slaughterhouse. Ash had to deal with the remnants of not only his mistakes, but his father's, too, on his own.

Protecting her was his job.

What about his father? Ash knew in his heart that eventually, he would have found the strength to let his father in again, to try to figure out how to forgive him. If he was sick, then that put a pressure on him to figure his shit out way too fast. It put scheduled finality on forgiveness—something that Ash was incapable of doing right now.

How could he forgive his father for killing his mother?

Tayshia re-entered the living room twenty minutes after she'd left. She was toting a large fuzzy brown blanket and her phone, and she wore joggers and a cropped hoodie with the hood up. The lengths of her new hair were gathered up into a pink satin bonnet. Her gaze snapped up from the floor as she entered the room, and she ran her tongue along the front of her top teeth.

"Whachu lookin' at, white boy?"

He couldn't help but crack a lazy grin at that. He stretched a hand out, palm-side up along the couch cushions. She froze in the process of returning to her side of the couch, narrowing her eyes.

"Answer the question."

"You look cute. Come here."

"Why would I want to sit next to your stank-ass?" she said, but her lips were twitching upward.

"*Come here!*" he said, raising his voice through a smile. "Cuddle me."

She rolled her eyes and made a show of marching over to him. Fanning the blanket, she shook it out to straighten it, and then plopped down beside him. He let the empty potato chip bag float to the floor and started to curl in toward her, legs still outstretched with his feet on the floor, then stopped.

"What?" she asked.

He gave her the most innocent, toothy smile he could muster. "You forgot to turn off the hallway light."

"Oh, no, you don't! I *just* sat down. I'm not turning off the—"

"Please, Tayshia!" he whined, taking her by the arm and shaking her. "I don't wanna get up!"

"—for your lazy-ass, bitch-ass, stupid-ass—"

"I'm tired. My legs are tired. Every part of me is tired."

"*Of what?!*"

"Carrying my half of this—"

"Don't you dare say relationship." She spluttered a laugh and held a finger up. "Don't you *dare*."

"...Of this relationship."

He laughed as he raised his arm to ward off her childish slap.

"And look!" she yelled, leaning past him to point at the chip bag. "You used to give me so much shit for my mess, and now you're just gonna drop that on the *floor*?"

"Please, my sweet." He threw a dramatic hand across his forehead. "Turn off the light. It burns my porcelain white skin as I run my hands through my tousled blond hair, and bite my bottom lip while staring at myself in the mirror. Because you see, today is the day my parents have sold me to my favorite band, and—"

"Because you're a vampire," she muttered to cut him off, throwing her side of the blanket aside and stomping around the couch. "A lazy, stupid, messy, pothead *vampire*."

Ash hadn't seen her be this playful—nor had he seen himself as such—in weeks. It helped him to forget about everything that was going wrong. It even made him want to forget their volatile relationship was the cause of all this.

If you could call it that.

"Thank you, my precious, sweet, angelic girl," he cooed as she returned to his side. "I'll give you everything you ever want and more."

"For turning off the damn light? Fine. Send me five hundred dollars."

"Get my phone."

"Oh, stop. Don't even try it."

The problem was that he *would* send her the money. He *would* give her everything. She *was* his girl.

He would do anything for her.

They settled in. Ash turned on his side and pulled his legs up onto the cushions, shouldering the back of the couch. Tayshia rested her legs over his, slightly positioned on her side with the top half of her facing forward. She then pulled up the video app on her phone, the one that she, Ji Hyun, and their friends had found the dance they'd learned today.

For the next hour, Ash was able to zone into a single-minded place with her as she scrolled through video after video. Some were funny, having them both in stitches until it felt like he was doing crunches, giving him the melodic sound of her laughter to memorize. Some were informative, about things like neurodivergence, eating disorders, and trauma. Those ones made him tighten his hold around her, pressing the occasional kiss to her shoulder over the fabric of her hoodie. And some were about the metalcore scene, with videos about top songs, going to shows, and what it was like to be a Scene kid back in the 2000's.

"Why are you getting *those* videos?" he asked.

"I had fun at the show. I actually really liked the music."

He gave a mock-gasp. "Did I inadvertently turn you into a Scene kid?"

"Perhaps," she said with a giggle. "My music library now has Thy Art is Murder."

"Hold up. Are you serious?"

She nodded.

"They're heavy," he said appreciatively, his gaze flickering up and down her face. "I kinda like that."

She gave him an impassive look. "Next up is a tattoo."

"That can be arranged."

"Yes, it can, if we go to Seattle with Ji Hyun and Andre."

"We are going."

"Well, they said they're getting tattoos. Are you gonna get one?"

"Probably. Why not? Are you?"

"Maybe," she said, dragging the syllables in a lilt. She scrolled to the next video—it was about someone's personal top ten post-hardcore bands. "What would I even get?"

"Something special to you, something important, something funny, something pretty. Tattoos are art. They can be anything you want."

She turned her face toward him and her gaze fell to the roses and chains on his neck. There was a faint smile on her lips. "You mean like the one you got for me?"

"Yes."

"Some would call you creepy."

"If that were the case, then some would call you an adrenaline junkie. *Canoodling* with your stalker? Why, Miss Tayshia Marie Cole, I do declare you've got quite the penchant for danger, haven't you?"

"Do me a favor." She dragged a deadpan stare in his direction. "Never try any form of accent ever again."

He wrinkled his nose, and she went back to her phone. She finished the video and then scrolled to the next one.

"Wait," Ash said, his hand sliding over her bare abdomen, "go back. What song is the top one? I liked it."

"Read it on the screen, fool." Gingerly, she covered his hand with her own. Her body was tense. He had a feeling she didn't like him touching her stomach, but he didn't move. She'd say so if she wanted him to.

"Shit, that's their first singer, so the song must be from their first or second album. I love that band. Pull it up and play the whole thing."

"A whole album?"

"Yeah. Okay, pick...That one."

Tayshia did so, and the moment the first song began, he tightened his arms around her. Burying his face in her neck, he slid his hand back across her abdomen and curved his arm until his fingers were caressing her lower back.

Tayshia started to say something, but Ash interrupted her, eyes trained on the silver chain around her neck. Whatever pendant she wore was hidden beneath her top.

"Are you wearing your necklace again?"

"My necklace? Oh, um..." She looked up at him, tilting her head back to do so. "I put it back on after my shower. We ended up having a nice night, and it got me thinking about everything. I feel like I should try to go back to the beginning, before everything happened. I didn't go to Paris until after we went to the caverns."

Ash knew that.

"Were you wearing it when..." He trailed off, swallowing hard against the sudden ache in his throat.

"Yes," she replied softly, her fingers coming up to pull the amethyst out of her hoodie and play with its jagged edges—jagged edges that fit perfectly into the cracks of his. "I was wearing it when he raped me."

They were quiet for a few beats of the song.

There was something heart-rending about that for Ash. The fact that he was in jail, probably getting into a fight with some other inmate while across the world, Tayshia was in Hell. Trapped under the darkness with nothing but the glittering lights of the Eiffel Tower, a menacing reminder of the beauty that was being ripped away from her.

"Why did you keep it?" he asked. "Be honest."

She took her time answering.

"Because it represented something special to me. Even though we didn't really get along or know each other that well, you were nicer to me that night than Kieran had ever been. Than anyone had ever been, really. You didn't lie. You didn't mock me or make underhanded comments. There weren't any microaggressions, no jokes meant to make fun, no attempts to hurt my feelings. You were just you. No matter what, all throughout high school, that's who you were. Yourself. And I still liked you. That made me realize that I could be myself, too. So when I went to Paris..." Tayshia trailed off, staring into the space between the paraphernalia-strewn glass coffee table and Ash's knees. "When I went to Paris, I didn't take it off because it was a reminder."

Her silence after her sentence ended was telling. Telling enough for Ash to feel like holding her tighter. Cradling her, keeping her safe from her own memories.

"That was a long time ago," she said, her tone suddenly clipped. "Now, it's harder to wear it all the time. I'm sorry that I always take it off. I don't mean to hurt your feelings."

"Don't be sorry," he said, tone gentle as he laid kisses to her temple, cheekbone, and the hinge of her jaw. "Until it represents what it used to, take it off whenever you need to. I'm not going anywhere."

"You say that like you think the only thing keeping you here is this crystal." She closed her fingers around it, tight as a clamp. Her body remained tense, taut as the string of a bow.

"The only thing keeping me here is you. With or without them, I'd still choose you."

She didn't look at him. Didn't say anything. She lost herself in silence and thought, and Ash did the same. He knew she didn't have the capacity to make a statement like that right now. She wasn't in the place to make life decisions and big choices.

Neither was he.

"I'll always choose you," he said, tilting his chin so he could kiss her where her neck met her jawline. "My precious..." He placed a kiss slightly below her jaw, on her neck, pulling her closer beneath the warmth of the blanket that swaddled them. "...Sweet..." Another, this time, pulling aside the neckline of her cropped hoodie so he could taste the junction of her shoulder and neck. "...Angelic girl." A final kiss, right to her pulse.

She shivered.

"How cheesy."

"You like cheesy."

"No, I like the praise though."

He hummed. "I know you do."

Tayshia's body melted against his as he continued to kiss her neck, his lips and tongue igniting fire in the trails they blazed. She gripped her phone tight in her hands, the music still playing. The screen turned off, plunging them into darkness beneath the blanket. The heat coming from their bodies was nearly unbearable. It felt like it was boiling his blood, scorching his insides.

"Thought you said you were tired," she whispered in accusation, fingers curled into the fabric of his shirt. "Seems like you got a lot of energy."

"I *am* tired. This will help me sleep."

"Mm-hm," she said, the suspicion in her tone evident. She didn't believe him. Didn't have to.

"All right," he said, breathing a laugh into the dark space. He moved his hand to her hip as he leaned away from her. "I'll stop."

"*No!*" she cried, and then she let out a nervous laugh. "No. I'm just confused."

"Confused about what?"

"I thought you hated me."

If he'd been able to see in the dark of the blanket, he knew he'd likely see her frowning the way she did when she was unbearably sad. The despondence was audible in her tone, as though she'd been holding it in for a while and it had been poisoning her.

Ash felt his stomach twist, and not with desire. It was his fault she felt that way. And to her credit, he had been so angry that he felt like he hated her this past week. And so had she.

But it affected her more.

"I could never hate you, Tayshia. Do you hear me? *Never*."

His fingers slid along the right side of her jaw, turning her face toward his so he could capture her lips. There was something like surrender in the way she let her head tilt back so he could kiss her the way she liked best: with a bruising mouth, tender tongue, and the experience to know what the fuck he wanted to do with her.

His right hand snaked between the cushion and her body, pressing flat to her back to arch her closer. His left hand smoothed up to her waist with a featherlight touch, like a bird gently skimming the surface of the sea. He felt her trembling as her sensitive skin was touched; felt her hips already beginning to roll.

Tayshia's hand slid up his chest, sending electric currents spreading outward from the tips of her fingers as she trailed them up to the hair at the nape of his neck. Her fingers curled inward, nails scraping his skin, and then she pulled herself closer to his body. The way she clutched him close, panted for air between kisses, and writhed against the couch weighed him down with desire and erased his mind.

It was a frenzy after that.

Ash's fingers dug into the flesh of her thigh and pulled. She took the hint, adjusting herself so he could pull the joggers off of her body. As he continued to kiss her, she untied the drawstrings on his sweatpants. He lifted his hips so she could push them over the swell of his rear. Tayshia gripped the blanket so it wouldn't break light into their dark little corner of the universe, and then she was hovering above him.

"Are you sure?" he whispered, a tiny flame of guilt burning at the back of his head. "I've been so—*fuck!* Oh, my *God.*"

Tayshia had sunk down onto him without care or warning, saying nothing as she took what she wanted and lost herself to what he could give. He was nothing but a lamb for the slaughter; fodder for her insatiable hunger. His hands cinched her waist, holding tight as she forced him to feel her. To feel her body as it gripped him, slick and warm and wet. His arms took over, hands gripping tight as he moved her harder against him, up and down. His back arched, stomach coiling tight enough to make him groan.

"Ash."

"Yeah?"

"From below. Hard."

Letting his hands trail down to her hips, he turned his face toward her and brushed his lips against her cheek. "Is that what you want, sweet girl? Tell me what you want."

"I want you to do what I ask you to do. And I want to make you come for me."

"You wanna be in control?" He mouthed at the skin below her jaw, panting when the slickness of her heat clenched around him.

"Yeah," she whimpered.

"That's right. You're in control. You're in—*ah*—control."

One more roll of her hips and his feet were flat on the floor, toes curling into the carpet as he slammed his hips upward, fucking into her like he was worshiping a goddess. The tightness of her channel pulled him deeper than bodies could go. Deeper than the oceans of the Earth, and deeper still.

Good *God*.

She fell forward like a limp rag doll, holding herself on her knees while he used her body, and burying her wails into the curve of his shoulder.

"Fuck, baby," he said, and it was a whine as he found solace in the soft skin of her throat. He noticed the scent of her body wash—lavender and vanilla, and it made him want to breathe her in forever. He felt his stomach coiling tighter. Too tight. "Please—*God*, fucking..."

She reached down with her left hand and pushed his hips flat again. Before he could question her, she was the one to take over. The one to slam her hips to meet his. The one that was going to decide how this ended.

It felt too good. Too good, and too intense to simply sit there while she fucked him to the edge of the universe and back. The roll of her hips was sublime, ecstasy mixed with determination. The pleasure mounted with each lift and fall of her hips.

Tayshia slid the fingers of her right hand along the palm of his left, twining their fingers together. She forced his elbow to bend so she could pin his hand to the top of the couch behind his head. He held her hand tightly, whimpering in the depths of his chest as he relished in the ability to pretend he was restrained. Every movement of her body became unable to ignore, from the shivering of her muscles to the twist of her waist as she made herself hit the right spot every time she bore down on him, to the small sounds she was trying so desperately to hide. The small sounds that he could tell were well-obscured sobs.

"I know," he whispered in a cooing tone, his other hand stroking along her thigh and up to her hip. "I know, baby. It feels so good for you, doesn't it?"

Her response was to whimper and gasp, utterly focused and determined.

Ash felt it rising up, coming towards him like an earthquake rolling across the bed of the sea. His cock throbbed, pulsing with his yearning to fall apart for her. He felt helpless. Like if he didn't want to come, she wouldn't let him breathe until he did. He closed his eyes to the darkness and his entire body began to clench, tensing for the end.

He moaned louder than he probably should have, desperation causing him to push the blanket off of them so he could get a cool breath. The light from the TV flooding his vision gave him a shadowed view of her face. It was burning from within, a galaxy of stars and incineration. She was Hecate incarnate.

"Oh, fuck," he breathed. "You're gonna make me *fucking* come."

"Hold it," she commanded, her hand moving from his hip to his throat. She leaned forward on her knees, the pressure of her body pinning their hands choking the breath out of his lungs. "I just need…A second…Just a little longer."

His breath rattled as she squeezed. Her hips jerked, faster and harder. Hard enough to bruise. He was right on the edge, every vein singing as he thrust up from below. He was ten thousand percent certain he was going to come inside of her. He was too far gone to give a damn.

"Please, please," he whispered, the words falling unbidden from his lips like rainwater from a grey sky. His need was a knife slicing through the center of his chest. "Please—fuck—*please come, Tayshia*. I can't hold it. I can't fucking hold it."

"Yes, you can," she said, her voice altogether much too sweet for how sinful she was being.

"I can't, I can't, I can't," he hissed through clenched teeth. His eyes rolled up into his head. "I'm sorry, baby, I'm so sorry."

It ripped across his psyche, the tidal wave of his orgasm crashing into him. He cried out another gravelly *fuck* as he grabbed her hips and dragged her down onto his cock as far as he could. It felt so good that he couldn't see straight. Couldn't *think* straight. He gave her everything he had to give, spilling himself into her with all of his guilt, his fervor, and his care for her. The waves of pleasure dragged a couple more moans out of him, and then his head fell back against the couch.

Tayshia smiled, as though this was a triumph for her and not a failure on his part. She panted for breath, still tight around his softening cock, her body thrumming with the delicious electricity that had just run through her own. She opened her mouth, starting to speak, but Ash was already moving.

He grabbed her by the hips and lifted her off of him. She let out a squeak as he turned his body so he was lying on the couch, taking her with him, and yanked her cunt directly onto his mouth. Tayshia yelped as all of the muscles in her body convulsed. His tongue laved her clit, and her thighs tightened around his head. She made a strangled sound that he'd never heard from her before, her nails scraping his scalp as she grabbed hold of his hair. He could taste the muskiness of her arousal and his come. The spice of her dominance and his submission. Her fury and his contrition.

She cried out again as his fingers reached around to slip inside of her from behind, searching and probing. Her body didn't seem to know what to do — move backward to focus on his fingers inside her, or grind downward to focus on his tongue — and she wailed.

"*Oh*, harder," she groaned, her voice a constrained plea. "Suck harder. Harder, harder, harder."

Ash obeyed, and she spread her thighs wider, leaning forward to slap her hands down on the couch. Her hips jerked again, tiny movements against the flat of his wet tongue. He moved his fingers faster, slamming them inside of her in a way that had her cheeks moving and the veins in his forearm flexing.

"Come on," he growled into her, slapping her rear with one hand. She let out a whispered plea, her entire body slipping forward. "Come on my tongue. I want it."

"I am," she whined. "I'm going to. Right...Right...*Now*."

And then she came, violently and with a sobbing, keening moan, her pelvis rolling to meet the cadence of his tongue as he tasted the depths of her. He moaned too, from the sheer eroticism of it. From the way the taste of her seemed to explode in his mouth, from the way she'd absolutely fucked him to the cosmos and dropped him to Earth without a care where he landed.

"Did I or did I not tell you I was going to fuck you on this couch?" he said, his hands sliding to cup her face so he could pull her up a bit more. "That was the best sex I've ever had in my entire life."

"And it'll be the last sex you have in your entire life if I don't wake up to five hundred dollars in my bank account. Peace out."

Her head plopped onto his chest and within moments, they'd both passed out.

☼☼☼

They woke to lavender skies, silver stars, and the world they hadn't seen in what felt like ages.

Those purple skies spread like a faint cloud of smoke above them, punctured by the pinprick lights of the stars that usually twinkled bright enough to light their way. If not for the moon, it'd be too dark to see much of anything. The white gardenias were thick and lush as they cascaded down the hill and across the grass for miles, leading to the mountains in the distance. The flowers, representing his mother, multiplying like they were trying to consume the Earth. The mountain range, his father, rumbling as though each mountain was about to erupt. The ocean, Tayshia, presented as a stormy sea instead of the calm, whispering waters he'd grown accustomed to.

None of this was normal, was it?

Ash sat up in the grass on the hill and saw Tayshia already standing. She had her hands on her hips, her back to him, while the hem of her gauzy white dress rustled in the arid wind. It hung off of the horrific image she'd conjured for herself, of bones that breathed.

Interestingly, she hadn't changed any other aspects of her appearance. She seemed to like her hair enough to leave it in the style she wore in the real world. That had to mean something.

"It feels different," she said, and she didn't sound calm.

"No, it doesn't." Ash stood up, dusting grass off the back of his joggers.

"Yes, it does. It feels different. Something's wrong."

"It's *my* dream world. Nothing's wrong with it."

She whirled to face him, her eyes wild as panic glittered like dark stars in her eyes. "Listen to me, Ash. Something is wrong. It's hot. Can you not feel how hot it is? The ocean is wild. The mountains sound like volcanoes. Something's wrong."

Now that he thought about it, the wind should not have felt arid or hot. It should have felt cool. Between the coastline being in the distance to the west of them and the moon glowing as silver as the stars above them, there shouldn't be any heat at all. The mountains had never rumbled. The sea had only ever crashed upon them once, and that was after a moment that signified their feelings becoming a truth they could no longer deny.

Something really was wrong.

"Let's check it out," he said, gesturing for her to lead the way.

They headed down the hill in subdued silence. Ash hoped nothing was wrong. Because already, the two times he'd been in her dream world were strange, haunted memories. Nightmares that lived in waking. But his world had always been safe.

What if it wasn't safe anymore?

Tayshia came to a stop at the edge of the flowers, leaving him to come to an abrupt halt behind her.

"I don't think we should walk in them," she said.

"Why?"

"I don't know. I can just feel it in my gut. Let me see one first."

He waited while she leaned over to pluck one of the flowers out of the mass of gardenias. A mass that was so thick that now that he was standing here before it, he realized he couldn't seem to decipher. The flowers were all growing into and around one another. Tayshia had a difficult time separating one from the convoluted mess of white petals and dark green leaves. Finally, she was able to break one away.

She stood, brought it to her nose, took a deep inhale.

"It smells good, like normal," she said. "Maybe I'm imagining it."

"Maybe."

He held his hand out for the gardenia. She handed it to him.

"Jesus, fuck!" he exclaimed as a sharp pain stung his fingertips. He shook his hand out, bringing his thumb to his mouth so he could suck at it.

"Did it just burn you?"

He nodded.

She whirled around and grabbed a large clump of them, running her fingers over the leaves and petals. Nothing happened. They remained soft and pliant beneath her touch. But when Ash reached out to touch them, the burn was like nothing he'd felt before. It felt hot, like flames were scorching his skin.

He ripped his hand away, stumbling backward a few steps. The look of horror on his face mirrored her own.

"This is because of your father," she said. "It has to be."

Ash froze, struggling to control the sudden panic of his own that rose up. He didn't want to talk about his father. Not here. Not where it was safe.

She continued. "The thing about my dream world that's different is that we can only seem to access it when I'm having a vivid nightmare about that night, and you can't seem to interact with it unless it lets you. With yours, we can come here whenever we want. But now that the mountains are shaking, and the ocean is unstable, and the flowers are hurting you? It's becoming a nightmare for you. And what does this world represent to you?"

"Everyone I care about."

"And what's the one you're most worried about right now?" He was silent. "Your father. And like it or not, you do care about him. You care enough to save his letters in that box, don't you? Don't you?"

He nodded.

"In my dream world, you are the deciding factor. And now, here I am, and I can make these flowers burn you. What does that say?"

"That I'm struggling."

"Exactly. You're struggling with your father. And that's why I think we should go see him. Tomorrow."

Ash felt the shock sinking down into the pit of his stomach. The stable world he'd created was starting to fall apart. They may not have known what *these crystals were actually meant to do, but they did know that they could learn how to navigate their dreams, and how to make them make sense in the real world. And in the real world, he was crumbling.*

Did he really want to let his father take this from him? This was the one safe place he had with Tayshia. They didn't fight here. Nothing could hurt her. There was no Paris, no Eiffel Tower, no eating disorder, no pain. But if he didn't give it a shot and face his dad to at least try *to make sense of his anger, then he could lose their last sanctuary from the wildfires of their reality.*

As she marched back up the hill, speaking her thoughts aloud about his father, how well the chance to look him in the eye would help, Ash leaned down to pick up a gardenia. One that Tayshia hadn't touched.

He felt no burn.

CHAPTER FIVE

The first time Ash's dad hit him, the shock hurt worse than the blow.

He'd done something stupid—forgot to turn the TV off before bed, or something—and his father had been so infuriated by this that he slammed Ash's nine-year-old head against the wall in the hallway. His mother had run to his side, the horror and anger in her tone seeming far away from the daze Gabriel had put him in.

His dad had just taken him to the movies earlier that day. They'd had lunch at McDonald's and spent the car ride home singing to eighties music at the top of their lungs. It had only been a couple of hours since they got home and his father had gone out to work on the garden. He had then come inside to tell Ash to get ready for bed, so he did. Lizette was in Ash's bedroom, putting away his clothes. He had just brushed his teeth, and then—

"I've told you time and fucking time again to turn the fucking TV off before you go upstairs, you little shit!"

The day after that, when his mother had to drag Ash away from the couch to keep him from accidentally sitting on a needle that Gabriel had stuffed down the couch cushions, Ash realized that something was wrong with his father. That something had changed. That whoever he used to be was fading, burning away to nothing.

His father's flowers died, leaving behind the thorns of a man unknown.

Tayshia's voice cut into the fog of his thoughts.

"Your phone is going off, Ash."

He blinked, glancing over at her from where he stood staring at the balcony through the sliding glass door. She was in the process of doing her make-up, with a false lash on one eye and the second one pinched between her thumb and forefinger. She wore a high-waisted pencil skirt that hemmed at her knees, thick red tights, and a red oversized turtleneck knit. Her long fluffy hair was loose about her arms, pinned back at her hairline by two silver clips.

She always looked so beautiful.

Saying nothing, Ash went to the coffee table to pick up the vibrating phone. Across the screen flashed Ryo's name and a picture of the three of them—Ryo, Ash, and Steven—from this Christmas. He clicked the green button.

"Hey," he said.

"Hey, kid. I was just calling to see how you were doing."

"My dad call you?"

"Yes, he did. Told me you had called the prison to request visitation."

Ash sighed, turning to the balcony so he could absentmindedly trace invisible designs on the cold glass with one finger. "I'm still not even sure I want to do this, but Tayshia and I called the school to tell them we had family emergencies, so we might as well."

"I don't want to push my opinion on you, son, but I think you're making the right choice."

"I'm not ready to forgive him. I'm not sure I even want to. In fact, if it weren't for Tayshia opening up the damn letter, I wouldn't even know he was sick. I didn't exactly read the other ones."

"You go at your own pace, son. Today doesn't have to be about anything other than answers."

That would require Ash to know what questions to ask.

"Tayshia will be there with me," he said instead. "Maybe I can let it be about that."

"I'm sure your father would want to apologize to her and on behalf of her father."

"Yeah."

"Well, son, I better let you go. You guys have a little ways to drive to get to Salem, so you'd better get on the road." Ryo's voice held a chipper tone to it, light and hopeful. "Keep your head up. No matter what happened, forgiveness is for you. Not for anyone else. You take as long as you need."

"Thanks, Ryo."

They hung up. Ash stared at the phone, the fear clinging to the edges of his heart and stomach.

He didn't want to talk to Gabriel. He was going to ask him why he hadn't responded to any of his letters, why he never called, why he never came to visit. He was going to make it all about himself, ask him if he was a *"good dad,"* to pressure Ash into saying yes.

They both knew the answer was no.

"Ash?" Tayshia stood beside him, both of her lashes on and her lips lightly glossed. She smiled. "Are you ready?"

He returned the smile, but it was hollow. He fidgeted with the lapels of his blazer, which he felt stupid for wearing. It was like dressing up for his own execution. "No."

"Then I'll hold your hand the whole time. And I won't let go until you ask me to."

The ice around his heart began to melt, droplets of frigid water cascading to calm the fires in his belly. Maybe everything would be okay if he just focused on Tayshia. Focusing on her had always been the thing that kept him going, kept his heart beating and mind drifting forward.

Ash curved his fingers around the side of her neck and pulled her against him, pressing a soft kiss to the center of her forehead. He let his lips linger, feeling her arms winding their way around his waist.

Tayshia would help him through the flames.

☼☼☼

The cubicle visitation room was full, so they were currently waiting in the entry area to be brought to the in-person visitation room. A corrections officer had been paged and was now on their way down to retrieve them.

Sign-in had been too effortless. So effortless that it felt mocking. The woman at the front desk was kind and had a big smile, which agitated Ash even further. He was here to see the man who ruined his life, and the woman was *smiling* as though he missed him. He wanted to tell her he was here to see for himself if his father was going to be dead soon, but unfortunately, Tayshia wouldn't find that as funny as he would. She was a little bummed that they had to confiscate her hair clips.

They'd already been through the first metal detector, so all there was left to do was wait.

Tayshia's fingers were warm and soft, linked between his own. They gave him something to revolve his thoughts around as they spun a galaxy in his head. His emotions were dying stars, circling toward the hole at the center, the hole that he hoped would devour them. His hatred, his anger, his pain, his grief, his confusion. The feeling of abandonment. The memories of his father when he gardened. The memories of his father when he beat him.

He felt like a small child.

The double doors swung open. A short, stout officer came strolling out, his baton swinging at his hip and the light brown of his skin shining beneath the fluorescent lights. He had a full head of glossy black hair and his nametag read Officer Maxwell.

"Morning, guys," he said. "Have a good drive?"

"Yeah," Ash said.

"I've never actually been to Salem," Tayshia added. "So it's a lot of new scenery. It's really pretty, though."

"Oh, really? Well, while you're here, I recommend you go to this little diner downtown. I'll give you the address when you get done, but we've got a time limit, so why don't I take you guys up there."

Ash couldn't seem to find words now that his throat had gotten dryer, so Tayshia squeezed his hand and answered for him.

"We're ready."

"Then follow me."

They followed Officer Maxwell through the double doors and down a hall to the left. An elevator awaited them at the end, one that they had to walk past several doors and offices to get to. When they got on it, Ash and Tayshia stood on one side and the officer went to the other.

"This isn't the prisoner's elevator—don't worry," Officer Maxwell said.

"Where are we going?" Tayshia asked.

"We're headed up to the third floor visitation room."

Ash wasn't sure how to feel. Guilty? Scared? Maybe both. The self-hatred was so overwhelming that for a moment, Ash wondered if he was feeling a fraction of the pain Tayshia must feel every day to want to purge.

Fuck. That was selfish. It was selfish to think that. The reason why things were so tense between him and Tayshia was because he was selfish. The reason why he hadn't read his father's letters was because he was selfish.

He was *selfish*, and he deserved this anxiety.

"You nervous, kid?" Officer Maxwell said, his hands on his belt and ankles crossed as he leaned against the wall.

Ash couldn't speak.

Tayshia looked up at him with an expression he'd never seen on her face before. It was like she was looking at a wounded animal that she wanted to free from a bear trap. "He's a little nervous. This is his father, you know. It can be stressful."

How did she sound so sure of herself? So confident?

When did she start to shine so brightly?

Officer Maxwell nodded. "Don't worry. I've seen people with much worse charges than your father still have visitors and loved ones. You don't have to feel guilty about a thing."

"It's not that," Tayshia said. "We have a complicated situation."

"What are your guys' names?"

"I'm Tayshia Cole. This is Ash Robards. His—"

The Officer cut her off, though not in a rude manner. "Ahh, I see. I followed the court case in the papers." He crossed his arms and tilted his head to the side, his gaze falling to their twined fingers. "I'm guessing you found a way to solve your family differences?"

Tayshia covered their held hands with her other one. "I'd say we did."

"No wonder you're both dressed so nice." The elevator dinged and shuddered to a stop on the second floor. Officer Maxwell grinned. "You're meeting your boyfriend's dad."

Ash did not have the mental capacity to think about boyfriending or girlfriending right now.

They exited the elevator. Everything blurred for Ash as they were led to another set of doors, which opened to a short hallway with windows on both sides. The windows on the left overlooked the grassy knolls outside the penitentiary. The windows on the right looked into the visitation room, which was empty of people at the moment but full of sectioned tables and chairs. There was a blond corrections officer stationed outside the door, his blue uniform crisp and clean.

"Go ahead and leave your cell phones and wallets in that bin there, right beside the guard," Officer Maxwell instructed. The officer who stood watch by the door gave them a smile and a wave. "He won't take anything, don't worry. He's already here eight hours a day—I doubt he wants to move in."

The officers both laughed. Tayshia gave a slight titter. Ash mustered nothing except more panic.

"There's one more metal detector to go through to get into the visitation room, and then it'll just be the five of us," Officer Maxwell went on, counting off the names on his fingers. "You two, me, your father, and another correctional officer who's assigned to him. Also, you can't touch each other or him. You'll have to let go of each other."

Tayshia let go of Ash's hand. It felt like she was ripping his skin off.

"Ready?" said Officer Maxwell.

"I'm ready," Tayshia said, tilting her head back to look up at Ash. "Are you?"

He nodded, finding that his throat felt too constricted to say anything. His knees were trembling. His palms were clammy with sweat. He wished he could reach for her. Anything. Anything at all.

He needed her, he needed her, he needed her.

They dropped their things off in the plastic bin and walked through the metal detector one-by-one. The room was colder than the hall had been, and Tayshia rubbed her arms in spite of the thick sweater she wore. They followed Officer Maxwell to a table close to the prisoner's side door, took their seats beside one another, and waited. The officer went to the right, to stand by the wall with a serious expression on his face.

"Should be any minute now," Officer Maxwell said. "Just sit tight."

His father was going to be right on the other side of that door. He didn't know what he was going to look like, how hurt he'd be, or what look would be in his eyes. Ash only knew that the time had come. There was no going back now. No more avoiding. No more running from his problems.

A buzzer sounded, fairly close. Close enough for Ash to know it was his father and his guard.

Fuck.

Fuck, fuck, fuck.

I wish I could have something, anything, he thought. *I can't breathe. I can't fucking breathe. I can't —*

"Ash?"

Ash tore his panicked gaze away from the door and looked down at Tayshia. Her concern shone up at him like the sun. He wished he could kiss her and let her light burn him away.

"Are you all right?"

"I'm cool."

She bit her lower lip, and he saw it flickering across her face. A deeper worry that made him want to curl around her and let her absorb him. Anything to rescue him from this horrible feeling.

"You can do this, Ash," she murmured, though he could tell Officer Maxwell had heard. "And so can I. He shot my father. He abused you. We can *both* face this together."

"Together," he repeated.

"Together."

The door swung open. Chains jangled. Footsteps thudded heavy and slow on the linoleum, so unbearably slow. The corrections officers were speaking, but Ash couldn't hear them. Couldn't see or feel anything other than pure, white-hot terror. His fingernails dug into his thighs.

This was a mistake. A fucking bad, bad *choice. The worst decision I've ever made.*

Ash kept his gaze cast down.

"You've got thirty minutes," the officer who had brought his father in said. He did not sound as friendly as Maxwell and the guy who was watching the metal detector. "I'll give warnings."

"Hello, Mr. Robards," Tayshia said, her voice almost melodic with how much positivity she threaded into it. She sounded like she was talking to a customer at a retail store. "You might not remember me. My name is—"

"I'm having trouble hearing you, miss. I apologize."

His voice was rough, grating against a sore throat. Weak. Weaker than he remembered it. Certainly meeker than when he would scream at Ash.

I can't breathe. This is too hard. I shouldn't have come here.

"I said, you might not remember me," Tayshia said, raising her voice and leaning forward a bit. Ash could smell her perfume. It was sweet. Floral. Calming. "My name is Tayshia Cole."

"Hello, Tayshia." Ash felt Gabriel's eyes on him, boring holes into his downturned face. "Hello, son."

Twenty minutes. It's just twenty. I can do this. I can do this.

"Ash, it's okay," Tayshia whispered, an anchor in the raging storm that scorched his confidence. "Look up."

He did.

"Hey, dad."

Gabriel sat in the chair across from them, wearing the blue uniform of a prisoner. His black hair, which was stringy and hung in scraggly ropes nearly to his elbows, was tucked behind his ears. His back was hunched, as though it might hurt to try and straighten it. His skin was as pale as a sheet, with a sickly-green tinge to it, and his chest heaved as though he were having trouble breathing. He kept swallowing, again and again, but Ash couldn't tell if it was from nervousness or not. His eyes seemed to have sunken deep into the hollows of his face, the bags under them dark and prominent and one of them seeming to be permanently closed. His mouth appeared situated into a permanent frown, even when he tried to crack a smile. It looked like he'd aged thirty years since Ash last saw him.

He did not look well.

The handcuffs around his wrists made noises as he lifted a tremulous hand to wave at them both.

"It's good to see you, son. You've got so many tattoos now," he said, his one-eyed gaze flickering over Ash's neck and hands.

"He's got them everywhere—his back, chest, and arms," Tayshia said, sounding as though she were talking about something she was proud of. "They're all so beautiful."

"I've always found them to be kinda...Kinda nice." Gabriel stopped to take a breath, then chuckled. "Sorry about that. My lungs aren't what they used to be. Nothing really is."

Ash wanted to yell at him. He wanted to scream into his face and tell him, *of course nothing's what it used to be! You destroyed everything!*

But all he could do was shake his leg and stare.

"I'm sure I can guess why you're here, Miss Tayshia," his father said slowly, his words slurring together a bit. His smile was faint, and there was a sadness to it. "The apology you're owed."

Tayshia didn't reply, crossing one leg over the other and her arms over her chest. Her facial expression was patient, open, and kind. Kinder than Ash had ever seen her look. He could tell that this moment was more important to her than she let on.

"I am sorry," his father said, looking at her the best he could from beneath an eyelid that drooped. "I am sorry for what I put you and your father through. I can only imagine the pain and suffering that I caused, and..." He stopped to catch his breath. "I want you to know that I know and understand the wrong I caused, and how terrified you must have been. I almost hurt you and in the process, I hurt your father. I—"

"And that hurt me anyway," Tayshia said, but she did not sound angry.

"Yes. I hurt you. And I am sorry."

Ash wanted to sneer. His apology was shit. Everything about him was shit. He didn't want him to speak to Tayshia, let alone breathe her air.

"Thank you, Mr. Robards," Tayshia said. "I forgive you. And my father—my parents, actually—both forgave you a long time ago."

How could she forgive him so easily? How did her heart have the strength to do that?

"I'm surprised," Gabriel said, a bit breathless as he clasped his hands on the table before him, "to see the two of you here together. But I am glad you've made a friendship."

Ash spat his words out. "We're not friends. We're together."

"Is that so? How nice."

"You don't seem surprised," Tayshia said.

"I am not." When he looked at Tayshia, it was like he was viewing her through a haze of grey fog. "You're a very beautiful girl. I saw the way my son tried to protect you that day in the ice cream shop."

"Don't fucking lie," Ash snarled. "I just stood there, and you know it."

Gabriel cleared his throat. "I assumed there might be something there between you."

"And you tried to shoot her *anyway*?"

The silence tortured the already-strained atmosphere. Ash nearly lost it, remembering how his father aimed the gun at her, how her father had to push her out of the way.

"Yes, he's wonderful," Tayshia said when it became unbearable, offering Ash a shy smile as though his outburst hadn't happened. "You raised a very good person."

"That's great to hear," Gabriel replied. "Does he take care of you like a man should?"

"He protects me and makes sure I have everything I could ever need. I feel so safe with him that I can't explain it. He makes me happier than you can imagine."

"Well, in that case, he had better marry you."

Tayshia let out an easy laugh, looking up at Ash through her lashes. He couldn't muster a smile in return, not when he was this agitated. If it weren't for the fact that Tayshia's words and face were so God-damned beautiful, he'd snap and remind his father that he stopped "raising" him the moment he jabbed himself with the first needle. It was Lizette who made Ash into the man he was now.

"So, you read my letter, I hope," Gabriel said slowly, like it took all the effort he had to say it.

"I did," Tayshia said. "We're both so sorry to hear that you're sick."

"What's wrong with you?" Ash said.

"Ash," she scolded. "Be kind."

He scoffed and averted his eyes to the right, catching the blank gaze of Officer Maxwell before he returned it to his father.

"Third-stage Parkinsons, I'm afraid."

Ash went cold all over his body, sheets of ice wrapping him, making him hypothermic.

His father wasn't just sick. He was dying.

"I've known for a long time," Gabriel said. "My wife and I—"

"Don't," Ash closed his eyes. "Don't talk about her."

Tayshia gave him a curious look before she turned her gaze back to his father. "I'm so, so sorry, Mr. Robards. When did you find out?"

"When Ash had just gotten into junior high. I was diagnosed a little before he turned thirteen. I was born in 1955, you know. I'm a lot older than his mo—Just older than the average father for someone your age." He paused to swallow. "So, you know, we wanted to keep it from him so he didn't worry."

"And it still didn't stop you from shooting yourself up, smoking, getting high, and stealing money from a drug dealer? Wow." Ash draped his words in sarcasm. "Tell us how you came to the conclusion that beating the shit out of your son somehow served as a good treatment plan."

"Ashley!" Tayshia snapped, speaking to him through clenched teeth with pursed lips and a furious glint to her eyes. "You better *knock* it off."

Ash ground his own teeth together.

"How long do the doctors say you have while it progresses?" Tayshia asked, the gentleness returning.

Gabriel said, "It could take months or years. There's no way to know. What I know is that the days are long and things are difficult."

Ash couldn't take it anymore. He felt like his body was a cage and air was expanding inside of it, trying to burst forth and annihilate him. He was tired of hearing his father's sob story.

Ryo was right. Today needed to be about answers, because he was never coming back.

"Fifteen minutes," the officer at the prisoners' side door called out.

"Why did you do it?" Ash blurted out, his hands shaking as they clenched in the fabric of his pants. "Why did you fuck up so royally that you destroyed *everything*? I want to know. I *deserve* to know."

Tayshia reached for his shoulder, but a sharp warning—*"No touching, young lady,"* – from Officer Maxwell stopped her. She pulled her hand back, but her facial expression remained pinched and worried.

Gabriel pursed his lips. It seemed like he was trying to either decide what to say, or how to condense it to fit into their small time frame. And when he did speak, though it was punctuated with breaks and pauses and heavy breaths, he seemed determined to get it out.

"I've never pretended that I was a good man during those times, son. I was a terrible man, a horrific father, and a reprehensible husband. I failed you both, in more ways than I can count on my hands. I treated you like afterthoughts when you should have been my stars, moon, and sun. I failed you when I hit you, and I failed you when I brought you to Ricky and got you involved with his men. I failed you the day I brought you to that ice cream shop."

Ash's eyes stung. His throat ached. He felt like he was going to die trying to hold the emotions back.

"It's my fault you're suffering. It's my fault that your mother died. I know that's why you won't answer my letters. And I'm sorry. I'm sorry I was such a bad parent. I'm sorry that I failed you. I love you, and I'm sorry that I never showed that."

"What..." Tayshia interjected. "What actually happened to your wife?"

Gabriel opened his mouth to speak, but Ash cut him off.

He had to. He didn't want Tayshia to know. Didn't want her to find out why he was so terrified every time she got down on her knees. Why he knew that her time on this Earth was finite so long as she let her disorder control her body and life.

"She had a heart attack," Ash said. "It doesn't matter."

"How old was she?"

"Forty-seven."

Tayshia appeared confused. "That's so young for a heart attack."

"Ten minutes," Officer Maxwell announced.

Ash could feel his father staring at him. He was going to speak. He was going to say something to him that he'd never be able to forget.

"She would have done anything for you, son. She *did* do everything for you. She was the best mother and wife anyone could ever have asked for."

No, no, no, no, no. Don't cry. Do not cry.

Lizette had done her best to work with the hand she'd been dealt. A troublemaking, partying son selling drugs to his classmates and people on the streets all because he was a stupid kid who wanted to buy tattoos and fuck everything that walked. An abusive, drug addict husband who found solace in the bruised artwork he could paint upon his family's bodies. She hadn't had the strength to fight for herself. Ash had fought for her every time he sat on that bottom step of the stairs and listened to her binge and purge so she wouldn't be alone when she was in pain.

"Don't let her poor choices dictate how you receive my apology."

It wasn't a fucking choice. If it was a choice, Tayshia wouldn't be doing the same thing that mom did. If it was a choice, I wouldn't be so scared of losing her. If it was a choice, she'd stop.

It was a good thing Lizette died before she saw what a failure Ash had become.

"I hope you'll forgive her for leaving you."

"*Shut the fuck up!*" Ash couldn't contain his anger, the rage that sent flames spiraling upward into his face from his heart. "Mom didn't *leave* me. You *killed* her. It's *your* fault she's gone. There's nothing for me to forgive her for, and you're disgusting for even insinuating that."

Tayshia watched with wide, terrified eyes. Ash knew she'd never seen him look this angry before, and that was saying something. He didn't want to scare her, but he couldn't *handle* this.

Gabriel's one open eye shone, his body seeming to deflate even more than it already had.

"Please. Can't you find it in your heart to forgive me for it all? Can't you give me a chance to at least offer you the peace of mind to know that I've made it right?"

"You mean offer *you* the peace of mind so you can die knowing that your conscience is clear?" Ash slammed his hands on the table and leaned forward, hissing at his father with all of the ire he had thrumming through his veins for him. "You're not sorry because you know what you did was wrong. You're sorry because you can't accept blame for anything and you don't want to die a bad man. Well, guess what? It doesn't matter how many apologies you give, you're still a piece of *shit*, and my mom is *still dead*."

Just like that, the veil that Ash had known his father was wearing all along seemed to dissipate in his one good eye. The glimmer there went from pitiable to ferocious, a shadow that died as a ray of sunlight pierced it.

"If you want to make that choice, then that's fine, Ash. But remember that when you make a choice like that, I might not always be around for you to have another chance to forgive me. What if I die and you never get the chance to make things right with us?"

The span of one broken heartbeat passed, and just like that, Ash felt like he was back in the courtroom. Like the cops were hauling him away, and he was watching his mother collapse. Like he was still screaming her name. Like he could see Bertha crying, panicking. Back then, he'd felt like he was staring into the depths of space. Back then, he'd felt like a star, alone in the darkness as it shone for no one.

He feared going back to that loneliness.

"Then, I guess I'll just suffer through the grief, won't I?"

"I'm *dying*, son. And I'm trying to apologize." Gabriel's voice had passion. Desperation. An undercurrent of indignation.

"I won't accept the apology of a dead man."

Ash stood up, Tayshia scrambling to follow suit. He turned away from his father for the last time, facing Officer Maxwell.

"I'm ready to go."

He nodded and headed for the door.

"Son, please—"

"Come on, Tayshia," Ash said, ignoring his father. "I want to go home."

"Good-bye, Mr. Robards," Tayshia said, soft voice sounding remorseful. "Again, I'm so sorry to hear about you being sick. Please, have a good day, all right?"

Gabriel didn't respond.

Ash walked through the metal detector and, without looking up to see into the room through the windows, he gathered his phone and car keys from the bin. Tayshia approached from behind, retrieving her phone.

Officer Maxwell was quiet as he held the door open for them. The furrow to his brow and the careful way he avoided his gaze but chose to give Tayshia a gentle smile, showed him that the visitation he'd just witnessed was not one of the better ones. The sympathy, the pity. Ash recognized those.

He knew he should be proud of himself for facing this — for facing his pain — but it was overwhelming. It was so overwhelming that his body ached and shook. He wanted to leave so he could remember how to function.

Anything to escape this suffocation.

CHAPTER SIX

On the way out, Ash stopped at the place where they'd signed in.

"Can you please put me on whatever list there is where prisoners can't send mail to me?"

"Uh…" The woman's mouth hung open and she adjusted her glasses on the bridge of her nose. "That's not something we can do. But we can take a request to hold onto the letters that a prisoner sends to you specifically."

Good. He wouldn't pick them up.

"That's fine," Ash said, voice flat.

"Ash, are you sure?" Tayshia whispered, but he didn't acknowledge her.

He was certain.

When he had successfully filled out the form and turned it in, he blazed out of the building as fast as he could. He knew he shouldn't walk so fast. He was six-foot-fucking-four and Tayshia could barely keep up. But he was losing it. He was barely holding himself in one piece.

At the car, he exploded.

"Fucking piece of shit! Fucking – " He kicked the wheel of his car over and over, enraged as the memories of his father's stupid fucking narcissistic face flashed before his mind. They'd be etched into his mind forever, a reminder emblazoned in dying starfire. " *– piece – of – fucking – shit – asshole – with – his – stupid – fucking – face!*"

"Ash. Ash! Ash, please!" Tayshia pushed herself between him and the car. Her hands slid up his chest, over the lapels of his blazer, and cupped his fury-heated face. "Please talk to me. Talk to me, okay?"

"He took her away from me," he hissed, gripping her wrists. "Do you understand? She was *all* I had. And he took her away from me. He wanted to talk about his stars and his moon and his sun? Well, she was *my* fucking stars. *My* moon. *My* sun. And now everything's just dark."

Tayshia's lower lip quivered and her eyes filled. She blinked the tears back, shaking her head.

"I'm sorry, Ash. I wish I could make it better, but there's nothing that can."

"You know what my last words to her were? That I was sorry. That I was so fucking sorry to her for being such an absolute waste of a son. A fucking...God, fucking dammit." He tried to pull his face out of her hands.

"You're not a waste, Ashley Robards." Her fingers tightened their hold as she forced him to look her directly in the eyes. "Do you hear me? You are *not* a waste. Don't you know what you mean to me? You're *my* stars. *My* moon. *My* sun. And everything is so bright when I'm with you. You're not a waste. You're my everything."

No.

No.

He was not going to cry in front of her. He wasn't going to cry in front of anyone.

As though it caused him physical pain, he gripped her hands and pulled them down, away from his cheeks. He held them against his chest. "I need to go home. We need to go. I just want to go."

"Okay," she said gently, taking her hands back. She walked back around the car, opening the passenger's side door. "And when we get home, we can take a nap."

"After lunch," he said curtly, his gaze snapping across the roof of the car.

"Yeah. After lunch."

God, what the Hell was wrong with him?

Tayshia had just said the exact words he needed to hear. The words he'd been yearning to hear from her ever since he realized he was falling for her.

And his first choice was to ensure he reminded her of the rules.

He turned the car on and pulled out of the lot, happy to finally be leaving his past behind. The source of his pain could rot there in that prison, and he wouldn't bat an eye. His father didn't deserve to die with forgiveness. With acceptance. With peace.

Let him perish.

"Ash, what happened to your mother?" Tayshia's voice rang into the silence of the car, a ripper at the seams of his barely-held-together composition. "What happened that led to her heart attack?"

Ash's self-hatred, fear, and anger at his father coalesced into one flame and extinguished itself. His mind went as blank as space without stars, leaving him nearly catatonic. If he entertained that conversation, he would dissociate.

"Tayshia, baby, you are absolutely everything to me, but please, for the love of God, don't talk."

They drove in dead silence all the way home, the scenery seeming to be louder than any thought Ash could conjure up. He didn't want to think about anything. He wanted to pretend this day never happened.

How was he supposed to wipe the sight of his father from his mind? It had eradicated the memory he had of him, turning him into something lamentable. Someone who deserved pity. Gabriel didn't deserve pity. He deserved to be held accountable for what he had done, and he hoped that Satan held him accountable for the next three thousand years.

If it weren't for his father's abuse, Lizette would never have needed purging to cope.

If it weren't for the abuse that Tayshia had suffered, she wouldn't need purging to cope.

The parallels sickened him.

It took them an hour to get into the mountains and back to Crystal Springs. It was strangely sunny for a February day, and the snow seemed to be melting for the first time in weeks. It didn't snow often in Oregon anyway, but it was so much more common in the mountains that it hadn't been out of place. Now that it was disappearing, it felt like the world was returning.

They picked up some fast food on the way home. Ash got a burger and fries while Tayshia got a chicken salad and water. While Ash picked at his fries clear until they pulled into their parking spot, Tayshia held tight to the container without once looking down at it.

Inside the apartment, Ash went to the table and set the remainder of his food down so he could take his blazer off. When he was left in his button-up and slacks, he unbuttoned his cuffs, rolled his sleeves up to his elbows, and took his seat. He felt imbecilic for dressing up for such a shit-show of a meeting, even though proper attire was required at the penitentiary. His father didn't deserve for anyone to be on ceremony before him.

Tayshia sat down in her usual seat, gingerly opening the salad lid and tearing the packaging on her utensils. They ate in silence, Ash's leg shaking beneath the table from the moment he sat to eat to the moment he took his last bite. His throat felt tight. Every time he swallowed, it almost hurt.

"Are you ready for a nap?" Tayshia asked after she'd picked at half of her salad.

Ash's elbows were resting on the table, his fingers interlaced in front of his mouth and chin on the pads of his thumbs. He'd been staring absentmindedly at her salad to the point where it had blurred, his hair falling across his forehead and into his eyes. He hadn't had the energy to move, let alone push his hair back.

"Eat, baby," he murmured.

"I am. I'm just taking my time. And I'm tired."

Without moving his hands or face, his eyes met hers. "Eat."

He didn't have the energy for a fight right now. He *did* want to take a nap. He wanted to wrap himself around her, pillow his head on her chest, and fall asleep.

The fire died in her eyes, and she picked up her fork.

He watched her eat, contemplative as he sifted through his complicated emotions. They needed boxes. The only way he was going to be able to cope with seeing his father and the feelings that it brought up was if he compartmentalized everything and gave it a place to be. Anger in the red box. Fear in the black one. Grief in the blue. Confusion went inside green. Hatred went into the orange. All of the colors were neat, side-by-side, exactly where they were supposed to be. That's how it *should* have been—separate and safe.

But even as he placed them into their boxes, he could feel the lids coming off. The hinges were rusted. The locks wouldn't clasp. The wood rotted.

The blue box remained open.

When Tayshia's container was empty, she got up to throw it away. Ash followed her, and they both came to a mutual stop at the entrance of the hallway. She looked up at him. He looked down at her.

He was so tired.

"I'm proud of you," Tayshia said. "I think you were very strong, and that while what you said to your father was harsh, it was necessary. He needed to know how he hurt you, and it needed to be free of anything holding you back. You were assertive. You didn't let him steamroll over you. I think it's a milestone. I think he was cruel and selfish and refused to accept blame. And I think it was horrible of him to use your mother against you. But you were strong, and I'm proud of you for that. Why haven't you gone to see him before now, Ash?"

Ash thought about his answer. Truly thought about it. Steeped the words in consideration and drank the conclusion like tea.

"Because I want him to suffer the way I have."

Her fingers sought his hands. Wrapped around them as though she were trying to lead him down a path. Which he supposed she had been leading him down a path for weeks. A path that he hoped ended in eternity. Her thumbs were soft on the back of his hands, spreading warmth through his heart and curling it deep into his abdomen. Her gaze lowered to his chest for a moment before crawling back up to his face.

"You won't suffer forever," she said. "I promise."

He held it together while her hands slipped out of his. He held it together while they headed down the hall to the safety and quiet of his bedroom. He held it together while she twisted her hair into a protective braid and clambered onto the bed. He held it together while she pulled the blinds down to give them darkness, and he held it together while she pulled the coverlet aside and beckoned him with a small curve of her lips.

He held it together until he couldn't anymore.

When she was settled beneath the blankets, waiting for him, and he was still standing there with only one button of his shirt undone, he froze.

Ash was trying to keep his edges together, trying to keep it all from spilling out. The emotions in those boxes, those colorful boxes that wanted him to break down. The sheer intensity of knowing that he'd been in a room with the father he'd tried to disown. The father who could never stop being his father, even though Ash had tried to stop being his son.

His eyes stung.

Tayshia sat up. Her puzzled look quickly faded into one of understanding. It spelled sympathy in the way her brows met. Sorrow in the tilt of her head. She set the blanket aside and climbed out of the bed, coming to stand in front of him.

"Ash," she said, her soft voice seeming to become swallowed up by the grey darkness of the Winter mid-afternoon. "She didn't choose to leave you. Your mother would never leave you, not for anything in the world, and I can tell you that with one hundred percent certainty."

He wanted it to stop. He wanted to stop feeling like vines were wrapped around his throat, squeezing and choking and strangling. He wanted to stop feeling so frightened of losing everything, of losing Tayshia.

He wanted to cry.

"She was your stars and your moon and your sun..." She took a step closer to him and placed her hand flat on the center of his chest. He wondered if she could feel his heart beating a tattoo against the inside of the bone. "...And you were her world."

Why was she so blurry?

He closed his eyes to the press of her hand against his cheek. Her touch filled him with a warmth that chased away the last of his faculties. He inhaled sharply through his teeth, his chin trembling. He couldn't hold the tidal wave back. It was the sea, and he was naught but a raft with a broken mast.

The first tear fell.

"Ash." Tayshia reached her other hand up, until she held his face, cradling it. "Look at me."

He obeyed.

The sincerity in Tayshia's eyes was something he'd only ever seen in his dreams. It was the same sincerity she had when she was lying in the gardenias, looking up at him with the trust that she had only shared with him.

It all came rushing up.

His mother. Tayshia's disorder. His father. Death. Sickness. Sadness. Paris. The mistakes that he'd made. The mistakes he would inevitably make because he couldn't stop fucking things up. The way he'd hurt her. The way he'd hurt his father. The way his father had hurt him. His broken friendship with Elijah.

Everything was falling apart.

"I'm trying so hard," he whispered, his voice cracking as he held a whimper in the cage of his chest. "But I can't breathe."

"I know." Her tone was soft, a soothing cajole. "I know how hard it is to keep breathing when you feel ruined."

Tayshia rose up onto the tips of her toes, her fingers brushing the nape of his neck so she could pull him down to meet her. She pressed her lips to his ear. When she spoke, though her tone was a whisper, it barreled through his body with all the force of a shooting star.

"Cry. Just don't lose yourself to how bad it hurts."

Ash fell into shambles, his pieces scattering like dust across the cosmos. Those pieces fluttered across the landscape of his wounded heart, pulling sobs out of him that wracked his entire body. He dropped his head into the crook of her neck as his arms wrapped around her waist in a bruising grip. He wept so hard that it would be humiliating if anyone other than her heard it, the pain sending him careening through fire.

He leaned into Tayshia. Physically. Metaphorically. Emotionally. And she held him. She held him with what little of herself she could give him, and it was more treasured to him than diamond. He knew that no matter what happened between them—whether she learned to trust him or not—he would cherish this moment.

She held him through it all, soothing him, pressing chaste kisses to the side of his neck and head. Wherever she could reach. The heat of her body, the solidness of it, was like the warmth of sunlight on a spring day.

Tayshia was in sharp contrast to him. Firm where he shook. Calm where he spiraled. Quiet where his sobs echoed. Steady where he gasped past the spasms of grief in his chest. He hadn't realized that this was exactly what he needed since the moment they closed the door of his cell. Someone. Anyone.

Her.

When the emotions retreated back into the box he wanted to keep them safe in, he pulled back. He moved his hand towards his cheek, preparing to wipe them, but Tayshia's fingers beat him to it. They swiped beneath his eyelashes, which he could feel clinging together. He knew he must look red in the face and splotchy, but he didn't care.

"Are you all right?" she asked.

He nodded and sniffled, his throat too raw. His migraine was already starting.

"I think we should lay down."

"Yeah?" he said, his voice cracked and raspy.

"Will you lay down with me?"

"Yeah."

He was already walking her backward towards the bed.

"Do you need something from me?" she whispered, her head tilting back as they reached the mattress. Her eyelids fluttered as his hands came up to hold her jaw with the sides of his forefingers and the pads of his thumbs.

"Yeah. I do."

He dropped his lips to hers, soft yet heated. His head turned first to the left side, then to the right, his eyes opening to give her a smoldering look that she returned. Their lips met again, their tongues mutually agreeing to greet each other in her mouth.

She was his everything.

Tayshia moaned into his mouth, kissing him back slowly. The strokes of her tongue were languorous in the way they rose to meet his. Her hands clenched in the fabric of his button-up, twisting tight as she fought to stay on her toes. Ash dominated the kiss in a way that showed her not only his gratitude for letting him break down, but his desire for her and the way that it would never abate.

He would always choose her.

He parted from her, his gaze flitting up and down her face as he took in the sight of her flushed cheeks and swollen lips. The way she panted slightly. The way she trembled in his arms. The way she fit against him, like she completed the parts of him that were missing.

"Do you remember the first time we were ever together?" he asked.

Her facial expression softened and she nodded.

He brushed his nose against hers. "What do you remember? Tell me."

"I remember how gentle you were, how caring. You were patient with me even though I was so jumpy and scared. You couldn't have known then, but you were the first person I was with since Paris."

As she spoke, he began to caress her. Gently. With care. Patiently smoothing his touch down her waist, around her lower back, up her spine. Running his lips slowly, slowly, slowly down the line of her jaw and her throat, worshipping her the way she deserved. In any way that helped him forget about everything else.

"I remember how shy you were," he whispered, his hands slipping beneath the hem of her knit sweater so he could peel it over her head. The fact that her hair was braided gave him full access to her body as it was revealed, clad in a camisole, no brassiere, and her skirt. "How you covered your face to hide how hard you were blushing."

"I was nervous," she said, the corner of her mouth lifting up into a smile. "You were intimidating. You still are. You're so experienced and all I have is nightmares."

He paused, pulling back to give her a sad look. "Tayshia..."

"Well, Kieran and I had stopped any sort of messing around by then and even when we had, it was different than it was with you. It was cold and it was rushed. But you…You were warm. You were slow. And you made me feel good."

"And you liked when I made you feel good?" he asked between kisses to her neck. His heart had begun its familiar, steady pounding. The fire was stoking itself in his lower body. The migraine from crying wasn't so prominent anymore. But the drained feeling, the fuzziness in his head, and the desperate way he wanted to be as close to her as possible showed him that he needed her for a reason. "When I called you my sweet girl?"

When his lips brushed the shell of her ear, teeth nipping the way he knew she liked, her head lolled to the side with a heavy sigh.

"Yeah," she moaned. "I love it."

"You want me to make you feel good right now, sweet girl?"

"Uh-huh."

"You have to do something for me."

"Anything you want."

"Make me forget."

She opened her eyes to look into his and answered by throwing her arms around his neck. Their lips slammed together with a fervent desire that Ash hadn't realized could reach these heights just because he'd wept. Their kisses were brief and successive, nothing like the drawn-out ones they'd shared before. This time, it felt like it was just a means to an end. A pathway to getting as close to each other as possible. He didn't know how she felt, but he knew that after being in such a vulnerable state, he just wanted to sink inside of her and chase it all away.

CHAPTER SEVEN

The days until Valentine's Day weekend passed by in a blur.

School was hard to focus on, but with the end of the year looming around the corner and him on the way to getting his associates, Ash had to try. He didn't feel like going to Christ Rising for another year, didn't want to attend another community college, and wasn't sure if he wanted to go to a university. He didn't know how he was supposed to focus on that when his dad was sick, Tayshia was running around trying to usurp his fucking reign, and he didn't know what he was good at.

Talking out of his ass, apparently, because Tayshia still didn't seem to grasp that he hadn't set the rules to be cute.

She thought he didn't see her pushing her food around on her plate to make it look like she'd eaten. That he didn't see her going to cupboards multiple times throughout the evenings just to close them without pulling anything down. He had to forbid her from organizing the fridge because she wouldn't stop.

When Valentine's Day rolled around, he knew he couldn't safely get her chocolates or take her out to eat. He didn't want to argue with her that day, either, so he sent her 500 dollars to wake up to. After school, she went to get her nails done, saying her friend, who she used to go to the buffet with, was taking her. Ash made her promise he could trust her. Then, he went to a florist and got her the hugest bouquet of roses and gardenias that he could carry. It was so large, someone had to lead him back to his car. Tayshia had loved coming home to them, of course, setting the bouquet gingerly on the table before throwing herself up into his arms and wrapping her legs around his waist.

He fucked her on the carpet between the couch and the front door before a relatively calm dinner, and then again against the wall in the hallway on their way to bed. All-in-all, it was a pretty damn good Valentine's Day.

It didn't matter because on Thursday, they fell apart again.

They were having lunch in the cafeteria. It wasn't as full that day as Ash was used to seeing, so they were able to have the end of one whole table to themselves. They sat near the windows that overlooked the edges of the forest outside. Ash had seen Andre sitting with Elijah, who barely acknowledged him with a second glance.

Ash could recall a time when all they did was laugh together. They played video games, ran around outside, had sleepovers, went camping with Ash's dad. The first time Ash skateboarded, it was with Elijah. When his dad left, Ash was there for him. When his mother died, Elijah was there, taking care of everything.

He'd always been his best friend.

Now, Ash didn't like the way Elijah looked at his girl.

Tayshia had asked to get her food by herself, without him hovering in the line, so Ash got his food first and sat down before her. She walked over a bit after, balancing her plate and drink in her hands. She sat beside him, and they both faced the window.

"All right," he said. "Let's see what you got."

Tayshia nodded, her eyes seeming wild as she looked out the window. She'd chosen something he knew she found to be safe: a caesar salad, crispy chicken strips, a soup of some sort, and a couple of chocolate chip cookies. Ash knew it was likely overwhelming for her, but she'd said she wanted to get it by herself, so he was going to let her get it by herself.

It was just too bad she'd very obviously thrown half of the original portion sizes away.

"Next time, please try not to throw half of it away," he said, his voice firm. "Okay?"

"Okay."

He glanced over at her, startled to see her looking right back at him. It felt like her face was open; her gaze clear in a way that he'd been desperate to witness. Like she was a book with all of its pages exposed at the same time. Like she had words that she wanted him to read and a message she wanted him to receive.

It felt like he'd forgotten how to read.

He had to remember that while telling Kieran her secret was wrong, it wasn't the only problem. It had merely exposed the issues they had yet to overcome, and the ones underlying. It exposed her lies and her manipulations. The extent of her illness. The danger. If their secrets had never come to light, Ash feared that they would have crashed and burned. And he couldn't think of anything worse than losing her.

They ate in silence, both seeming to be more focused on listening to the students around them prattle on about this and that.

His gaze fell to his plate, where he saw the food mingling together like an arrangement to be painted. It looked so harmless. So normal and unassuming. How could it be the one thing destroying *everything* right now? How could it be the one thing that had the power to take away everyone he cared about? His mother. Tayshia. Hell, even his father had looked awful enough for Ash to question if the prison was feeding him proper meals.

And here it was. Food.

How could something so crucial to life be so destructive?

When he was done eating, he felt exhausted. Each bite he took had taken all of the energy he had stored within his body. He scrubbed his face with his hands and then dragged his fingers through his hair. He wished things didn't have to be so complicated. That things hadn't changed. He just wanted to go to sleep and pull Tayshia into his dreams with him forever.

"I'm full," she announced.

Ash glanced down. "There's still food on your tray."

"I know." She shot a wary glance in the direction of the students who were still chattering. "But I'm full now."

They shared a look that felt like electricity running back and forth between them, currents zapping, invigorating them with anger.

"Can you maybe try to eat the rest of it, please?"

"I did try," she replied, "but I'm full."

He considered letting it go. He considered dropping the topic, allowing it to fade into the nether with the rest of the things he often tried to ignore. But the more he thought about it, the more it dug its claws in, hooking into the flesh of his psyche like it wanted to rip him into pieces.

"Tayshia. I'm gonna need you to pick up your fork now."

She beseeched him with the pull of her eyebrows. "I'm being honest. I'm full. I can't eat another bite, I *swear*."

"Pick it up," he hissed, "and eat."

A ways down from them, some younger students had fallen silent in the sort of way that told Ash they were eavesdropping. He wanted to turn to them and give them a look, snap at them, *something*—but the last thing he wanted to deal with was gossip. They'd finally stopped caring about the fact that he'd gone to jail. He didn't need them misunderstanding and thinking he was trying to force her to eat out of pure cruelty.

He *really* didn't want to draw Elijah's attention.

"*I'm full.*"

Full off of a quarter of a meal?

She was lying.

Ash had to fight to contain his ire behind a woven net of decorum, calm, and reasonability.

"Do not lie to me. Finish the rest of your lunch."

"But—"

"If you don't, then you'll have to make it up at dinner."

Tayshia's eyes widened. She wasn't prepared for that. It made her just as angry as he felt.

"I told you that I'm full, Ash." She spit out her words like curses. "That means that I'm full. I'm not going to overstuff myself just to make you happy. I ate a normal amount of food, and that should be good enough."

"*I* decide what's good enough," he growled back, no longer caring about their surroundings. "*I* decide when you've eaten enough. If you wanted to be able to decide that for yourself, then you should have thought about that before you put us in this situation."

She gestured between the two of them with her hand. "*Us*?! The situation I put *us* into?! What, do you mean *Paris*?"

When he didn't reply, she looked horrified.

"Last I checked, my body was mine. *You* came into *my* memory."

"So I should just sit by and watch you kill yourself. Is that it? You want me to just fuck around and find out what you look like, sprawled in front of the toilet, *dead*?"

Her lips twisted as she bit the inside of her cheek. No answer.

"Exactly. The fact that we're sitting here, fighting over the fact that you're going above and beyond to try and get out of eating like, four fucking bites insinuates that we're in this together."

"*This*? What—what—what is *this*? Could you be talking about the disorder you seem to think I have? Or could it perhaps be the fact that you verbally abuse me to try to fix it? Wait—you said, '*put us in this situation.*' Do you mean the situation where you inserted yourself into my life like the overbearing, controlling asshole you are? Or maybe it's simpler than that." She slammed her hands down flat on the table and pushed herself to her feet. "Maybe you're talking about the fact that the most painful, *horrific* night in my life was not only viewed, but *experienced* by you without my permission?"

His amethyst necklace suddenly felt like it weighed as much as the moon. He couldn't breathe. His heart took a dive right into the pits of Hell where, by the anger blazing in her eyes, he could tell hers already was.

"Fuck you, Ash."

Ash watched her go, his hands shaking as he pulled them through his hair again in agitation. He felt sick to his stomach, like it was curdling in his body as he sat there and stewed in his own regrets. Several people stared at him with their jaws agape. From the look in their eyes, they didn't seem to know whether to be shocked or amused. It was humiliating.

In a lot of ways, she was right.

He was pulled into a memory that he never would have seen if not for the crystals. She would never have shared that part of herself with him otherwise. And by extension, they wouldn't be together. It didn't matter if she was suffering alone—it was never his right to be a part of that experience. It was never his place, and it never would be. There was nothing anyone could say or do to take that pain away from her. She'd been violated twice.

But how could she blame him for something he couldn't control? He didn't know what would happen when they broke those crystals. He couldn't possibly have known that they would give them the power to dreamwalk. If he could go back, he wouldn't have seen her memory at all.

Did that excuse her killing herself for the sake of coping? Did it excuse the binging and the purging and the starving? Did it excuse the way she'd used her body to manipulate him into buying her binge food? If it wasn't his job to keep her alive and she didn't want to fight for herself, then who would?

Who else but him?

He wasn't going to let her walk away from this. Not from him. Not from their relationship.

He would fight for her, like he promised.

☼☼☼

After school and a tense, charged car ride, it began the second they got into the house.

Tayshia had nearly made it to her bedroom door by the time Ash caught up to her. He grabbed her hand and tugged to stop her, whipping her around. Her back hit her bedroom door, a cry of indignation escaping her lips. He pointed a threatening finger in her face, his fury burning so bright in his eyes that it could light the entire countryside.

"Don't you *ever* take Paris and use it against me like that, do you hear me? If you do it again, we're done. Do you hear me? We'll be *done*."

Fear flashed through her eyes like lightning, and then she shoved his hand out of the way.

"Why don't you understand?!" she cried. "Do you not grasp that my body isn't even mine anymore? No part of it belongs to me except what I can control. The *only* thing that's mine to control is food. And all you care about is making me into your image of what you think I should look like. You just want my body in the state that you want it so you can own it."

"Don't you fucking dare. Don't disrespect me like that. I'm *nothing* like that man."

"I wasn't aware you were owed respect for *my* trauma."

He opened his mouth, but the words he originally wanted to say had died in his throat. Instead, they were replaced with something new. Something dangerous. Something as dark as the shadows in the windowless hallway that twisted their way around them right now.

Ash took a step closer to her, until each breath she took brought their chests together.

"Do you not realize how irrevocably Paris changed me? Do you not grasp that I would take a bullet to the *chest* for you, Tayshia? I'm not trying to control you. I'm not even trying to save you. I'm just trying to love you, and you won't *let* me."

Wait —

But he couldn't take it back. It was true.

The minute she let him, he would fall.

"Stop. Don't say that."

"Why not?" His whisper grated harshly to his own ears. He kept his hands at his sides, even though they tingled with the urge to touch her. "Is it so horrible to think that you're worth something to me?"

"*Stop*," she said, covering her face with her hands. "Please, please stop."

"No. You have value, Tayshia. You have value, and the value that you have is enough for me to want to go to these lengths to protect you. Even from yourself."

"Ash! It was just—just four bites of food! It's not that—it's not that *deep*. I—I—"

He batted her hands away from her face and grabbed her chin, cutting her words off as he forced it upward.

"It's not just four bites of food. It's everything. It's all the times you won't eat the first bite, and all the times you won't eat the last. It's all the times you get down on your knees in front of *that*—" He pointed down the hall towards the bathroom. "—place and risk not getting back up. I don't want another fucking grave to visit. I want *you*."

"I don't want to understand. I don't *want* you to want me. I just want to...I want..."

She didn't have to finish her sentence.

"I will do *anything* to make sure you stay alive," he said. "I don't care how toxic I have to get. I don't care if you hate me. I'm sorry that I'm so hard on you. But I'll never fucking apologize for doing what it takes to make sure I don't have to watch another person I care about die."

There was a moment of silence before her eyes widened yet again, the words settling into her psyche with the speed of a shooting star.

And she slapped him.

So hard that his head whipped to the side and he staggered backwards faster than the sting. Faster than the realization that she'd just hit him. And even though he'd once told her never to do that again, he knew he deserved it.

"If you use my rape to serve your condescending agenda ever again, we're through."

When he looked down at her, holding a stunned hand to his throbbing cheek, she looked like she was on fire.

"Yeah. That's right, little boy. You're afraid to lose me, too."

He stood there long after she'd slammed her bedroom door shut, leaving him in the darkness of the empty hallway.

CHAPTER EIGHT

"Did you hear from them?"

Ash tore his eyes off the road to glance at Tayshia. She sat with her sock-clad feet up in the seat and her arms wrapped around her legs. Her combat boots were on the floor, and she'd tossed her dress coat on top of Ash's in the backseat. She had a dark smoky eye shadow dusted onto her eyelids and her lips were stained red.

"Yeah," he said, looking down at his phone for a second while driving with one hand. "I heard from my tattoo artist first, and he said he's in Seattle for the weekend at a shop downtown. And then Andre said Ji Hyun's sick. She has the flu."

"Oh, so they're not coming?"

He shook his head. "It's just us. We have our own hotel room, anyway."

"It's probably for the best. I think we should make some promises."

Ash raised his eyebrow, letting his phone fall into the center console. "What kind-of promises?"

"To each other," she said, reaching to turn the music volume down. "I think we've been fighting too much."

He looked at her sidelong.

"Yes, part of it is my fault," she said pointedly, "but a lot of it is yours, too. It takes two of us to argue and your temper is out of control. It scares me."

Ash, who had been about to interject, closed his mouth. He looked at her, his heart twisting and shrinking in his chest. On instinct, he slid his hand to curve over the top of one of her knees.

"I'm sorry, baby. I don't want to scare you. That's not at all anything that I've ever wanted."

"Well," she said, covering his hand with her own, "you're terrifying."

He didn't know how to respond. She was right. His temper was short and hot, and when it exploded, he toed the line. That wasn't okay. What if something made him snap and he hurt her?

"If I ever hurt you that badly," he said quietly, "I will literally walk into traffic."

"Don't be so dramatic. That's rude to do to other people. Walk into the ocean instead. It's much cleaner."

The laughter came easy and with it, a lighter mood. Ash liked it better when they were getting along. They were on their way to Seattle, going on their first overnight trip completely by themselves. Did he really want to ruin it by arguing and snapping? They'd just made it through their first Valentine's Day together, too. Did he want to put a stain on *all* of their firsts?

"All right," he said, his hand moving to caress her cheek with his knuckles, keeping his eyes on the road. "I'll make you a promise. No fighting on this trip. I'll keep my temper. And I'll treat you the way you deserve, okay?"

She gave him a cheesy, eyes-closed smile, pushing her face into the touch of his hand. "Okay."

"You're so cute. Turn my music back up, brat."

"*Just* cute?"

"You're fucking beautiful. How's that?"

"Passable, but only because you actually gave me 500 dollars on Valentine's Day."

Rolling his eyes, he kept one hand on the wheel while he leaned over to kiss her. She clutched his face and surprised him with a huge, prolonged smack of her lips, causing him to nearly swerve into the next lane.

"What a great start to our trip," he said. "You try to kill us both."

☼☼☼

The trip took two-and-a-half hours, and the rain put Tayshia to sleep. She woke bright-eyed and bushy-tailed when they arrived, excited to see the city that she'd never been to before. After handling the hotel, which was a rather nice high-rise overlooking downtown Seattle and the Puget Sound, they headed downstairs and decided to walk around Pike Place.

They watched the men tossing the fish around with the crowd of people who had gathered to see, staying underneath the awning of the entrance floor to keep out of the rain. Most people clapped and cheered along with their performance, except for Ash who simply didn't do those sorts of things unless it was at a hardcore show. She seemed to be having the time of her life though, clutching his arm so she could pull herself onto her tip-toes and see over everyone's heads. He ended up embarrassing her a little by wrapping his arms around her from behind and lifting her a foot or two into the air.

"Well, I can see," she remarked, clutching his forearms and giggling her way through the rest of the performance.

Wandering Pike Place took more than a couple of hours. It was a convoluted mess of shops that twisted a few floors underground. No matter where they went, they were either going uphill or downhill. There were bookstores, clothing stores, trinket shops, and a comic book store that Ash loved perusing. He bought several things, including a few *manga* for her to read.

She seemed to have no trouble hanging onto his hand and pulling him in every direction. She dragged him into a Japanese stationary shop to buy more notebooks than she probably needed, and into a store filled with so many porcelain antiques that he didn't know where to look. They traversed the cramped aisles until she hit what she called the *"jackpot."* He was then forced under pain of death to buy an entire set of glazed porcelain ducks for the kitchen. His debit card would have cried if he didn't have all that insurance money.

He didn't mind. Seeing her face light up was worth every penny he spent, especially after all the darkness she'd faced.

At some point, she said she was hungry. He was so happy to hear it that he dropped the vinyl record he was thinking of purchasing, tugged on her hand, and whisked her out of Pike Place. They used his phone to check for the best restaurant to get dinner before their evening tattoo appointment, and decided to go to Hard Rock Cafe. He'd been there before, but Tayshia seemed like she'd simply perish if she didn't get to go.

Across the street on the top level, there was a grocery store with all sorts of snacks and foods from all over the continent of Asia. She picked out several different types of candy, claiming it was for when they were relaxing in the hotel room that night, and then they went to the register. As the cashier cheerfully rang them up, chatting with Ash about their trip, Tayshia looked up.

Her eyes got wider and rounder than he'd ever seen them.

"What? What is it?"

"Duck," she squeaked out, pointing above his head. *"Duck!"*

"Goose," the cashier said.

After giving the cashier an amused look, Ash glanced up to see a wide selection of stuffed animal backpacks hanging off of hooks. They ringed the entire entrance to the open-air shop. And right where she was pointing was a yellow duck backpack with soft, fuzzy fur. He reached up with ease and took it down, handing it to her. She looked dizzy with happiness as she clutched it close.

"What a nice boyfriend you have," the cashier said, her facial expression mischievous.

"Thank you, Ash," Tayshia said, hopping up to kiss him on the cheek, and then frantically stuffing her candy and purse into the backpack. She pulled it on over her coat and when she turned around to show him, the rosy-cheeked smile she cast him over her shoulder made him blush. "So cute, right?"

"Adorable," he said, his gaze focused on her face. Then, he nodded to the cashier as he took the receipt. "Thank you so much."

They headed out and up the hilly street towards the restaurant. It wasn't as crowded here as Pike Place had been, but he had a feeling they'd have to wait a bit for a table since it was Friday night. The mid-February air was cold and frigid, but the failing sun provided enough warmth to keep the snow from sticking to anything other than Tayshia's hair.

She swung their clasped hands between them as she practically skipped up to the crosswalk. Ash was in awe. He'd never seen her in such good spirits. It was bittersweet.

He knew it wouldn't last.

As they waited for the crosswalk to signal that they could go, she held up her hand. The snowflakes landed in the creases of her brown skin, melting upon contact with the lighter color of her palms. Her smile was radiant, so radiant that it made her glow from the inside-out.

He was so close to the one thing he wanted most: for her smile to make it all the way up to her eyes.

At the restaurant, the hostess told them that they were just in time for the dinner rush to begin, so they'd gotten *very* lucky. She took them to a booth with a wide table and cushioned benches, where they slid in on each side. The fit was tight, but Tayshia didn't seem to notice.

That was a relief. He wanted her to stay as happy as she was right now for as long as possible.

She ate like normal. Ash was so ecstatic to see it that it felt like he was floating up to the sky. She didn't seem anxious or upset, and she laughed and smiled at the snarky remarks he made. He knew not to get too excited about it all. They were together, they were both wearing their crystals, and they were having a good time.

That did not mean that she was better.

Her amethyst was clasped around her neck, sitting pretty against the long-sleeved black shirt she'd worn that day. She'd also chosen to wear high-heeled black boots and a pair of high-waisted leather pants that were skin-tight from hip to ankle. When they'd stopped in the hotel room to check it out, she'd run a flatiron over her hair to make it as straight as possible, and put on the pair of hoop earrings he'd gotten her for her birthday. But now that they'd been in the rain, it had started to curl up again.

"I see you were going for Megan Fox chic today," he said as he chewed a bite of his burger, speaking of his everyday skinny jeans and V-neck combo.

"Shut up, you MGK look-alike. I wanted to look like a city girl. What's more city girl than leather pants and a turtleneck?"

"Nudity."

"Ash, shut up. For God's sake." She laughed around a mouthful of food. "If you don't like my outfit, you'll just have to accept it. It's what I'm wearing."

"Tayshia, you look beautiful. I like your outfit almost as much as I like you."

"Stop playing."

They ate in comfortable silence for a while, both of their gazes flitting about the classic-rock themed restaurant. Over the speaker, The Black Keys played softly. The establishment wasn't too full, but there were enough people that they weren't looking around at nothing.

"So, you're getting another tattoo," she said. "Color me shocked."

"You wish you were as daring as me."

"As if you don't already have 3,500 all over your twenty-foot tall body. You don't need another one."

"But I want another one," he purred, smirking and setting his fork down. He bit his lip, leaning back nonchalantly in the seat and sinking down into it. "Are you telling me I can't have what I want?"

She scowled and threw her gaze up towards the ceiling. "Ash, you *always* get whatever you want."

"Oh, I know. I have you."

She hid her smile in a bite of food. "You're laying it on thick today."

"How much thicker do I need to lay it on to convince you?"

"Convince me to what? To go with you while you get another unnecessary tattoo?" The fork disappeared into her mouth again. She gave him a thoughtful look. "I'm gonna need another 500 dollars."

"If you go with me to get a tattoo, my beautiful, illustrious, stunning girl, I will…Not give you another 500 dollars. But I'll continue to pay your rent and all the bills until the end of time. And since I'm older than you, you can call me your sugar daddy. How's that?"

She spluttered on her water and began to laugh uncontrollably. A hand pressed to her stomach as her eyes twinkled with amusement. She leveled an incredulous look in his direction.

"Is this what I have to look forward to?!" she said, still giggling. "An eternity of you getting more tattoos while you bribe me to get them, too?! Yeah, sure I'll get a *tattoo*."

"You'll do it? No backing out—you'll *actually* do it?"

"What? No, I can't get a tattoo. What would my parents say?"

"Probably the same thing they said when they realized you were with me."

"Ash. I *cannot* get a tattoo!"

"Why not?"

"Because."

"Why not?"

"It's certifiable."

"Certifiable? You think I'm crazy?"

"No, but—well, actually. I mean…?" She let out a nervous laugh. "I can't get a tattoo."

"Why not?"

"What would I even get?"

He shrugged. "Anything. Most of mine don't mean anything. A few do, like the ones I got for you and my mom. But the rest are just fuck-all."

She leaned back, tapping a finger to her chin. "Can I get something small?"

"No," he said. "Cover your entire back."

At the look of horror on her face, he held the inside of his fist to his lips to cover his smile as he burst out laughing. He waved his other hand in dismissal, shaking his head.

"Tayshia, I'm *playing* with you. You can get something small, dork. They're not going to laugh at you for it. They get people coming in for the *stupidest* shit all the time."

She shot him a stern look and then sighed. "I'll think about it."

He grinned.

CHAPTER NINE

When Ash held the door open for Tayshia to duck underneath his arm, his gaze swept the expanse of the medium-sized shop. There were five open stations scattered around the edges of the room, separated by walls and decorated to match the aesthetics of the artists who were assigned to them. Three of the stations currently had artists, including Ash's artist.

The death metal playing over the speakers, coupled with the buzz of tattoo machines, felt like a familiar comfort to him, but in a somber way. He remembered using that buzz to fill the void in his chest. After long nights spent crying over his mother in his cell, trying not to let his cellmate hear, the tattoo needle was the only solace he seemed able to find back then.

As they walked up to the counter, where a girl with baby bangs and bright green hair stood, Ash spotted his tattoo artist in the far right corner. He was using someone else's station since he was just traveling.

Diego had his black hair slicked back against the top of his head, the sides shaved to reveal the tattoos he had there. His light brown skin was so decorated in colorful tattoos that not a speck of bare flesh remained save for that of his face. He looked up from wiping down the chair, and his charcoal-colored eyes lit up.

"Ayy, it's Ash fuckin' Robards! How you been?! It's good to see you!"

"Ayy, it's me! What's up, man?"

Ash's face split into a grin as he went around the counter to greet his friend with a warm, solid hug. He returned to Tayshia's side, his hand going to the back of her neck beneath her hair.

"Not much, not much." Diego looked genuinely happy to see him. "I thought I wouldn't be seeing you again for a while. You said you were going back to school."

"Yeah, I did," Ash said with a laugh. "Still am. I'm in this prerequisites program at my old high school. It lets you get your associates before going to a university."

"Oh, nice. So, what are we thinking today?"

As they conversed, one of the other artists in the shop looked up from the woman he was tattooing the forearm of. His gaze washed over Ash, who was now leaning over the counter with his hands flat on top of it, and then it landed on Tayshia. It swept the length of her body and then back up to her face. There it stayed, lingering and appreciative.

Tayshia didn't seem to notice. She was too busy looking at the shop, taking in the sights of the décor and the ink drawings that the artists had smattered all over the walls. She bobbed her head absentmindedly to the music, her hands curved along the front edge of the counter and tapping away to the tune. She had her beige dress coat and her new backpack on, and she stuck out like Christmas lights amongst the black and red of the shop.

"All right, let's get this shit going," Diego said. "Follow me to the chair."

Tayshia's heels clacked against the wooden floor as she and Ash followed him over to the station. They took off their coats and hung them on a rack in the corner. Then, she sat down on a stool that Diego pulled up on the other side of the chair.

Diego took the other stool, beginning to prepare his tools and ink.

"Where's it gonna be?"

"On my chest."

"You sure we got room left, or did you want filler?"

Ash reached over the back of his head to tug his long-sleeved shirt off. His eyes met Tayshia's as he stood there, shirtless, and handed it to her. He could see her struggling not to look at his torso and it made him want to smirk.

He wanted to tell her it was okay to look.

"Yeah, we got some room here between the snake and the clock. And I want it to be a raven."

Diego studied the tattoos on his neck and chest, gaze moving from the chains and roses down to the twin serpents, thorns, and celestial things that spanned the skin. He nodded to himself, then went back to preparing the ink and tattoo gun.

"Yeah, there's some room. I'll fill in the extra space, and then add the bird below it."

"You mean right there?" Ash gestured to himself.

"Yes, there. On your sternum, where the snake's tails come down."

He lowered himself into the tattooing chair. "Do you think we could do it black-and-grey but with like, a hint of red?"

"Yeah, we can do that, McGreedy."

"Shut your ass up."

Ash jolted when he felt gentle fingers sliding gently against his back, horizontal along the spines of the dragon's head. They trailed its neck, traveling over its vertebrae on their way to the tail. As Tayshia traced each spike on its wings, he felt a shiver run through him. His skin rippled. She hadn't seen his back tattoo yet, so he let her appreciate said dragon in silence.

Diego cleared his throat. "Okay, go ahead and lay back."

"Why, wanna fuck me or something?"

"Now *you* shut up."

Tayshia's fingers dragged away from his body as Ash laid back. He lifted one knee, resting his foot on the seat as Diego pushed a lever to make it recline. Ash stretched his left arm up and tucked his hand behind his head. His right hand, he let trail down to hang off of the chair. His fingers were within millimeters of Tayshia's knee and the top of her calf.

After putting on latex gloves and wiping Ash's skin down, Diego began. So did the buzzing.

Ash gritted his teeth against the initial pain as the needle pressed into his skin. It started underneath his collarbone and etched its way towards his heart. As it vibrated down to his bones, he fell into the familiarity of it. It was something he knew. Something he could expect.

Something that made him forget.

"So, whatever happened with that girl?" Ash asked. "The one you were seeing in August."

Diego chuckled, his gaze focused on his work. "Gone."

"No."

"Yes. Gone. She got out of there with the quickness."

"Ah, that sucks. You—" Ash hissed as the needle swirled up over the slope of the place where his collarbones nearly met. "You said you really liked her."

"I did." Diego's eyebrows shot up. "But I dunno. We went to this club and she was like, dancing with these guys. I thought it was suspicious. And I walked up to her and it just became a situation. You know how it is."

"Yeah."

Ash's fingers drifted up along the outside of Tayshia's calf, but he kept his eyes focused on the bite of the needle in his flesh. It hurt like a burn—it was his chest, after all—but it felt so insignificant compared to what he felt inside every day since his father ruined his life. Since he took everything within him and turned it to shadows.

"Hey, you remember when I gave you this one?" Diego asked with a laugh, gesturing to one of the star systems tattooed on Ash's ribcage. When Ash nodded, he continued, "You were *tore* up."

"He was? What happened?" Tayshia sounded curious.

"Oh, he was crazy. Fought everyone who started anything with him. It was ridiculous. Well one day, he—"

"I'll tell it," Ash growled. "Tayshia, it was nothing. People liked to pick on me. I don't like being picked on. It just happened to be a *lot* of guys in there that didn't like the look of me."

"No, don't lie to her. You know you started some of them—*yes, you did,* Ash. Don't look at me like that!"

"He's lying, Tayshia, baby. Don't listen to him. I was a poor, victimized angel."

"Now, I *know* he lyin'," Tayshia said, and then all three of them laughed. "Okay, but for real. What actually happened?"

"You wanna tell it, Pinocchio?" Diego teased. "That's what I thought. Okay, so there was this guy who'd been giving him shit for days. Like, just *days* of harassing him in the caf, in the yard, in the halls. Well, they got assigned to do laundry together one day. Somehow, Ash thought it was a good idea to respond to the guy's bullshit by slamming his head in the washer."

Tayshia gasped. "Did he *die*?"

"No, silly," Ash said. "He beat the fuck out of me. Duh."

"And then he came to get a tattoo from me the next day, Ash did. Made me tattoo right over the bruise. He's a masochist, I tell you."

"A sadist, too," Tayshia added, earning herself a pinch to the calf.

"So, why's this one sitting so still?" Diego asked, raising his voice in a pleasant tone. "You just here to watch?"

Ash gave Tayshia a half of a smile, watching as she lifted one of the arms that she'd folded in her lap to wave a hand.

"Oh, yeah. I'm just here to watch him," she said. "I don't have any tattoos."

Diego arched one eyebrow and exchanged amused glances with Ash, who spoke.

"I've been trying to convince her to get one. I don't think she's changed her mind yet."

Diego said, "Come on. What, are you worried about your mom having a panic attack?"

Ash cringed, but Tayshia seemed to take it in stride.

"No, I am not," she said, chuckling through her blatant lie. "I'm more worried about the pain. I don't know if I can handle it. My tolerance is so low."

As if on cue, Ash hissed again. He sucked air in through his teeth as Diego's needle outlined the left side of the raven's face beside his sternum. Tayshia grimaced.

"It's really not that bad," Diego said. "Tell her, Ash."

"It really isn't." His chest was on fire. Literally burning in excruciating flames. "It's like a scratch."

"That doesn't look like it would feel like a scratch."

"Because he's lying to you, baby doll," Diego said, throwing his head back to laugh. "For real, though—what matters is where you get the damn thing. If you want it on your upper arm, it's no big deal. If you fuck around and get your first tattoo on your face, then you're gonna have a bad time."

"Yeah, get a face tattoo, Tayshia."

She stared at him. "You get a face tattoo."

"No, you."

They narrowed their eyes at one another. His fingers curled around her calf and he squeezed. Then, like wildfire ripping through a dying forest, evil spread her smile wide.

"If you get one on your face," she said, "then I'll get a tattoo."

Diego burst out laughing, so hard that he had to lift the needle. Ash glared at him, then shot her a wicked grin.

"All right."

"Wait, really?"

"Yeah."

"Boy, you got to be either stupid or insane. I'm not sure which."

"Which one makes you want to fuck me?"

Diego laughed again, his head thrown back. "You guys are cracking me up. Just go see Tomas over there. He'll fix you right up."

She smoothed out the front of her shirt and then crossed her arms over her chest. "What should I get?"

"Are you asking me? Are you serious?" Diego looked like he found her words horrifying. He looked at Ash. "Is she serious?"

A flash of panic crossed her face, so Ash jumped to action.

"She's kidding. Tayshia, you can get anything. It can be something you like, or you can just let the artist do whatever. What's important to you?"

"Gardenias."

Ash felt something in his heart warming up, melting like snow beneath sunlight. He reached out to grip her hip in a show of affection, and then he looked at Diego.

"Well, then you can tattoo a gardenia on my face when we're done with this."

"Sure," Diego replied as the needle moved across to the other side of Ash's chest.

"And there you go."

Tayshia sighed and glanced across the shop. "I'll go over there, to that guy."

"Tomas," Diego supplied.

"Tomas."

In the silence that followed after she walked away, Ash felt excited. He wondered how the tattoo would look. There was something intriguing about the idea of Tayshia having one. He imagined he would never stop touching it, no matter where she got it.

"That your girl?" Diego asked.

"Yeah," Ash said, voice a bit hoarse from laughing.

"She's hot."

"So you wanna die. Okay. All right."

"Shut up," Diego said, both of them laughing. He resumed tattooing. "Anyway, about that girl from the summer. She—"

"Diego?"

"Hm?"

"Call her baby doll again, and I'll cut you."

The tattoo gun continued to buzz, even as it stopped moving. Diego gave him an incredulous look, to which Ash responded with a slow smirk.

Diego rolled his eyes. "I can't with you."

Ash ran his tongue along his top teeth and glanced over to the right, across the shop at Tayshia. The artist who had been looking at her when they entered the building was talking to her, his hands moving about as he described something. She had her arms crossed, her body language closed off, and something didn't sit right with Ash. Something about the way the guy—Tomas—looked at her made a serpent deep inside of his abdomen curl and twist in warning.

Then, when Tayshia sat down in the chair and pulled her turtleneck off over her head, revealing her pink silk camisole so she could expose her shoulder, he felt the serpent rise.

The look on her face showed her discomfort.

"Di," he said, his gaze trained upon every movement of Tomas' hands.

"Yeah?"

"Who is Tomas?"

"Oh, him? Yeah, he's new. They say he been here about a month. He's got nice shading skills. Why?"

Ash said nothing, flinching when Diego's needle hit a tender spot. He clenched his teeth, watching the way Tayshia turned her face away from Tomas's needle as he begun. She looked over at Ash, glaring at him.

"She's gonna kick your ass tonight, Ash," Diego said as he worked. "I can tell she's the type to cry."

"She doesn't look like she's crying to me."

Diego glanced over and let out another laugh. "You're right. She looks pissed off. Looks like you're just getting the ass-kicking tonight. Anyway, will you let me finish telling you about the shit that happened?"

"Yeah."

Ash fell silent, alternating between listening to Diego and feeling the pain of the needle. As the time wore on, going from thirty minutes to an hour, the burning increased to the point that it was starting to wear on him. He rested one hand on his stomach and slung the other arm across his eyes to block out the light. The anxiety began to pound in his veins and expand in his chest.

"Don't fuck it up. Quit bouncing your leg," Diego said, his voice a concentrated murmur as he shaded in parts of the raven's feathers. The needle ran back and forth, back and forth over his skin. It felt like it was being rubbed raw.

"Fuck," Ash growled. "Don't fucking talk to me."

"Rude."

Ash's brows twitched together beneath his arm. He hadn't forgotten how bad his other chest tattoos had hurt, but he supposed he'd been too distracted by other things to put it to the forefront of his mind.

In the distance, beneath the sound of the loud music, he could hear the murmur of Tayshia's voice. It mingled with Tomas' laughter and made the serpent in Ash's stomach launch itself up to his chest.

It was taking Tomas way too long to tattoo a fucking flower.

"That shit should have taken twenty minutes," Ash said through his teeth, trying to bear the feeling of the needles on his sternum.

"Don't be ridiculous. An hour at least."

"Well, what size is she getting? Can you look?"

"I'm legit trying to tattoo you right now."

"Just fucking *look*, will you?"

After a pause, Diego said, "It's the front, top, and side of her shoulder. He's got the outline done and he's starting the shading now."

"Stupid."

Diego chuckled but said nothing.

More time passed and soon, he could hear Tayshia's laughter. He couldn't tell if it was fake or real and it made him want to spring up and walk over there. He just wanted to see what they were doing. To know what they were talking about.

What if Tomas was making her uncomfortable? What if the only reason why she was laughing was to disarm him into thinking she wasn't? What if this was like Paris, when she tried to talk her way out of—

"Di, I gotta go over there. Like, you don't understand."

"No, you don't," Diego replied. "And quit bouncing your fucking leg."

"They're laughing too much."

"Because he's hitting on her."

Ash felt a violent rage flaring within his body, but Diego anticipated it. He lifted the needle from Ash's skin and pressed his hand flat to his shoulder.

"If you get up, I swear to God."

"You just told me that—"

"Tomas hits on every girl who comes in here that's even remotely attractive to him." Diego sounded annoyed. He brought the needle back to Ash's skin, and none-too-gently. "Now, suck it up, shut up, and lay there. And quit bouncing your *fuckin'* leg."

Ash grumbled curse words to himself, keeping his forearm over his eyes to stave off the headache.

Even with water breaks, he could feel himself reaching his limit by the time another hour had passed. The combination of the scraping needles, Tayshia and Tomas' barely audible and amiable conversation, and the thought of her freaking out and breaking down later made him want to scream.

Tayshia's voice came to fruition beside him. "How's it going so far?"

Ash lifted his arm a bit, cracking open one eye. He hoped she could see how irritated he was.

"It feels like Hell," he snarled. "How'd it go for you, Chatty Cathy?"

She sat down on the stool. With a ginger hand, she pulled the neckline of her shirt aside, revealing the plastic covering her new tattoo.

It was indeed a gardenia, black-and-grey in color, and it spanned the majority of her shoulder. The petals stretched over the end of her collarbone, down towards her bicep, and around the side as though reaching toward her back. The leaves as well as the bottoms of the petals looked like they'd been shaded darker than the rest of the tattoo. It really was gorgeous work, but Ash hated the fact that Tomas had had his hands on her.

He knew he was being ridiculous. Possessive and too protective, but it was difficult. It was difficult knowing what she'd been through and how hard it was for her to even get to a point where Ash could touch her. For another man to have his hands all over her? It bothered him.

But she looked happy.

"He said you can even shower with this plastic on it. Isn't that cool?"

"Mm," Ash said.

"Well, do you guys like it?"

"Oh, Hell yeah," Diego said. "It looks sick. Tomas always does such clean lines."

"I really like it," she replied, still sounding excitable and energetic. "It didn't even hurt as bad as I thought. Well, I mean, some parts did, but for the most part, it was just like, a vibration."

"Even better," Diego said, and then he resumed the shading on Ash's tattoo.

"So, do you like it, Ash?"

"Yes," he said, his teeth still clenched.

"You don't sound like you do."

"Well, I do."

Diego cleared his throat. "He's in a lot of pain. Just ignore him."

"Fuck you."

Tayshia tutted. "Ash, don't be rude."

"Rude is his middle name," Diego said. "Ah-ah. Shut your mouth, Ash. Just be quiet until I'm done. We got like, fifteen minutes to go on this."

Ash scowled heavily, covering both eyes with his arm again. He heard the stool cushion shifting as Tayshia sat down, and then he felt her fingers curving over the top of his raised knee. She squeezed to comfort him.

"It looks really beautiful," she said to Diego. "I really like the red and I love the way you added those broken chain links around the bird's feet."

"Looks good, doesn't it? It goes really well with the chains on his neck."

The two of them engaged in light conversation for the remainder of the time. Then, when Ash thought his muscles might start shaking from the prolonged exposure to the pain of the needles, Diego turned off the machine. The buzzing went silent and Ash felt relief flooding his body like a wave from an ocean of reprieve.

He sat up, feeling Tayshia's hand on the back of his left shoulder, assisting him as he rose. His head throbbed, chest pulsing and burning. He was going to need weed after this.

"So, where do you want it?" Diego asked.

What?

Oh, fuck.

That was right. He'd forgotten already.

The face tattoo.

"Right underneath my temple."

"Like on the cheekbone?"

"Yeah."

The buzzing began again. Ash wanted to scream.

"Wait," Tayshia said through laughter. "You don't have to anymore."

"Are you serious?" Ash said, incredulous.

"I'm not going to make you tattoo your *face*, Ash. Come on."

Ash exchanged glances with Diego, who turned off the tattoo gun. The relief Ash felt almost eradicated the pain of his freshly-tattooed chest.

"Anyway," Diego said, "why don't you get up and check it out?"

Ash went to the mirror on the wall.

"Okay, this is fucking sick," he said, admiring the new additions to his chest tattoo. "I forgive you for letting me berate you in the chair."

"Oh, *thanks*," Diego said.

The snakes that rippled along Ash's collarbones like they were traversing the planes of his upper body were now completed by a surrounding of smoke shading. The chains wrapped around the roses' petals on his neck hung into broken links that rained down around the red-shaded. Ash felt the broken chains represented the way he felt about his life. That the chains didn't matter anymore, even though they were still wrapped around him. His past and his future. He could be restrained if he looked up, and free if he looked down.

Restrained if he held onto his mother. Free if he held onto Tayshia.

Still chained.

Tayshia stood beside him. In their reflection, he could see her ogling him. Her gaze was almost hungry as it took in the sights of not just the new tattoos, but the ones on his arms, abdomen, and the backs of his hands. Finally, she met his eyes.

Hers burned.

"I like your tattoo," he said with a small smile.

"Thanks. I like yours. All of them."

He leaned down to give her a quick kiss on the cheek, then turned to Diego to ask him if he had any weed. Diego did, selling him enough for a relaxing night. He tucked it into his pocket for later. Following that, they covered his chest with a special lotion and then applied the same sealing plastic film that Tayshia had on her shoulder.

After Ash paid for both of their tattoos—with much gratitude from Tayshia—they left with his hand curving into her waist, tugging her tight against his side. The moment they rounded the corner into the alley between the tattoo parlor and the building beside it, he had her pressed up against the brick wall.

He slammed his forearm above her head, his lips attaching to hers the moment his flesh hit brick. Tayshia threw her arms around his neck and pulled herself onto her toes, her tongue shoving its way into his mouth and exploring its depths as though it were the first time. She whimpered when her freshly-tattooed skin stretched but seemed to push through it as her fingers found their way into the hair at the back of his head.

"You're mine," he growled, his hand wrapping lightly around her throat and his lips brushing her jawline. "Aren't you?"

"Of course I'm yours. Why do you sound so scared?"

Ash didn't like that Tomas had touched her. He didn't like that he had talked to her, or made her laugh. He didn't like it because Tomas didn't know her like he did. He didn't know what she truly found funny. He didn't know how she liked to be touched. He didn't know how long it had taken for her to be comfortable enough to show her body to someone like that.

He didn't know what she sounded like when she cried. He didn't know how much pain she was in every waking moment of every day. He would never know what it felt like to hear her screams, to feel her sobbing in his arms.

Tomas would never see her roots, so why should he get to see her petals when she bloomed?

"Because the thought of anyone—especially a man—touching you without knowing how beautiful you are inside makes me angrier than I thought. I'm the only one who knows what it takes to make you happy."

"It was just a tattoo."

He pressed his forehead against hers and took a deep breath.

"And you're my everything."

The space between them stretched as wide as the distance between their stars and then their lips met. They met again and again, soft and gentle, and then hard and bruising. He cupped her face with his hands and pinned her to the wall with his body. Her hands curved over his shoulders like she wanted him to envelop her and keep her safe. They kissed, mindless of the fact that the sidewalk just beyond the mouth of the alley they were currently making out in was crowded and full.

Ash cared about this girl. He genuinely cared about her. He wanted to take everything bad that had ever happened to her and burn it. He wanted to take the memories she had of Paris and send them down to Hell so they could never return to plague her. He would do anything for her and if he ever lost her—to a man or to her disorder—he'd do whatever he could to get her back.

He would do absolutely fucking anything for her.

CHAPTER TEN

Tayshia's eyes were guarded as she watched Ash enter the extravagant hotel lobby behind her. There was a heavy air about both of them, pervading Ash's painted-on disguise. He could feel the day weighing him down, slowly peeling away the layers of his false strength. He felt drained.

What happened when they went home tomorrow, and she went back to being sad?

"Should we do room service for a snack later?" she asked, pressing the button on the elevator.

"Sure. As long as you eat."

"I will."

Ding.

The elevator doors opened and they stepped inside. The people on it smiled at them and stepped out, and then they were alone. Ash pressed the button for their floor—the ninth—and the elevator began to ascend.

He looked down at her, watching the way she stared blankly at the wall, and he knew she was likely dreading the return home, too.

"Why?" he asked.

She lifted her gaze from the floor. "Why what?"

"Why were you so happy today?"

There was something electric that charged across the tense silence between them, like their hearts were reaching for one another. Ash felt like he was handing his to her, but she was too frightened to give hers in return.

"Because," she said in a muted tone, "This was a city. Cities scare me because a city is where that man hurt me. I think he would be miserable if he knew I was happy." She paused. "And I wish I could make him suffer the way I will."

Ash remembered. He remembered saying those words because they'd been the most honest words he'd ever shared with her. He'd wanted his father to suffer the same way he knew that he would. It wasn't fair that Ash should have to burn in fires that Gabriel had set.

As long as she was burning, she wanted the man in Paris to burn, too.

He dropped his hand to his side, his fingers brushing hers. She jolted but didn't move away. Taking it as permission, he threaded his fingers through hers. When she looked up, he trapped her gaze with his own.

"You won't suffer forever," he said. "I promise."

Ding.

The elevator doors opened, and her hand drifted out of his own. He followed her down the hall, hoping that she hadn't hit rock bottom yet. Watching her padding softly along the carpet in her pretty outfit and her cute duck backpack and her sexy heeled boots. Watching her leave her happy day behind, ready to return to her cloak of sadness.

"Would you like to shower?" she asked when they were in the darkness of the room as she took her boots off.

"Nah, that's okay. You can go first."

The light of the bedside lamp flooded the room, illuminating the nice furniture and her unreadable facial expression.

"I meant with me."

He sat down in the armchair, leaning down to untie the laces on his shoes. For anyone else, a shower together would be nothing out of the ordinary. For them, it was everything.

They were awake.

"I mean, only if you want me to," he said, removing his shoes and socks and then standing up again. "Do you want me to shower with you?"

"I do."

She dropped her new bag onto the dresser, took her coat off and hung it on the chair, and went into the bathroom.

Ash stood there for a few minutes, debating. The only time he'd ever seen her completely nude was in her memory. In Paris. In *pain*.

The light in the bathroom turned on. She'd left the door open, so it shone out into the miniature hallway. Ash heard the water flow, slamming against the floor of the tub.

Was she ready for this?

Was *he*?

He pulled his shirt off and headed for the bathroom.

Steam had already begun to rise, floating up to greet the glass of the mirror. It fogged it like flames, fire licking up the walls of a burning house. Ash looked at the closed curtain, his pulse pounding as he unbuckled his belt. It dropped to the floor with a clink.

This was a *big* milestone.

He turned and glanced at himself in what was left of the clear parts of the mirror. Glanced at the tattoos that littered every inch of his upper body and wondered if the fact that they were there meant he wasn't as vulnerable as she was. It felt unfair—his scars were obscured.

"Are you coming?" she asked softly, poking her head out around the curtain. Her curly hair ran down her back and swung by her elbows. Dark makeup ran down her face from beneath her eyes, making her appear as though she were on some sort of hard drugs, or like she'd been drinking for hours. "The water's warm."

"Yeah," he said he unbuttoned his jeans. "Are you okay?"

She nodded, watching him remove his jeans before lifting her eyes as he walked closer. They held each other's gazes as he removed his boxers. He stood before her, as naked as he could be, and took a deep breath.

"Ready?" he asked, brushing his fingers back through his hair.

"Yes."

She skulked backward, pulling the curtain aside with her. The shower was a moderate size, so there was plenty of room for his tall form to crowd into it. He felt the hot water cascading over his skin, down his chest and spine, droplets soaking his hair. He pushed it all the way back.

Tayshia stood with her arms wrapped around her body—one across her chest and the other across her stomach. She couldn't seem to make eye contact with him, the droplets clinging to her lashes flinging every which way as she looked to the left, right, up, and down. He could see that she was terrified.

He was so, *so* fucking proud of her.

"Come here," he said softly, his fingers fluttering along her waist as he folded her in his arms. "It's okay."

She trembled as though she were standing in the center of a barren, frozen wasteland. The Arctic surrounded her, swallowing her in snow as she existed beneath the starlight. Frost decorated the planes of her body like it wanted to turn her into a sad Roman sculpture with forlorn eyes and a downturned mouth.

He pulled her chin up with the side of his knuckle. Her body shook harder. She immediately put her head down again.

One.

"Come on. You can do this for me. Look into my eyes."

He pulled her chin up a second time. Her gaze darted up, and then her head turned down again.

Two.

"It's you and me. Just you and me. No one else here."

A third. This time, her gaze trained itself upward.

After a moment, her face screwed up as though she were losing control. She turned away, squeezing her eyes shut. The shower water running down her face in desolate rivulets made it look like she was crying. They crossed and split apart, creating Eiffel Towers on her cheeks.

His fingers found her chin and jaw once more. His hand curled around her chin to hold it there, even as she continued to quiver.

Three.

"Just you…And me."

She tried to pull away again, tried to turn her entire body as the intensity of his stare became too much. But the time for hiding had come and gone. That was the past—their past, even if things had moved as fast as they had for them. What they had now was their future. Their healing. The mending of their trust.

His fingers slid along her jaw and pulled her face back towards him. She fought against it, but he was stronger than her. He forced her to look up at him. She closed her eyes.

Four.

"Tayshia, open your eyes for me. *Please.*"

Two agonizing seconds crawled by, and then she opened her beautiful eyes.

Five.

"I won't look away. Even if you don't want me to look at you. If you keep your eyes on me, you'll always have something to count on."

They spent the rest of the shower like that, barely moving, looking into each other's eyes. There were several times where it became so overwhelming that Ash himself wanted to look away, but he didn't. He refused. He would look at her until eternity came, and then longer.

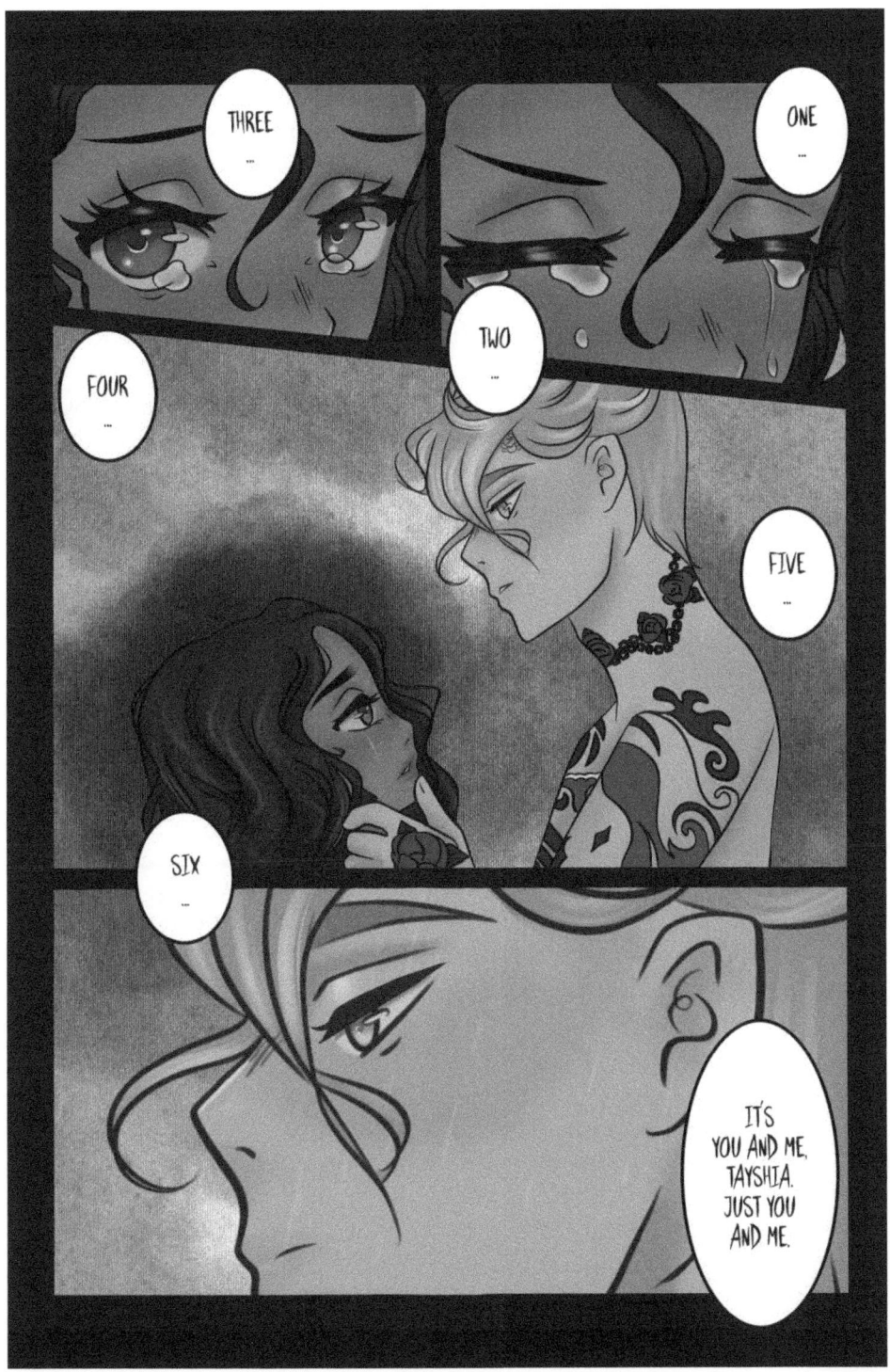

And she looked right back at him. He could see it there—the determination as she fought against her own fears and insecurities. The determination as she fought the trauma and the pain that draped over her naked body. Her brow furrowed several times, as though it were taking an immense amount of concentration, but she never lowered her gaze.

Ash wanted her to know that no matter what, he wasn't going to give up on her. As long as she tried. As long as she fought.

Until the stars burned out, and the snow melted, and the moonlight faded, and the seas dried up, and the sun died, and the shadows receded, he would look at her.

Finally, when the water started to lose its heat, they stepped away from one another and began to actually shower. They moved in silence, alternating between tasks. When she washed her scalp between braids, he washed his body with soap and a cloth. When he ran conditioner to the ends of his hair, she was running a razor over her legs. They both were careful not to agitate the wraps on their tattoos, washing around them with ginger hands.

Ash finished first. He dried off with a towel and then went out into the main room. Slipping his legs into a pair of grey sweatpants and a black shirt with long sleeves, he prepared for bed. He sat down in the armchair with his weed and rolling paper. While he smoked, he stared at himself in the vanity mirror across the room and lost himself in thought.

The sounds of the water ceased.

Ash brought the joint to his lips and took a deep drag, holding the smoke in for as long as his lungs could handle. It burned, aching in a delicious way as he coughed. He exhaled, watching the thick smoke curl out and leave behind an excellent, buzzing high. It tingled through his veins.

The bathroom door opened and Tayshia stepped out.

Completely nude.

Ash, whose head was resting back on the top of the chair, looked down through his lashes at her. She stood there, her hair wet and skin dry, her face clean of all the make-up. Her hands were in tight fists at her sides, and she kept shifting her weight from one nervous foot to the other. She looked gorgeous, the way the lamplight cast gold over the brown of her skin. The way it illuminated every part of her that she'd hid thus far, and every part that he'd seen.

He lifted his head, the joint feeling like an afterthought between the fore and middle fingers of his left hand.

"This is me," she said on the wake of a short breath. In measured increments, she lifted her gaze from the floor to meet his across the room. "This is my body. I don't like it. I don't like anything about it. But when you..." She closed her eyes and took a second, then opened them with another determined look. "When you look at me, and you fight for me the way you do? I feel like I can see myself loving it one day."

Ash sat up and leaned forward, his elbows resting on his thighs. He looked at the floor and then up at her. "I can't be the one to make you love yourself."

She took a step closer, her hands starting rising to cover herself. They stopped and went back to her bare sides.

"No, you can't. And you won't be the one to do it. But you've helped me see the path to being able to do it myself."

He brought the joint back to his lips and sucked in the smoke. "What are you trying to tell me?"

She watched the smoke curl up towards the ceiling upon his exhale, and then looked down at him again. He saw her trembling.

"This is what's left of me, Ash."

Walking closer, she stopped in front of the chair, her knees brushing against his.

"It's all I have."

He studied her while he took another drag and blew the smoke out to the side. She blinked slowly, and it was like she was dragging her lashes upward through molasses.

"It's what I can give you."

Ash remained motionless as she leaned down to press a kiss against his lips. It was soft. Tender, the way her lips moved against his and her fingers held his face. She kissed him like she were sealing a declaration. Then, she pulled back.

"If you want me, I'm yours."

She settled atop his lap. Without saying anything, she took the joint from him and put it between her lips. Her eyelids fluttered closed as she took in the smoke and blew it out above them. As her head tilted back, her damp hair falling down to her lower back, Ash's gaze ran down the length of her upper body. Her bare breasts, her waist, her collarbones and the line of her neck. The curls he'd run his fingers through to get to her core many times before.

It was like they were in limbo, floating in the darkness, reaching for one another. Sometimes, it felt like their fingers were brushing. Sometimes it even felt like they were holding hands. But then, just as soon as he felt it, it was like she was gone again, floating off into shadows that shattered like glass.

She passed the joint back to him, an almost-satisfied smile on her face as her bloodshot eyes studied his hand. She lifted it in both of hers, her fingers playing with his rings. She twisted them around his fingers in turn, successive motions from left to right.

He gave her a lazy smirk around the smoke. "What're you doing?"

She didn't speak, instead choosing to pull his hand closer. His fingertips brushed her sternum.

He twisted his hand and wrapped it around one of her wrists. They both breathed laughs as he pulled and she pitched forward against him. Their lips brushed and he felt her free hand sliding into his hair. He tried to press his lips against hers, but she kept pulling her head back in minute distances. Not too far, but just enough to keep him chasing her.

The spring in his abdomen coiled tight enough to steal his breath.

Their lips brushed again. They both smiled as he tightened his hold on her wrist until he felt her fingers curling.

"You're making me angry," Ash murmured, his voice hoarse from smoking.

"How so?"

"You're annoying me."

"Hmm. You should probably punish me for it."

When her fingers twirled the ring on his middle finger again, he realized that it tickled, and that was why he was so on edge. In two fluid movements, Ash let go of her wrist, batted her hand away, and wrapped his hand around her throat. She sucked in her breath and looked down at him with a mischievous, close-lipped smile playing about her full lips. She stole the joint from him and held it.

Ash didn't smile, his expression serious as he trailed his now-free hand down the center of her chest. Her breathing hitched. Her pulse fluttered beneath his fingers. He squeezed the sides of her neck until he heard her breath rattle.

"I thought your body was yours," he murmured, his eyes drinking in the sight of her breasts heaving with the exertion of trying to get in a full breath.

"My body doesn't belong to anyone," she choked out, her head falling back as his fingers twirled one nipple and then the second. Her hips jerked, and he felt himself growing hard beneath the softness of her body. "But you can borrow it for a little while."

"Yeah?"

"You can have me."

Fuck.

Using his hold on her throat, Ash pulled her forward until her back arched and her hair fell around them like a wet curtain. Her face turned and he heard her struggling to breathe in his ear. He covered her breast with his whole hand, massaging it with just the right amount of pressure to make her squirm. He pressed a kiss to the spot below her ear so he could feel her shiver against him.

"Tell me first. I need to hear you say it."

"If I could give my body to anyone," she choked out, "it would be you."

Ash let go of her throat, looking up at her as he took the joint from her. It was almost gone. She gasped for a breath of air, her hands pressed flat to his chest, antagonizing his tattoo in a way that he masochistically liked. His other hand slid over the curve of her rear, down the back of her thigh, and towards her core.

He felt her cunt, hot and wet as his fingertips circled it, and he sucked in more smoke. Her hips moved backward, jolting when the tip of his finger slipped inside and then pulled back out. The smoke filled their faces, and she breathed it in. His fingers went deeper inside of her, then ran down and forward to find her clit. He swirled it, as gently as possible.

"Do you deserve it?"

"I don't deserve it," she said with a loud gasp, her eyes rolling up into her head.

Ash's stomach clenched again. His fingers searched outside of her core, feeling how wet she was for him. Tayshia leaned forward, arching her lower body even more. Her forehead rested against his shoulder as she stifled a whimper. He looked down the length of her bare back, the joint resting between his fore and middle fingers again.

"What *do* you deserve?"

"I don't know," Tayshia groaned, her face buried in his neck. She rolled her hips, trying to get his finger to slide inside of her.

He obliged, feeling smoke sliding past his lips as he sunk two fingers deep into her body from behind. He groaned when he felt her body pulling him deeper. Two seconds passed, and then he couldn't take it anymore. He handed her the almost finished joint, which she took in a bit of a daze, and then his hand was around her neck again, ensuring she kept her face against his throat.

His fingers began to pound into her. Shudders rippled through her body as she moved backwards to meet the thrusts.

"Tell me what you deserve," he said. Ordered it like he had the right. "Come on. You can do it. Tell me."

"I deserve you."

"Tell me who you belong to." He squeezed her throat tighter and moved his fingers harder, curling them as best he could from this angle.

"*Oh, my—*" Her voice was a whine now. "You. I belong to you. Ash, please."

He let go of her throat. She placed one hand on his shoulder as he pulled his fingers out of her, pushed them between their bodies, and slid them back inside of her from the front. He curved his thumb so her clit would rub against his knuckle, and then he watched her.

"Tell me you're mine. Fuck my fingers and tell me you're mine."

"I'm yours."

"Now ask me nicely, baby. Be a good girl and ask me for your reward."

"Please, let me—let me come on them. Let me—*God, fuck*—let me come—"

He used his other hand, massaging her clit gently while he slammed his other fingers brutally inside of her body. Every part of her seemed to vibrate. The concentrated expression on her face broke apart like waves upon the sand. She came with a loud moan, her head falling back as she shook and trembled above him in her euphoria.

Ash stood up, causing her to have to stand quickly to keep him from carrying her. He took the joint from her, which was pretty much gone, and tapped it out on the ashtray. The moment he turned back to her, they were upon each other. He grabbed her face and pulled her up into a wild, passionate kiss that came straight from the depths of his soul. She kissed him back with just as much fervor, as though she'd been waiting for her entire life to kiss him right here, right in this vulnerable moment.

"Do you want me," he asked through kisses and brushes of his tongue against hers, "to fuck you the way you deserve?"

"After everything I've put you through? Yeah," she breathed, her head falling to the side as he kissed his way down to her pulse. His tongue tasted it, and she let out a cry. "I want you to punish me."

"It might hurt."

"Good."

Their eyes met.

His clothes were off within three blinks, his shirt across the room and his sweatshirt on the floor beside them. They were both naked. Both vulnerable.

Raw.

Ash pinned her down horizontally across the bed, his rings pressing marks into her throat and his other hand curved beneath her knee to pull it up by his ribs. He wasn't going to waste any time.

"It's just you and me," he whispered as the head of his cock found her entrance and split her wide. "Look at me. Just you and me."

She nodded, her expression slowly twisting as he slid inside of her body. Their gazes remained connected as he began to thrust. Her expression continued to twist until suddenly, tears began to slip out of the outer corners of her eyes. She let out a sob, causing a lance of panic to spike through him. He nearly pulled out, but her fingers gripped his hips, stilling him before he could.

"Keep going," she pleaded with a sniffle. "Please."

"Are you okay?"

"Mm-hm. I just like you so much, it's a lot of feelings. I feel so connected to you."

Her words sent a wave of sudden need through him. He kissed her tears, tasting them as his hips slammed against hers. They lost themselves to it, the loud sounds that echoed throughout the room. The sounds warred with the wails leaving her lips as he fucked her so hard he saw novae bursting in front of his eyes.

He stood up on the floor beside the bed, grabbing her hips and dragging her down onto his cock. He wanted to watch himself dive in and come back out. It felt good, little pieces of the galaxy raining down his spine and the backs of his thighs, right to his center.

"You're such a good girl," he growled, fingers digging into her flesh as he gazed down at her. Watched her lips curl up into a blissful smile. "You feel so good on my cock. Fucking—*oh, fuck*. Say it. Tell me how good you are."

"I'm so good for you."

He went harder, and her back arched up off of the bed. The groan that left her lips came from deep within her chest, tearing out of her throat as though he'd expelled it from her body. The walls of her cunt gripped him like a velvet vice and he felt himself hurdling closer to the edge of space and time.

Ash pitched forward, his hand smacking down on the comforter beside her head. His other hand found her apex and began to play with it the way that she liked. It made her twitch and whimper, the way *he* liked. His gaze flickered up and down her face, taking it in.

"I'm gonna make you come now."

She nodded because it was all she could manage.

"Put your feet on the mattress and spread your legs."

As she did what he told her to do, Ash began to thrust again. Hard. Brutal. Punishing. Tayshia threw her head back in a deep, screaming moan. She sounded desperate, hips writhing, hand wrapping around his wrist by her head.

"*Oh—my—God.* Ash. Ash, please. Please, please, please. I'm gonna—*fuck*. Please tell me—Tell me I'm—"

"Sweet? Good? Everything?" His tongue curved around her ear and her entire body jerked. Her legs shook so violently that he knew she wouldn't be able to walk if she were upright. "What do you want?"

"Tell me how you're fucking me."

"I'm fucking you so good, aren't I?"

"It's good. It feels so good. Wait. Wait, wait. I'm—"

His hips stuttered in their pace as she clenched around him, her body starting to go rigid. Her breaths stuttered. When she looked at him, it was almost like she was shocked he could make her feel this way. His stomach clenched tight, so tight he couldn't breathe.

"Come for me, sweet girl," he practically cooed, his hand soft against her side. "*Fuck*—Come for me now. Come on. You can do it. Help me come."

When she finally did, her body gripped him so tightly that his own orgasm slammed through him like a lightning bolt. It spread outward from his spine and into the furthest reaches of his limbs. It was all he could do not to collapse on top of her. He pulled out of her body, painting her abdomen with his come as he followed her over the edge of the stars, where they soared together.

"I had the best day," Tayshia whispered into his ear when they were cleaned up and curled together beneath the comforter. "Thank you for all my presents and for dinner and for being so nice to me."

He hummed sleepily, legs tangled with hers and arms wrapped around her naked body. The skin-to-skin contact, the unbearable warmth, the softness. Everything was so perfect right now. So perfect that he was certain they'd never fight again. She wasn't cured, but everything looked so hopeful right now. All they needed to do was keep making steps.

"I was proud of you today," he murmured. "You don't understand how proud."

"Really?"

"Every step you take in the right direction makes me proud."

She burrowed closer to him, her fingers stroking melodies and notes along his upper back, his shoulder blades, the nape of his neck. She kissed him again, their tongues dancing languidly to the tune of her songwriting. When they pulled away, it was because they were both so tired they were drifting off.

"Things are going to get better, Ash. You'll see."

Ash held her face and kissed her a few more times, as quick and gentle as a summer breeze. This was all he manage in his exhaustion, in his anxiety. Everything was so absolutely *perfect*.

He couldn't shake the feeling that everything was going to fall apart.

CHAPTER ELEVEN

Something was vibrating.

Ash stirred from a deep sleep, groggily lifting his head from Tayshia's bare chest. She inhaled through her nose, still fast asleep as he unfurled his arms from around her waist. The vibrating continued, nonstop and annoying.

It was his cell phone.

Ash cursed beneath his breath as he reached onto the bedside table and snatched the phone up. Blinking and bleary-eyed, he peered at the screen.

It was Ryo.

"Yeah?" Ash said into the receiver, voice hoarse. He rubbed the heel of his palm against one eye, ignoring the sound of Tayshia sighing as she started to wake. "It's seven in the morning."

"Hey, kid. I'm sorry to bother you, but we need to have a little talk."

It was something in his voice. A note to a discordant song, one that made Ash's heart drop and stomach swim. Something was wrong.

He sat up, the coverlet falling from his chest and gathering at his waist. He pulled his knees up beneath it, resting his elbows on his kneecaps as he held the phone to his ear.

"Is Steven okay?"

"Is something wrong?" Tayshia asked quietly, her own voice a raspy croak. She sounded tired.

"It's not Steven. It's—It isn't him." Ryo heaved a great sigh, the notes in his voice settling into steady ones of resignation. "It's your dad."

Water rushed past Ash's ears.

"Ash, I'm so sorry. He passed away."

Ice settled into every crevice on Ash's body, outside and in. His skin pulled taut, frozen and brittle. His organs were icebergs in the

Arctic sea that was his blood. His bones were icicles, his muscles ice floes.

Winter erased every feeling inside of his heart, rendering him empty and numb.

Behind him, Tayshia had sat up and folded her legs beneath her. Ash could feel that her legs were shaking from the intensity of the situation. The air between them was tense, though not for the reasons it usually was.

"When?" Ash asked, his tone as flat and cold as a lake in the dead of January

"Last night. I got the call just this morning."

"How'd he die?"

Ryo hesitated, staying silent.

"Ryo," Ash growled, "Tell me how he died."

"He took his own life, Ash." Ryo's voice shook. In the background, Ash could hear Steven speaking in soothing tones, but couldn't tell what he was saying. "I'm so, so sorry. He was very sick. He was looking down a tunnel, and he was going through a lot of turmoil. His disease would have progressed to the point of chronic pain. Maybe he didn't want to suffer."

Ash glared off into the darkness of the hotel room, his fingers curling tight around his cell phone. A sudden eruption of rage blasted through his chest. He pulled the phone away, holding it so tight against his forehead that he thought he might crack his own skull.

He knew why his father had done this, and it had nothing to do with his illness.

"Okay," he said.

When Ryo replied, it was through obvious tears. "I don't want you to worry about anything. I was his emergency contact, so I'll handle everything. I'll be calling and texting you more but for right now, keep next Friday free."

"Only a week?"

"Did you want to go with a full body burial?"

"I don't care what you do with him," he said, abrupt in his delivery. "We'll be at the funeral."

"Okay. Keep your phone on you. The funeral director will likely call the cemetery scheduling office sometime in the next few days to schedule it. Someone will have to call you to get permission to use the family plot."

"Fine."

"Do you want to talk about—"

"No. I should go. Tayshia and I need to get on the road, I guess. We're in Seattle."

"All right." Ryo didn't sound like he approved of his behavior, but did it matter? He knew how much he hated his dad. "I'll talk to you later. I love you."

"Love you. Bye."

Ash hung up the phone and tossed it onto the bed, near Tayshia. He swung his legs around to place his feet on the floor, leaning down to grab his boxers and pull them on. He stood up and walked over to the last of the rolling paper and weed that he'd bought from Diego, and he rolled himself a joint. Using his lighter to light it, he stuck it into the corner of his mouth and went to grab his jeans, inhaling the burn and blowing the smoke out without dropping it.

Tayshia watched him from the bed as he pulled his pants up and slung them low on his hips. Forlorn, she gave him a mournful look, gathering the sheet close to her chest to cover her nudity.

Ash used his middle and ring finger to take the joint and hold it away from him while he grabbed his phone. He held it to his lips and took a drag while he checked his text messages. There was one from Diego asking to hang out soon, and another from Andre saying Ji Hyun's fever had finally broken around three in the morning. He used his thumb to reply to them.

"Are you sure you don't want to be involved in the process?" Tayshia asked, her voice small. "I'm afraid you'll regret it if you don't take part in it."

"Why would I want to?" he said, giving Tayshia a lifeless stare. "We both know why he did this."

She averted her eyes, fidgeting with the blanket in her lap. "He knew you'd forgive him eventually."

"No, he didn't. That's why he fucking killed himself, Tayshia." His fingers were agitated as he tucked the joint between his lips again, pulling his shirt on carefully. He mussed up his hair with his fingers and when he spoke, a cloud of smoke billowed forth. "He thought he could punish me for not doing what he wanted. He's a narcissist, like I said he was. I'm not helping with *shit*."

"I'm so sorry, Ash," she said, her voice breaking, shattering as she dissolved into tears. She hung her head, shoulders shaking as she pressed the knuckles of her left hand to her eyes. "I never should have made you go see him. This is all my fault. If I hadn't convinced you, he never would have asked for your forgiveness, and maybe he'd be alive."

"Tayshia," he said softly, the only emotion he seemed able to muster being sympathy and concern for her. He'd seen her break down before, but never for something like this. He wasn't going to let his selfish, poor excuse for a father ruin her. "Stop crying."

"I just..." She covered her mouth and wept harder. "I'm so sorry. I shouldn't have pressured you. I'm ruining *everything*."

Ash crossed the room to her, placing a hand on the mattress so he could lean down to kiss her. He peppered her with affection and comfort—her lips, cheeks, and the line of her jaw. Her tears tasted like salt, but they weren't enough to melt the ice that he had frozen into.

"It's not your fault. Don't cry," he whispered, his words somewhat brusque. "This is his fault. He did this. And he did it because I wouldn't give him what he wanted. So, let's just go home."

☼☼☼

In the five days that passed before the funeral, time blurred.

During the day, Tayshia took care of everything. She did the dishes, picked up after him, cooked the meals, did the laundry, vacuumed the floor. She picked up the mail and piled it neatly on the kitchen counter near her porcelain ducks. She called the school and informed them that Ash would be out for a few weeks, that she would only be gone for one week, and that she would need their assignments prepared by the teachers. She called her parents and told them that she wasn't going to come for spring break the following month because Ash's dad had passed away

Andre and Ji Hyun came over every day after school. Ji Hyun helped Tayshia with dinner and kept her company. Andre sat on the couch and played video games with Ash, who remained as silent as the grave his father would be in by the end of the week. They would smoke weed to the point of near-catatonia, and it provided Ash some solace from his confusing emotions. Andre tried to bring some life to the room, talking and making jokes, but all Ash seemed able to muster was a monotonous, short response.

Still, he stayed, and that was what mattered.

Elijah tried to come by, the door having been answered by Ji Hyun while Tayshia was arms-deep in dishwater. He was carrying a large bouquet of sympathy flowers that Tayshia added to the large bouquet of Valentine's flowers Ash had gotten for her, and he'd also brought a tray of desserts that his mother had baked for him. Ji Hyun took those and put them on the counter bar.

His eyes found Ash's across the room for a moment before Ash simply returned them to the TV. He didn't want to see Elijah, but neither did he have the energy to care enough to hate him right now. It could wait.

After a brief conversation with everyone else *but* him, Elijah promised to be at the funeral, and then left.

"It's good of him to try. He ain't even have to do all that, and he did," Andre said, the only remark he made. "He's good people."

Ash didn't think so, and he couldn't place why.

On the morning of the third day, Ash got a text from Ryo.

Your father's been cremated. I went to the prison and picked up his effects. There's a letter for you. Would you like it?

Tayshia, who had been beside him on the couch when he got the text, carefully slid his phone out of his hand. Without a word, she tapped out a reply of *yes*. Ash didn't argue. He was so numb inside, so empty, so tired.

She knew he wouldn't read it.

On the fourth day, Ash got a call from Steven. He answered it and put it on speakerphone, dropping the phone onto his chest. Slouched down low on the couch while he played video games with Andre again, he listened to what his godfather had to say.

"Hi, honey. I really, really hope you're doing okay. Are you hanging in there?"

"Yeah," was all Ash said.

"Okay, that's good. Well, I was just calling because Ryo needs to go to handle something at work. He took time off for—for everything, you know, so...Anyway, he wants me to tell you that you're going to get a call from your father's lawyer here in the next couple of weeks. He just got off the phone with him before he left, but didn't have time to call you."

"What for?"

"For your father's life insurance."

A tiny flicker of confusion entered Ash's self-imposed prison of emptiness. "He was paying into *life insurance*?"

"Yes, for you. I think he was paying into it since you were seven, just like your mother. He kept paying even when he got into prison. He had a savings account, apparently. Well, and he also did some work from prison. They do have jobs there sometimes, you know. I'm sure it helped keep him busy."

He had a savings.

A fucking *savings*.

While he was selling drugs and spending Ricky's money on shit, he was tucking some of it aside for savings and insurance. What the fuck?

"Why?"

"Because you're his son, Ash."

Ash couldn't deal with this. The fact that his father could destroy their family, kill himself because Ash wouldn't accept his apology, all while paying into *life insurance* for him so he could try to bribe him with money after his death?

"What a fucking asshole," he spat out. "I love you, Steven, but I gotta go."

"What? Oh, uh—okay. I love you, too, son. Before you go, did you want to help us with the headstone? We're trying to think of what to write."

"Nah. I'll see you at the funeral."

Ash pressed the end button and went back to playing the game.

"Are you sure you don't want to help with that?" Andre asked quietly. Ji Hyun and Tayshia were chatting amiably in the kitchen while they cooked. "You might have something you want to say."

"Anything I might have said died with him when he killed himself. I don't give a fuck what they put on it. He's lucky they're handling it. If it were up to me, he'd be getting a fucking rock."

"Well…All right, then."

At night, Ash was insatiable.

He'd wake in the darkness, his fingers seeking Tayshia out in bed, brushing her cheeks to wake her so he could tell her he needed her. So he could whisper and plead against her hair, her neck, her shoulder. She'd say yes, letting him roll her beneath him so he could bring her to a quivering, soft orgasm with his fingers or tongue. He'd tell her she was an angel, she'd tell him to be gentle. He'd hiss curses into her ear, she'd plead with him to fuck her harder. He'd pin her legs open, sliding in and out of her body as though it could chase the conflict away.

She'd try to cling to him but he wouldn't let her, snapping at her to stop touching him, to put her hands beneath her back, to stuff them under the pillow. She'd push her throat up into the circle of his fingers, groaning and rolling her eyes as he brought her the euphoria he so desperately wished he could have. The safety and the peace of knowing that she hadn't lost anyone the way he had. The confidence to know she would always have someone alive to care about her.

Ash had nothing. No mom. No dad. And the one girl he cared about seemed Hell-bent on dying.

He made her look him in the eyes when she came, finding that if he got lost in the cosmos that swirled in her eyes, the galaxies that tied them together, then he could forget.

For a little while.

Then, in the darkness, while they were trembling and catching their breath, he'd pull her close and whisper the only words his heart seemed able to chant.

"I have no one left but you."

☼☼☼

From the depths of the grey sky came rain.

Torrents and torrents of it, dumping from the clouds without reprieve from the morning of the funeral until the time they set foot on the wet grass of the cemetery. Grass so wet that puddles had gathered between its blades, soaking into the soles of Ash's shoes. The Earth seemed to mourn where Ash had no desire to. It was cold, though not cold enough to do much more than pinch at his nose, and not even the hint of a breeze existed.

There was something mildly comical about the cliche way Tayshia clung to his arm while he held a black umbrella over their heads. They were head-to-toe in the same shade of black, donning somber expressions like masks.

Well, for Ash it was a mask.

Andre and Ji Hyun exited their car, draped in black as well. They embraced a stiff, emotionless Ash and a warm, sympathetic Tayshia. Expressing their condolences, they stood with them while they waited for the others to arrive.

Ash hated this. He didn't care about his father. He was a piece of shit. He was the person that had destroyed their family, and the person who had tried to get one last jab in by punishing him for holding his forgiveness hostage. How was it fair that he could ruin their family, get to escape the consequences, and then leave Ash to deal with the aftermath? He just wanted Ash to regret not accepting his apology. He wanted him to know that he was a bad son, and that he'd killed his father because of it.

Tayshia took both of her hands and slid them down, intertwining all ten of her fingers with five of his. He could feel her gaze on him, but his own was glued to the wet parking lot beneath them. Watching the drops of rain as they glanced off of the black asphalt. Staring into the continuum of space and time. Looking at a bleak future down the barrel.

He imagined the universe would take her next.

Soon, Ryo, Steven, and Elijah arrived. They offered their condolences, Steven spending an extra amount of time embracing him. Ash remained rigid, still as stone. He knew everyone else felt something, but he didn't want them to force him to feel something that wasn't there. He hated his dad. He felt nothing but repulsion for him and his choices.

At ten-o-clock AM on the dot, the pastor arrived to read the rites.

As everyone headed up the hill towards the Robards family plot—which had only one spot left—Elijah lingered toward the back with Tayshia and Ash. He wore black slacks and a black peacoat much like Ash's. His hands rested in the pockets of his slacks, a nonchalance to his body that Ash envied.

"Hey, man," Elijah murmured. "Are you doing okay? I know we haven't talked."

"I'm fine," Ash said.

"Well, I know your guys' relationship was complicated. I just wanted to make sure you were good."

Ash looked down at him, their gazes meeting with a form of clarity and understanding that he didn't like. It was the knowledge that Elijah knew they weren't friends anymore and that there was nothing they could do to repair it. The cognizance of them both knowing that he was here out of respect, not because he wanted to mend things.

"Well, I'm fine."

Tayshia gave Elijah a look that Ash couldn't see, the two of them exchanging glances.

The priest's eulogy was perfectly adequate, with all the right words and phrases meant to bring solace to anyone who cared about Gabriel Robards. Everyone stared at the grave, underneath which he was buried, listening to the pastor in silence. When he was done, he offered final condolences and took his leave.

Everyone stood there for a while, the silence thick beneath the fall of endless rain. As they left one-by-one in a blur, Ash realized that he was feeling emptier and emptier. The boxes on his emotions were all shut tight, tight enough to suffocate air. He felt nothing. Absolutely nothing.

By the time only he and Tayshia remained, he'd gone numb.

Gabriel's headstone lay right beside Lizette's, much smaller but no less beautifully carved. While the latter was made of polished white marble, Gabriel's consisted of solid, smooth grey stone. They looked like monoliths compared to how small Ash's spirit had shrunk. Even when gazing upon his mother's grave, his heart was a void.

Lizette Ann Robards. 1970-2017. Beloved Mother. May you find solace and peace in a place where the sun bathes your wings.

Gabriel Lee Robards. 1955-2019. Husband. Father. First and foremost, a human being.

He was alone.

Ash was completely and utterly alone, and no amount of wishing and hoping was going to keep Tayshia alive. Nothing would make her fit into his cracks and crevices. She didn't want to. And now that his father had sewn those cracks up tight, he wasn't sure she'd be able to get back inside his heart when he came out on the other side.

He knew he'd feel this someday. He knew it would hurt. It would hurt so bad, he wouldn't be able to breathe. And when that day came, what if his cracks ripped open?

What if his heart awoke, and she wasn't there?

"My condolences."

Ash and Tayshia turned to look behind them. There, emerging from the hazy curtain of rain on the hill, came the redheaded man with the spider tattoo. He had a coat and jeans on, with the hood up and not a care in the world for the water dripping and rolling down his face. In his hand, he held a small bouquet of chrysanthemums. His smile was not sinister, however it made Ash feel uncomfortable.

He stiffened, a protective hand wrapping around the back of Tayshia's neck.

"Relax," the redhead said, the skin of his spider tattoo wet on his cheek. "I'm here on Ricky's behalf."

"For what?" Ash growled the words, wishing he could whisk Tayshia away on the back of a dragon.

"To pay respects to a fallen rival."

They watched as the man leaned down to place the bouquet amongst the flowers that Steven and Ryo had brought, the chrysanthemums mixing visually well with the lilies, orchids, and carnations. The man plucked one of them out and placed it at the foot of Lizette's headstone. Then, he stood back up.

"Ricky was devastated to hear what happened. You should know that your father died having owed him quite a bit of money but given the circumstances, Ricky's decided to forgive that debt. So, you can rest easy."

Ash bit his tongue. He wouldn't have paid a cent of his father's debts.

The redheaded man smiled down at Tayshia, who shifted closer to Ash's side, slightly behind him.

"Morning to you."

Before Ash could try and stop her, Tayshia responded.

"Thank you. Can I ask your name?"

His lips curled up into a Cheshire grin. He passed the pad of his thumb across his lower lip, dragging rainwater along it. His gaze was hungry, much too hungry to be considered innocent.

"Caden."

Recognition dawned on Ash. *That* was his name. He couldn't believe he'd forgotten it.

Caden was the main dealer, and Ricky's right-hand man. He was the one who managed all of the other dealers, sending them where they were supposed to go and keeping track of the minutiae. He was also the person who handled punishment and rewards. Punishments that Gabriel had often passed along to Ash.

He was feral.

"You look gorgeous in black, Tayshia," he said. The sound of her name rolling off of his tongue made Ash sick to his stomach. At the show weeks ago, Caden had heard her name and remembered it after all this time? "What a pretty girl you are."

Caden placed a hand on Ash's shoulder as he passed him, and then headed off down the hill.

Ash's gaze lingered after him on his way down the hill, remaining until his crimson hair disappeared from view. When he turned to look down at Tayshia, she appeared worried.

"That was so unnecessary," she said. "I think we should be careful."

"Agreed."

He didn't want to tell her how brutal Caden could be unless it was absolutely necessary. Because if Ash remembered correctly,

Caden didn't care if someone was a man or a woman. He would beat the fuck out of anyone who crossed him.

Suddenly, Tayshia's phone began to ring, the bright jangling of the melody jarring them both. She let go of Ash's hand so she could pull it out of her coat pocket.

"It's my dad. I'll send it to voicemail."

"No, go ahead and answer it," Ash said. "I'll wait here."

"Okay."

"And here." He handed her the umbrella handle. "Take it. I'll be fine."

After some reluctance, she took the umbrella and walked away to answer her still-ringing phone.

Ash let the rain soak him as he turned back to his parents' graves. He allowed the emptiness to provide him with solace, the only comfort he needed after such a trying year. Gazing down at the graves, at the remnants of his parents, he wondered how one person was supposed to hold the loss and the hatred and the pain and the sadness in one heart.

Where was normal located in the chaotic star system that was his life? Where was peace? Healing? Where was happiness?

Why did it feel so out of reach?

Tayshia approached from the side. "Here. He wants to talk to you."

He tore his eyes away from the gravestones and looked down. She was holding her phone out to him. Shock and instinct had his hand withdrawing from his coat pocket to take it from her, knowing that it was going to be her father's voice that he heard. As he held it to his ear, Tayshia held the umbrella over them both, having to raise her arms quite a bit to accommodate for their large height difference. It didn't matter much, given that he was already dripping.

"Hello," he said, voice shaking with the nervousness that seemed to always exist around her father. "Mr. Cole."

"Terrence," he corrected, the deep baritone of his voice seeming louder than the speaker itself. "Hi, Ash. I know you're probably going through a rough time right now. I wanted to offer my condolences and see how you're holding up."

"I'm fine."

He heaved a sigh. "You see, I know you're not. You're pretending to be. And that's okay. But you should ask yourself why."

There was no pretense. This was how he truly felt. He didn't care.

He hated his dad.

"He fucking left me. I wouldn't accept an apology, so he just kills himself to punish me? What a selfish bastard."

"No. Listen." Mr. Cole paused, as though he wanted to be sure Ash was listening. "You can't look at it that way. If you do, you'll never find peace. You will never become the man you're meant to be if you let this hatred burn you up."

Too late. I'm already burning.

"Easier said than done, Mr. Cole."

"Ash, I want you to hear me. If you listen to nothing else in regards to your father, please listen to this: if I can forgive him, then so can you."

Here was the victim of his father's mistakes, Mr. Terrence Cole. The man Gabriel shot in cold blood. A man who had the right to damn him should he see fit.

And he'd forgiven him.

Ash closed his eyes before letting them flutter open. He clutched the phone tight.

"I was supposed to have more time."

Tayshia looked up at him, sharp and curious, but didn't say anything.

"I know, Ash. I know. But you know, sometimes we don't get that. We don't get to have all the time in the world to heal the way others want us to. And that's okay — it's okay to not be able to forgive him yet. Someday, you will. Then, one day, you'll wake up and you won't feel so empty."

Ash could barely focus on the rest of the conversation. The exchanging of pleasantries was like smoke, floating in one ear and out through the other. The deepness of Mr. Cole's voice, the din of the heavy rainfall, the sound of his own beating heart. It all coalesced into one word to explain why he felt like he was burning.

Purgatory.

When the conversation was over, he gave Tayshia her phone back. She accepted it, fixing him with a look that he couldn't read. Was it sympathy he saw there? Or was it compassion? He needed them both, yet he couldn't think of anything worse than being taken care of because his father had made a choice to tear his son down on his way up to Heaven.

They headed down the hill, hand-in-hand, her shining like a star and him as empty as a black hole.

CHAPTER TWELVE

Time had passed as quickly as the snow had melted, like the rain had simply washed the days away.

The torrential downpour had continued the day after the funeral, clear until the current day: Wednesday. Grey and somber outside, the dark atmosphere seeped into the apartment and warred with the shadows of Ash's disposition. If the day was dark, his spirit was darker.

Now, it was Thursday. Five days since the funeral. Five days since the emotional turmoil had rolled in like fog over the moors.

Ash hadn't been to school in almost two weeks, but Tayshia had been dutiful in bringing the classwork that his teachers had given her. Andre and Ji Hyun had kept up with their new routine of coming over every day when school let out, giving Ash something to focus on that wasn't the numbness that his wretched father had left behind. They played video games, smoked weed, and ate food while Ji Hyun and Tayshia sat on the couch beside each other and played their consoles. It was just like the week before, and it was routine.

He supposed everyone felt there was safety in routine.

Typically, they went home before too long but today, Andre and Ji Hyun had decided to stay the night. spring break started on Monday and they were planning on skipping school the next day

"You guys can sleep on the couch," Tayshia said, her hands on her hips. She moved from her spot in front of Ash's side of the couch and walked toward the hallway. Ash, Andre, and Ji Hyun watched her go. "I don't think we have any extra blankets in Ash's room, but I'll see."

"Do you have any in your room?" Ji Hyun said, standing up and adjusting the hem of her sweater. She'd gotten a new perfume and today she smelt of cinnamon. It pervaded, even through the smell of marijuana smoke. "I can go grab them if you do."

"*No!*" Tayshia came darting back out of the hall. Her eyes were wide with something akin to panic, but filtered through embarrassment. "No, no one can go in my room right now. But Ash doesn't have any blankets, so maybe you guys shouldn't sleep over. It would be too cold and uncomfortable on the couch without any."

I guess that means she never cleaned her room, Ash thought as his thumbs clicked and flew across the game controller. They'd been gaming since Andre brought the girls home from school. Since Ash was off school for bereavement, he had been playing since that morning.

Andre took a drag off of Ash's blunt. He held the smoke in his lungs, speaking in a strained voice. "I mean, I don't need one. Babe, do you need one?"

"I would *like* one, yes," Ji Hyun replied with an incredulous laugh. She then looked at Tayshia. "We could go and buy some blankets."

"That sounds good to me."

Ji Hyun turned and held her hand out to Andre, who barked a laugh.

"You wildin'," he said.

"No, I'm not. Gimme."

Andre rolled his eyes and sat up on the couch, reaching into the back pocket of his jeans for his wallet. "Lemme guess—you want enough for your nails, too?"

"I wanna get my nails done," Tayshia said, as though everyone was making plans without her. "We should."

"It's only six, so let's do it," Ji Hyun said. She snapped her fingers, and shook her hand palm-side up. "With the quickness, please."

"I'm just making sure I memorize how much I give you. I'm taxing you at the end of the year."

"Andre!"

Ash would have laughed if he weren't currently floating in a fog so thick he could only focus on weed and the video game.

"Here's two hundred," Andre said. "Don't go gettin' them five inch long claws, or I will *destroy* you."

Ji Hyun merely smirked, bending down to peck him on the cheek.

Tayshia put her hands behind her back, giving Ash an almost nervous look. Eggshells seemed to have been crunching beneath her feet in the five days since the funeral. She tread carefully around him, saying nothing unless absolutely necessary, lest she shatter the tension and awaken whatever beast lay dormant in him. It wasn't that she was scared of him — the issue was that she was scared of what would happen when he finally broke.

If he broke.

Ash was determined never to let those boxes open. It was better that he remain indifferent, a blank slate for a new story to tell its tales upon. Because if he tried to tell his own, the ending might not be the best and the character arc? Well, it would be shit.

"Tay, come here," Ash said, pulling his debit card out of his wallet. As she walked around the couch and coffee table to approach him, he held it out to her, slid between his fore and middle fingers. "Take my card."

"But you already gave me money on Valentine's," she protested. "I haven't spent any of it."

"I know. It's okay, just take it. Get your nails done."

"Ash, this is too much."

"Nothing's too much. Take the card."

"Girl, take it. Are you crazy?" Ji Hyun leaned forward and snatched Ash's card out of his hand. "*Thank* you."

Ash leaned forward and lifted his chin. Tayshia took the hint and leaned down, her fingers soft against his cheeks as she gave him what was perhaps the gentlest kiss she'd ever given him. So gentle, it was like a whisper against his skin.

"There's food on the stove for you," she said quietly. "I made you some chicken."

"Mm."

She tucked a bit of her puffy hair behind her ear, giving him a small wave before going to put her coat on by the dining room table.

The girls walked out the door with the keys to Andre's car jangling in Ji Hyun's hold. Andre picked his controller up and jumped back into the current game they were working on, immediately launching into a playful tirade against how endearingly high maintenance Ji Hyun had become. But the entire time he did that, Ash's mind was elsewhere.

What the Hell was wrong with Tayshia?

☼☼☼

Between games, Ash went to use the bathroom.

He was getting a bit hungry and his thumbs ached from pressing the controller buttons for so long. Tayshia's chicken was probably cold by now, so he would need to heat it up. And that fact became evident as he walked in the kitchen and saw it sitting there on the stove, the baking dish full of untouched chicken parmesan.

Andre cussed at the screen, beginning to rant to Ash from the living room about something one of the opposite teammates had done in the game. Ash tuned him out as he pulled a plate down from the cupboard and used a spatula to scoop himself some of the food. There wasn't much there to begin with, but—

Wait.

Why was there only enough for one person?

Ash frowned, sliding the food off of the spatula and onto his plate. His brows furrowing, he slowly turned to face the bar and dining room beyond it. Setting his plate down, he rested his hands on the edge of the counter. He hung his head, staring at the plate while his mind raced with fast, frantic thoughts.

When had she last eaten?

The day his father passed, they hadn't stopped to eat anything on the way home because he'd been so in his head. Andre and Ji Hyun had come over at his request right after they got home. They arrived after he stepped out of the shower. He couldn't remember what happened after that, if they all ate together, or if everyone ate sporadically through the night…?

He had no idea what she'd eaten all week. All he remembered was her continually bringing him plates and bowls. Eggs at breakfast. Sandwiches at lunch. Steak for dinner. Bags of chips or stacks of cookies. Cans of soda. He never needed to ask—she just knew by the way he started shifting on the couch when he was hungry. And he'd been so focused on drowning his consciousness in video games during the day that by the time he was reaching for her at night, the rules he'd set for her meals were nowhere in his realm of thought.

They were just existing. She'd bring him food, he'd eat it, and then she went to sleep before him. There was one night where he didn't fall into the bed until nearly four in the morning.

Had she eaten?

He couldn't remember. He couldn't *fucking* remember.

She cooked him three meals a day, prepared him snacks even when he wasn't hungry. She cleaned and she handled what needed to be dealt with, and she did her homework while he was doing his. He'd thanked her more times than he could count, and now? Now, he just felt stupid.

He hadn't been paying attention.

The world shattered around him, shards of realization crushing him beneath the weight of his own failure. The boxes within his mind shook and tore open, lids disintegrating as his emotions burst forth. They swirled together, a raging storm that set his hands to shaking.

The thoughts continued as he shoved the plate into the microwave and angrily slammed his fingertip against the number buttons.

I don't have time for this, he thought, his blood running as hot as molten rock. *This is out of control. My dad fucking died, and the first thing she does is find a way to get around being unable to purge? She just starves herself? What the fuck is wrong with her? What the actual fuck is wrong with her?*

Ash ate with angry hands and swallowed with a tight, livid throat. He stood in the kitchen after his plate was emptied, glaring at a sink that was not full enough. The things she'd used to prepare the meal were there, but there were no plates and no forks. Nothing to indicate that she'd eaten any of it.

It was several moments before he realized that Andre had been saying his name.

"Yeah?" Ash said, his tone tight.

"I need you to come help me with this. They're kicking my literal ass." Andre's eyes narrowed. "Wait, are you good? You sound like you're pissed."

"I'm fine," Ash lied.

He dropped his fork into the sink and came to join him. When he sat on the couch, his agitation ran so thick in his veins that he couldn't relax. He perched on the edge of the cushion, his knees pressed against the edge of the coffee table. Andre eyed him, then pressed the start button so they could play.

She's going to do what the fuck I say, and that's just it. When it comes to eating, she can't be trusted to put any importance on her life. So I guess I'm gonna have to be the one to —

"Ash."

— make her take her life seriously. I mean, what does she expect? That she'll just be able to starve and purge forever? That it won't kill her because she's somehow the exception? Has she —

"Ash, he's killing you."

— lost her —

"Hello?! Ash! That guy's killing you!"

— fucking mind?

Ash's character died, causing Andre's character to become overwhelmed by the enemy and die, too. The game was over.

Andre whirled on him, still seated on the couch. "Bro, that guy literally got you with a headshot because you were just standing there! What the Hell? We were so close!"

Ash blinked himself out of his fiery reverie. He was so angry that he felt like he was floating outside of his body.

"I'm fine," he said.

"Are you kidding me? Whatever the Hell's going on with you, you better figure it out before the next game. You're giving me bad vibes, and I'm not havin' it. Headass."

They started a new game. Even though this time, Ash was careful not to let his thoughts get the best of him and get their characters killed again, to sever them was impossible. He was too angry, too passionate about this. Too lost to it. Once, he'd read that there were black holes that could destroy galaxies. That could tear them asunder, consume the stars, and leave behind an abyss.

I'm justified. I am justified in doing whatever I can to make her stop. Whatever I can to fight her disorder until we win. If I can smoke this bitch out, then it won't have such a strong hold on her.

She's not gonna fucking die on me.

☼☼☼

When Tayshia and Ji Hyun came home, Ash was ready. His energy was so high that he could barely sit still. Andre's weed was almost gone, he'd smoked that much. And as the girls walked in, still chatting happily about whatever it was they were laughing about, Ash was packing the last bowl of weed they had.

"Look at my nails!" Ji Hyun gushed, prancing over to Andre to flash her bright green nails. They were long and curved slightly. They looked like she'd have trouble writing with them.

Tayshia crept over, still bundled up in her dress coat. Her hesitance to be near him made sense to him now that he knew the depths she would sink to in order to control her environment.

She paused, like she wasn't sure she should bother, and then showed him the nails on both of her hands. Her precious hands. She looked so nervous, so hopeful. So unlike herself.

He glanced at them, gaze dancing along the deep bordeaux color that she'd chosen, the rhinestone decals, the tiny snowflakes she'd gotten painted onto each thumb.

As angry as he was, he cared about her. He was angry *because* he cared about her. He didn't understand her disorder. Why couldn't she just...Stop? Why wasn't he enough to make her happy? Maybe anger wasn't the problem.

Maybe she made him sad.

"They're pretty, baby," he said, voice subdued and hoarse from the smoking. He knew his eyes were red as Hellfire; they felt dry and heavy. "Do you like them?"

"Thank you. Yes, I do," she said, and then her smile faded. Her throat bobbed as she swallowed. "And here's your card."

Ash took the debit card back from her, tossing it onto the coffee table beside the wallet he'd discarded there. He leaned forward with his elbows on his thighs, dropping his head into his hand so he could drag his fingers through his messy blond hair. A sigh escaped him.

"Ay, you, uh..." Ash's eyes met Andre's. "You think you and Ji Hyun could give us some time to talk? I don't know if a sleepover is a good idea tonight."

The awkwardness was palpable.

"Yeah, sure. Let's get back in the car, Ji," Andre said, setting the controller down on the coffee table and rising to his feet. "We'll see you guys tomorrow."

Ash said nothing, the tension in the room mounting with every step that their friends took. Ji Hyun still had her coat on, so the deathlike silence in the living room while Andre shrugged into his coat was agony. They left, plunging Ash and Tayshia into a silence so deep and so dark that it was as though all the stars had gone out.

She stood by the coffee table, shifting from left foot to right. She fidgeted with her new acrylics, red almonds clicking and clicking and clicking. By the expression on her face and the way her gaze flit about the room, she already knew what he was going to say. She knew she was in trouble.

"I was distracted," he said, picking up the pipe. He allowed her to wallow in her dread as he lit the bowl and inhaled. The smoke cut into his lungs, burning as he held it. Then, after he blew it out, his gaze burned into her, devouring the silence. "I was distracted, and you took advantage of me."

Like an autumn leaf, her face fell. Her brows came together, the fear so prominent on her face that he almost changed his mind about confronting her. But the fear also meant that he was right—she hadn't been eating, and she'd been doing it on purpose. She'd done it *knowing* that she was taking advantage of the fact that he was distracted.

She opened her mouth several times, averting her eyes as she struggled for an answer. For another lie.

And he watched her try, smoke surrounding them as he took his time finishing what was in the pipe. As he took his time scraping the resin out of the bowl so he could smoke that, too. She stood there the entire time, not saying a word. Not opening her mouth again.

Finally, he spoke, his eyes burning into hers.

"When was the last time you ate?"

She jolted, the words causing every minute of her life to flash across her face like lightning. The look of terror in her eyes was so absolute that for a second, the ocean of Ash's anger ebbed like a receding tide. It was clear she was frightened of him.

But then, the terror dissipated, leaving indignance in its wake. She balled her hands into fists at her sides and raised her chin.

"Friday. Before our tattoo appointment."

Ash closed his eyes. He needed to ease his storm. He needed to ease it and calm down, or else he was going to explode.

"I won't bother trying to hide it," she went on. "I don't want to eat unless I can get rid of it. I'm not going to. You can't force me to eat, so you'll just have to let me purge, or cry about it. Because I'm gonna do it anyway."

The tide stretched back away from the shore. It rose into a colossal tidal wave that loomed over Ash's temper and crashed down upon it. He slammed the pipe down on the glass coffee table.

"Have you lost your *fucking* mind? What makes you think that I would ever *let* you purge?"

She took a step back, but spat out, "It's not about you *letting* me do anything. It's about you understanding what you *can't* do. And no matter what you think, you can't make me do anything—*including* eat."

"I can do whatever the fuck I want where this is concerned," Ash said, slapping his hands on his thighs and standing up. All six feet and four inches of him, towering over her to the point where she had to crane her neck just to manage eye contact with him. "Your ass has been sitting outside Death's door, just waiting for him to answer your annoying, impatient knocks for months. I've had it. When it comes to your disorder, I'm taking control."

"My *disorder*?! *What* disorder?"

"Um, your *eating* disorder," he said with a snide curl of his lip. "You know, the thing that's made us both go completely *insane*."

"I do not—That's—I do not have an eating disorder. I have coping mechanisms, but that doesn't mean that I have an actual disorder."

"Binging and purging are symptoms of an eating disorder."

"Oh, thank God. Doctor Robards is here." She threw her hands up with a mirthless laugh. "Doctor Robards is here, and now I'm diagnosed. Healing is at hand."

Ash's anger flashed like a lightbulb going out inside of him. "So does spending half of your day on your knees in front of the toilet by choice *not* mean something? Skipping meals and starving yourself for a week? Manipulating me into buying you binge food so you can get back on your knees as soon as possible? I mean, yeah. I'd say those things constitute having some sort of disorder."

"A disorder is like an addiction, Ash. That means it's something that isn't under the control of the person suffering from it. An outside factor that controls the individual."

"You want me to get you a fucking mirror, or...?"

Something went dead in her eyes. Dead, and somehow desolate.

She turned and walked away, shaking her head in denial as she rounded the couch. "I do not have one of those. You do *not* know what you're talking about."

"Tayshia, *stop* walking," he snarled. "I'm talking to you."

She spun to glare at him. "I have everything under control! People with eating disorders don't!"

"You have it under control. Okay."

"I can stop whenever I want. I simply choose not to."

The fact that she didn't think she actually had a disorder was so terrifying that it was laughable. Her obliviousness would get her killed. She was going to die without him, and that was why he didn't feel bad about setting the rules in the first place.

He should never have let his father get under his skin. *This* was what mattered. *Tayshia* is who mattered.

"If it was that simple," he said, walking around the coffee table so he could approach her, "then you wouldn't have fought me so hard on eating after I set the rules, and you wouldn't have starved yourself for six days."

"Except that it *is* that simple. I said I choose not to. That implies that my choice is tantamount."

"Your choice to move one step closer to death every time you purge is *tantamount*." He stretched the syllables of the last word in a mocking tone, using his fingers to mark the air quotations.

"Tantamount to what?"

"To the fact that you have a problem, Tayshia! You have a problem, and I made it too easy for it to grow. I got distracted and I let you hurt yourself."

"And now you've decided to make my life a living Hell to deal with your guilt."

"Guilt? What do I have to feel guilty for?" He was shouting now, heedless of the thin apartment complex walls. "Caring about you? Wanting to save you? Wanting you to *live*?!"

He could tell by the set of her jaw that her teeth were gritted. The ire danced in her eyes. She stomped away a few steps before she whirled on him again. "Because you know you've been horrible to me, and too controlling, and—and—And mean. You've been much meaner than you need to be, all because you feel guilty!"

"Except that I don't. I think you're sick and that you're incapable of taking care of yourself. And so I've taken it upon myself to—"

"Taken it upon yourself to *what*, Ash? Tell me what to do? Insult me? Make me feel like shit about myself? Well, you're doing a damn good job! And the only thing that I could do to cope with the way you make me feel is the one thing you won't let me do!"

"I said you could do it, actually. I said you could purge. Just as long as you do it where I can see."

"Do you not see why that's a problem?!"

"Oh, I know exactly what the fuck I'm doing. No one in their right mind would willingly throw up their food in front of anyone. You're ashamed of it, which is why you hide behind closed doors and a closed mind. It's the reason why you hide it from everyone you know and the reason why you're so angry with me right now. You're not pissed at me because I won't let you do it. You're pissed at me because I'm making it harder for you to do it where no one can see. I'm forcing you to face it for how disgusting it is."

Something shifted in her eyes—something that showed him he'd struck her right where it hurt—and a quick glance downward showed him that she'd clenched her fists again, by the hem of the coat she had yet to remove. When she returned her gaze to him, her eyes were shining. Tears had gathered in them like rainwater collecting in the center of a flower where the petals met.

"I'm not disgusting."

Pain wrenched through him as he realized what he'd said and that in her mind, there was a filter. The endless torment of having to watch the person he cared for hurt herself again and again meant nothing to this filter. It would turn anything he said into the worst version of itself because that's what the disorder needed to breed.

Darkness.

"I didn't say you were. Do not twist my words."

A tear slipped down her cheek. She lifted her hand to wipe it away, but Ash caught her wrist before she could. She looked away as he swiped his fingers through the track, disrupting her sadness with a tenderness he only held for her. There was no one else he cared for more than her.

"I know that what I'm doing is infuriating," he said, "but what you have to understand is that these are the consequences for your actions."

She wrenched her hand out of his grasp. "What *actions*? And who says you get to be the one to decide the consequences! You're not my dad, you're not a judge, and you're not a doctor. You're not even my boyfriend."

That hurt.

That hurt, and so it made him mad.

"But I'm fucking you like one, so what does that make you? My whore?"

Her jaw dropped.

"I won't enable you, Tayshia. You took advantage of my ignorance to get me to buy you binge food. You took advantage of the fact that my fucking *dad* died and used my distraction to starve yourself. *No one* is going to manipulate me like my father did, least of all *you*."

"It's my body!" Another angry tear fell down her cheek, and she let it. "I shouldn't have to manipulate you into letting me do whatever I want with it in the *first* place!"

He took a step toward her. She jolted, stumbling to the side to get away, moving too fast knocking into the side of the couch.

"And I don't feel the least bit guilty," he said, his presence pressuring her to move around the couch with the sheer intensity of his glare. As she backed away, he advanced on her. "I don't feel guilty for doing what I have to do to keep you alive. If you don't care about yourself enough to do it, then someone has to. If that makes me a shitty person, then I don't give a fuck. But what you're not gonna do is tell me I feel guilty when I don't."

"That's just like you," she said, stopping beside the edge of the kitchen counter, in the space between it and the back of the short end of the sectional. "Telling my secrets when it serves you best. What's left after that? Are you gonna tell them how you called me a pathetic bitch, too?"

The images that flashed across his mind brought the heat of the anger in his blood to a dangerous boil. Remembering that day during winter break, the day Kieran and his friends had jumped him. He'd been in so much pain. He would have done anything Tayshia asked him to do.

He ground his teeth together, fighting the urge to turn around and leave. He felt the fury like flames in his head.

She'd *asked* him to treat her that way. He hadn't wanted to. He hadn't *wanted* to cross those lines. But she begged him.

"You *are* a bitch."

"And you just love to say it, don't you?"

When had she moved backward, and when had he followed?

When did they get into the hallway?

When had she gotten this close to him?

What the fuck was going on?

Ash had never had this little control over his faculties. He'd never felt this hateful yet at the same time so attracted to a girl. It was like every time she did this—every time she pulled this dark energy out of him—she was setting him aflame with the same fire that she suffered in.

"Don't act like you don't beg me."

Her smile was faint, but the look in her eyes was as vicious as a defiant cat. "And you're always so eager to oblige, aren't you?"

"About as eager as you are every time you beg me to let you come." He smirked, hoping it looked as cruel as he felt like being. "If I didn't know any better, I'd say you like being my whore."

"I want to slap you."

He slammed his hand against the wall by her head, watching the way she flinched. "If you do, you'll lose that fucking hand."

"Maybe I should do it anyway."

"And maybe I should show you what it's like when you beg me for something, and I don't let you have it," he whispered, his tone sinister. "Do you know what I could do to you?"

Her eyes simply shifted back and forth between his, searching them as though it were a challenge. Like she was daring him to do something. "It would be the last step, wouldn't it?"

"Last step before what?" He leaned down closer to her, his hand sliding down the wall a few inches as a result. He tilted his head to the side, rising to the silent challenge she was posing. "You weigh me down for the rest of your life with your fucking problems?"

"The last step before you have complete and utter control over my body. Because that's what this is all about, isn't it? You'll do anything to get that control. Take care of me. Believe my lies so it fits your narrative of me. Tell me all the reasons why you're making rules for me so you can pretend you're saving me." She whispered her taunts, too, her breath hot against his lips from below. "Don't you want to save me, Ash?"

His other hand snapped up to grip her hair at the back, dragging her head backward. She needed to know just how thin the ice had melted.

All this consternation, and he could tell they were just dancing. They were ballroom dancing, swirling around a dead body in the center of the room. He felt like the body was her.

And his partner was a ghost.

"I'm getting to the end of my rope with you."

She let out a bitter laugh. "Why don't you punish me for it?"

"Why do you keep taunting me? Huh? Why do you keep fucking *taunting* me?!"

"Because the only way I can get what I want from you is if I provoke you into it! I don't want you to take care of me! I don't want you to embrace me, or hold me, or tell me everything's gonna be okay! Don't you get that?"

As she spoke, he felt the shock rendering his hold on her hair loose. She was moving forward. He was stumbling back. His back hit the wall.

The tables had turned.

"I want you to lose control with me, over and over again until you go completely insane. I want you to crash and burn. I don't want you to save me. I want you to *fuck* me!"

Alarm bells were going off in his head, he was sure of it. By the way they set his heart to racing, they filled him with a sense of urgency that he was unable to ignore. An urgency that spelled out what she meant.

She wanted him to treat her like she didn't matter because the thought of mattering to someone was too unbearable. If she accepted his feelings, then she'd have to admit that she deserved to be loved. She didn't think she deserved that.

She knows she's a disappointment to me, he thought, *because she can't pull herself out. And she doesn't want me to pull her out because then she won't have the only thing she can control.*

Tayshia wanted him to treat her like he hated her the way she hated herself.

Ash moved forward until she was pinned between his body and the opposite wall. Her breathing hitched higher as his left hand curved around the front of her neck, forcing her head to tilt back again. His eyes met hers, as intense as flames.

And then he kissed her.

He could tell she was trying to come alive by the way she turned her head and ran her tongue along his lower lip. He felt her desire by the way she slipped it inside his mouth with silent desperation and clung to his shoulders. He sensed her need by the way she whimpered into his mouth and tried to command the kiss in her own way, even as the hard press of his body kept her from being able to go onto her tip-toes. It kept her vigilant, kept her straining to keep them connected in spite of the fact that he was the one who had the power to decide when it ended. They were swimming together, but he was pulling her deeper into the ocean.

"Why?" he whispered.

"Because." Her gaze sliced through the shadows to meet his. "I want you to be as broken as me."

"I already am."

Tayshia took several deep breaths and then, on the last exhale, she moaned as though the mere thought of it overwhelmed her. She threw her arms around his neck, gripping the back of it so she could pull him down to her level. She kissed him with a vengeance, her tongue shoving its way into his mouth without preamble. It was all he could do to keep up.

He dragged his mouth in kisses down the side of her neck. His fingers clawed at her coat, ripping the sides of it open so he could get to the tee shirt she was wearing. His fingers clawed at that, too. So much so that he tore it from neckline to hem, exposing her chest.

Ash's large hands grabbed at her body, his hand against her ribcage and his left holding her waist. He pulled her onto her toes, bending her back a little as he leaned down so he could worship her breasts. Tayshia's head fell backward, fingers sliding into the scruffy shorter hair at the back of his head, tugging at it. She shook and writhed in his arms as his tongue caressed, laved, and sucked its way around the peak.

She shivered, thighs shifting together as she swayed backward and they hit the wall together. When he pulled her nipple between his teeth, then closed his lips around it, she let out a high-pitched keening noise.

Ash wrapped one arm around her waist and the other around her lower back, picking her up. His head tilted up to kiss her as he carried her to the bedroom with the full intent of throwing her onto the bed. But then she was all-out *mauling* his mouth, her hands gripping his cheeks and legs wrapping around his waist, and he found he didn't think they had the time to walk the extra steps.

So he placed her on the dresser.

The chest full of his father's letters was virtually nonexistent to them as they played games with their tongues and mapped constellations on each other's bodies with their hands. Their kissing was frenetic, as though it were the last chance they had to kiss for all eternity. And inside his head, all he heard was her voice, chanting *I want you to fuck me* over and over and over.

His fingernails dug into the outsides of her thighs, dragging her to the edge of the dresser so that they bracketed his waist. They ground against one another, the frenzy of their need swelling to a crescendo from which there would be no slowing.

"Ash."

He kissed her neck again, listening to the heaving of her breath and the melodic sound of her sighs. He couldn't think. Didn't *want* to think.

"Ash, wait, wait, wait."

He'd been so numb for the past week. The only time he felt anything was when he was inside of her.

"*Stop!*"

Tayshia slammed her hand flat against Ash's chest and shoved him backward. Her still-healing tattoo was on display as she pulled the torn sides of her shirt closed, the ripped neckline having fallen down. Her facial expression was mournful, despairing in the way it tugged at his heart.

Firelight in the Dark

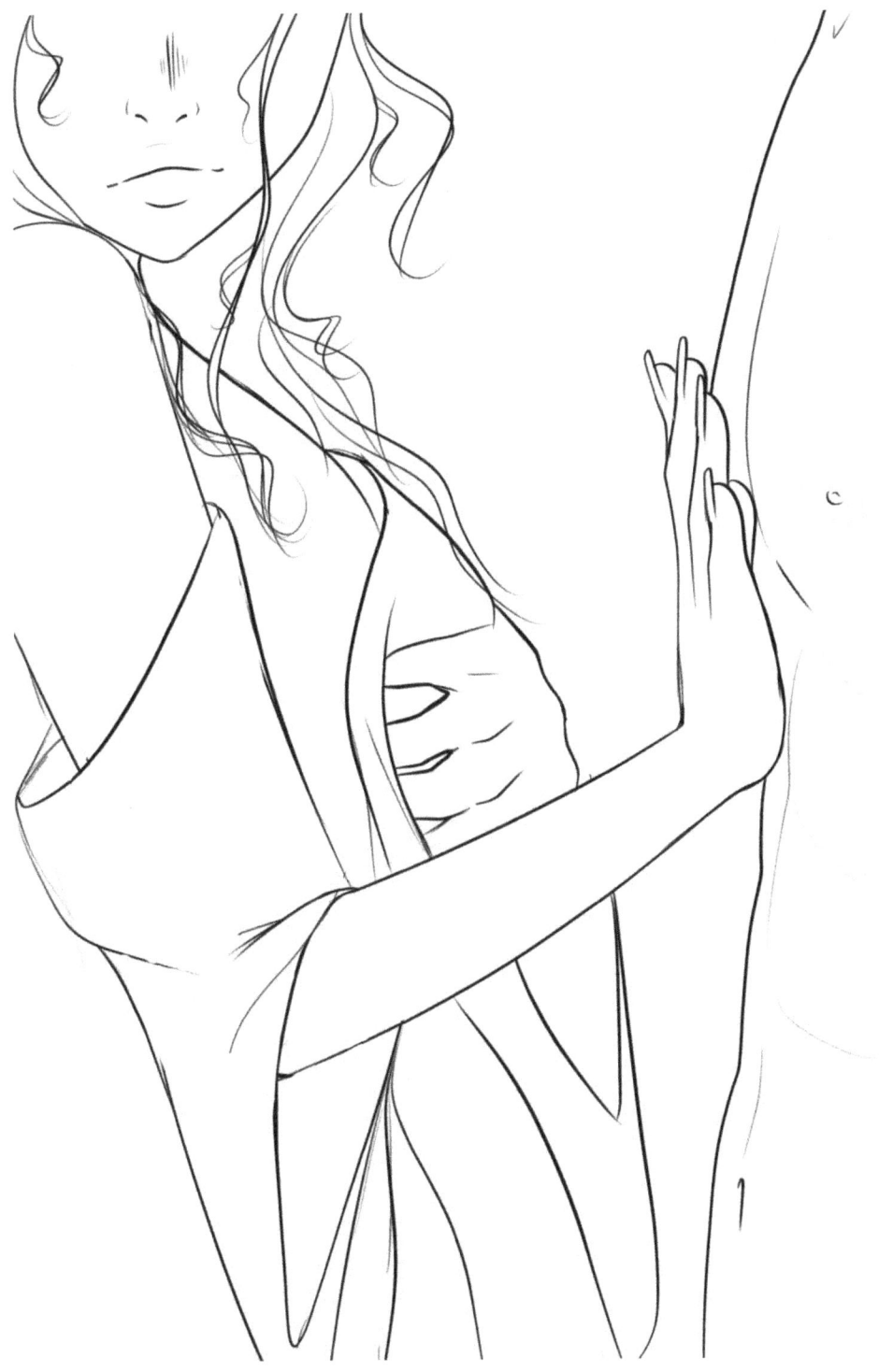

Concerned, he tried to reach for her, to cup her face in his hands, but she pushed them away. She placed her other hand flat on his chest, holding him firmly at arm's length.

"No, Ash."

Confusion filled him.

"Did I hurt you?"

"This isn't about me," she said, and her eyes were mournful as she dragged them up to his face. "This is about you."

"What?"

"This fight, these feelings, the way we're dealing with it? It's not just because of me and what I did. It's because of you and how you're running away from what you really feel."

His brows twitched together."

"You need to feel it, Ash. You need to feel the loss, or it's going to eat you up and spit you out like poison. We can fight tomorrow. But today? You need to feel this."

Her words sunk in like stones, cutting through the icy numbness that had plagued him since his father passed.

Oh.

Panic. It was spreading down from his head and out through his body. Anxiety wrapped around his limbs, causing him to tremble. And there, amidst the panic, was a helplessness that he didn't know how to manage.

Because she was right.

But to admit that would mean letting her win the argument. It would be letting her think he actually thought she was healthy and sane and not disordered. If he agreed with her, then the focus would be diverted from the problem at hand: her fucking eating disorder.

"You know what I need?" he said. "I need you to get the fuck out of my room."

She didn't move, the shock registering on her face in stages as she realized what he was saying. "I—oh, I wasn't—I just—I didn't want us to hide behind sex like we always do!"

"*Get the fuck out!*"

Tayshia's face crumpled, her head jerking backward as though he'd just hit her. He was too angry. Too overwhelmed to care. She didn't care about him, anyway. If she did, she wouldn't have just manipulated him after a fight *about* her manipulation.

She jumped down from the dresser and slunk out of the room like a chastised fox, her head down and steps quiet. When she was gone and Ash was alone, it hit him.

He was grieving his dad.

Chapter Thirteen

"You ready to go?"

Ash glanced up from his phone. Andre stood at the front door, holding it open as cold air from the rainy night blasted in. On the couch, Ji Hyun and Tayshia were playing the game that Ash and Andre had been playing nonstop. Though they weren't doing so hot at it, they were giggling and falling about. Something about headshots seemed to send them into orbit.

If things weren't so broken and mangled between he and Tayshia, he might have had the wherewithal to think it was cute.

"Yeah," he said, the agitation in his veins making his hands shake. He needed weed, which was the reason why they were going to Andre's apartment. He needed weed, a huge break from the Hellhole he lived in, and some time away from Tayshia. "Let's go."

Ash pulled his hoodie on over his tee shirt, then picked his black snapback up from the arm of the couch where he'd set it. He put it on backwards and headed for the door.

"You're not gonna kiss your woman good-bye?!" Ji Hyun practically screeched, stopping them when Ash was outside the apartment and Andre had just finished laying a kiss on her lips. She looked disturbed. "What the Hell is wrong with you, Ash?"

Ash's eyes sought Tayshia's for a moment.

The last thing they wanted to do was kiss each other right now. Things were *fucked* between them.

"It's okay," Tayshia said with a wave of her hand, her voice shaking. "I'm not feeling well. I don't want to get him sick."

Ji Hyun narrowed her eyes. "You don't *seem* sick."

"She threw up this morning." Ash's voice cut back into the house, across the room.

Because she had. He'd finally managed to get to sleep around three, but had woken at six to have a bathroom trip. As he'd neared the door, the familiarity of seeing the light on underneath it was almost nostalgic.

When she'd left the bathroom that morning, stumbling and swaying against the door frame, she nearly fainted upon seeing him. He'd at least had the decency to catch her as she fell against his chest. And he couldn't be cruel to her, either, no matter how angry he was. It would be imbecilic of him to wonder why she'd do it, especially after he'd kicked her out of his room the way he had that evening.

But not even middle-of-the-night epiphanies could bring a sense of normalcy back to their connection, and he'd let go of her, hands leaving her skin like a star shooting across a dark sky. She'd gone on to bed. He'd gone to the bathroom.

They'd taken their necklaces off.

"Well, damn," Andre interjected. "You better not give us something."

"It's not like that," Tayshia said with a meek smile. "You guys go ahead."

Ash stared at her, stared at the way her smile shook. The way she donned a mask so their friends wouldn't see the way she was trying not to crumble. His heart broke, rending in two in his chest.

All he had to do was go back inside. All he had to do was kiss her, and everything would be better. They could go back to the way things were.

"We'll see you guys," Ash said softly. "And we'll be back in like, an hour."

Ji Hyun didn't seem convinced, but the sympathetic look she sent in Tayshia's direction showed him that she knew they were lying.

"Ash, are you *okay*?" Andre said when they were in the darkness of the parking lot. His concerned expression made Ash feel guilty. Because he wasn't all right, and neither was Tayshia.

"I'm fine," he lied.

"I don't know. It seems like something's off. Is this because of your pops?"

"Bruh, I'm *fine*," Ash snapped, opening the driver's side door of his car. They were taking it because he had more gas in his tank. "Stop asking."

The car ride was silent between them, the metalcore music seeming to further agitate him where it otherwise would soothe. Andre was tense, but he seemed to know better than to say anything. They were so quiet that when they finally did arrive at his apartment, Andre immediately loaded up the bong without so much as a word.

"You go first," he said, holding it out to Ash. "You need it more than I do."

Thank God.

Ash was quick to take a hit, the heat and bite of the smoke in his lungs a welcome reprieve from the cold turmoil he'd been suffering from. Andre watched him carefully and then, when Ash passed him the bong, he spoke.

"Something's up."

Ash said nothing, listening to the clicking of the lighter. He gazed at the far wall, eyes blank.

"What happened?" Andre continued. "You guys were so tight. Seems like something got fucked up."

"Something did get fucked up." Ash leaned back against the couch, running his fingers repeatedly through his hair from root to tip. "But I can't explain it, and I don't want to talk about it."

"Okay. Well, just talk to me if you need to. You know I...Ash?"

Ash was on the verge of tears. He'd dug the heels of his palms into his eyes, pressing, trying to keep them inside. His chest heaved.

"What's up, man?" Andre asked, his voice subdued. He set the bong on the coffee table. Ash heard the thunk of glass against wood. "I'm here for you."

Ash took several deep breaths, trying as hard as he could to keep himself from breaking down to sob. He pulled his hands away from his eyes, his vision of the bong and his best friend now blurry. He felt embarrassed and overwhelmed — no one other than Tayshia had seen him cry.

"Man, I can't explain this shit."

"Then don't try. Just let yourself feel. Things are going to be rocky with her for a little while. But she's not going anywhere, I can tell you that for sure."

Andre didn't understand and never would. He didn't know how bad things were. He didn't know how sick Tayshia was, how sick Ash was for the way he treated her. He and Tayshia were two stars, consuming one another as they spun around and around in the depths of darkness where no other stars surrounded them.

"You're not gonna break up with her, are you?"

"We're not even together."

"But Ji called her your girlfriend. You didn't correct her."

Ash was quiet for a second, before snatching the bong back up. "Well, she's mine, isn't she?"

"Good enough."

He'd thought about it.

He'd thought about giving up, cutting his losses, leaving her. Just letting her kill herself slowly so he didn't have to lose anyone else. Ridding his life of the selfishness and the manipulation and the lies.

But he couldn't.

The thought of not waking up to her in his arms, of not hearing her laugh as they lounged on their couch, of not seeing her in their dreams underneath that lavender sky. The thought of her not sitting there playing her little monster game while he played his own games, of not feeling her fingers threaded through his own when their bodies were pressed so tight together that they were one, of not knowing what it would be like to love her. The thought of never getting to see her smile reach her eyes.

It was out of the question.

Ash opened his mouth to say something, but his phone buzzed. He pulled it out of his back pocket, glancing at the screen. It was Tayshia. He set it down, choosing not to answer it.

"I just need to have a clear head to think," he said. "I don't want to end things with her. I would literally rather die. But we're not doing well, no."

"Man, just stop and think for a second. Of *course* you're—"

Bzzt. Bzzt. Bzzt. Bzzt. Bzzt.

She was calling again.

When Ash made no move to answer it, Andre went on.

"Of course you're not doing well. Your pops just passed."

"Yeah, but I *hated* him."

"That doesn't mean you aren't grieving. He took something important from you: the time you needed to be able to forgive him."

Ash had hardly the time to mull that over before his phone was ringing again. Buzzing and buzzing and buzzing. It kept going, each call fading into the next with less than two seconds between each one. It filled him with anxiety that made his fingers tremble and the center of his chest swell with it. It grew to the breaking point, and then exploded.

"Why the *fuck* is she calling me so many times?!" he shouted, the angry outburst drawing Andre's perturbed gaze.

"Yo, chill. Maybe she thinks you forgot something."

"Okay, well she's calling me fifteen fucking times in a fucking row! I'm here because I need a God damn break from her shit!"

Andre's frown lines deepened. "What shit? What does she do?"

"I told you I can't explain it. It's not—"

Bzzt.

Ash nearly hucked his phone across the room.

"I'm going to lose my mind," he said. "I want her to leave me alone right now. I want her to leave me alone."

"All right, all right. Just breathe, dude." Andre leaned over and picked the phone up. "Shit, she did call fifteen times. But the new one's a text."

"What does it say?"

"Tell me your passcode."

He did, and then Andre's eyes were scanning the screen. His expression was confused. "Who's Caden?"

The broken gears in Ash's mind turned and clicked painfully into place.

He lunged across the couch and grabbed the phone out of his hand, frantically taking in the words of her text.

Literally Caden is here at the fucking door.

"Fuck," he said aloud. "Fuck, fuck, fuck, fuck, *fuck*! We have to go. Come on, come on, come on! Let's go!"

"Go? Go where?"

Ash was on his feet, his entire body shaking and thrumming with fear and anger. He pressed her name on the top of the conversation and then pressed *call*. He held the phone to his ear as it rang.

"Get up," he said, snapping his fingers in his friend's direction as he headed for the front door. "We're going. We've gotta go. Get in the car."

"Okay, okay, okay!" Andre sprinted out the door after him. "What the Hell is happening?"

Tayshia picked up before Ash could answer.

"Ash," she whispered, her tone strained and frantic. "Ash, they're here. They're at the door. They're—"

Ji Hyun's voice in the background cut her off. "We opened the door because we thought they left."

"I don't know," Tayshia said, breathless. "We—And we thought it would be okay to—to look out the door, and then we—we heard them on the stairs. And they came back. They fucking came back up the stairs. They—"

"Why would you open the door?!" Ash snarled, tucking the phone between his ear and shoulder as he slammed his car keys into the driver's side door. Andre was still coming down the stairs. "Why the *fuck* would you open the door?!"

"Stop yelling at her!" Ji Hyun's voice came through the speaker. "We both opened the door. We weren't sure."

"Yeah, and we were just curious. We didn't know how they knew where we lived."

"Where are you right now?" Ash's car was already flying down the road, the phone in his right hand and his left hand on the wheel. His seatbelt wasn't on, but Andre was in the process of clicking his into the holster. "Are you inside?"

"We came back to your room," Tayshia whispered. "They were knocking."

"Shit," Ash cursed, glaring out the window as they came up to a red light. "Okay, well just stay there. We're coming."

She was quiet for a second, the only sound coming from a still-panicking Ji Hyun.

"Ash, I'm scared. They keep knocking."

"Well, then you shouldn't have opened the fucking door!" he shouted, his voice ringing in the car. "That was a pretty stupid thing to do."

"Hang up that phone." Andre's voice was as dark as night. His glare seared into the side of Ash's face. "You better hang that fucking phone up right now, Ash."

Ash gave him a strange look and said to Tayshia, "Look, I want you to stay in my room. Lock the door, just in case."

"Okay."

"And do not open that bedroom door, *no matter what*."

"What if they come in?"

"They won't."

"But what if they do?"

Ash sighed and started to reply, but the sound of Andre clearing his throat reminded him that he'd pissed him off, and he needed to hang up.

"We're on our way."

"But—"

"Tayshia, listen to me. I'm not gonna let anyone hurt you. I am on my way. I'll be there soon."

It took a while for her to answer. When it came, it was a choked whisper. "Okay."

"Don't be scared."

In the background, Ji Hyun let out a gasp. "God, they're knocking again. Why won't they just *leave*?!"

"Fuck. I'm coming, all right? Keep that door locked for me, baby. Just keep it locked."

"Please hurry," Tayshia said.

The moment Ash hung up, Andre was on him.

"You don't talk to your girl like that, do you hear me? Look at me, Ash." Ash did, his fingers clenching around his phone in his lap as he saw the anger in Andre's eyes. "You don't talk to your girl like that. All right? Okay?"

"Yeah, fine."

"I'm serious. Do not ever yell at her like that in front of me again."

Ash chewed at the inside of his cheek. He'd never been at the brunt end of Andre's anger before, especially not for something he already knew he felt bad about. He didn't *want* to yell at her. He didn't *like* the side of him that had been coming. It was the frustration that was getting to him, turning him into a person he didn't want to be.

Tayshia had set him on fire.

"I know you been through some shit lately," Andre continued, his voice a bit gentler. "But that's your *girl*. She's the one been holdin' you down since day one. You seen the shit she did for you these past two weeks? You don't fuck with that."

Ash tipped his head back against the seat, his mind clouded. "It's complicated."

"No. That shit ain't complicated. That's a blessing. You're blessed, man. Don't fuck it up."

They were both quiet as Ash drove down the highway as fast as he could get away with going. Ash couldn't stop his mind from traversing wild planes, imagining all sorts of horrible scenarios. He hadn't heard of anyone in Ricky's gang *killing* anyone, but violence was never out of the question for them. And for Caden, it didn't matter who was at the brunt end of his fist. He could and would hurt Tayshia if it served his agenda.

In any case, Andre was right. Tayshia may have lied to him for the sake of her disorder, but never once had she faked her feelings for him. Those were real. She'd taken care of him after his dad's death because she cared. She'd stopped him the previous night because she cared. She'd given her body to him, having the courage to show herself in her full nudity *because she cared*.

"So who is Caden?" Andre asked.

"Remember how I used to sell for that guy Ricky? And my dad, too? Well, Caden's like, his second. Like if Ricky is number one, then Caden is—"

"Number two."

"Yeah," Ash said with a nod, glancing at him and then back to the road. "And we ran into him after that show."

"Oh, shit." Andre held the side of his fist to his mouth, staring at Ash with wide eyes. "In January."

"Yeah."

"Well, fuck. Okay. Well, what's his deal?"

"I don't know. That's the problem. I don't think he had any interest in me—or in Tayshia—until he saw me. I didn't recognize him and I noticed he was standing too close to the girls, so I—"

"*That was him?!*"

Ash nodded.

"You think he's gonna break in and kill her?!"

"No, you weirdo." Ash gave him a revolted once-over. "Fuck outta here with that. No one's going to kill her."

"Don't you think if they were feeling froggy, they would have jumped by now?" Andre said with a measure of sarcasm that made Ash roll his eyes. "

"Some kid who went to the public high school used to sell for Ricky, too. Can't remember his name. Caden let him postpone his payments for two months. Kid thought he was getting off, picking up more shit every week, selling it and keeping the money. Just like my dad."

"And what did he do?"

"He beat the shit out of him. His girlfriend was with him, and he beat the shit out of her, too," Ash said. "Caden don't give a fuck."

"Oh…" Andre shook his head. "Well, shit. I guess you better put that pedal down to the floor, my boy. My girlfriend's there, too."

Ash was way ahead of him.

✧✧✧

They were coming down the stairs right as Ash and Andre arrived.

First came two men that Ash didn't recognize—a raven-haired one his age, and a blonde one who looked a bit older than the thirty-year-old Caden. Caden himself brought up the rear, twirling his car keys around his finger. He wore a pair of black joggers and a grey tee-shirt with a wide neckline that revealed the thorns he had tattooed across his collarbones. His hair had been freshly shorn on the sides, leaving a shock of red at the top of his head that fell into his eyes. Upon seeing Ash, his thin lips spread into a vicious grin that brought a twinkle to his eyes.

"Well, well, well," he drawled. "What a surprise. And here we thought you'd be home for us to come visit."

Ash didn't think. He couldn't. There was nothing in his head. The sound of his voice coupled with the fact that he had just harassed the girls wiped his mind free of all thoughts that didn't involve his fist in Caden's face. It was like a switch turned off, leaving nothing but darkness and one flame of rage burning at the center.

He lunged.

Caden didn't budge, but the other two men who were with him jumped back and away. Andre side-stepped and whipped around, putting himself between Ash and the others. He placed a hand on his chest, holding him back with a finger in his face and both of their chests heaving.

"Don't fuck with him," he growled, his eyes glinting dangerously. "Look at his hand."

Ash's gaze darted past Andre and down. Caden's hand was low at his side. There, attached to his keys, was a switchblade. It was out, the sharp point glinting beneath the lights of the apartment complex stairwell.

"Don't worry. I wasn't gonna stab you. I was just gonna cut you a little," Caden said, bringing the blade up to his mouth so he could lick the edge. His spider tattoo seemed darker, like he'd gotten it touched up since the funeral. It was a reminder of what he was capable of.

He would bite, and he had venom.

"What the fuck are you doing here, at my house?" Ash said, waving a hand to tell Andre to move away from him.

"I told you. I wanted to visit you." He gave a mock pout. "You don't want to see me?"

"Preferably not."

"Aw. Well, I missed you and little Tayshia. I thought if you weren't home, I could at least see her."

Andre was quick to hold Ash back again, this time struggling a bit as he tried to shove him to the side. The anger was white-hot, blinding him to all else but Caden's thin neck. He wanted to slit his throat. In that moment, Ash forgot every argument he and Tayshia ever had. In that moment, she was priceless.

She was his.

"If you touch her — if you so much as *look* at her, I'll — "

"You'll what?" Caden said, sauntering a couple of steps forward. The keys were back to twirling, his pointer finger extended. "Point your little toy gun at me? We both know you don't have the balls to use it."

Andre and Ash carefully avoided each other's gazes. They both knew he didn't have that gun.

Caden couldn't know.

"Listen to me, Ash," he said, one hand slipping into the front pocket of his jeans while he continued to twirl those keys. "I'm not trying to cause problems or scare our poor, sweet Tayshia. I'm just concerned."

The tension mounted, causing Ash's hands to clench into fists at his sides. He wanted to kill him. He wanted Caden dead.

"What could you possibly be concerned about?" he bit out. "I don't owe you shit, my dad is dead, Ricky forgave him. What the Hell do you want?"

Caden crossed the distance to stand in front of him. It wasn't often that other men were as tall as Ash, but Caden was at eye level. They were equally intimidating and thus, could not intimidate each other.

But when he ran the tip of the knife up the front of Ash's throat, forcing his head back, he felt a tiny flicker of fear run through the fire that burned in his mind.

He glared at him from beneath his lashes. The bite of the blade was strong, but not strong enough to break the skin unless he swallowed. It was cold outside — much colder than it had been lately since today hadn't rained. Caden didn't seem bothered by it in the slightest.

"If you want me to be less interested in you," he murmured, the smile fading and becoming replaced by a flatness to his eyes and tone, "then try being a little more boring."

With that, he flicked the knife away from Ash's chin, nearly cutting him. Caden signaled to the quiet men that had flanked him, and then the three of them left.

Their car doors slamming snapped Ash out of his angry reverie. He glanced over his shoulder, turning to watch the blue Oldsmobile

Caden drove zoom out of the parking lot. The engine was loud and obnoxious.

"We'll deal with it if we have to," Andre said.

An icy shiver rippled through Ash's spine. He shook his head. "No. This is my thing. I'll deal with it."

"He had a knife, bro."

"Yeah, well...He sells drugs in a fucking gang." Ash rubbed the back of his neck with his hand. "What do you expect him to carry? A floss pick?"

"Ash." Andre gave him a deadpan look. "Just promise me you'll find a way to lay low. You can't stay in this apartment right now. Find somewhere to go. A hotel, or something."

He was right. It was too dangerous to stay here while Caden's eye was on them. If they went somewhere else, Ash would only have to get Tayshia to school for a week before spring break began, and then they could *really* lay low. And Caden was unpredictable—he might very well get bored of them if they weren't in a place where he could find them.

Without waiting for Ash, Andre bounded up the stairs two at a time. Ash followed, overtaking him with his much longer legs. He pulled his keys out and unlocked the deadbolt first, then the door itself. Andre pushed past him, frantic, and Ash turned around to lock the door from the inside.

"Babe? *Babe!* Come out!" Andre called.

The bedroom door wrenched open, and then Ji Hyun was *running* down the hall. She cried out in relief as she threw her arms around his neck and lamented her fears, telling him how scared she was.

In spite of the awkwardness that had been there before he left, Ash moved beyond them and into the hall. Tayshia had just made it two steps outside the bedroom door when his hands were on her waist, crowding her back into the room. He folded her in his embrace, dropping gentle kisses to her face and the side of her throat.

"I could have lost you," he whispered. "I thought I might."

She pressed her face into his chest. He could feel her shaking, trying not to bring attention to it, and it melted something in his heart. Caden was terrifying, and she didn't know much about him.

"You must have been so scared," he said, fingers tangling in her hair so he could drag her head back. He looked at her from beneath his lashes. "I'm sorry I yelled at you. I didn't help at all."

Tayshia shook her head, not saying anything as she pressed her forehead against his chest again. She burrowed into him like he was safety from a storm, and she was defenseless. Overcome with an emotion he didn't quite understand, he dropped his head onto her, his cheek brushing soft, fluffy curls, and feathered more kisses to the side of her head. His hands smoothed low on her hips, then up the center of her back.

What if Caden had broken in? What if he'd gotten home and found her and Ji Hyun both dead, blood spilled on the carpet and silence filling the room? What if the last time he'd truly spoken to her had been an argument, or that phone call where he'd screamed at her?

The confusing emotion roiled, churning and making his heart ache.

If anything ever happened to Tayshia, he would spiral.

Slow and sure, he lowered his lips to hers, kissing her with something insatiable and hungry. His fingers moved behind her head, curling as he used her hair as an anchor. He tugged her head backward, dragged it there so he could devour her mouth in a way he never had before. He didn't want anything left by the time he was done kissing her, reminding her how much he cared for her.

She made him feel alive and without her, there was nothing.

Tayshia pressed closer to him, her hands sliding up to cup his face, the tips of her acrylics tickling his skin. As she kissed him back, the familiar heat of desire started to take root and grow in his body. To grow like flowers with petals of fire.

Ash slowed his kiss further, using a soft tentativeness that spoke not of insecurity, but of necessity. Of concern. He wanted to show her that he was sorry for their arguments. That he was sorry he wasn't there when Caden was. And when she tilted her head, trying to kiss up into his mouth in a way that told him that she needed him, his aching heartbeat felt steady.

He pulled back and rested his forehead against hers, the two of them breathless. He caressed her everywhere that he could, cherishing her with his fingers against her cheeks, her waist, her neck, her arms. Everything that he held dear. Her hands were on his shoulders and now, they slid to his chest and gripped his hoodie again. They stood there for a while in the darkness, swaying slightly as he embraced her, as he worshipped her with his caress. The song was one of their hearts — one that no one else could hear.

"Do you realize what I would do for you?" he said, his voice rumbling in his chest. He thought of the gun he'd tossed, and of the way he'd attacked Kieran. "What I've *done* for you?"

Still clutching him, she let her head drop back again so she could look at him. There was a shine to her eyes, but he couldn't be sure if it was tears or just the moonlight.

"What if he comes back?" she said, voice trembling. "What if he hurts me? I can't go through it again. I can't have what happened in Paris ever—"

Ash felt a flash of pain that morphed into a violent rage. One that he had to force back.

"You listen to me. No one will *ever* hurt you like that again. Do you hear me? *No one*. You are safe, Tayshia. You've always been safe with me. If he touches you, he'll find out what happens when I stop caring about what happens to me."

She stared at him for a moment longer, a frown on her face that seemed to deepen. Before he could remark on it, she'd buried her face in his chest again and wrapped her arms around his waist. He felt her hands clutching beneath where his hood fell, pulling, holding him tight, and he buried his face in the crook of her neck and shoulder. She smelled of rose. Of lavender. Of gardenias.

Of something to be cherished.

CHAPTER FOURTEEN

Later, after Andre and Ji Hyun were fast asleep on the couch, Ash tugged Tayshia into his bedroom with him.

Things still weren't good between them, but there was something about the way she'd stared through the TV instead of at it while they were watching a movie tonight that told him something was wrong.

He had a feeling this would normally be the moment where she purged.

"I think," Ash said as he pulled the covers back, "that we should figure out what to do about Caden. I don't like that he came here. There's no reason for him to do that. And while I get why he came to my dad's funeral, I think it's still weird."

"Yes," she said as she slowly pushed her hair up into her satin bonnet. There were things unsaid between them, shards of glass that they were treading around. The argument. The fact that he'd yelled at her on the phone. The fact that he hadn't kissed her good-bye. The fact that he'd caught her purging and hadn't said anything to her about it. "He knows where we live, and that's not good."

"No, it's not," Ash agreed. "We could go to a hotel? Just to lay low for a little while."

She opened her mouth, inhaling to speak, then closed it.

"What were you about to say?" Ash asked.

"I wasn't—I was just gonna suggest something. I don't know if you'll be on board with the idea."

He tilted his head to the side, waiting.

"What if we went to your house? The one that you grew up in? No one's been there in over a year. I think it would be the least likely place they'd check because it'd be so obvious—they would assume that you wouldn't want to go back there, so I don't think they'd even think to check it. And if we just go there for a few weeks, maybe that'll be enough time for Caden to find something else more interesting than us. If we go to your house, that could be the best solution."

Move into his childhood home? The home that was filled with memories and items from his past that he'd rather not ever see again? The home that by the grace of God and the vigilance of his godparents, no one had broken into? His bedroom was likely exactly the way he'd left it.

"No."

"Okay."

Ash raised an eyebrow. "Really? You're not gonna try to convince me?"

She shook her head. If it were daylight, he had a feeling she'd be blushing. How unlike her. She should be arguing with him, lashing out, trying to explain how stupid he was being. How they were in danger because of him.

"You gonna stand there all night, or come to bed?" he said, turning to look down at her in the moonlight that peeked in through the window.

"You...I don't know," she mumbled.

Ash crossed his tattooed arms over his bare chest. His new tattoo was still healing, ridged from the scabs, but the soreness had long since dissipated.

"Are you okay?"

She shook her head.

"Are you still scared?"

She nodded.

"Of who?"

Her silence was enough of an answer. She wasn't scared of Caden—not truly. Him knocking on the door was a scary situation, but it didn't go deeper than that for her.

"You're scared of me," he said, his tone resigned. "Right. What do you want to do about it?"

She tugged her sleeves down over her hands. "Talk about it."

"All right, fine." He sighed and sat down on the edge of the bed, placing his hands behind him and leaning back. "What do you want to start with?"

"Do you think I'm repulsive?"

Okay. That was not what he thought she wanted to talk about.

"What?"

"I said, do you think I'm repulsive?" The moonlight made her brown eyes look hazel as she waited for his reply.

"Of course not. Why would you even think that?"

"During our argument yesterday, you…" She averted her gaze, playing with one sleeve. "You seemed so angry that for a second, I honestly believed you thought I was repulsive. That you didn't want to be with me anymore."

He wanted to tell her that would never happen, but he bit his tongue.

"And then I thought about it all day, thought about a way that I could fix the thing that's destroying us. My…Disorder." The word seemed to taste bitter to her. "And I remembered what we did that day, during Winter Break. You seemed so in control and after it happened, things were so good between us for a while. And for me, I liked the feeling of being helpless. Of letting you handle everything. I liked when you said the things to me that I say to myself. And then I pieced everything together."

He remembered it. It'd been like tasting an expensive, aged wine: delicious, smooth, and borderline forbidden. He nodded, his expression curious and his heart beating rapidly in his chest.

"I liked it when you degraded me because I know you care about me. It takes the things I say to myself and it makes them false. An act. A lie. And when we did that stuff together, I felt like they weren't true. For the first time, the horrible words I say to myself—that I'm pathetic, that I'm bad, that I'm needy and annoying and worthless and needy—they felt like they weren't real. Like you took them away and made them yours so you could throw them away afterward."

I was in control, he thought, *so she didn't have to be.*

"And I just get so tired sometimes," she whispered. "So…I have a proposal."

He knew what she was going to propose, but he needed to hear her say it. To speak the words into reality so he could feel them sink in and tell him what he already knew about himself from the moment he first wrapped his hand around her throat.

Control was something he needed, too.

"What's the proposal?"

"Well, I—I just—I—"

"Just say it, Tayshia."

"Your temper is—it's scary. It's scary because it's unpredictable. And it makes me feel like you think I'm disgusting, or that you hate me, so—"

"I told you yesterday," he said, temper already flaring. "Don't twist my words."

A panicked look crossed her face and she stepped forward, waving both of her hands and shaking her head back and forth. "No, no. That's not what I'm saying. Not at all."

"Then what *are* you saying? You're acting really weird."

"If you don't think I'm repulsive, but you keep finding yourself so mad at me that you feel like you might hate me...I'd rather you channel it into something else. And, since you won't let me—let me purge..." She seemed to be losing steam, embarrassment mounting as the words fell from her lips. "I think we could both find some control in something else."

Figuring it out was like moving through molasses. And the moment he did, he moved his elbows to his thighs and leaned forward. Fingers lacing together, he looked down at the floor to contemplate.

The problem was not what she wanted. He could give her what she wanted, and he would. He wanted to, even if it came from a dark part of himself. Every time they had an argument, this was how they solved it. With their bodies. With sex. With the push and pull of their hands, the press of their fingers to each other's skin. It wasn't healthy.

But was it healthy for them to fight all the time? Was it healthy for her to binge and purge and starve? Was it healthy for him to scream at her? None of this was healthy.

He looked up from the carpet.

"You're not afraid of Caden, and you're not afraid of me," he said decisively. "You're scared of what's going to happen now that you've realized that you can't purge forever. You're scared because you think you've found a possible new coping mechanism, and you think I'll say no."

After some hesitation, she nodded.

"So, what do you want?"

It took her several attempts before she was finally able to say it. Even then, she said it with her head down and an uncharacteristic shyness to her voice.

"The way you talked to me, the way you controlled me and made me feel helpless? I want you to do that again. Every time you get mad, I want you to take it out on me."

"To punish you?"

"Yes. I want you to punish me."

"Because you can't punish yourself if you can't purge."

"Yes."

It was fucked. It was completely fucked.

"You know, there's such a thing as therapy," he muttered.

"*No!*" She took several quick steps forward, a desperate look on her face. "I don't want to go to a therapist or any doctors. I'm *sure* this is what I need. It's what I want. I--"

Ash held up a hand for silence. She was getting to the point of babbling.

"Just calm down and talk to me."

"Do you ever get angry enough to hurt me?"

"No," he said. "To hurt other people, yes. People like Kieran, or Caden."

"That's not what this would be," she insisted, and then she came to stand between his legs. He felt her sleeves against his face as she cupped his cheeks with her hands, forcing him to look up at her. "Think of it like a solution to the problem. It will solve *everything*."

"You want me to hurt you."

"Not *hurt* me." She bit her lower lip. "I want you to use me. To make me do the things you want me to do. To take the bad words and make them good."

The darkness in his body spread, reaching his eyes. "Tell me why."

"It makes me feel safe."

"How?"

"Because it's you."

Ash closed his eyes for a moment, his hands on the verge of clenching into fists. The energy in his body had mounted. His friends were sleeping in the living room, but he didn't care.

He was going to give her what she wanted because he wanted it, too.

"And you won't purge? You won't binge or starve? You'll follow the rules, you'll eat, and you'll stop fighting me on it?"

"I promise." When he raised his eyebrows, she sat down beside him and wrapped her arms around his neck from the side. Her forearms laid flat across his chest and back, her chin resting on his shoulder with her forehead nuzzling into his hair. He turned his face toward her, their cheeks pressing together, right as she whispered, "*I promise.*"

There was no indecision. No walls, no qualms. Nothing more he needed to convince himself. He hadn't been hesitant all those weeks ago because he didn't *want* to do those things with her. He'd been hesitant because he *did*. And with her past, he didn't want to hurt her.

But now she was telling him to do whatever he wanted, as long as he took care of her.

He could do that.

"Okay," he said. "We'll do it."

"Really?"

"Yes. I'll take control so you don't have to."

"Okay. And will you call me names like you did?"

"Names?"

"Like...Like whore and slut."

"Is that what you want?"

She nodded enthusiastically, her eyes bright. "That's exactly what I need to hear."

"All right. Then I will. But if you want to stop, just say so."

"Do I say—say stop, or should I make up a word?"

His brows twitched together. "Why would you need to make up a word?"

"Um...Well, I..." Her fingers were drumming on the bare skin of his shoulder. "There's things you do that I like, that I might say wait or stop, but I don't really mean it."

Ash needed to remember that she wasn't experienced, even if remembering the reason why was painful. She was bound to have things she wanted to do that she was too scared to put a name to, and things that she liked that she didn't know the names of in the first place.

"It's called overstimulation," he murmured, the darkness continuing to inch outward from his belly and into the rest of his body. His skin felt like it was on fire. "It means you like it when you're sensitive, and I keep going."

"Yes." She looked away from him, likely blushing again. "That. I like that."

"I can do that."

"Then I guess I can just make it simple. If I don't want to do something, I'll say no. If something is too far, I'll say that it's too far. But if I say wait, stop, please, or—or I can't, then we—we keep going. Okay?"

"Stand up and take off your clothes."

A squeak escaped her throat. "What?"

He turned his head, regarding her as though he had no interest in anything at all. "Stand up…and take off your clothes."

"But Andre and Ji Hyun are here."

"I don't care. You said you wanted to do this when I was angry with you. Well, I'm angry with you. So take off your clothes. Now, Tayshia."

She leapt to her feet, hands shaking as she reached for the hem of the large hoodie and pulled it off over her head. It left her standing there, trembling in naught but her leggings, tank top, and bra. Ash watched patiently as she shimmied out of her leggings, peeling them off of her body and dropping them on top of the discarded hoodie. She was shaking so hard that he could see the involuntary shivers rolling through her limbs.

"Breathe," he said, his tone soft. "If you want to stop, just tell me no. Just like you said."

She nodded her head, reaching behind her to unclasp her bra. She let the straps slide down before she dropped it onto the floor. But then, right as her fingers hooked beneath her panties to take them off, too, Ash spoke.

"Stop." He stood up, jerking his head toward the bed. "Lay down. And take off your bonnet. I want to put my hands in your hair."

She did, still shaking in spite of the fact that her breathing was even. Glancing up at him, she pulled her bonnet off, the soft, fluffy curls of her weave tumbling down. Then, she laid back against the pillows.

Ash got onto the bed, still wearing his joggers, and sat back on his knees with her feet on either side of his kneecaps. His fingers sought the waistband of her dark panties at her hips, causing her to jolt when they brushed her skin.

"*Breathe*. It's just me. Say no if you want me to stop."

"K-Keep going," she stammered out. "T-Take them o-off."

Slowly, he tugged her underwear down, leaving her completely nude before him. Her fingers twitched in the comforter by her hips, like she wanted to cover herself but was forcing herself not to. She couldn't seem to meet his gaze, which burned on her as bright as a star.

Ash crawled over her, giving her barely enough time to spread her thighs to accommodate him before he was above her. He placed his right hand on the blankets beside her shoulder and, driven by greed and curiosity and an iniquitous lust, he held her panties up before her.

"Open your mouth."

She stared at him in confusion. "What?"

"I said open your mouth."

She parted her lips.

Ash watched her with indifference as he threaded the garment into her mouth. He hoped she could taste herself, could feel how wet she was as the microfiber moved across her tongue. There were so many things he wanted to do to her—to do *with* her—and none of them required her voice.

When the fabric was successfully placed inside her mouth, he couldn't help but smirk.

Perfect.

He remained hovering over her, allowing the possessive, near-predatory energy he usually held back to come over him. His hand smoothed from her knee down to the crease of her thigh and pelvis. He slid his thumb to the right, pressing soothing circles into her pubic bone, mindless of the curls she had there.

"Stop shaking," he murmured, gaze falling down to her lower half. His hand moved back up, then down again. Massaging her. Calming her. "No matter what, you're always gonna be safe with me."

At the confused look on her face, he paused, remembering their deal. Their compromise.

She didn't want him to be nice.

"Don't you know how pathetic I think it is that you can't calm down?" Her eyes widened. "I'd much rather tell you to suck it up and spread your legs. But this is your last chance. If you want me to stop, tell me to stop now."

Distress threaded into the lines of Tayshia's furrowed brow as she made muffled noises of dissent. She placed her hands by her head and spread her thighs a bit more.

He got the hint.

"If you wake my friends up, I'll fuck you until you cry," he breathed into her ear. "And I'll make sure they know what a whore you are."

She moaned.

She *moaned*, and it was the last bit of encouragement and confirmation that he needed to know that this was exactly the way she wanted it.

Later, as they laid there with her curling around him, clutching at him in her sleep like he might fade away if she didn't, Ash realized that if he ever lost her, he'd never recover. He'd be so desolate, so completely devoid of purpose, that life would mean nothing. He'd throw himself into the sun for her.

He needed to protect her. From herself. From Caden. From everything.

They had to go to his house.

Chapter Fifteen

March 2019

Hiding his car in the garage made Ash's heart ache in a way that differed from the way he felt about Tayshia. In a way that ran deeper than the sea and took his anxiety higher than the sun.

H wanted to run away from it.

It was days after the incident with Caden, and the first Monday of March had arrived. Tayshia had already finished school, Ash having dropped her off and picked her up, and they were now at his godparents' house for one night before they moved in. They were discussing things over dinner.

At his place at the table, Ash could see into the remnants of his father's garden, could see into the past, into destruction. While Steven and Ryo had informed Ash that they thought it would be better if they went to the police and filed a report, they also said that they were going to keep an eye on them from their windows. Tayshia listened and offered suggestions. Ash gazed out the window with his chin in his hand, his forearm and elbows resting on the table.

The plants were brown. Mottled and shrunken. Dead rose bushes reached up wooden climbers like the deceased reaching for Heaven. Blackened petals were so brittle that he could see them drifting down to the Earth of their own accord, hoping to be buried. The ghost of his father on his hands and knees in the dirt, tilling the soil and preparing it for something beautiful, only to spend less than a year destroying it with indifference and addiction. And beyond the death, he could see the window of his kitchen. The kitchen where his mother had baked her last birthday cake for him, where she'd given him the gift that helped bring him and Tayshia together.

The necklace he wasn't wearing.

"And for the days that you have to go to school this week," Steven was saying, "since I'm the one who's always at home, I'll use my bird-watching binoculars to keep an eye out for the Oldsmobile."

"But you have to promise me this isn't anything too serious," Ryo interjected. "Ash. *Ash.*"

Ash jolted, tearing his eyes off the window. "Huh?"

"You need to promise me this isn't anything serious. That you're just laying low. I'm not about to lose my kid." His godfather was staring him down with a stern glint in his eye.

Ash's stomach did a flip and for a moment, he wished Ryo was his father, that Steven was his second father, and that he'd been able to grow up with them.

But then, he felt guilt sinking deep into his core.

He'd never wish for another mother.

"It's not anything serious," Ash lied. "Once spring break is over, we'll go back home."

Tayshia didn't look at him, keeping her gaze on the plate of food in front of her. She'd eaten half of it and was struggling through the last half, but Ash wasn't going to bother her about it. She knew the rules. She knew the agreement.

"I mean, this is a good idea overall," Steven said. "I just *know* that house is full of dust and needs a good cleaning."

"And I can take care of that," Tayshia said in a bright voice, pushing the food around on her plate. "I don't mind keeping myself busy cleaning."

"Which is a miracle," Ash said, trying to lighten his own mood by making a joke.

She fixed him with a playful look. "I may have been a bit messier before, but I've changed. At least, I'm trying."

In spite of his godparents, Ash reached over to squeeze her hand. She *was* trying. Albeit, in an unorthodox way, but she was trying. That was more than he could ask for.

"Eh, you're all right."

Her glare wasn't that heated, but it was a glare nonetheless. "Shut your ass *up*, jerk!"

Steven and Ash laughed, Ryo hiding a smile by shaking his head and taking a bite of his lasagna.

After dinner, Ash and Tayshia went up to the guest room for bed. They were both tired after packing their clothes all day, and they were both so tired that neither of them could keep their eyes open for more than five minutes. The next day was the big day—the day Ash finally stepped into his past and let the memories do whatever it was that they were going to do—and he couldn't wait to sleep so he could forget about it.

"Do you think we should put our necklaces back on?" he said when they were snuggled up under the covers. They were facing each other, studying each other's faces in the moonlight.

Tayshia placed her hands together on her pillow and adjusted so that the side of her head lay upon them. "Do you want to?"

He thought back to the way his dream flowers had burned him. How the sea had churned and the mountains had shook. It scared him. It meant that something wasn't right within himself.

"I'm too..." He hesitated, feeling nervous to share this part of himself with her. It was like the day he'd cried in front of her. He hadn't wanted to. He didn't want to seem weak when she needed him to be the one that was strong. "I'm scared to."

"Me, too," she said, and it was an admittance. "I think something was wrong when we were there before, because I thought your dream was trying to tell us that you needed to see your dad."

He pulled his hand out from beneath the covers and rested it against her cheek, the tips of his long fingers brushing against the satin of her hair bonnet. "As long as you know that I don't need the crystals to know I like you."

Her lips curved up and her eyelids fluttered shut. She tilted her chin upward for a kiss but instead of pushing forward, he rose up on his right elbow and rolled her onto her back. His gaze traversed her face, and then he pressed a kiss to her lips that was as soft as the petals of a flower. Her fingers reached to hold his cheeks, pulling him close.

When he pulled back, she gave him a serious look. "I just wanna say that I'm really glad you have your godparents. I think Ryo and Steven really love you, and I think that's exactly what you need."

"I'm glad I have them, too. You have no idea." His gaze softened again. "But I'm glad I have you, too. You're all I need."

"Boy, you better stop."

But she smiled into their kiss.

☼☼☼

When he'd walked up to the brown house with its red door on Christmas Eve, it was different.

There had been a measure of safety in it, knowing deep down that he wasn't going to enter. That he wasn't going to open that door, with its smooth crimson paint. That he wasn't going to open the past and sink inside it. He hadn't been more afraid than was natural for someone who knew he wasn't going to cross a line.

Now, knowing that he had no choice but to cross it, he feared he would drown.

Tayshia stepped onto the porch first, turning to watch him carry both of their bags up the steps. His hands were clammy and tremulous as he pulled the keys out of his pocket—the keys that Ryo had given him along with his father's effects from the prison—and inserted them into the lock.

"You ready?" Tayshia asked.

"No," he said truthfully. "But I'm going to keep you safe. So, we're going inside."

The pace of his heartbeat increased to an overwhelming speed as he turned the key. The locks tumbled and clicked, the sound of it seeming to echo across the porch.

And then he stood there.

"Ash," Tayshia said softly, stepping closer to him. "We can't stand out here like this. What if they drive by?"

"I know," he said harshly, then lowered his voice. "I know, baby. I just—I need a second."

This was it.

This was the last chance he had to turn back.

They could go get a hotel. He didn't mind spending the money. Honestly, with his father's life insurance coming sometime in the next year, there was no reason to stress about a necessary hotel stay. It would be easier.

Maybe he could sell the house and pay some trash collectors to come gather everything up so he wouldn't have to look at it. Maybe he could burn the entire house down, and his memories with it.

But then Tayshia placed her hand on his, covering it over the doorknob. Their eyes met and the small, encouraging smile she gave him was all the reminder he needed that he wasn't alone.

"Let's do it together, okay?" she said. "We can count down."

"Okay. Yes. We'll count."

"Five…"

His heart beat faster.

"Four…"

Breathe, he thought to himself, closing his eyes and hanging his head for a second. When he did, he felt her pressing her forehead against his, standing on the tips of her toes to do so.

"Three…"

Her breath was warm against his lips, the fingers of her other hand soft on the side of his neck.

"Two…"

He held his breath, feeling it spinning in his chest like a pulsar lost in space.

"One."

He opened his eyes to look into hers and it was there that he saw safety. And then, just like the two times he'd showered with her — In dreams and in reality — he felt like the stars had aligned for this one moment, to help him overcome his fears. He had Tayshia. She was by his side.

He was not alone.

Turning the doorknob, they entered the brown house with the red door.

Everything was exactly where Lizette left it.

From the jacket discarded on the back of a green dining room chair, to the empty white mug on the oak coffee table beside an open photo album. From the unopened mail on the mahogany table in the hall by the front door, to the blue slippers tossed haphazardly beside the black suede couch. From the knit maroon blanket and pale green pillows on said couch to the dead tulips she must have bought for herself sitting in a dusty porcelain vase on the center of the dining room table.

Everything was *exactly* where she left it before she never came home.

Tayshia brought the bags inside and locked the door behind them, sealing them in the dim lighting that made it through the closed windows. Only the kitchen blinds were open, and Ash could see winter sunlight trailing around the corner, into the dining room from where he stood.

He couldn't breathe.

"Why don't you show me around?" Tayshia said, her voice quiet in the oppressive shadows of the house that was no longer a home. She took his hand, threading her fingers between his. "I want to see where you grew up."

He looked at her through panicked vision, feeling his breath rattling in his chest. "Why?"

"Because it's part of you."

"I don't want it to be."

"But it is." She placed her other hand on the center of his chest, warm and firm. His heart jumped to meet her palm. "Just like Paris is a part of me. Show me who you are, Ash. Show me who you are in spite of it."

He squeezed her hand so tight it hurt. "What if it breaks me?"

"Then I'll pick up your pieces and put you back together, just like you do for me."

It took him a second to collect himself, to keep from telling her he loved her just for saying that. He didn't know how he felt, and he didn't want to sort through those emotions while he was trying to sort through his fear and grief. Grief so immense and all-encompassing that were it not for her hand upon him, he might have forgotten he was solid. His mother was gone. His father was gone.

Ash was the only one left.

"We'll start in the living room," she said, tugging him over.

The photo album.

"No, let's...Let's start in the kitchen." He pulled on her arm, causing her to stumble around to put her back to his front. He kept hold of her hand and put his other on her waist as they walked into the kitchen.

It looked exactly as he remembered it, with eggshell cupboards, white countertops, and a white refrigerator. The sink was aluminum with a faucet and while there were no dirty dishes left behind, there was still a scrub brush and sponge in the bottom of it. Above the sink was the window overlooking part of the garden and those horrible, lifeless plants, the blinds still up as though his mother had wanted to look at it and remember a better time. The floor was the standard kitchen linoleum, off-white in color, and the dishwasher was one of the old yellow ones from the late nineties. It looked out of place but gazing upon it flickered nostalgia in his mind.

"My grandpa put that in," he said.

"What?"

"The dishwasher." He curled his arms around her waist and held her tight, resting his chin on top of her head. "He put that in right after I was born."

"And you were born in 1998, right?"

"Mm-hm. You, too?"

"Yes, I'm a little younger than you." She rested her head back against his chest as they stood there, rocking slightly to that song that only they knew. "I'm surprised that the dishwasher still works."

"My dad kept fixing it up. Every time it broke down, he yanked it out and got on the floor to make it work again. I guess my mom liked the way it ran and didn't want to get rid of it. Well, and I think it was also because it represented something to him."

"You think it works now?"

"I guess we'll find out. Or you will, since you appointed yourself the Cleaning Queen."

"I *am* the queen. Show me the next room."

Ash took her into the dining room. She wandered over to the flowers, reaching out to touch one of the dark, dead petals. It dropped to the table amongst the others that had fallen. A pout on her face and a curious glint in her eyes, Tayshia stood by the dining room window, which did not have blinds or a curtain, but whose view was obscured by the climbers and those dead roses that reached for Heaven. It was so large that she looked like a painting in the center of a clear canvas, her fluffy hair hanging down her back and her hands pressed to the cold glass.

"It must have been beautiful when it was taken care of," she said.

"It was." Ash came to stand beside her, slipping his hands into the back pockets of his jeans. "He used to win awards, you know. Sold so many flowers every year that it paid for things. But then, somehow, he changed. I don't know what happened or how he got into it, but he started doing drugs. Then he was selling. Then he convinced *me* to help sell. And that's when everything went to shit."

"Maybe you should fix it up," she suggested, looking up at him and removing her hands from the panes. "The garden. Maybe that's what you could do over Spring Break."

Ash raised his eyebrow. "You mean take it all apart and plant new flowers?"

"Yeah, and we can go to the hardware store and pick them out. You could make it beautiful again, and that could help you feel better about the house. And once I clean up in here, maybe then you might even think about staying."

He wanted to protest. He had to remember that she didn't know the extent. She didn't know how bad his father got, how he'd be out in the garden doing absolutely nothing for hours because he was so high, digging in the same spot and filling it back up while muttering nonsense. Tayshia didn't know how his father used to beat him for the tiniest sleights, then brought him apology gifts as though it could heal his broken arm, or a bruised rib faster. She wasn't aware of the fact that his mother had died of a heart attack at the age of forty-seven because she was Bulimic.

But the look in her eyes shone so hopeful, so innocent and pure in her hope, that he would have given her anything.

"Okay," he said. "I'll fix up the garden this Spring Break while you do the cleaning. Deal?"

"Deal. And then we'll talk about moving in?"

"Yeah. We'll talk about it."

"Okay, next room. What's that? The bathroom?"

She started toward the downstairs bathroom by the stairs—toward his mother's bathroom—and he lunged forward to stop her. He slammed his hand flat on the door to keep it shut.

"It's just a bathroom," he said. "It doesn't have any meaning to me at all. We don't need to go in there."

"Okay? Calm down."

"Sorry." He cleared his throat and ran an anxious hand through his hair. "Come on. I'll show you my room."

Adrenaline pumped through his veins at the near-miss. He hadn't wanted her to see the bathroom because *he* didn't want to see the bathroom. It was his mother's prison. She was tormented there, tormented by herself and the demons that Gabriel had unleashed. And even though she had found peace in death, there were parts of her spirit in there that Ash didn't want to touch.

That place was haunted.

Ash led her up the stairs. The stairwell felt cramped with how tall he was and how close they were getting to his bedroom. His bedroom was not a place he wanted to be, either, but it wasn't as painful.

He opened the door, letting them into a room that still smelled faintly of incense. He was surprised that it had lasted that long. Tayshia wandered in and around the edges, fingers moving over his things, feeling memories beneath her hands. She gazed around at the black decor, the rumpled covers on the bed, the deathcore band posters that adorned his walls, the small TV and game console in the corner. The same console his father had given him for his birthday after hitting him.

Being in this room was skin-crawling. It felt like the eyes of his younger self were watching him from all four walls. The only reprieve was the window overlooking the street and the neighbors across it, and even then, it seemed like the sunlight couldn't break through. The room was so dark. It *felt* dark.

And everything was exactly the way he left it.

"It definitely looks like your room," she said. "It's cozy and comfortable. Are we gonna sleep in here?"

"Uh…" His hands shook again, and he hid it by crossing his arms over his shoulder. "I guess you can if you want. I'm taking the couch."

"That's fair. I'll miss you, though."

"You could always sleep on my chest."

They smirked at each other, and then Tayshia crossed the small space to him. She wrapped her arms around his neck and let her head fall back so she could gaze up at him through lidded eyes.

"As much as I like you, are you sure it's a good idea we defile your childhood home with the things I let you do to me?"

His smirk widened into a roguish grin as he uncrossed his arms and slid them around her waist. "You're the one who asked me to defile you."

"Maybe I want you to defile me on the couch."

"Maybe I will."

"And maybe I want you to defile me in your bedroom."

"Maybe… Maybe I will."

His panic rose.

Ash staunched them by hugging her so tight around the middle that she let out an *oof*. She giggled, squealing as he spun her around and then set her on her feet again.

It didn't have to be miserable the *whole* time.

They decided to sit down on his carpet and play video games for a while, taking turns on the controller as he showed her how to play one of his favorite fantasy games. She loved the fact that the female character could summon things, so she had no qualms playing for hours.

At one point, when she was arms-deep in a temple trying to get a new summon, Ash had to use the bathroom. He didn't want to use the one downstairs for obvious reasons, so he had only one other option: his parent's bathroom, which was located inside their bedroom. The bedroom was across the hall and down a ways from Ash's room, and the door was shut.

He had no choice.

Ash took a second to steady his breath, and then walked into his parents bedroom.

The master bedroom was the largest room in the house, with a rectangular, L-shaped set-up. There was a large chiffarobe to the left, a big dresser along the far wall, two windows with the curtains drawn shut, and a massive King-sized bed with four posters and an ornate wooden headboard with slats. The comforter had an interesting striped pattern of muted pastel greens and oranges, with matching pillows that seemed to cascade along the headboard and mattress. They had a large flat screen TV and entertainment center stacked with DVDs adjacent to the bed, and there were crystal floor lamps in the corners on either side of the windows. Ash could tell his mother must have stopped sleeping in here after he and Gabriel were arrested.

It was the cleanest room in the house.

He stood there for a while, bladder screaming at him while he tried to orient himself to his surroundings. Entering the room had been like entering the event horizon of a black hole. He was being torn to shreds, stretched to his limit, and crushed into nothing all at once.

The most vivid memory Ash had of his parents' room was when he was a kid. It was Christmas, and he was so excited, he woke before the sun was even up. Sneaking down the stairs, he'd peeked into the living room to see a beautiful Christmas setup, with the lights glittering and sparkling in white and blue, tinsel shining amongst them. The presents were all colors — reds and greens and silvers and blue — and they were stacked up in a way that was meant to look magical. And it *was* magical. He'd never forgotten it. He'd barreled into his parents' room and jumped onto their bed, begging them to wake up. Santa had come

That was five years before everything fell apart.

After he went to the bathroom, he laid down on his parents' bed, right on his father's side. He crossed his ankles and settled back against the pillows with his hands clasped over his chest. He gazed up at the ceiling, at the dusty, immobile fan with the gold filigree, and he let the truth sink in.

His mother was dead. His father was dead. Tayshia was going to die. He had no control over anything in his life. Nothing ever went the way he hoped or dreamed or wanted. He'd been to jail, so the possibility of a job was futile even if he went on to university. He wasn't getting good grades in school and now, with bereavement, he had stacks and stacks of take-home classwork that he was turning in, but not doing well on. And Tayshia was going to fucking *die*.

Maybe he should die, too.

☼☼☼

They fought that night.

And it wasn't because of anything she did in particular. It was because of his anxiety, and his inability to see a reason to live if she didn't care enough about herself to try. Because it didn't matter what they did, she was always going to have those thoughts in the back of her mind. Those thoughts that told her she was worthless and that she didn't deserve to live. And he would, too. He would never see a purpose in his own life.

They were dancing in flames, expecting not to burn.

After a dinner where Tayshia once again struggled through her meal but managed to finish everything on her plate, they went into the living room to watch a movie. But the moment they sat down, Tayshia noticed the open photo album. It was large and square, full of scrapbook photos of Ash's childhood. Tayshia picked it up and held it in her lap, mindless of the empty coffee mug that was on the table.

His mother must have been looking at his baby pictures before his trial.

God, it hurt so bad. It hurt so fucking *bad*. He couldn't breathe. There were chains wrapped around his neck, his heart, his stomach. He felt like he was suffocating. Like he'd already suffocated, and he was crossing the River Styx, waiting for the gates to Hades to open just for him.

And Tayshia was just sitting there, pointing out pictures of him. His ultrasound, him in diapers, him with his toys, him with his first missing tooth. His first Christmas, his first birthday, his first time at a theme park. The time he got into Lizette's lipstick and she'd taken a picture of him before spanking him on the rear. When he was nine and he got scuffed up riding a bike that he'd stolen from a kid at school, and his father had taken a photo of that before marching him to the kid's house to return it. Ash standing front and center before his father's garden in the Spring, smiling a missing-teeth grin and holding his father's blue ribbon award for the best roses in the country.

He felt sick.

But as she turned the pages, moving later and later through his life, he could see it. He could see the way his mother's light had diminished. How she wasted away as not only the disorder, but also her husband snuffed her out. As he took her spirit and split it into several pieces so he could pick and choose the ones he wanted, instead of just accepting his wife the way she was. Tayshia was watching his mother die in pictures, and all she seemed to care to see was Ash growing up.

The picture that unraveled him was something nondescript.

It was a photo of his mother and father at their wedding. Lizette was pregnant. They were at the reception and his mother was seated in a white wicker chair, surrounded by beautiful roses that looked only half as vivid as his father's had been. She wore a flowing white gown with long sleeves and a sweetheart neckline, and there was a crown of daisies ringing her skull. In the process of eating cake with her hands, she was smiling up at the camera with such rosy cheeks and happiness shining in her eyes that it speared through Ash's core and set him alight with an epiphany.

His father had taken his mother from him. But Tayshia? Tayshia was taking *herself* away from him. She was leaving him slowly, bit-by-bit.

She was going to *die*.

"Can you put that fucking thing *down*?!" he shouted, the suddenness of it causing Tayshia to let out a cry of terror. She dropped the photo album to the floor, where it lay upside-down between the couch, their feet, and the coffee table. The light of the muted TV flashed across their faces, warmed by the living room floor lamp, and the horror seemed to darken her eyes to a molten brown.

"Why are you yelling at me?" she said, her voice low and angry.

"I don't want to look at that shit! Why would you think I want to see it?" He stood up, so agitated that his legs were restless. "I could barely come into this fucking place, and the first thing you want is a tour, and to sleep with me in my bedroom, and to see the bathroom, and now, you wanna look at my *baby pictures*?!"

"Ash, I'm your *girlfriend*. Of course I'd want to see your baby pictures!"

"*When the fuck did I ask you to be my girlfriend?!*"

Her jaw dropped.

Ash was panicking. He'd lost it. His entire body was shaking. His chest was spasming in hyperventilation. He was angry and sad and overwhelmed and in anguish, all at the same time. He wanted to punch the wall. He wanted to punch the *fucking* wall.

"Why are you doing this?" she said, her voice small and tearful. She sniffled, tears escaping, slipping down her cheeks. "Why are you being so *mean* to me?! I didn't do anything *wrong!*"

"Because you won't stop forcing me to feel things that I don't want to fucking feel!" he yelled, holding his hands to his chest. "I don't want to feel the shit I feel for you. It's overwhelming. It freaks me out. I can't function anymore. I can't think anymore. I'm angry all the time and when I'm not angry, I want to throw myself in front of bullets for you, and that's not what I fucking want for my life!"

The train was coming off the tracks. The threads had unraveled. Stars were bursting, dying, scorching. His mind was a battlefield, screaming with red smoke and gunpowder and dying soldiers.

"Well it's good to know that you only want me when your *feelings* make you feel comfortable!"

"It's not about that! It's about the things that I want, and the fact that *you're* keeping me from them!"

"The things you want? What are you talking about?! I've given you everything!"

"But I don't *want* you!"

No.

No, no, no.

No!

Why the fuck had he just said that? Why? Why would he say something so untrue and so stupid and so *wrong*? Of all the ways he could hurt her, he'd just hurt her with the worst words. They'd just come out, and they'd come out completely wrong.

He'd meant to say that he didn't want her like *this*. He didn't want her sick and dying and leaving him. He wanted her to be as happy and rosy-cheeked as his mother had looked on her wedding day. He wanted her smile to reach her eyes.

But he couldn't bear to watch Tayshia die.

Tayshia began to quake. The panic had overtaken her and her eyes were wild. Tormented. He'd just taken her heart and her mind and everything she'd given him and stamped it out beneath his feet. He'd ruined her.

She burst into gut-wrenching, devastated sobs that Ash knew came from the deepest, darkest part of her heart. She buried her face in her hands and wept there on the couch as though it'd been building up for hours. As though she couldn't bear to get up.

"Aw, no, come on," he groaned, dragging both hands through his hair as he started toward her. He reached for her, trying to take her by the elbows, to stop her. The desperation clawed at his belly. "Tayshia, I'm sorry. I didn't mean that. I didn't mean it. Please talk to me. Please. I'm so sorry."

She shoved him away, her entire body shaking so hard that he thought she might faint. She was gasping between sobs, shaking her head.

"Don't touch me! *Don't touch me!*" she screamed, her tear-filled eyes glaring up at him in agony and betrayal. "Don't you fucking *touch me!*"

As she stormed up the stairs and slammed his bedroom door shut, he sank down onto the couch and listened to the sound of her sobs for all the hours it took for him to fall asleep. They sounded just like the ones that had torn out of her throat in Paris, the moment she collapsed at the foot of that hotel room bed and lamented how broken she was.

He hoped he burned.

CHAPTER SIXTEEN

Spring break began to the tune of a somber song.

They had not spoken a single word to each other since the argument. When he got up to take her to school or pick her up, they didn't look at each other. At dinner, they didn't talk to each other. At night, he slept on the couch and she slept in his room. They both used the bathroom upstairs, but even in the awkward moments where they bumped into one another, she kept her eyes down and he kept his face turned away.

Everything was ruined.

Ash tried to make things right. He made her breakfast, lunch, and dinner, and he didn't hound her about finishing everything on her plate. The day after their argument over the photo album, she woke up with a migraine that he could sense from a mile away. He'd made sure she had NSAIDs and water at her door all day. He bought her a bouquet of roses and gardenias—since they'd left the Valentine's one dying at home on the table—and placed them outside the bedroom door in the morning so she'd wake up to them.

When she'd taken the dead flowers out of his mother's vase and put them inside of it, he'd had a small sliver of hope. But he hadn't gotten so much as a snippet of eye contact.

Not that he deserved it. What he'd said was the absolute *worst* thing he could have said. If he could go back to that day and just suck it up, just *look* at the pictures with her, then they'd be happy right now. She wouldn't have cried herself to sleep.

Why was this house so poisonous?

By the time the first day of Spring Break rolled around, he hadn't heard her voice in so long that when she came down to the living room in the morning on that Sunday and spoke to him, he nearly dropping his pipe onto the floor.

"What did you say?" he said, his voice hoarse from sleep and disuse. He was still shirtless in his joggers, barefoot and with his blond hair a tousled mess atop his head. "I didn't hear you."

Her facial expression was neither sour nor chipper. It was as flat as the state of Florida.

"Can we go to the hardware store now? I want to get all the cleaning supplies and gardening stuff."

"Uh…Sure. Yeah. Yeah, we can go." He raised his pipe and lighter. "Just let me smoke, and then I'll get dressed."

She nodded and went to sit at the dining room table to scroll on her phone.

Ash tried not to get *too* excited as he finished smoking the bowl he'd packed. He knew she hadn't forgiven him, and she might never forgive him. He hadn't even apologized yet. But the chance that she might let him hold her hand was enough to lighten his heart the most infinitesimal of amounts.

After dressing in a pair of low-slung skinny jeans, one of his band hoodies, and a backwards snapback, he jogged downstairs to meet her.

"Ready to get out of here?"

She nodded again, tucking her phone into her fuzzy duck backpack. She wore a pair of black tights, a black A-line dress, and her dress coat. Her hair was pulled to one side of her head, falling forward over her shoulder.

Neither of them were wearing their crystals, and he didn't know if they ever would again.

One silent drive later where Ash made the heat as high as she always liked it, he was out of the car and running around it to open her door for her before she unbuckled her seatbelt. She paused at the sight of it, her gaze carefully avoiding his own as she climbed out of the car. It wasn't raining that day, but the weather was still a bit nippy. It made her cheeks flush, reddening the brown skin of her nose.

His fingers tingled with the desire to take her by the hand, but he didn't. Better not to push things, especially when she was walking at least a foot apart from him. She never did that. She usually liked to walk right next to him and slightly behind so she could feel safe and led.

God, he'd fucked up so badly.

They wandered the hardware store with a cart, throwing in everything they thought they'd need. Tayshia didn't speak to him, and he didn't speak to her. The only time they used their voices was to ask a store clerk to procure things for them. The closest they came was when Tayshia's eyes lit up at the sight of a box of string lights. She'd opened her mouth, then closed it with a nasal exhale, her eyes going dark. As she'd reached up to put the item back, he'd snatched it up and put it in the cart so he could buy it for her. He'd grabbed five more boxes, just for good measure. They were going in the garden.

It didn't even get him a smile.

Ash grabbed everything he remembered his father using for the garden in its prime, and then some. Tayshia picked up every cleaning supply item that was possibly necessary. And when their cart was full and he'd purchased everything, they took it to the trunk and backseat of his car. They had to crack the window so the end of the broom and fancy mop he'd bought could fit, but it worked. Then, they drove home to drop it off and drove all the way back to get the flowers.

Picking out the flowers was the closest he got to having her speak to him. It was more like she was making gasps and exclamations under her breath to no one in particular, marveling at the flowers she thought were prettiest and would match the best. She kept checking the flowers' information on her phone, seeing when they bloomed and how well they'd last through the Spring and Summer. It was clear to Ash that she wanted the garden to look the best it could be, when he didn't deserve to have that type of attention from her. It was so cute that it made his heart ache.

He wished she would talk to him.

She chatted up the cashier as Ash paid, enthusiastically telling her about the garden plans, spring break, and their shopping habits.

"That backpack is so cute!" the cashier gasped after Tayshia and he had turned to go. "Where did you get that?"

"Thanks! My boyfriend got it..." And she trailed off, only for a second. A second that felt like ten years to Ash as he remembered the words he'd shouted at her not days ago. Her smile to the cashier was forced, her lips quivering in a way that only Ash could pick up on. "I got it in Seattle last month."

"Oh, nice. I love Seattle. Did you go to Pike Place?"

"Mm-hm," Tayshia nodded. "That's where I got this backpack. It's really cute and it holds a lot."

"I might have to get one on my next trip. I'll keep a look-out."

Such an innocent, harmless interaction. The cashier had no idea the depths of what Ash and Tayshia were enduring together.

Before they left the wide, open exit of the hardware store, Ash stopped the cart and reached for her hand. He tugged her around, her eyes going wide as he brought his hands up to cup the sides of her head. With a sad frown on his face, he pulled her against his chest. He wrapped one arm around her shoulders while he dropped a lingering kiss onto the top of her head. He had no right to do it, and she had every right to push him away.

But he did. And she didn't.

✧✧✧

While Tayshia started her cleaning journey in the living room with a duster, Ash went out into the garden. He left the back door open with the gardening supplies situated in the doorframe and on the concrete step that led to the dead, yellow grass.

It wasn't as difficult to be in the garden as he'd thought it would be. It felt airless, the life and beauty that his father had once breathed into having been exhaled like dragon's breath, scorching the ground.

He took stock of the garden's state, his hands on his hips as he inspected it. Lots of weeds, everything was dead, soil was probably dry and hard as Hell. The rose climbers were sturdy and able to be reused after a good paint job. He could put a few more in on the edges of the garden and hang the string lights from them so they stretched over it like a sparkling roof. It would be a big undertaking with the planting, but if he worked all day until dark--Hell, if he got floodlights and worked into the night--he could have it looking pretty good by the day they left.

Ash worked through the day, using gloves to keep himself from getting hurt as he pulled the thorny, dead rose bushes from the climbers. He dropped them into his father's old, rusty wheelbarrow so he could put them in the bin they'd always used for yard waste. He had plans to schedule someone to come pick it up when he had a chance to get to his phone.

With the roses gone and the climbers exposed, he could see that it would be best if he built some trellises. Flat, simple, tall ones that he could place vertically along the edge of the garden that, when the roses grew and started to climb, would create a corridor of roses.

He rubbed his chin.

Perhaps he could put some cobblestones down the center of the garden, too, to create a winding path. The flowers Tayshia had picked could adorn the ground on the sides, and they'd grow thick and lush by April since they'd bought buds instead of seeds. With the string lights, she'd probably love to be outside in it every time they came here.

The vivid, dreamlike image of he and Tayshia dancing on the cobblestones amongst the lights and flowers, with the moon shining above them, was so painful that he had to sit down and rest. He wiped his brow and looked at the half-empty garden with its dry, packed soil, and sighed.

This wasn't going to be a one-week thing. He could get the trellis, path, and flowers planted by the end of Spring Break if he focused and worked from sun-up to sun-down like his father had done when he was young, but it would need to be cared for.

If he wanted the garden to last, he was going to have to come back to the house.

At some point, he started to feel his feet blistering. The all-black Vans he was wearing were not conducive to gardening, so he was forced to hunt his father's brown work boots down. He felt sick as he tied them on, but he knew it was better than blistering. It was about noon by then, the pre-spring sun high in the sky, and he was pouring sweat. He took his shirt off, heaving a sigh of relief as the damp fabric peeled away from his feverish skin and still-healing chest tattoo, and got back to work.

Glancing across the yard as he dragged another clump of weeds out of the soil, he could see Steven and Ryo standing in front of the sink through their window. They were talking, laughing and embracing one another. As if on cue, they both turned to look and grinned widely, waving a greeting to him. He raised his own hand in greeting, painting a smile on his face that masked the turmoil he suffered inside.

No reason for them to know how bad things were.

On one of his many trips into the house for water, he stepped into the kitchen to see that Tayshia had finished the living room and was now working on the kitchen. She was on her hands and knees in a pair of leggings and a crop top, with her hair piled on top of her head, a silk scarf wrapped around it. She was scrubbing so hard at a spot in the linoleum that she didn't notice him standing there in the laundry room.

"Tayshia. *Tayshia*. Hey, *Tayshia*."

Her head snapped up. "Huh? What?"

The first words she'd spoken directly to him in days, and it was nearly three in the afternoon.

"Can you get me some water so I don't get dirt all over the floor?"

"Oh, yes. I can." She spoke to him like he was a customer, and she worked a register. "One second."

Ash watched as she used the edge of the counter to drag herself up, her arm shaking slightly and breath heavy. It seemed that she was tired. He had way too much energy for someone who'd been weeding and hauling dead plants all day.

Tayshia filled a glass from the cupboard and dumped it out to ensure there was no dust, and then she filled it again. Her gaze traversed his body, lingering on tattoos she'd never seen in the daylight, and she walked over to pass him the glass. As he drank it, he kept his eyes on her, trying to think of something to say but coming up with nothing.

"Thanks," he said after he swallowed.

She nodded, and that was that.

Ash got down on his hands and knees, too. He had too. He'd tried to use the tool to really rip the soil up and while it had worked, there were problems. There were roots from God-knows-what twisting in random places—roots he'd missed while weeding—and the hoe just wasn't enough. The soil needed muscle and a good hacking with a handheld so he could have the ability to mix it with the sphagnum peat moss that he'd bought.

Thunk.

Something solid.

The handheld had hit something solid.

"Fuck," he muttered to himself in annoyance. "There better not be rocks in here."

How could there be rocks in the soil that his father had meticulously tilled and cared for for *years?* It didn't matter if the garden was dead; rocks didn't migrate. If Ash had to go out of his way to remove rocks from the soil, he'd never get the garden done by the following Sunday. And he was determined to prove to himself that he could.

He went back to the other tools and supplies and searched for the hand cultivator. When he found it, he hefted it in his left hand and went to the far edge of the garden. He began to work, going through and breaking up the soil to try and turn over whatever it was that was in there. He worked his way through, finding nothing, until he got to the spot at the center—the spot where he'd found the obstruction.

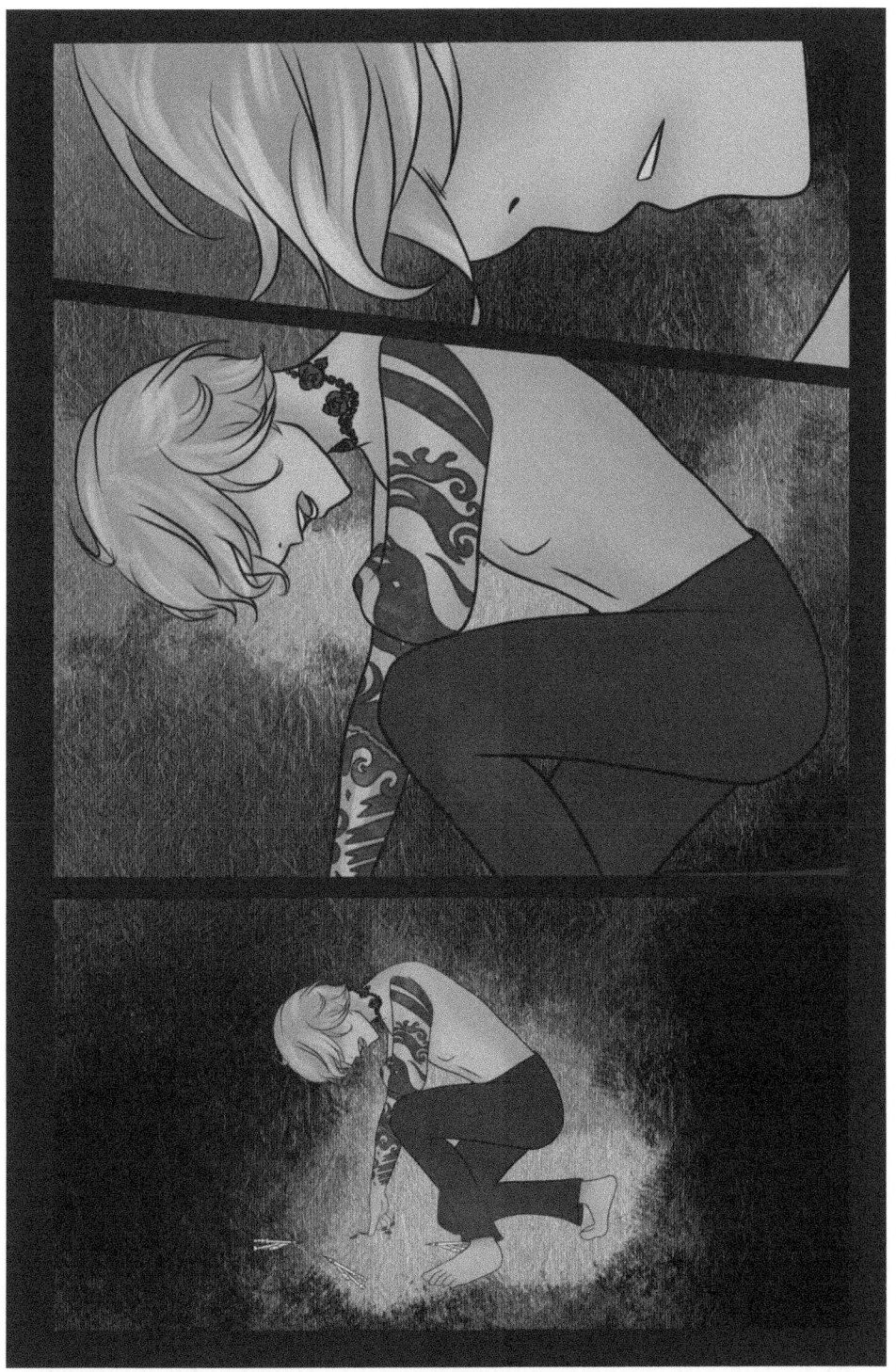

As the soil came apart, clumps tumbling in every direction, the obstruction was unearthed. Several of them, in fact.

Needles.

Empty pill bottles.

Blackened spoons.

The things his father had used to destroy their family. The things he'd used to destroy himself. And here they were, buried in the garden that had not only helped to feed their family, but had once been buried beneath the plants he'd let die.

The same dead plants Ash had just spent hours removing.

Fury swirled within him, heating like the parts of a star that burned the fastest. Hot stellar winds blazed through him, scorching the path he'd been slowly paving to calmness.

All the times his father was out in the garden, high off his mind on PCP, he was burying everything. He was *burying* the things he'd done, his sins, his shortcomings. No doubt he hadn't wanted Ricky to see it, because he hadn't seemed to mind burning spoons and shooting himself up in front of Ash and Lizette.

If he wasn't already six feet under, Ash would have turned this garden into a grave.

☼☼☼

Ash went back inside when the sun was too low and the sky's light was a dark, midnight blue. It was cold, too cold to work, and his knuckles felt like they were frozen. He'd gotten the entire garden ready to be planted and now, he was going to go back to the Hardware store before it closed to buy flood lights and the things he needed for the trellises.

There was a pile of drug paraphernalia covered in dirt in a trash bag on the step. He didn't know yet how he was going to get rid of it, but he planned on asking Ryo for help later. The anger inside of him still burned bright, and the agitation was so fierce that anything could have set him off.

He was so exhausted by the time he locked the back door that he nearly fell over while he was taking his father's boots off. And with his mind so preoccupied by his indecision over whether or not to just buy pre-made trellises, he didn't think to look at the floor when he walked into the kitchen. He tripped.

There were storage containers *all over* the floor. They were all his mother's, her having collected them over the years every time she went to the grocery store, and had taken up an entire cupboard while he was growing up. And there they were, scattered all over the floor as Tayshia worked on organizing them.

"What the Hell are these doing all over the floor?! I literally just tripped over one."

Tayshia's head whipped in his direction. She still had that scarf on, but now she was dressed in nothing but a giant tee shirt. The rest of the kitchen was pristine and sparkling clean, so it seemed like the storage cupboard was the last on her list.

"Do *not* lose your temper with me, little boy," she said in a low, dangerous tone. "You are in *no* position to disrespect me after what you said."

He said nothing after that, choosing to kick some of the containers aside so he could start cooking. He was so tired and so angry with his father for ruining his fucking life that he simply didn't have the patience to cope with Tayshia's mess.

Why couldn't she have stacked them on the counter and sorted them that way? Why did she need to stack everything with its lid on? It made more sense to stack them together—contained within their same-size containers, and pile the lids on top of one another as nicely as possible.

When he nearly tripped again while carrying the boiling noodles over to the strainer he'd placed in the sink, his temper flared once more.

"Tayshia, *please* get this shit out of my way, baby, okay?" he growled, using endearments even though he was pissed. "I almost spilled hot water all over your precious fucking head. All right? I don't want you to get hurt."

"Well, why are you cooking amongst the containers, then?" she retorted, reaching back into the depths of the cupboard to place another closed container there.

"I'm not *cooking amongst the containers*. I'm cooking our dinner in the kitchen, where you're supposed to be able to cook without shit all over the floor."

"Why don't you pick them up?"

"Why don't *you*?" He placed one hand on his hip and the other on the sink and glowered down at her. "You're the one that put them all over the floor!"

"I'm almost done!" Her brows were furrowed and eyes wide in indignation as she glared up into his face from the floor. "Can you not see that I only have like twenty more to do?"

"Why don't you just stack them inside of each other?"

"Because I don't want to."

"Why not?"

"*Because.*" She resumed her work.

"Tayshia, *why*?"

"I want everything to be exactly like this. You don't *get* it. I just want it to be easy for me to pull a container out."

"For what? Your negative-one meals per day?" he said with a sneer.

She said nothing after that, so he went back to cooking. When it was done, he got two plates down from the cupboard and set them on the counter.

"I'm not eating tonight, so you might as well put that back," she said.

Ash felt a flash of rage so sudden that he nearly threw a plate at the wall. No, she wasn't going to do this right now. No fucking way in Hell. "What?"

"I said, I'm not—"

"I *heard* what you said. I'm trying to figure out if you left your sanity back at the apartment. You're *eating*."

"I'm not hungry tonight and since I'm an adult..." She made a sound of exertion as she placed the last container in the cupboard, and then used the counter again to stand up. When she was standing, she crossed her arms over her chest and craned her neck to look at him. "...I'm not going to eat."

Ash closed his eyes and pinched the bridge of his nose. "You're acting out. That's what this is."

"You're not my parent, so I'm not *acting out*."

"Yes, you are. You've been eating just fine for the past two days, and with no argument. But now, out of nowhere, you're not hungry?"

"You're not about to make me do anything after what you said."

"Tayshia." His tone was murderous. "If you don't eat, then—"

"What?" She looked up at him with one eyebrow raised. "You'll tell me you don't want me?"

He was silent.

"Yeah. That's what I thought."

She did not eat that night.

CHAPTER SEVENTEEN

Ash woke to the feeling of Tayshia shaking him with a violence so absolute, his lonely dreams shattered and he woke with a start. The couch was so comfortable that he felt like he was floating on a cloud. Outside, the light was still a dark cobalt, signifying that the sun hadn't yet peeked over the horizon, but night had passed.

He was on his stomach, arms hugging his mother's pillow with his hair tousled into his eyes from a solid sleep. But upon feeling her shake him again and again, whispering his name, he realized he was not still dreaming. He was awake.

And something was wrong.

"What? What?!" he cried, heart racing as he rolled and looked up at her through bleary vision.

"I don't feel good," she said, her tone quiet and terrified, her eyes wide. Her bonnet was still on and she was clad in naught but his tee shirt. It was the morning after she'd refused to eat—after the storage container argument—and things were bound to be awkward later.

But for now, it was an emergency.

Ash yawned and sat up, rubbing his knuckle against one eye. "What's the matter?"

"My chest feels cold," she said, and her voice shook. "It feels—it feels cold, and my arms feel like they're shaking. I don't know. I don't know how to explain it. It was like—like I was fine and everything was working okay, and then it felt like something dropped."

Alarmed, the last vestiges of his slumber shattered and he reached for her hand to tug her closer. One hand went to her lower back and the other reached up to her chin, tilting it down so he could inspect her face. Which, of course her face had nothing to do with what she'd just described, but he didn't know what to do besides check her over.

"Does anything hurt? Are you breathing okay?"

"I feel like I can breathe fine. But my heart like..." She lowered her gaze as though she were ashamed to tell him. "It fluttered. It didn't hurt, but it felt weird. And now it feels like my arms are—they're tingling? I don't know. Ash, I don't know. I don't—"

"Shh, shh," he whispered, curving one arm around her waist and pulling her down onto the couch across his lap. He laid her down on top of him, his other hand sliding into the depths of her curls to press her head against his chest. "You're shaking, baby."

"It doesn't feel right. I don't feel right. I feel sick. I feel sick. I don't feel right."

"It's all right, Tayshia, don't worry. I've got you no matter what." He pressed a kiss to her forehead, then to her cheek, then to her lips. "Let's get up and go to the urgent care as soon as it opens. A doctor there can check you out. Okay? Does that work?"

"I don't know." Her fingers twisted in his shirt. "What if they weigh me?"

"That's not a big..." He trailed off. It *was* a big deal. It could set her off worse than she already was. "I'll go in with you and I'll ask them to make sure you're weighed backwards. How is that?"

"You will?"

"Yeah," he said with a lopsided grin before he gave her one last forehead kiss. "Let's get ready so we can get down there before everyone else starts showing up. You know how urgent care gets. We can catch breakfast when you're done."

"But what if I'm dying?"

You are, he wanted to say. *You* are *dying.*

But he couldn't.

"You won't. I won't let anything happen to you." He held her closer, feeling the warmth of her body, the fragility of her spirit, and the trembling of her fear. It was bittersweet, knowing that there had been no forgiveness on her part, and no apology on his. But this was more important. "I promise you."

After getting dressed for a rainy day, Tayshia called him into his parents' bathroom to help her with her hair. She'd taken her weave out the night before so when she took her bonnet off, her natural kinky curls needed to be unbraided and picked out so she could put them into two larger braids until she had time to put the weave back in. Ash gladly set the arguments aside—given that they were mostly his fault—and helped her. They worked together with two pick combs, water, and a detangling cream to remove the hair that had shed while it was braided up.

By the time it was fluffy and defying gravity just the way it was meant to, Ash's arms were tired. He leaned against the bathroom wall with his arms crossed, watching with interest as she pulled her hair back into two braids on either side of her head. She had synthetic hair that she'd retrieved from her room sitting on the counter, and it looked fairly real. She fed the hair into each braid as she went and, with the extra hair, she was able to make the first braid reach thin to her hips.

"I love your hair," he said quietly, watching her fingers moving faster than he could ever hope to manage himself. He could hear her nails clicking together as she worked.

Her expression was disbelieving, her lips pursed. "Mm-hm."

"No, I'm serious."

"I doubt it," she said. "I haven't ever heard a single person compliment my natural hair. Not even my mom."

"First of all, that's fucked. Fuck your mom for that," he said, resting the side of his head against the doorframe and ignoring the reprimanding look she sent him in the mirror. "Second of all, I've always thought your hair was beautiful. I always liked how you did different styles when I'd see you in class. I'll admit, I didn't understand it, but I understand you now."

She raised one eyebrow. "Because my race and culture are things you need to *understand* for them to become acceptable?"

"Of course not," he said, moving closer. He slid his arms around her from behind, bending down to rest his chin on her shoulder. "I've come to realize that there's beauty in the things we don't understand, and that learning to understand them is the best way to unlearn those things you told me about after you went job hunting that one time. There's a lot I have to unlearn and want to unlearn, and you don't need my permission to be beautiful. You just are. I've *always* liked your hair. I just didn't have a reason to tell you. It's not like we got along in high school."

"I struggle to see where you deserve the medal for your musings." She continued to braid her second braid, but the corners of her lips were twitching upward in the faintest of smiles. "My tall, white King."

Ash burst out laughing and pressed a series of playful kisses to her cheek before his chin returned to her shoulder.

"I don't deserve a medal," he said. "And I don't want one. I have the only thing I want. But what I need is to put the work in, so I can earn the right to be by your side. Your hair is amazing, exactly the way it is."

"But I don't need your permission for it to be amazing."

"No. But I think it's stunning anyway. There's a lot of things about you that I find stunning. But I won't deny that I'm ashamed of the way I acted at the mall that day. It feels unforgivable, in a lot of ways. I tried to be your savior when it wasn't my place, and that was wrong."

He grew lost in thought, in guilt that ran deeper than his mother's death and his poor choices. In the type of guilt that fear exacerbated.

What if Tayshia died, and he never got to finish proving himself to her?

"It's something you have to work to unlearn," she said after a moment, resting the back of her head against the front of his shoulder. Her hands moved to cover his as she looked at his reflection through her lashes. Her eyebrows lifted upward as she spoke. "You can't be my white savior or my white knight. But you can unlearn the things you were taught, and you can learn when to fight and when to lay the sword down."

Ash watched her as she spoke, watched the strength seem to weave its way through her words without her needing to be overt about it, and he realized something about her. Something that smashed into him like a blow directly to the heart. Something that showed him that no matter what she'd been through—the trauma, the pain, the suffering—she was someone who could always say that she'd survived.

Yes, she wasn't well. Yes, she needed help. But the incident in Paris hadn't destroyed her. It had taken the pieces of her heart that she'd already cherished and showed her how important it was to keep them intact. Her disorder was a result of her trying to get them back because she didn't understand that they had never been taken away from her. But he was looking at her now, listening to her words, watching the proud way she lifted her chin while she looked at him in the mirror, and he could see those pieces shining like diamonds in her eyes.

She was forged in flame.

"You're so beautiful," he breathed, gazing into her reflection as though she might disintegrate if he looked away. "You're everything."

When she smiled, for the briefest moment, he thought it reached her eyes. He could imagine it as vividly as he could see her standing in front of him right now. The soft curve of her lips, the way her eyes would twinkle as she shone from within. Her happiness would be so absolute that he wouldn't have to worry about her anymore.

But then it was gone, dissipating like smoke in the wind.

"It's just too bad," she said, her tone of voice pulling taut. "From the sincerity in your voice, I might have believed you *wanted* someone beautiful and everything." She stopped beside him on her way out of the bathroom, looking her up and down. "Guess that would be wrong."

Ash dragged his hands down his face after she left the room. He could be under no facade. She was not going to easily forgive him for what he'd said, nor was she required to. His hope that things could return to normal was delusional.

He needed to figure out how to overcome his shame so he could fucking *apologize*.

Once he'd washed up, he jogged down the stairs to meet her. Tayshia was in the kitchen, drinking a glass of water when he entered. She turned to look up at him as he came to stand beside her.

"Maybe we should stay home," she said.

"Are you insane? You woke me up at six in the morning, freaking out because your heart--"

"I know." She set the glass in the sink and rested her hands on the front edge of it. "I'm just concerned, and I feel fine now."

"Concerned about what?"

"I feel fine now. I really do."

Ash narrowed his eyes, the concern coiling in his heart like a snake. "I don't want to argue this morning. It's literally seven in the AM. I'm tired. You're tired. Let's just go to the urgent care, have you checked out, and then—"

"They're gonna weigh me."

"Well, *yes*. But we already talked about that."

She chewed her lower lip, her gaze shifting about like a cornered animal. "I don't know. I don't really know if I can—if I want to do this. I'm concerned, Ash."

Ash sighed and took her by the shoulders. He ducked his head so he could look her in the eyes. And even though he felt sick with guilt over how he'd hurt her, he didn't look away.

"I'll be right there with you the whole time. All that's gonna happen is they're going to ask you questions, check whatever needs to be checked, and send you on your way."

He could see her thoughts racing in the way she bit at the inside of her cheek, at the way she stared at him without really *seeing* him. She was freaking out, and there was nothing he could do about it.

"Let's just go," she said abruptly, and then she turned around to go to the door to the garage.

"What's the real reason you don't want to go?" he asked, following her. Steven had already responded to Ash's text, telling him they were good to go and that there was no sign of any Oldsmobiles on the street, so he pressed the garage door button on the wall. It creaked on its way up, and the spring morning rushed in to greet them with sunrise and a light breeze.

"You know why."

They got into the car, Tayshia standing immobile by the passenger's side while Ash paused by the driver's side with his keys jangling in his hands. Just by looking at her, he could tell she wasn't well. She looked like a gust of wind would take her out to sea.

"You gonna tell me with your words, or just wait for me to read your mind?"

She shot him a nasty look. "You have no problem controlling everything else about me. Why not just make a couple new rules and force me to tell you? Better yet—why don't you decide I'm better? I'll be healed. Magic."

They drove in silence that was as awkward as it was tense. Ash wanted to say something, anything, but her energy was so negative that he felt too suffocated to speak.

"You seem bothered," was all he managed to come up with as they pulled up to a red light around the corner from the medical park.

"I *am* bothered."

"Stay bothered."

"Tayshia, I mean it," he snapped. "You're going to the doctor. We are here, and that's it. You can complain about it later."

"I feel *fine!*" she cried, heedless of the other cars and people walking on the sidewalk, on their way to work and appointments. "I don't *want* to go in when there's nothing wrong with me!"

A flash of anger slammed through him, but he stuffed it into the box where it belonged. He had no right to be angry with her right now. It was more important that he get her into that doctor's office. If her heart had given her trouble enough to want to wake him up from a dead sleep, then it was imperative that she go.

"I don't care what you want," he said quietly, hand on the wheel as he turned into the parking lot. It was fairly full, which didn't surprise him. He could see quite a few parents toting their kids into dentist and doctors' offices. "I've told you that before—I do not care what I have to do to make you better.

"You can't *make* me better," she spat out nastily, arms crossed over her chest and the seatbelt strap. "It's stupid to try."

"Then I guess I'm a fucking idiot."

He parked the car close to the doors of the urgent care. It was double-sided: an emergency dentist on the left and the urgent care on the right. Ash turned his head, and their eyes met across the center console. She was glaring at him, pointed daggers that felt as sharp as they were deadly.

"I hate you so much, Ash."

He deserved that. It hurt, but he deserved it.

"Report me, then." He got out of the car. "Take my hand, Tayshia."

"No."

"Come *on*."

"*No.*"

"*You* were the one who wanted help this morning! You said—"

"I know what I said. But I changed my mind."

"Tayshia." He used his sternest voice. "It's time to go. *Now.*"

Like the changing of the tides, she turned to beseech with the most pitiful, pleading look in her eyes that he had ever seen.

"Ash, *please*. They're going to weigh me. They *always* weigh you at the doctor's office! And if they find out that I'm purging and that *that's* why my heart is acting up, then they'll refer me to some stupid treatment center or therapist, and then--"

"That's not my problem." He turned to the side, holding his hand out again and snapping his fingers. "Let's *go*."

"Ash, I am *begging* you."

"I said *you're going*. Get your ass out here before I drag you."

Tayshia narrowed her eyes a fraction. The distance between them seemed to stretch further and further, like she was drowning, floating out to sea and he was stuck on the shore, trying to throw her a rope. Or like they were running in opposite directions because if they went toward one another, they'd have to face the thing that was trying to control them both.

Her disorder.

He should have smoked a damn joint before leaving.

Ash leaned into the car and forcibly unbuckled her seatbelt. She let out a cry of indignation, struggling against him as he grabbed her as gently as he could by the upper arms and hauled her out of the car. He let her go as soon as she was far enough away from the car for him to slam the door shut. He whirled around, livid, gripping her chin and pulling her forward against him.

"You're going to the doctor and you're going to tell them everything that you've been doing to yourself," he said, his ire overflowing like boiling water. "And you're not going to skimp on a single thing. The time for lying and hiding is *over*, Tayshia."

Her panic grew, intensifying like dark storm clouds in the sky. Her face crumpled, her mask falling apart. The telltale signs of tears began to glimmer in the corners of her eyes, shining like the amethysts they both no longer wore. Her terror looked as real as he'd ever seen it.

But he didn't trust her.

"Don't give me the false dramatics," he snapped, letting go of her chin and grabbing her hand in a tight grip. He pushed forward and started walking, tugging even as she tried to pull against him. There were people looking at them, watching her act like a child, but he didn't care.

She was going into that office.

"I'm not faking it," she whined. "Ash! I don't want to go! Ash, *please*!"

He ignored her pleading, marching them all the way down the aisle of cars and towards the sidewalk that led to the urgent care doors. As they stepped onto the concrete, he felt her defeat as tangibly as he felt the breeze rustling through his hair. It was the beginning of a very green spring, but to Ash, it all just felt grey. Grey like the sidewalk, like the walls of the buildings, like the color of his heart.

He just wanted her to be *fixed* already.

When he felt her wrist twisting in his hold again, he whirled around to tell her to knock it off. Instead, he was met with the sight of her trying to curl her fingers around his. Surprised, he allowed it, feeling her fingers sliding between his and twining together. Her facial expression was naught but a glorified pout as she averted her eyes to the parking lot and the busy street past it.

She looked like everything that she'd been fighting for was lost to things she understood enough to not want them to devour her, and pain she did not understand why she deserved. Standing there with her toes turned slightly in and her lips curved down into a deep frown, he saw that her shoulders were slumped. Her hand was so tentative within his own, and there was nothing beautiful about the fear he had that he would break her fingers by mistake.

She seemed so emotionally frail that his heart broke.

"What?" he said.

"I'll go in." she mumbled, closing her eyes as though she were in pain.

"Yeah?"

"I'll tell them the truth."

He tilted his head and scrutinized her, wanting to ensure it really was surrender that he was witnessing.

Seeing her there, watching her appear as though she wanted to simply crumble into pieces on the sidewalk, he felt something come over him that was familiar. It was familiar, yet it had been ages since he felt it. It was the same feeling that had made it so easy for her to manipulate him into thinking it was *okay* that she purged as long as he was there to take care of her. The feeling that only came about when it seemed like she was trying to engage in something other than self-destruction.

Hope.

This was so hard, staying angry with her. The line between hatred and affection was such a blurry, fragile thing. Every fiber in his being told him that being with her would be too hard—too painful, too difficult. She would rip his heart out of his chest and eat it, just to throw it up later so it didn't poison her inside.

But what if he walked away…And she died?

Was he only here, holding her hand because he was afraid she would die? Were any of his feelings for her real? Or were they just lingering nightmares from his mother's death?

How could his feelings be real if it was so easy for him to be cruel to her?

His gaze dropped down to her neck, devoid of the necklace that had brought them together. The necklace that had softened his heart and helped him see her for the precious gem she was. Before he knew just how deep the disorder's roots had sunken into her soil.

Her roots.

If he couldn't be there to tend her roots, how could he say he deserved her when she bloomed?

Ash tugged on her hand again, causing her to stumble forward again. She fell into him, looking up at him with a shy expression — the same look she used to give him before everything got so fucked up. Before she sunk into her desperation and he shattered into his anger.

Cupping the back of her head, he pressed her face into his chest and held her there. He dropped his lips to the top of her head, placing a lingering kiss that almost hurt. It ached in his heart, like it could never be mended. Even if she got better, the past six months together would forever be a scar.

Tayshia wrapped her free arm around his waist, embracing him. He could hardly feel it, she had so little strength. Her fingers felt colder than ice in-between his own.

He wished he could drop her off at the urgent care and leave her there.

He wished he could take her to the hospital and leave her there.

He wished he could take her into his dreams and leave her there.

"If they send me away," she said, "would you come with me until they told you to leave?"

"You're strong enough to do it on your own."

"What if I don't want to do it alone?"

God. Fuck.

Fuck.

This felt like sliding a sharp blade between his ribs, slow and steady on its way to his heart.

"There are some things that we want that we just can't have," he said, emotion gnawing at his throat. "And some things that we have to do alone."

"Yes," she mumbled into the fabric of his shirt, "but it doesn't stop me from wishing it were different."

"You and me both."

She was his entire world.

The realization stole his breath away, leaving him suspended in the space between light and darkness. Even when he was angry, she was his everything. Even when she was hissing vitriol at him, she was it for him.

Here, with her hand in his own, he could feel their destinies intertwining.

Ash let her go and, before he could break down, he turned away. Keeping a tight hold on her hand, he tugged her along the sidewalk.

When they got into the office, they checked in. He stood behind Tayshia while she gave them her information and told them she was coming in for a heart problem. They told her it'd be a forty minute wait because there were others who'd checked in before them, and then they made their way through the large, very full waiting room to find seats. One they were seated, Ash instinctively put his hand in Tayshia's lap, where she clutched it like a lifeline and stared at the floor.

There was a middle-aged man staring at them over the top of a magazine, watery grey eyes peering out at them from beneath tufts of sandy eyebrow hairs. His expression was not kind, but it was curious.

"Aren't you that kid from the news a year ago?"

A couple of people looked over, and Ash gave him a puzzled look. Not because he was wrong, but because he couldn't understand what God told him he had the right to speak to him about it in the doctor's office.

"Wait a minute. Yes, you are. You're the kid from the news. And you, girl—you were in the paper, too. Your dads got into it at the old ice cream shop, and then *your* dad shot the place up." His eyes fell to Tayshia's lap, where she was gripping Ash's hand so tight his fingers were going numb. The man made a disgusted noise. "Aren't you supposed to be in jail? What does your *dad* think about you dating the son of the man who shot him?"

Ash just stared at him. He hadn't had anyone recognize him in public in a while. Not since the elderly woman at the store last year. Having it happen here was a shock, but he couldn't react. He wasn't about to cause a scene in front of all these people with their kids.

Apparently, Tayshia had a different plan in mind.

"Why don't you just shut the fuck up and mind your business?" she hissed, her eyes as cold as ice chips. "Huh? How 'bout that?"

Ash blinked down at her in surprise. She didn't *ever* have public outbursts like this. Temper tantrums around him, yes. Angry arguments with her parents, yes. But with random people she didn't know?

The man scoffed and went back to his paper.

It took a while for people to stop looking at them. One child stared for five solid minutes before his mother noticed and quietly told him it was rude to stare. Tayshia seemed incredibly mortified, gripping his hand even tighter as she kept her head down.

Ash was a different person now than he was in September, but he could feel some of his old shame starting to rise. The shame he'd felt having hurt all those people, having terrified them. He'd always been ashamed of his father, but the ice cream shop? That was his fault. He hadn't done enough to try and stop him. He'd just stood there and let it all happen.

Maybe he *was* a bad person. After all, he seemed to have no problems hurting Tayshia when she asked him to. Yet here she was, sitting beside him, holding onto him with a desperation that he'd never seen from her before. She was *terrified*, and he was the only thing keeping her sane.

He let go of her hand, ignoring the temporary look of dismay on her face as he wrapped his arm around her and pulled her as close to his side as she could go with the arms of their seats between them. She turned towards him and placed a hand on his chest, fingers bunching the fabric to hide her trembling. He kissed her temple and whispered against her skin that everything would be okay.

The mother with the staring child caught Ash's eye, offering him a warm smile. She'd seen the entire thing. Somehow, Ash could tell that her smile was more than just a polite acknowledgment.

That was enough for him.

Time passed, and people came and went. Tayshia got more and more nervous as the minutes ticked by, to the point that when a nurse came out and called her name, she jolted as though she'd been asleep. Ash kept his arm around her as they headed over to the door that the nurse was holding open.

"Good morning, guys," the nurse said brightly, her blonde hair swept back into a ponytail and her glasses rimmed in tortoiseshell. She held a clipboard in one hand. "How are we doing today?"

"We're good," Ash said. "She's a little nervous."

"Well, there's no need to be nervous, Tayshia," the nurse said. "My name is Nurse Michaels, and the doctor who's going to be seeing you today is *great*. You're in good hands." She looked up at Ash, who towered over them both. "Will you be coming back with her?"

"Yes," Tayshia said quickly. "I need him there."

"Don't worry, I'll come." Ash rubbed her upper arm and raised his eyebrow at the nurse. "That's okay, right?"

"Absolutely. If you guys will just follow me, then?"

CHAPTER EIGHTEEN

Ash reached to hold the door open for all three of them, and then they headed down a small hallway. Ash paid little attention to the doors and the computer and files areas, instead keeping his attention on Tayshia. She was saying unintelligible things under her breath and her gaze was darting about like she was trying to follow a faerie's dance.

They came to a stop by a scale. It was one of the standard medical ones, with a tall column and wide platform for someone to stand on. It looked harmless to Ash but to Tayshia, it was likely ominous and threatening.

"So, we just have to weigh you first," Nurse Michaels said, turning to face them. Her brows furrowed together. "Are you all right?"

"I'm f-fine," Tayshia squeaked out.

"Can we just—" Ash scratched the back of his head. "Can you weigh her backwards?"

"Oh, yes." Nurse Michaels' eyes widened and she looked Tayshia over, a sweeping of her gaze downward. "Of course. Go ahead and step backwards on the scale."

"And don't tell me what it says," Tayshia said. "Please."

The nurse gave her a troubled look and then agreed, and Tayshia stepped on the scale. Ash looked away out of respect and then, when the nurse said she was done, he turned back in time to see Tayshia coming toward him. He wrapped his arms around her for a moment, and then turned her around. Nurse Michaels gave them both an encouraging smile, and then led them into a nearby doctor's office. Ash stood in the corner of the room, arms crossed over his chest and one ankle crossed over the other.

Once the door was closed, she went to the computer and started clicking things with the mouse.

"All right, so first what I need to do is ask some preliminary questions. It's just for our records and to add to yours. It'll be questions about your medical history and current symptoms. Is that okay?"

"Yes," Tayshia said as she sat down on the edge of the paper-covered bed. She gripped the hem of her sweater.

Nurse Michaels ran through all the questions, starting with confirming her name and birthdate, and moving into family history. Tayshia answered all the questions to the best of her ability, until it came to the point where Nurse Michaels asked her about her prior mental health history. She didn't seem to know how to answer it.

"I've never been diagnosed with anything," she mumbled.

Nurse Michaels exchanged glances with Ash before fixating her attention solely on Tayshia. "Any concerns you have about possible symptoms of something don't have to be discussed with me. You can mention them to the doctor. Unless you'd like me to make a note of something in your chart for when we send the information from this visit to your primary care provider?"

"Uh, I don't have one. I mean, I *do*, but he's in Medford. I haven't seen him since August."

"Right, but we'll send it to him down there, so anything you need marked down, you can tell either me or the doctor today."

Tayshia glanced back at Ash.

"Be honest," he said.

She sighed with a defeated pout and then hung her head. "I might be Bulimic."

"Okay," Nurse Michaels said, and she typed some things down. Ash recognized her tone. It was professional. Intentionally distant.

The tone of someone whose suspicions had been confirmed.

When they were done, Nurse Michaels told them that the doctor would be in soon, and to have a good day. Her gaze lingered on Ash with a certain measure of sympathy, and then she was gone, sealing them inside the room by themselves.

Ash pushed away from the wall and came around to stand by Tayshia and the bed. He put his hand on her shoulder, thumb massaging comforting circles into the muscle of the junction.

"Holding up okay?" he murmured.

"So far, I guess." She didn't look up from the floor. "It was really hard to say it out loud."

His hand slid to cup her cheek, his thumb tilting her face up. "You're doing your best. That's what matters to me. Okay?"

Another nod, and then she leaned forward until her forehead rested against the part of his chest that ached. He was so glad they were here, finally in a place where she could get some help of some sort, but he was worried about her. She was a house of cards waiting to collapse.

He curved his arms around her in a warm, firm embrace, holding her in silence until a knock sounded at the door. At that point, he moved away from her and went back to the corner.

A tall woman with thick, black locs entered the room, the deep umber of her skin glinting rich beneath the fluorescent lights. When she smiled, it was both bright and welcoming, the white of her teeth offset by the white of her lab coat. Her eyes twinkled dark brown, nearly onyx as she held her hand out to Tayshia and shook it. She shook Ash's hand, too.

"Good morning, you two. My name is Doctor Igwe." She sat down on the swivel stool that Nurse Michaels had used at the computer and started messing around with something on the screen. "So, I'm going to be taking notes while you're speaking, just so your appointment summary is as accurate as possible. As long as that's all right, can we begin?"

Tayshia nodded.

Doctor Igwe smiled again. "Great. That's wonderful. What brings you in today?"

"I woke up with heart problems this morning," Tayshia explained, fingers twisting her sweater anxiously. "Like, my heart stopped for a second and then fluttered. It skipped beats."

"Hm, that is concerning." Doctor Igwe frowned, her fingers flying across the keyboard. She then turned in the stool so she could better address Tayshia. "Did you have any trouble breathing, or any pain?"

Tayshia shook her head. "It was just...Cold? I don't know. My chest felt really cold and my hands were shaky and kind-of sweaty. And my heart fluttered and I *did* have to catch my breath. That's why I woke my boyfriend up. Because I was scared something really bad was happening."

Ash closed his eyes for a second, not caring one iota about Tayshia calling him her boyfriend again.

Was this how his mother had felt before she passed out in the courtroom? Was this the precursor to Tayshia's death?

"All right. Well, typically, I would order an EKG for this situation—which I'm going to do—but what I'm concerned about first is the whys and the hows." Doctor Igwe crossed her legs and clasped her hands over her knees. "I see Nurse Michaels recorded your answer for the question about prior history with eating disorders. Can you tell me a little bit about that?"

Ash cracked his neck in discomfort. This was it. The moment. Either Tayshia lied and fucked up what little chance she had at survival, or she told the truth and spiraled afterward.

"I—" Tayshia cut herself off, her head hanging once again. "I don't know."

She sounded like she was going to cry.

Ash pushed away from the wall again, coming to her side in an instant. The doctor gave him a small smile as he approached and perched on the bed. He began to rub Tayshia's back in soothing circles. There were tears dripping down her cheeks, one-by-one, like raindrops etching their way down a car window.

"Sorry," she whispered. "This is really hard."

"I know," Doctor Igwe said. "These topics can be difficult, but you're making the right choice seeking help. We want you healthy and well, and we don't want you hurting and in pain, okay? I'm sure your boyfriend here would agree."

"He would," Ash murmured.

Tayshia nodded, looking up at him through her tears. He gave her a nod of his own, hoping to encourage her the way the doctor was attempting to. She let out a resigned sigh and sat up straight.

"I have a really bad relationship with food. I don't like it being inside of my body. I love it, love the way it tastes, and like eating...I just don't like when it's inside me. So, I throw up everything I eat. It doesn't matter whether it's healthy food or junk food, I get rid of it as soon as I can after I eat it. There have been times where I've purged more than ten times. My record is seventeen once, because I started in the early morning and did it all day. That was this summer when I was still at home, before school."

Seventeen times? He wanted to be sick at the thought. After catching her purging the times that he had, he never wanted to see it happen again. She'd looked so exhausted, shuddering as the endorphins flooded her body and tricked her into thinking she was flying. That things were better and that she didn't hurt anymore. That she was in control.

But to him, she just looked sick.

"How often do you eat your meals?" the doctor asked, her fingers typing on the keyboard again. "And are you still purging to that volume now?"

"Well, we have a…System now," she said, shooting Ash a brief look. "I eat three meals a day, and we eat them together. But that's only been for a few weeks, I'd say. Before that, I went about a month without digesting anything intentionally. It might have been a little more than a month. I'm sure I digested a little, because I'm sitting here, alive, but yeah. I throw up *everything*."

There was no reason for Doctor Igwe to know that their system was a little bit fucked up, and very much steeped in volatility and argument. Better to let her think it was a good temporary solution.

"That may be, Tayshia, but it is because you are an outlier," the doctor said in a grave tone, turning from the computer again. "Not only is going without food that long dangerous to your health, but so is the constant purging. Every time you eat, your stomach starts the digestion process." She held a hand over her stomach, gesticulating to describe what she was trying to paint the picture of. "That's when the acid starts getting ready to process the food you've just eaten. When you purge it, it burns everything on the way up. You could get acid burns on your esophagus and in your mouth."

"I know that," Tayshia said. "I just don't care."

Doctor Igwe's smile didn't falter, but it was sympathetic. "But there are people who do. People like your boyfriend and I'm sure your family and friends. And *I* care. I want you to understand what you're doing to your body, and I want to be honest with you."

"About what?"

"Knowing how often you purge, your symptoms don't seem too out of place. And what's more concerning is the fact that you experienced that flutter. What that's called is a heart palpitation."

Ash's hand slid up to Tayshia's shoulder, where it remained. He needed to stay calm and not let his facial expression shift. He needed to keep his thoughts free and clear of anything that had to do with his mother.

"Okay," Tayshia replied.

"One of the most dangerous aspects to purging is what it does to your heart. You can be any weight, at any stage of your disorder, and at any age, and have a heart attack. You could purge one time or one hundred, and your heart could stop."

Fuck, fuck, fuck, fuck, fuck —

"But I feel fine now," Tayshia protested, wiping the tears off of her cheeks. "My chest doesn't hurt, my heart is fine, and I—I'm *fine.*"

"That's why it's so deadly," Doctor Igwe said. "One minute, you're fine. The next, you're dead."

"Oh."

Ash couldn't help but slide his arm around Tayshia's waist, pulling her closer. His mind was at war with him, trying its best to force him to imagine what she would look like if she were dead. It was horrible.

"Tayshia, honey, have you sought medical help for this before?" Doctor Igwe asked, both her expression and voice kind. "With a primary care provider, or a hospital?"

"Once," Tayshia whispered, ducking her head down to watch her fingers play with the fabric of her sweater. "Before school started. I was feeling sick after not eating for a while. Because sometimes, I would try to starve all day, but I'm too weak for that. I think I made it five days before I fainted, and my parents took me to the doctor because I lied and said I'd been dizzy for no reason. When they left me alone with the doctor, I tried to tell him I wasn't eating."

"And what did he say?"

"He said that Black people don't typically have eating disorders, and that I was fine. He said the statistics don't support anything other than binge eating among Black women. And then he told me my vitals were okay, and that I was probably just stressed because of college starting. I gave up after that."

Doctor Igwe looked horrified, speechless with it. "Tayshia, I'm so sorry. I am *so* sorry."

"You never told me that," Ash said quietly, unable to understand how to cope with the rage that was coursing through his veins. He had no idea who this doctor was, but he legitimately hoped he perished. To think that Tayshia could have gotten help—that she'd *tried* to get help—and the doctor had let his prejudice and racist perspective control whether or not he did his fucking *job*? "Why didn't you tell me that?"

"It's humiliating," Tayshia said, her eyes shining with fresh tears. She swiped her fingers underneath her eyes to try and stop them. "It's embarrassing that no one cares about me enough to help me."

Doctor Igwe opened her mouth to speak, but Ash was quicker than her.

"*I* care about you, Tayshia. You know that. You *know* that. That doctor is a fucking asshole. He was wrong."

"And your feelings and experiences are valid," Doctor Igwe interjected, an erupting passion to her voice that almost made Ash want to cry. "I'm so sorry that he failed you. As a doctor, it was his job to treat you equally to his other patients and as a result of his malpractice, you haven't been able to get the help you need. I can definitely imagine the pain you've endured because of this, and I wish there was some way I could make it right. But what I can do is make sure that you get help, and make sure that I listen to you."

"I'm confused, though. I don't *look* like I have an eating disorder, so it just feels like none of this applies to me."

"Tayshia, you can be *any* weight and still have an eating disorder," Doctor Igwe said. "It doesn't matter your size, race, gender, or ethnicity. *Anyone* can have an eating disorder and it's *always* serious. What the previous doctor said to you was incorrect. The women of our community *are* able to have eating disorders, and we *are* the statistics that he told you don't exist. Just because something isn't reported doesn't mean it isn't happening."

Tayshia stared at the floor for so long that Ash realized she was dissociating. But by the time he realized it, she was speaking.

"I could be better now if he would have taken me seriously?"

Doctor Igwe sighed. "I can't say for sure. But I think it's definitely possible."

It was seconds before Tayshia dissolved into tears, burying her face in her hands and weeping unashamedly. Ash pulled her into his arms as fast as he could, his heart racing as he struggled to contain his anger and his turmoil. From Tayshia's previous doctor to the way his mother had died, today was overwhelming.

He wanted to fall apart.

"Why don't I give you two a moment, and I'll go order some tests," Doctor Igwe said quickly, rising to her feet. "When I get back, I'll ask a couple more questions."

"Thank you so much," Ash said, and then his attention was on the weeping girl wrapped in his embrace. He was so focused on her that he barely heard Doctor Igwe departing. "Tayshia. Tayshia, baby, it's okay. Everything's okay now."

"It's not," she sobbed. "It's not okay. I *tried* to get help, I did. And no one would help me."

"I know. But I'm here now. I'm helping you." His touch was smooth and gentle as he pulled her face up to look at him, wiped her tears, and hooked his fingers behind her ear in one fluid movement. His eyes searched her own, desperate for her to understand just how much he cared and how hard he would fight for her. "I'm not gonna let you die, okay? Okay?"

Tayshia fell into him again. He held her tighter, burying his face in the crook of her neck and shoulder. He couldn't imagine a life without her and yet he wasn't going to have to imagine it for much longer if no one took her seriously. The devastation of learning that she had tried to get help before being blatantly denied it was enough to grieve over.

"I'm here," he whispered. "I'm not ever going to leave you."

She clutched at the back of his shirt, her tears soaking the fabric as she wept.

The doctor returned ten minutes later, when Ash was in the process of clearing the stray tears from the borderline catatonic Tayshia's face. She was carrying a paper packet with her.

"Hi, you two. Everything all right now?"

"For the time being," Ash said. "It's just overwhelming for her."

"Of course it is, and completely understandable. I'm glad you came in today, though, Tayshia. We're gonna get you some help. The help you deserve."

Tayshia's gaze snapped up, her catatonia dissipating. "What?"

"I also wanted to tell you some other things that are common for people with eating disorders. I did include them in your appointment summary, but I figured it would be best if I explained them to you," Doctor Igwe said, handing the paper packet to Ash to take. "Some of the things that can happen besides heart arrhythmia and burns are just as life-threatening. For example, if you eat too much and purge, the strain could cause your stomach to rupture. That could kill you very quickly. Another danger is your electrolytes. If your Potassium drops too low, you could die. Other issues can be with your joints and your bones. I've seen disordered patients who ended up with osteoarthritis or early onset osteoporosis.

"There are also negative effects on your body that don't end in death, but that can lower your quality of life significantly. Hair loss, tooth decay and cavities with the probable loss of some of your teeth, short temper, dehydration, ulcers, your skin can get dry…The list is extensive, Tayshia. When was your last period?"

As Doctor Igwe turned to the computer, Tayshia answered. Strangely, there was an edge to her voice that hadn't been there since before they'd come into the building.

Why was Tayshia angry?

"In June."

"Of 2018?"

"Yes."

The doctor's brows twitched together as she typed it into the computer. "I'll have to reprint your summary. I'll be back. But I ordered you an EKG and blood work, and I'm ordering a pregnancy test. You can deny any of these tests if you want."

"No, I'll get them."

"Okay, good. That's good." Doctor Igwe seemed to have picked up on Tayshia's mood swing. "The last thing I wanted to talk to you about is treatment."

There it was.

"I don't want to go to treatment!" Tayshia said, the panic so audible in her tone that Ash feared she might leave the room. "That's not why I came in today. This is *urgent care*. It was just supposed to be for my random heart problem."

"No, honey, I'm just going to print out a list of referrals to therapists, treatment programs, and dieticians. That's all."

"I'm not *diagnosed* with anything, though. There's no need for treatment. I don't need to go to some hospital where they put a tube down my throat!"

"Tayshia, *please*," Ash said quietly. "Please just listen to her."

Tayshia narrowed her eyes at him and didn't reply.

"Right, well," the doctor said with caution, "I'm going to go ahead and print out the numbers anyway, and include them with your summary. And then you guys can talk about it when you get home. A thorough discussion should help you come to a good decision for your health. But Tayshia, I need to be honest with you. If your bloodwork comes back as concerning, I'm going to recommend you see a primary care provider as soon as possible."

That seemed to be the last straw.

"Why?!" Tayshia cried, scrambling to her feet. "So you can section me and force me into a mental hospital?! No!"

Before Ash realized what was going on, Tayshia had stormed out of the room. The doctor gave him a helpless look and a grimace. They exchanged some last-minute professional conversation, he accepted the appointment summary for her, and then hurried to find Tayshia.

Ash had known about his mother's eating disorder for so long and he'd never once told anyone. Never once even told her that he knew. If he had, he might have been able to save her from the heart attack her purging had almost undoubtedly caused. He had simply done what he could from afar, cleaning up after her so her shame wouldn't be discovered. He would sit on that bottom step and listen, wondering how it must feel to feel so out of control.

"We don't always get the things that we want."

But what did he want?

He kept making the wrong choices. Wrong choices that they both had to suffer for. Telling Kieran Tayshia's secret, violating her trust and safety. Buying her binge food and giving her space to get sicker. Yelling at her, controlling her, forcing her to eat. Telling her he didn't want her.

Why couldn't he make the right choice for once?

✧✧✧

Tayshia was standing at the car, and she wasn't mad anymore.

She was standing by the passenger's side door, shivering from the chilly morning with her arms wrapped around herself. There was a hollowness to her eyes that seemed like she would never be full. Her beauty was the sad beauty of the same roses that his father had planted for his mother. Full, rich, and alive in the ground. When freshly cut?

Dead in a week.

"Why did you get so angry?" he asked with a sigh, coming to stand beside her with his back to the car next to theirs. "She was just trying to help you."

"I know. I just... Freaked out. I guess having to face it sucks."

"To face the disorder?"

"And everything else I've done since." She lowered her gaze forlornly. "I'm a bad person, Ash. I've done horrible things to give the disorder space to breathe. I don't deserve good things."

Before he could speak, she tilted her chin up and looked him in the eyes.

"I want you to know that even if you don't want me — even if we don't get along later tonight, or come tomorrow, whatever — that I'm sorry. I'm sorry for asking you to buy me binge food, and for convincing you to. I should not have said to you that you were toxic like your father, and I shouldn't have told you to stop caring about me. It was hurtful. It was wrong. You may not be able to forgive me, but—"

"I forgive you," he said. "And I'm sorry, too. I'm sorry that I told you I didn't want you. It wasn't true, and I never should have said something so hurtful to you just because I was angry. It was wrong."

Her eyebrows rose.

"I forgive you for what you said," he continued, "but I don't forgive you for how you used me. I don't forgive you for manipulating me into enabling you. I told you I cared about you, and I meant that. The only thing that keeps me here is the way I feel about you." He set the paper packet on top of the car and cupped her face with both hands, feeling just how cold her skin was beneath his palms. "I'll forgive you when you forgive me. When we forgive each other for our mistakes—all of them—then I'll let you go. Until then, you're mine. And Tayshia?"

"Hm?"

"Call some of those numbers. They can give you help. Real help—help I can't give."

"No."

"No?"

"No." Her eyes blazed up at him, wild and afraid.

"I don't think you have a choice," he said, his voice gentle as he took her by the elbows and pulled her closer.

Her face grew pinched, screwing up with emotion as she fought back tears. "I have to have a choice. They can't force me to do anything I don't want to do. If I don't want to go, they can't make me."

"You're right. They can't. But I can."

She looked up at him, inhaling to speak, but he silenced her with his lips. It took a moment, but she melted into the kiss with her head tilted back and mouth open to him. A sigh escaped her and he devoured it, just as he devoured her with his tongue brushing against hers. Her fingers wrapped around the tops of his shoulders, gripping tight as she anchored herself to him and pushed onto the tips of her toes.

"And if they tell you to go to the hospital," he breathed out, pressing kisses along her jaw while his fingers trailed up the sides of her neck, "then you're going."

"But—"

"Hush," he said, and then he kissed her again.

Tayshia threw her arms around his neck and kissed him back, tasting him like a woman parched. Like she'd been dragging herself through a desert devoid of him for a century. She leaned into him and he held her, his hands sliding up her back in reverence. He could feel her heart beating against the cage of her chest, as though it were reaching for him.

Ash wondered if she knew how much he cherished her.

"Ash."

"Yes?" He kissed her cheek, then her cheekbone.

"What if I'm not really sick? What if it's all in my head? What if I'm—I'm faking it?"

"You're not faking it. It's real. It's valid. And even if you were, what healthy person pretends to have an eating disorder to the point where they're purging that many times a day?"

"But what if—"

"No," Ash growled, his hands starting to quiver. He closed his eyes. "No. You *are* sick. You *do* have a disorder. And you're valid. But if any of the new doctors you see tell you you need to go to treatment, then you're going to go. I cannot lose you. Do you understand me?"

"Yes," she whispered, lowering her head.

Ash felt like he was playing chess, adjusting his strategy and inching his pieces to the left and right, forward and back. Like if he made one wrong move, his army would fall. He had to make the right decisions. The right moves.

The right choices.

He grabbed her chin and dragged it back up. He gave her a serious look, holding her in place before he kissed her a third time.

Because he could feel it.

A storm, brewing on the horizon of not only their relationship, but their lives. Like heavy dark clouds of something destructive and unavoidable. Anger like thunder and worry like darkness. Anxiety, the heat in the air. When he looked at her, searching for those shattered pieces of her heart, it was like they were hidden by the rain.

CHAPTER NINETEEN

"You all right, Ash? You don't look okay."

Ash blinked himself out of a reverie, tearing his gaze away from Officer Cook's desktop. When he refocused it, it was to the sight of the officer's bushy eyebrows coming together, and his frown deepening beneath his mustache.

"I'm just tired," Ash said.

"Well, I know you said you've been working on your father's garden. It's good to keep yourself busy during your break." Officer Cook clasped his hands and leaned over the desk. "Just make sure you're not working yourself too hard."

If only he knew.

"Other than that, kid, how's everything been going?"

"My dad died."

Officer Cook's face fell. "Oh, *no*. Ash, I'm so, so sorry. I had no idea. What happened?"

"Killed himself," Ash mumbled, dropping his head into his hands for a moment as though he had a headache. He pushed his fingers through his hair and sat back in the chair, gaze falling to the carpeted floor. "Couple weeks ago. Or three. I don't really keep track."

"That's just awful." The sympathy on the officer's face was the same sympathy Ash had seen on his friends' and godparents' faces. He was tired of it. "I'm guessing you had the funeral, and everything...?"

"Yep."

Officer Cook paused, like he always did before he said something that was technically not in his job description.

"Did you call that number I gave you?"

Ash's heart skipped a beat. Of course he hadn't. He didn't *need* a therapist. He was overwhelmed, yeah, but he was *fine*. If anyone needed a therapist, it was Tayshia.

"No," he said. "No offense, Officer Cook, but I don't think that sort-of thing is for me."

"Why not?"

"Well, because I'm fine."

Officer Cook pursed his lips, looking down as he seemed to mull his thoughts over what he wanted to say next. When he spoke, there was an intensity to his gaze that in a lot of ways, reminded Ash of Ryo.

"Sometimes, as men, I think we forget that not everything that we've been taught about ourselves and the things we need are true. There's no weakness in therapy. There's no weakness in needing help or support. And, Ash, you've been through a *lot*. A lot more than even me at my old age, and I go to therapy every week. I just want to see you succeed in life and end your probation with a future. You're on the right track. I don't want to see you hurting."

The sting in Ash's eyes warned him in time to bottle his emotions up before he broke down in the middle of his probation appointment. He wasn't used to this—wasn't used to someone being this interested in his mental health and how he was doing. Sure, Ryo and Steven loved him like a son and gave him everything he needed in that respect, but Officer Cook seemed like he truly cared about him.

It was overwhelming.

"Call the number," Officer Cook continued, a note of passion in his voice. "Call the number and start there. Take the first step. That's the hardest part to recovering and once you get past it, you've got a long journey. I'm not kidding you. It's *long*. But it's so, *so* worth it, Ash. So worth it. I promise you."

He wouldn't. He wasn't going to. Ash was *not* seeing a therapist, and definitely not before Tayshia. He wasn't sick like her. He didn't need help. Why the Hell would he want to sit in a room with some stuffed shirt and tell him all of his problems when he was *fine*?

What the fuck did *he* have to recover from?

"Thanks, Officer Cook," was all he said.

The officer heaved a sigh that showed him that he knew Ash wasn't on board, but he didn't press him on it. He shuffled Ash's papers. "Your progress report wasn't too hot."

"Does it matter? It's not even part of probation." Ash didn't mean to sound annoyed, but having a probation appointment that Tuesday morning when he needed to get back to work on the garden was bothersome to him. He took accountability for what he'd done at the ice cream shop, but right now, his life was so fucked that the garden was the only thing he'd been able to control in months.

"Yes, it matters. Your grades and your future matter. Typically, when someone is on probation, we like to check in on their personal life and see how the job search is going. Going to school *is* your job. It's very much relevant to the terms of your probation."

Ash sighed and dropped his head back to look up at the ceiling. "I'm doing the homework, but my head's fucked right now. It's just a mess in there, so it's hard to focus on the classwork."

"I know it's spring break now, but how are you getting your work? Are you picking it up on a weekly or daily basis?" Officer Cook sounded curious.

"No, my girlfriend's been..." God dammit. He closed his eyes for a second. "I had someone bring it to me for the two weeks I was on leave before break started. I managed to get it done and got low grades anyway. The teachers were nice about it but said they couldn't give me special treatment."

Officer Cook opened his mouth, and Ash knew he wanted to ask him about the *girlfriend* portion of his statement. He didn't, however, choosing instead to focus on school.

"I'll call the school," Officer Cook said. "I don't want you to get special treatment, either, but they should have given you extensions so you could split your focus and work when you were able. The grieving period is a very sensitive time and you should not be expected to do homework while you're in that period. Ridiculous. It may be a program attached to the high school, but it's still college and colleges nowadays provide compassionate allowances for issues of mental health."

Ash flinched, resisting the urge to tell him he wasn't grieving. He *was* grieving, just not for the fact that his father had died. The grief came from multiple sources that all traced *back* to him, and it wasn't something that addled his mind. No, the grief was in his chest, and it burned there like a low fire meant to smoke and cook him from the inside-out.

"My mental health is fine," Ash said mutedly. "I just can't focus."

"Well, why is that?"

"I have a lot going on." He shook his head out. "Look, I really don't want to talk about my mental whatever, my dad, my girl, or anything like that. It's too much right now. I just want to focus on what we're supposed to for the appointment so I can get back. I have a schedule for the garden."

The look of sympathy returned. "Of course, of course. I shouldn't push you right now. Why don't we just let the appointment end now so you can get back and get focused on something good for the day?"

Ash nodded, relief chilling the fire in his heart.

"Anything else you need me to know?"

"Uh, well, I'm currently living at my old house for the week."

"Do you plan on staying?" Officer Cook picked up his pen and flipped to the first page of Ash's report. "Should I mark that address down?"

"I don't want to stay, no."

Officer Cook narrowed his eyes. "But it's a possibility."

Ash had resigned himself to it. Now that it was getting cleaner and the garden was on its way, he had a feeling that he might be able to see himself staying. And Tayshia seemed comfortable enough to the point where he'd heard her listening to music in his bedroom the night before and that very morning. Provided they didn't break up whatever it was that they had, it was a possibility that they could move there when the school year was up and the school ended the apartment leases.

"Yeah," he admitted to the officer as well as to himself. "It's a possibility."

"Okay, well, let's cross that bridge when we come to it. If you decide to stay past break, give me a call and we'll make the address update."

"Okay." Ash stood up to go. "If someone's living with me, do I need to report who?"

"Yes," Officer Cook said, sounding distracted as the pen scratched across Ash's report. "We need record of all persons living in the same household as you for the duration of your probation. And we have your current roommate down as Tayshia Cole, right?"

"Yeah."

The officer lowered his pen and raised his eyebrows, looking up at where Ash stood with an intrigued, almost mischievous expression. "And is she staying with you at your old house?"

"Yeah."

Officer Cook pursed his lips, but there was amusement there where Ash felt none. "Yes, you will need to report her as having come to the house with you. I'm happy to hear you found something good amongst it all, though. I hope you're treating her well."

"All right, well I'm gonna go," he said. "I'll see you next month."

"Get those grades up," the officer said, just like he'd said last time.

Ash acknowledged him with a hand in the air, and then he closed the office door behind him.

When he got home, he could hear Tayshia on the phone in the living room. Whoever it was, she hung up the second Ash got home and as he walked in the door, she turned the TV up. She sat back on the couch, curling her legs underneath her as she flipped through channels and stared resolutely at the screen. He wanted to ask her who she'd been talking to, but he refrained.

"Not cleaning today?" he asked, trying to make some sort of small talk after the rather intense day they'd had yesterday.

"I will," she snapped. "I just finished putting my weave in and I just want to sit for a while. Is that okay, or does that break your *rules*?"

Ash's fingers twitched through his hair in agitation. Right out of the gate, she was going to act like this? He knew he'd fucked up and hurt her, but what was the point of being nasty?

He didn't want to keep fighting.

"Whatever, Tayshia. I'm going to work outside."

She didn't say good-bye.

☼☼☼

By the time Ash went inside at dark, he was so mentally exhausted that he thought he might cry in the shower. As the dirt and sweat and oil ran down the length of his body and swirled into the drain, he fought not to. He was tired of crying, and he'd only done it twice since getting out of jail.

When were things going to get better?

The doctor's visit and the conversation they'd had afterward showed Ash that things weren't as clear-cut as they seemed, and they weren't getting any better. Tayshia was in such extreme denial that it was going to kill her. And whenever he thought about her dying, it made his chest hurt and his stomach roil with nausea.

After his shower, he dressed in nothing but a pair of grey sweatpants, his entire body aching from working all day. Tayshia was in the living room, perched on the edge of the couch like she had too much energy. Their eyes met on his way to the kitchen, and then she quickly looked away.

It was time for dinner.

He pulled out the cookware and food he'd need, followed by a knife and a cutting board for the vegetables. But as he pulled out a potato to start cutting it, Tayshia caught his attention. She'd sidled into the room, her hands behind her back. She had chosen another tee shirt of his from high school as a nightgown, and there were black socks on her feet. Her hair was down and not yet in her bonnet for the night. She wore an inscrutable expression on her face.

"How was your probation appointment?"

He paused before the knife could touch the potato. "What?"

"Your appointment today, this morning. How was it?"

"It was fine." He turned his head toward her, confused and suspicious. Why was she talking to him out of nowhere, after ignoring him all day? "Why?"

"You seemed drained when you got home."

"I *am* drained." He started to cut the potato, slicing it in half horizontally, then arranging the halves so he could cut them in half, too.

"Did you get a lot of the garden—"

"What do you want?" He had to cut her off. The suspicion in his gut told him to find out her angle, and immediately.

Tayshia averted her gaze and then stepped closer to him. "You."

What the Hell?

"Why would you want me to touch you after what I said?"

The chop of the knife was loud against the cutting board as she took her time responding. Ash's heart was racing, knowing she had to be lying. There was no way that she'd want to do *anything* with him.

"I want you to prove it."

"To prove what?" he said without looking up from the potatoes.

"That you're sorry."

He stopped cutting and looked at her seriously. "How?"

She moved closer, only a yard away. Her eyes were bright, shining with a desperation that he didn't think he understood. "Because I want you to make me feel better."

"Why? I'm the one who did something wrong."

"Because I've spent some time thinking about it today, and I know what went wrong. I think that when you said it, you were angry. And what did I tell you to do when you were angry with me?"

He couldn't breathe.

"You were overwhelmed and upset about the album not because I was looking at it, but because of something you saw in the pictures. I don't know what it was that you were truly upset about, but whatever it was, it was causing you pain. And you want to feel in control of it, right? To make that pain go away?" She slid her hands up his bare chest, tracing the lines of the new raven tattoo, over the roses and chains on his neck, and settled them upon his cheeks. "Use me."

He knew why he'd been angry and she would never understand. How could he tell her that his mother had died of the same eating disorder that Tayshia currently had? How could he tell her the most painful secret of his life without her panicking and thinking he'd always had an ulterior motive with her, that his feelings weren't real? His feelings *were* real, he was just stupid and had a poor temper.

However.

This was Tayshia. She was a master at manipulating him. She knew exactly what he wanted, what he needed, and how to get the things she wanted out of him.

"Is this because you don't want to eat?"

"We can eat after."

As she gazed up into his eyes, the rather simple epiphany that landed on Ash's psyche was enough to shatter the Earth he stood upon.

It was all about control. The eating disorder, the degradation kink, the arguments. The only way she could deal with the pain he caused was for him to cause a type of pain she could control.

Neither of them were in control of anything in their traumatic, shitty lives, and neither of them had the energy to stop the inevitable.

And it *was* inevitable.

The inevitability of the two of them coming together was almost as certain as the rise of the sun. Ash had a brief second to remember to drop the knife onto the counter before that inevitably came to fruition.

They threw themselves at one another with a frenzy, hands clawing and gripping and pulling and squeezing. All at once, they were no longer in the kitchen at his childhood home, the place of painful memories and a bleak future. They were in a world of their own making, traveling across planes and through starfields. Their tongues slid together, lips separating and crashing again and again. Her hands gripped the back of his neck, his shoulders, smoothed over his chest. The moment she had her wrists crossed behind his head, he gripped the backs of her thighs and pulled her up to his hips. She wrapped her legs around him, fingers cupping his face so she could kiss him with a fervor she'd never had before.

She was insatiable.

Tayshia ground her hips against the hardness that had grown in his pants, wrapping one arm around his neck and keeping the other on his cheek.

"I want you to show me how sorry you are," she whispered against his lips before kissing him again, tongue delving deep into his mouth. "But I want you to make everything my fault."

Everything *was* her fault.

Most of it.

Well, some of it.

"Yeah?" He tilted his chin upward and let his eyelids flutter open. A low fire burned in the depths of hers, stoking one to life within his when their gazes locked. "You want me to treat you like I hate you?"

"That's exactly what I want."

"Then let me fuck you on the table."

He carried her to the kitchen table, dropping her unceremoniously onto the heavy wood. In the next second, Ash's kisses were moving across the front of her neck and his hands were on her hips. He dragged her forward as far as he could, the movement causing her to gasp. The hem of her makeshift nightgown pulled taut, and his hands slid down to her knees where he dug his fingers into her flesh.

"Tell me what you're gonna do for me," he panted raggedly into her throat, fingers squeezing as he ground against her core. Her fingers twisted in his hair as she held his head close to the sensitive skin on her neck. "Tell me now."

"I'm gonna let you use me." Her voice came out in a strangled whine, one that he swallowed with his mouth.

His right hand came up to press flat on her chest, spanning her collarbones with his fingers. He pushed her onto her back with enough force to jostle the table and stood up tall, rearing over her, purposefully intimidating and dominant in the way he almost glared down at her. Her legs shook and chest stuttered as he lifted his other hand. A smirk curved his lips as he took his fingers and ran them through his hair.

"Did I scare you?"

She nodded, her brows pulling together as she looked at his tattoos, eyes bouncing around as though inspecting a piece of art.

"Do you like when I scare you?"

"Yes. You terrify me."

"Hm," he hummed, slowly placing his left hand on the table beside her so he could lean down and place his mouth near her ear. "That's pathetic."

The hand of his that was on her chest moved up to her hair, tugging her head to the side. His face dove toward her, tilting at the last moment to kiss her neck with a desperation that crested the top of a lustful wave. He suckled at the flesh there, hard and relentless. The mixture of pain and pleasure made her writhe, clawing her nails down his chest and letting out a series of meek, stammering pleas. He moved to form another mark on her neck, using his teeth and tongue this time, and her back lifted from the table. Ash felt the need growing inside of him, his stomach twisting and tightening.

"Sometimes, I think I'm done with you," he said as he stood up and, with his hand still twisting her hair and holding her, he dragged her panties off of her. "And then I remember that if I did that, I wouldn't get to fuck you anymore. What else are you good for?"

"Nothing," she moaned.

"That's right. Nothing."

His fingers slid between her trembling thighs. She was so turned on that just the light touch had her crooning, eyelids falling shut and hips canting as she rode the same wave that he did. Her fingers curved around the edge of the table, holding on for dear life as he teased her. Her face, though pinched, was beautiful in the raw way she gave in to the things he made her feel.

"You love this shit, don't you?" he said with a note of incredulity to his tone. "*Don't* you?"

Tayshia cried out when he turned his palm up and sunk his middle and ring fingers into her cunt, immediately setting a pace so brutal that the sounds echoed around the dining room. It was so fucked up, thinking about the fact that his family had fallen into shambles in this house, and now he was about to fuck someone on the table.

"Tell me what you need," he commanded. "Use your words."

"Call me names. Something. Anything. I need —"

He silenced her with his hand around her throat.

"Such a needy whore for me, aren't you? Fucking my fingers like you can't function unless you're coming around them. What do you think our friends would say if they saw you like this, legs spread and desperate? You'd feel so ashamed, wouldn't you?"

"Yes, I-I would," she stammered, brows twitching together as her hips continued to roll.

"Maybe I should invite them over."

Ash leaned forward, changing the angle, and he could tell she saw stars. Tayshia wailed, back arching and upper body twisting, head lolling to the side. His fingers squeezed the sides of her throat so hard that her breath was ragged. She kept saying *yes* and *please*, to the point where it was a mantra.

"You're nothing to me."

She came the moment the last letter left his mouth, her body squeezing his fingers like a vice and her eyes falling shut. Nonsense came from her lips, things that Ash couldn't quite hear.

He kept going.

"Too sensitive," she gasped, twisting beneath him, her hands gripping his wrists.

"I know."

"Ash, please! I'm too sensiti—" She broke off into another wail when he brought his soaking wet fingers to her clit and began circling it with a gentleness that had her hips twitching. "Oh, *God*."

"That's right," he cooed, studying her face as he brought her to the heights of the stars yet again. "You like it when I tell you you're nothing. That you're desperate and pathetic. *No, Tayshia* – open your *fucking* legs."

Tayshia had tried to close her thighs around his forearm but upon his order, she forced them apart again. Her facial expression was pained.

"Please. *Please*."

"Do you want to stop?"

She shook her head, her legs shaking so hard it rattled the table more than his fingers' thrusts did. "But—But I—"

"Are you gonna come?"

"Yes, yes. But—"

His heart skipped a beat. Concern flooded him, breaking through his current headspace, reminding him that she was precious and she was breakable and she was his.

"Does it hurt, baby?"

She nodded.

Ash slowed his pace. Her entire body went limp, one foot sliding off the table to hang down. Her fingers still dug into his forearms, pulling his hands closer, and she let out a squeak.

"Does *that* hurt?"

Tayshia shook her head, as slow as molasses, and then she promptly fell into a shuddering, convulsing, whimpering mess. He could feel her walls spasming as she came a second time, could feel her getting even wetter. And by the way she dug her fingernails into his skin, the way she bared her teeth in a hiss, the closing of her eyes, it was good.

She drove him fucking insane.

"What do you say?" he whispered.

"Oh, thank you," she sighed, a dreamy smile spreading across her face as her hands fell lax beside her shoulders. "Thank you."

"For...?"

"Taking care of me."

"Good girl. I'm gonna fuck you now, but if you want to stop, remember to say the word."

Breathless, she said, "Only if I say *no*. Anything else, keep going."

"Are you sure?"

"I'm *extremely* sure. I like the feeling of it, knowing that all I have to do is say one word, and it ends if I need it to. But I also like the feeling of controlled helplessness when I'm with you. I know you'd never truly hurt me, and there's something about the person I care about most degrading me that just makes everything feel less out of control."

Taken aback at her saying so much right in the middle, which she rarely did, he leaned down to give her a soft, lingering kiss on the lips. He tilted his head to the right, his tongue taking advantage of her parted lips. This kiss was sensual, unlike the frenzied one they'd begun with, and Tayshia held him tightly by the biceps. Like she didn't want to let him go.

His lips moved down to her neck, to her pulse, where he teased her into sighing. She moved her hands, placing them flat on his chest. Her fingernails dug into his flesh as her hips bucked between the hard table and his soft body. Ash's mind was going blank again, wiping clean as the heat between them enveloped him.

"Will you fuck me hard?" she managed to whisper when his tongue brushed along her collarbone. "Will you make me forget everything you said?"

"Mm-hm." His hands hooked beneath her knees and pulled her thighs wide.

Tayshia's hands were steady as she pulled the drawstrings of his sweatpants. She pushed them down a bit, eyes never leaving his, and placed her hand over his boxers, over the hardness that had grown there. It was like a shock to his system, the effect of marveling at how much her confidence had grown with him since their first kiss causing a shock to his system that went beyond how good it felt to have her hand on him.

Ash sucked in his breath and his head dropped toward her shoulder. He placed heavy, wet kisses to her neck that caused her hand to squeeze over him.

"God, you have the sweetest, softest fucking hands," he groaned between kisses. His hand curved around the underside of her jaw, forcing her head to the right, toward the living room, so he could lave her skin with more. Tayshia's hands worked to pull the waistband of his pants outward so she could slip her hand down inside. The minute she wrapped her fingers around his cock, he lost any last semblance of control that he'd maintained up until this point. "*Oh, fuck,* I'm going to make sure you know just how made for me you are. How much you're made to be fucked. What a dirty, *dirty* girl you are."

As he said the words, he scraped his teeth against the junction of her neck and shoulder and bit down, causing her to cry out once more. Ash reached down between them, his eyes blackened with something borderline demonic as he grabbed her wrist in a vice and pressed on her pulse. With a gasp, her fingers stretched out and released him. His hands went to her knees, pushing until her feet were on the table and her legs were spread obscenely wide.

"As much as I love the feeling of your hand around my cock..." he breathed, his lips ghosting over her own as his hips rocked forward, causing him to slide her wetness up over her apex. "I think my little whore needs her clit played with first, hm?"

She gasped when he slid back and then forward again. He moved his hand to push against the inside of her knee, opening her wider. A groan echoed in his chest as he slid back and forth, back and forth, grinding his length against her.

It felt good.

Very good.

Like dancing beneath starlight, or swimming in a moonlit sea. Like seeing sunlight burst through the shadows of a rainy day, or watching fire light up the darkest of nights.

She was everything.

"This pathetic, desperate, needy, selfish cunt is mine," he said as he continued his agonizingly-slow slide. "And it's perfect. Absolutely fucking perfect."

They both gasped. She was so wet that his passage over her core was slick. He moved his hips faster, his head falling back as he bit his lower lip. Tayshia let out a high-pitched moan, and the sound jolted through him at the same pace as the lightning-whip of pleasure.

Ash was determined to get her off this way, before he'd even made it inside of her. That in and of itself—that attentiveness—made her body bow off the table and her hips roll to work with the cadence of his.

"And I'm gonna fuck you," he continued with an edge to his voice. "Again and again and again. Until you can't walk because your legs are shaking so much. Until you recognize who you belong to. Until you realize that it doesn't matter what you or I say...Or how much we fight...Because I will *always* want you."

Each of his words was punctuated by a stroke and a slide. Tayshia quivered beneath him, writhing as she climbed up to the cosmos for yet another time that night. Her teeth clenched as she got closer and closer to falling apart.

He wasn't even inside yet.

"You're gonna come for me like this," he said, and it was a statement, not a question.

Even though it was not a question, she answered it anyway, on the cusp of a stuttering gasp.

"I'm g-gonna—gonna come f-for you."

Ash was pinning her too hard. She could barely move—no. She couldn't move. There was no escape from what was coming, what was racing toward her like a shooting star that aimed to incinerate. And he loved to see it.

"Your moans are so cute," he taunted, breathy and strained. "So cute and needy when you tell me you're gonna come."

"Oh, God." She squeezed her eyes shut as she whined, her hips trying to twist. It was coming. He could always tell when she was going to come. There was no reprieve and nothing to stop it. "Please, Ash, please."

"What are you asking for?"

Every time she tried to roll her hips, he pressed harder on her knees. Like he was keeping her away from the friction and the speed she needed to finish. His hips continued their slow, steady sliding, never going faster. Never giving her what she needed.

"Please let me."

"Let you what, sweet girl?"

"Let me come, okay?" Her eyes snapped open for a desperate, frantic moment as a wave of pleasure rocked through her, capped off by his infuriating pace over her clit. "Let me come. Please."

"You can come like this, can't you?"

He was still taunting her. He knew she couldn't.

"I can't. I really can't."

"I think you're lying. You lie about everything, baby. How am I supposed to believe you?"

"Ash, I'm sorry. I'm sorry I've lied so much. But I'm telling the truth."

"Mm, I dunno. Lying brats don't always get what they want."

Her chest rose and rose, spine arching as her hand reached blindly upward for nothing and found only the teetering vase of roses. When her fingers smacked into it, it toppled over and rolled to the edge of the table. When she pleaded again, it was pitched high and tight over the sound of the glass thudding on the carpet.

"Too bad." Gone was the gentle coo—returned was the tone he'd been using earlier. The one that warned her not to disobey. "If you want me to fuck you, you'll come exactly like this."

Tayshia let out a desperate sob, trying yet again to move her hips. She was near-delirious at the denial, unsure of what to do when she knew she needed more. Her hips were only able to rock with the slightest of movements. He supposed her thigh muscles were burning by now.

"Ash, please," she sobbed. "I'll do anything, *anything*. Please."

He looked at her then, the corner of his mouth tilting up as he leaned down to kiss her. Their tongues curled together, the mingling of their saliva causing his hips to snap forward faster.

And it was exactly what she needed.

Tayshia broke the kiss to cry out, her orgasm slamming into her with the full force of a comet and sending stars and planets careening through her mind. He could see it reflected in the brown irises of her eyes.

Right as she started to convulse, his hips pulled back far enough for him to notch her entrance. He slid deep inside of her while she was coming, and it nearly made him scream.

"Good fucking *night!*" Tayshia exclaimed, all of the air in her lungs rushing from her mouth as he bottomed out inside of her. Her arms wrapped over his shoulders, fingers clawing at his back as he began to thrust, not stopping to grant her a reprieve. The table rocked with the force of it. She was so tight, still shuddering from her climax, and it was *everything.*

"Fuck, fuck, fuck," Ash groaned, long and low as her walls clenched tight around him. He let go of her knee so he could curve his arm beneath her and place his hand flat on her lower back, angling her hips upward. His head dropped to her shoulder in a moan as he stroked as deep as he could go.

It soothed a place inside of him that made crystals shatter and stars die.

There was something very, very intense about this situation. Something about this connection he felt between them that only seemed to twine them closer together with every drag inside of her. He didn't know what the Hell it was, but it certainly felt like it was written in the stars.

Ash's hand found her throat and squeezed as he rose up above her, using his solid stance on the floor to intensify his movements. Harder and harder, his long, slender fingers curled inward and his rings pressed depressions into her flesh. All she could do was whine as the lack of air brought them both closer to yet another climax. Her eyes were as endlessly fierce as a galaxy.

"Come on," he bit out between gritted teeth, his eyebrows pulling together. "Fuck me just like that. Feels so fucking tight. So good. So fucking perfect."

Tayshia's hand brushed his chest and he jolted. Moaned, because she'd just done something good.

His nipples were sensitive.

She scrambled to pay them special attention, both of her hands coming up to pull at them, tweaking and twisting. It sent shockwaves down his spine. His hips jerked forward even harder, slamming so far up into her that there was no room for anything else, but not so hard as to hit her where it would hurt.

"Oh, fuck. Fuck." He was nearly whining, turning his face away as she struggled for air beneath him. All she could do was squeak and make whimpering noises as he unraveled above her. "Please. Please, fuck. Oh, my—you're gonna make me fucking come inside of you. You're gonna make me *fucking* come inside of you, you *fucking* slut."

Tayshia's eyes rolled up and she came again, suddenly and in a way that made Ash hover between limbo and someone's heaven. He released his hold on her throat, soothing it with gentle fingers as she groaned, clenching around him once more.

When she came down from the skies and her breathing had settled, he pulled out. She had only a second to be puzzled before he'd flipped her onto her stomach and kicked her legs apart. She let out a yelp as he grabbed her hips and pressed back into her, his fingers twisting in the back of the shirt she wore, and in the depths of her hair.

Ash rammed into her, hot and wet and fast and deep. She shrieked, her fingernails scrabbling at the tabletop as he fucked the air out of her and brought himself hurtling right back into space.

He was absolutely fucking gone.

"It's all right." He sounded delirious as his fingers began a slow assault on her clit even though she was squirming at the contrast of hard to gentle. "It's all right. You feel so good, baby. So fucking good. So fucking beautiful. You're so damn beautiful. I love this *fucking* cunt almost as much as I love you."

What.

Tayshia wasn't expecting to hear him say that, and neither was her *lovable* cunt, because his admission caused a second, smaller orgasm that rocked through her body and made her moan from the recesses of her chest. It was unexpected for both of them. So unexpected, in fact, that it brought him right to the edge in spite of its weakness.

"Shit—" Ash breathed a laugh, his hips stuttering as he paused, holding himself propped with one hand on the table. He could feel her core squeezing, pulling at him. He groaned again. He wasn't gonna be able to hold back. Not with her. Not when he'd just fucking told her he loved her like a God damned idiot. "Fuck it. Fucking *fuck* it."

Tayshia lay there, still shivering and whimpering, while he used her body, picking up the pace of his thrusts with one hand on her hip and the other wrapping around her throat from behind. She allowed herself to be a conduit for his desire, even as his hips snapped so hard that he feared she would bruise.

When she pressed her hand over his, pushing it tighter around her throat, her submission caused him to fall over the edge.

Ash moaned, shoving the back of her shirt up and pulling out so he could paint her back with his come. His fingers stroked up and down her side, sounds that made his toes curl falling from her lips. She smiled over her shoulder at him, a catlike grin that showed she was pleased and hopeful that it was as good for him as it was for her spreading on her pretty face. He tucked himself back into his sweatpants and then went to get a towel. When he cleaned her up, he was gentle, caring as he placed kisses on the warm skin that covered her spine. Then, he helped her stand on tremulous legs with weak knees.

She wrapped her arms around his neck and pulled him into a sweet kiss, after which she whispered *thank you* and *I feel wanted* against his lips.

That night, she slept on the couch with him, cascading over his body with her head pillowed on his chest. They did not talk about the confession, and they did not talk about the argument.

It was probably for the best.

CHAPTER TWENTY

"I'm picking you up at 2:30, right?"

Tayshia paused with one foot out of the car and her hand on the handle. She nodded, albeit a bit awkwardly since they hadn't exactly found a new normal yet.

"Okay, I'll be here," he replied, his hands positioned on the bottom of the steering wheel, his head tilted back against the seat. "Have a good day."

"Thanks." She got out of the car and shut the door behind her, turning back to give him a small, almost shy wave.

It was something.

Spring break was over and Monday had come. Ash had finished what he wanted to do in the garden, but he hadn't gotten a chance to get the lights up yet. He planned on doing that today so he could take Tayshia out there when night fell. She hadn't seen the full effect of the garden yet, and he was looking forward to surprising her.

There weren't as many lights as he wanted, so he stopped at the hardware store to get some more. Then, he headed to the grocery store to get some stuff for a nice dinner, a new bouquet of flowers as well as a replacement for his mother's broken vase, and more candles than was necessary. He planned on giving her a *real* apology tonight, and telling her how proud he was of her for making it through her doctor's appointment.

She deserved to be praised, and he was prepared to grovel.

He spent an hour or so in the garden, ensuring everything was the way he wanted it to be. If it didn't look like he'd brought the stars down from the sky for her, he was going to cancel somebody. He strung the lights up on the trellises and across the garden from the top of each one. He made a beautiful network of lights, cross-crossing and dangling, so that when she stepped onto that cobblestone path that he'd made, she felt like she was walking into the sky. Into the Milky Way. Into the universe.

When he was done, he headed next door to see Steven for lunch, and they talked for a while about the garden. Steven was more interested in the romantic at-home date than he was the flowers, but he expected that. He was hopelessly in love with Ryo, after all, and he told Ash all about the romantic dates they'd been on since they wed.

While he spoke, Ash couldn't help but feel excited. He wanted to know if Tayshia would speak like this with her friends after she saw what he had planned. If she would sit around a table and gush about how romantic it was, how beautiful the garden was, how much she loved it. It was easy, too, to imagine them living in some sort of normal, alternate reality where there was nothing bad, and where romantic dates were as common for them as they were for his godparents.

Sometimes, he grew tired of dreaming.

After lunch, Ash went home to start cooking. What he was making would take hours, and he wanted it to taste perfect. Food was already difficult enough for her, so he hoped that by ensuring it tasted the best it could, he would be able to help her overlook her anxiety surrounding it. He spent as long as he could preparing it exactly as the recipe asked, and he chopped the vegetables early so he wouldn't have to do it later. He also planned on taking her to the mall so he could buy her a new outfit.

It was around two-o-clock, thirty minutes before he was supposed to pick her up at school, when his phone began to ring.

He set down the knife he was using and walked over to the kitchen counter to pick up his phone, the sounds of its vibration rattling on the countertop. One glance at the screen had his heart skipping a beat and a frown painting itself upon his face.

Elijah.

Should he answer it? He wasn't sure. He and Elijah hadn't spoken in almost two months. They didn't look at each other and on the off chance that they did, they quickly looked away. It was as though they'd never met. The deterioration of their friendship had happened so quickly, and he still wasn't sure why.

Maybe he was calling because he wanted to try and work through the disconnect? It was that small flame of hope and possibility that caused Ash to press the green button.

"Hey—"

"Ash, I need you to come to Southside right now. Elijah won't wake up, he—he's not waking up, and there's blood everywhere, and I'm freaking out. Like, I'm freaking out. You need to—"

"Tayshia?"

"*Yes*, it's me! Can you listen to me? I need you to come to Southside *right now* and help us! There's blood everywhere, and Elijah won't wake up!"

Ash's vision was hazed in red.

"You're supposed to be in class."

"I was—I was but we—we left." She was breathless, panicked. Clearly terrified. But All Ash could focus on was the fact that she'd lied right after goading him into sex.

Again.

"Why are you with Elijah? Why are you using his *phone*?"

"*Why aren't you listening to me*?!" she screamed, louder than he'd ever heard her scream at him before. "Elijah is unconscious because we were at the buffet and we saw Caden and his friends or lackeys or whatever they are, and when we came out, I was sick of it. I'm just *sick* of it. So I confronted him and Elijah tried to stop me, but Caden—Caden started h-hitting him. And then one of the other—other guys, he—he slashed the tires so we can't leave. Now, can you get in the car and come help us?!"

He couldn't think, couldn't think, couldn't think.

Why was she with Elijah when she was supposed to be in school?

Why were they on the southern side of town?

Why was she using his phone?

Why were they at a buffet?

Why was Elijah unconscious?

Why—

Caden.

Caden.

He exploded.

"Are you fucking *stupid*?!" he roared, so angry that he couldn't see straight. He dragged a hand through his hair and curved it on the top of his skull, distraught. "No, wait. I forgot. You've been starving your fucking brain for *months*. So yeah, *of course* you'd do something so fucking idiotic!"

Tayshia was silent save for the sound of her anxious breathing.

"Where are you?"

"Old Country Buffet. It's in that shopping center—"

"I know where it is," he snapped. "And is Caden gone?"

"No." Her voice shook like she was about to cry. "They're just standing against the wall of one of the buildings. Watching us."

"And Elijah's unconscious."

"Yes. They beat him badly, Ash. Really bad. They slammed his head against the wall and it was concrete. And there's people here. A—a crowd. No one seems to know what to do."

"Literally there is a police department for a reason."

"Some people did call the police. But Elijah is *bleeding*. Doesn't that mean anything to you?!"

Ash clenched is teeth, resisting the urge to tell her that no, he didn't care.

"I need you," she said. "I'm scared."

"You should be. I'm on my way."

He hung up the phone.

Running for his keys, he snatched them up, tucked his phone into his back pocket, and was out in the garage in seconds. The car was on the road before the garage door had even reached the driveway again.

What the Hell was going on? Why would Tayshia *do* this? Why were she and Elijah off on a completely different side of town together, and what on God's green *Earth* would possess her to do something so stupid as to confront Caden? Something so *dangerous*. Did her death wish extend to physical pain and depravity? Caden was a *sadist*.

He shouldn't have shouted at her. He should *not* have shouted at her. She was panicking, begging him for help, and he'd fucked up yet again, letting his temper control the words that came out of his mouth.

Why the fuck was she with Elijah?

So much for a romantic dinner date.

✵✵✵

When Ash pulled into the rundown shopping center on the south side of town, the first thing he saw was that the courtyard was mostly vacant, but there indeed was a small crowd of people that had gathered. They seemed simultaneously confused, angry, and shocked, hands on hips and mouths moving in frantic conversation.

Most of the storefronts in the center were empty, had For Sale signs, or notices in their windows that indicated that they were going out of business. The few shops that were still open without issue--a hardware store, a clothing boutique, and a couple of restaurants--seemed to have closed their doors early for the day. The fountain at the center of the courtyard was dirty and rusted, the stone cracked, and the water that spewed from the mouth of the cliche dolphin had turned a sickly green.

This was Ricky's side of town.

He spotted Elijah's car as close to the buffet as he could possibly have gotten, and he could see Caden and several other men gathered by the wall of the buffet.

As he got out of the car and looked over the top of Elijah's car roof, he saw them.

Tayshia was on her knees on the ground beside a prone Elijah, and there was blood streaming from her nose. She'd worn a lavender sundress that day and the strap was torn, leaving her tattooed shoulder bare. There were scrapes all over her body.

Elijah looked awful, blood seeming to have been coming from multiple places on his body, soaking through the white of his torn shirt. His face was a mottled disaster—It would almost certainly swell to immense proportions in the coming days. There was so much blood on the right side of his head that it was pooling on the ground beside him.

What the Hell did they *do* to him?

Tayshia looked up. The moment her eyes locked with Ash's, the fear on her face melted into a deep relief.

"Ash!" she cried. "Please, come help me wake him up!"

At the sound of her voice, several members of the assembled crowd addressed him, hollering that the police were on their way. Ash ignored them, rushing around the car. He barely spared Caden and his companions a second glance. He sunk into a crouch beside Elijah, pressing two of his fingers against his neck.

His pulse was intact.

"Go open the back door of my car," he said.

Tayshia did as he asked. She came back right as Ash was hefting Elijah up in his arms and turning to face the car. He stepped off the curb and around the back of Elijah's car so he could get to his own, ignoring the fact that the blood was staining his grey shirt. Tayshia went to the other side so she could reach in and grab the undersides of Elijah's arms. She pulled while Ash held Elijah's calves, and then he was in. They shut the car doors at the same time and gazed at one another over the top of his car.

He was angry with her. More than angry. He was enraged. The questions that he'd been asking himself since he left his house were swirling inside his head, dancing to the tune of a furious song.

"I'm sorry," she said, her voice cracking. "I don't know what happened. I don't know why I walked up to them."

Ash simply stared at her, unsure of how to proceed. He couldn't accuse her of cheating because they weren't officially together. But he felt betrayed. Which feelings were valid? How was he supposed to look at her the same?

Wait.

Why was Tayshia's nose bleeding? Why was the strap of her sundress ripped? Why was she covered in scrapes?

New questions began to stir, churning like a stormy sea as he started to put the pieces together.

He moved around the car so fast that Tayshia backed away from him.

"I'm sorry, Ash!" she said, eyes wild and panicked. She held up hands that were bloody. "I'm sorry! I can explain—"

She cut herself off when Ash grabbed her wrists and twisted her hands so that he could glare down at her palms. It looked like while one hand was scraped, the other had been slashed with a blade of some sort.

The bloody nose was only the tip of the iceberg.

His horrified gaze traveled upward, scouring her body, suddenly seeing things he hadn't noticed before. Cuts and scrapes on her arms, her shoulders, across one collarbone. Blood trickling from scraped knees and a larger abrasion on her thigh that looked like she'd been dragged across the sidewalk. Her hair was a mess, one bun unraveling and the other loosened as though fingers had sunk into her hair and used the it for a handhold. Her left cheek was scraped from temple to chin and smeared with dark red.

When their eyes finally met again, he felt his fury catching fire, flaring into an inferno that burned like Hellfire.

"What did he do to you?"

"It's not—It was—"

Ash's hand lashed out and caught her gently by the chin. He lifted his own, speaking quietly.

"Tell me what he did to you. Now."

She looked down, her arms coming up to embrace herself, one hand curving into her own waist and the other crossing her chest to grip her shoulder. "There was a weird look in his eye, in Caden's. And I tried to run. But he caught me. He dragged me across the ground and they kicked me. That's when Elijah tried to help. They decided to beat him instead."

Every star in his mind died at once.

He could see it, displayed before his darkening vision like a horror movie. Tayshia, staggering backward as she realized Caden was not someone she could just *confront* like Kieran. That he was a monster, and that he didn't care if she was a girl. He could imagine what it must have felt like, turning and trying to run, only to have a man grab her by the hair and drag her kicking and screaming across the concrete. What fear she must have felt when she was on the ground, a group of people towering over her. What pain when their heavy shoes connected with her arms, sides, hips, legs, and face. He could imagine her pleading for them to stop.

Just like Paris.

Slowly, he turned his head to cast a fiery, murderous glance behind him.

Caden was leaning back against the wall of the building, one foot kicked back against the concrete and his arms crossed over his chest. The glint of his switchblade showed beneath his elbow, like he was showing off his half-hearted attempt at hiding it. His crimson hair had fallen into his eyes and across his spider tattoo, giving him a roguish look.

And he was smirking.

"Get in the car," Ash growled to Tayshia, not taking his eyes off of him.

"What are you going to do?"

At this, he turned his glare upon her. Her eyes widened and she took a step back.

"Get in the car, and don't get out."

He walked away without staying to see if she obeyed. Caden watched him approach without concern, his friends ceasing their conversations to turn and mirror their leader's condescending disposition. They varied in height and style of dress, but one thing remained constant between them.

They all had blood on their hands.

"Hi, Ash," Caden said in a sing-song tone. "Come to get a little taste of what we did to our precious Tayshia? Or you trying to figure out how to make some money?"

Ash came to a stop amidst the group, his gaze hot on Caden and his hands relaxed at his sides.

"I don't need any money."

"I mean, I can talk to Ricky for you." The patronizing tone set Ash's teeth to clenching. "He might let you stand guard at the door. Kind-of like a puppy."

Ash watched him like a predator stalking its unsuspecting prey. He did not raise his voice. "I don't need you to do shit, Caden."

Caden let out a short laugh. "So I'm guessing you want to know what I did to her. Did she give you the details, or should I start with the way she screamed when I dragged her by the hair?"

"Start with where you fucked up."

For the first time, Ash saw a flicker of something in Caden's eyes. Something he might have called nervousness if it didn't disappear as quickly as it did.

"Look, Ash." Caden placed a hand on Ash's shoulder. His eyes were glittering like black diamond. "We have a history, you and I. A relationship, if you want to call it that. We've known each other for years. That warrants you a modicum of respect. Which is why we stopped, and why I decided to play with that other guy. I *enjoy* this, Ash. I *enjoy* inflicting pain for the sheer sake of doing it."

Ash nodded, rubbing the line of his jaw with the side of his hand. He gazed off into the distance, into that angry red that tinged his vision with fury, and he pretended to seriously consider what Caden was telling him. Pretended he actually cared for one iota of Caden's opinions, excuses or existence. Pretended to listen while Caden spun his webs and bared his fangs.

"The sooner you realize that I will *never* stop finding it incredibly and *insanely* interesting to watch the way you lose your shit over your little girlfriend, the sooner you'll realize that beating the living shit out of her was the most fun I've had all year. She looks awfully pretty in black and blue, don't you think?"

The haze of red darkened, and Ash blacked out.

He hauled back and decked Caden across the face, fist flying and slamming into his to the tune of a satisfying crunch. Caden's head snapped backward. He staggered and hit the wall behind him. The guys around him shook their shock off and started towards Ash.

"*Leave him!*" Caden roared, rubbing his bloody nose with the back of his hand. The look he gave Ash was pure murder. "This is between him and I."

Caden rushed toward him, but he was ready and a Hell of a lot angrier. He sidestepped him at the last minute, using the low swing of his left hand to catch him right in the solar plexus. Caden ran right into it, the air rushing out of him with a sickly sound as he collapsed. Ash grabbed him by the front of the shirt, dragged him up to his knees, and hit him again. And again. And again. All with the silence that surrounds a burning star.

It was no contest.

The ease with which he was able to slam him sideways onto the concrete was almost comical. Ash landed on one knee, resting his forearm atop his thigh for support as he grated the spider tattoo against the ground with a vicious, twisting hand. Caden made a gurgling sound as blood from his now-missing front teeth erupted from his mouth. Ash leaned down closer, his lips nearing Caden's bleeding ear.

"If you touch what's mine again, I'll slit your throat and watch you drown."

He gave Caden one last shove to the head and stood up. He glanced at Caden's friends, who seemed to be terrified enough to back away at the mere wither of his stare. His knuckles were aching, but it was a good ache. A rightful one.

The ache that comes with vengeance.

Caden pushed himself up onto his hands and knees, spitting bright red blood out onto the pale concrete. Satisfied, Ash turned around and walked away, heading back for the cars. As he did, he heard the sirens in the distance, getting closer.

Shaking the pain out of his hands as he returned to the only person he cared about in the vicinity.

Her.

She was running to meet him before he'd even made it out of the courtyard and onto the pavement of the parking lot. When she connected with his body, throwing her arms around his neck, he couldn't help it. He wrapped his arms low around her waist and buried his face in the crook of her shoulder for a tiny respite. Just knowing that she'd gotten hurt because of him--*again*--was enough to make him forget about the fact that the reason why she'd run into Caden was because she and Elijah were here together, alone.

But only for a moment.

He placed his hands on her waist and pushed her back, glaring over her head at the sight of two police cars pulling into the lot. He could be under no illusions as to the reasons why he was here, why she was here, and why he was covered in the blood of four different people, including himself.

"Get in the car like I told you to, Tayshia," he said quietly, looking down into her eyes with as much of the betrayal he felt as he could muster into his own. "We need to get him to the hospital."

Before he could get into the car, a police officer approached him. After a small exchange of words in which Ash left out the fact that he'd fought Caden and that Elijah might be in critical condition, the police officer agreed to let him go to the hospital. Behind him, the sounds of the crowd hurling accusations towards Caden, demanding he be arrested could be heard.

The police officer was confident that they would not hear from Caden again, and he assured them that they'd send someone to the hospital to take Elijah and Tayshia's statements. Though this relieved Ash, it did nothing to assuage his anger. Tayshia had manipulated him one too many times.

There might not be a way back from this.

☼☼☼

"I'll stay until the police get here," Ash said, sinking down into the cushioned seat beside Tayshia. The emergency room was fairly empty, giving them plenty of spaces to have chosen while they waited for the doctors to tend to Elijah. "The nurse said he's gonna be okay, but that he has some internal bleeding."

Tayshia buried her bruised face in her hands for a moment, dragging her fingers beneath her eyes as though she had a headache. She'd already been seen by a doctor, who'd determined that she was in much better shape than Elijah was. A nurse had bandaged her up and sent her on her way. Now, they sat and waited for more news.

"I don't know what I was thinking," she said.

"Yeah, neither do I."

"I was just tired of Caden scaring us and controlling us. You didn't want to move back into your family home, and it's ruining us."

Ash bounced his leg as he placed his elbow on the arm of the chair and stroked his chin.

"The house isn't what's ruining us, Tayshia," he finally said, giving her a dark look. "You are."

She turned to look at him, her brow furrowed. "What?"

"Why were you with Elijah?"

"Not for the reasons you think."

"And what reasons do you assume I think?"

"I'm not cheating on you."

He struggled to contain his temper and maintain his calm, quiet tone. "Then what the fuck were you doing at a restaurant with him across town in the middle of the day?"

"It's hard to explain."

"Well, let me make it easier for you. I'm guessing every time you went out with *friends*, it was him?"

She was silent, her gaze lowered to the ground and her expression guilty.

"And I'm guessing that you found a way to manipulate and trick him into buying you food that you then purged in a bathroom somewhere. He probably has no idea what you're capable of."

Once again, she said nothing.

He leaned forward, hanging his head between his hands as he fought back the urge to cry.

She *was* ruining them. Every choice she made, every step she took, was a step in the direction of their destruction. Tayshia was destroying him, dissecting him limb from limb, and she was burning the pieces to ash simply because it served her.

He couldn't take it anymore.

"I'm so tired of tearing myself apart for you, of making decisions that put myself in danger emotionally or mentally or physically just to keep you safe. For you, someone who doesn't give a fuck about whether or not she lives or dies. And you know what?" He lifted his head and looked at her with tears of ire stinging his eyes, blurring his vision. "I'd do it again and again and a-fucking-gain. I'd hurt everyone who so much as *looks* at you wrong, and I'd kill them if I had to. Do you not grasp that? I would *kill* for you. And that's the fucking problem."

"Ash—"

"Don't. Just…Don't."

He stood up right as the nurse came through the double doors with a smile on her face.

"Good news! He's awake. Would you like to come see him?"

Ash glared down at Tayshia, who was trying to quickly wipe her tears before the nurse saw.

"She'll be right in."

CHAPTER TWENTY ONE

The days that had passed since what happened with Caden and Elijah were long and lonely.

When he'd returned home, he'd put all the food away in the refrigerator. He'd taken all the candles and put them in a drawer in the kitchen.

He left the flowers in the vase. He'd bought those to send a message—albeit a different message, but a message all the same. The embarrassment wasn't enough to overcome the anger. He was tired.

When Tayshia had returned from the hospital, bandaged in a few places, she informed him that the police had arrested Caden, and that they'd been looking at him for a long time. He would not be bothering them ever again.

They had gone back to not speaking. The only time they were in the general vicinity of each other was in his car to and from school, and at meals. After school, she stayed in the room the entire time and only came down for dinner. She acted like he and the roses weren't there, and so did he.

One day, he'd apologize for what he'd said, but not until he found out the truth behind her and Elijah's friendship. Something didn't sit right with him and even though he couldn't name it, he knew there was something more to the things he'd accused her of in the hospital hallway. There was something she was still hiding.

The night everything happened with Elijah, she came home when it was dark, having called Ryo for a ride home from the hospital. This surprised Ash. When she'd entered the house, he'd been watching TV on the couch and was even more surprised to see that Ryo had followed her inside. With tears still falling down her cheeks, she'd walked up to Ash's old bedroom without saying anything to him, leaving Ryo and Ash to talk.

"Elijah's gonna be just fine," he'd said, sitting down beside him on the couch. "They're keeping him for a couple of days, and his mom's there now. She'll make sure he gets the rest he needs. But he'll be back in school by Monday, just like you."

"Okay," Ash had said, turning the volume on the TV down. He cast Ryo a wary glance. "So, were you here for dinner, or something? I can heat something up."

"No, son. I'm here to have a little talk with you."

Suddenly, the tears had made sense.

Ash sat there while Ryo lectured him for his temper. The embarrassment had increased tenfold, sickening him and reminding him that if anyone saw the way they treated each other, they'd be horrified. Repulsed. There may even be some level of hatred. And from what Ryo said, Tayshia hadn't been able to keep it inside. She'd burst out into tears the second his godfather asked her how she was doing.

Their relationship felt like poison.

Now, it was another Monday, and Ash was returning to school. As always, he waited for her by the garage. She seemed to have a bit of trouble as they got in the car due to her bruises, but overall, she seemed all right. The ride was silent save for the music and the tapping of her thumbs on the screen of her phone. He was mildly curious as to who she was talking to, but he wasn't about to ask.

They went their separate ways after they entered the building, Tayshia's locker being on a different floor from his. He was unsurprised to get condolences left and right, including from people who had once given him nasty looks at the beginning of the year. Hell, even Kieran gave him a sympathetic nod.

It was annoying.

He wished more people knew what a shitty person his father was. He wished they knew that he wasn't grieving him, but the life he'd destroyed. The family he'd shattered. The mom he'd killed. He wished they knew he hated him.

It was sometime towards the middle of his second class that he got a text from Tayshia telling him that she was going to be in a meeting with an adviser at lunch, and that she wouldn't be there. He didn't have the energy to argue with her, but he sure as Hell didn't believe her, so he didn't reply.

He almost didn't go to the cafeteria, knowing how likely it was that Elijah would be there. But he was hungry, he had a headache, and he was in a bad mood.

What did it matter if he added another problem to his roster?

Everyone stared at him, leaning in to whisper to themselves as he walked over to his favorite table by the window. He paid them no mind. His headache raged on, having not abated since that morning. His classes had been an irritation, especially given the fact that his teachers seemed overly-sympathetic and talked to him in hushed tones, like a child who'd just had a bad dream.

Except it wasn't a dream. None of it was.

His dad was dead. He and Tayshia hated each other. There was nothing but pain. Cold, dark pain.

Why did everything have to *hurt* so much?

"You look like shit."

Ash glanced up, his forehead propped against his palm. His spoon was stirring through his stroganoff in an absent manner as he stared at the specks in the tabletop laminate until they blurred. He blinked to refocus his vision and saw that Elijah and Andre were sitting down across from him. Elijah looked a bit bruised up and he wore a compression wrap on his left wrist, but aside from a pretty wicked black eye, he seemed all right. He must have said something to Andre to explain the bruising, because he seemed uninterested in it.

"Yeah, well," Ash said. "I feel like shit."

"You sick?" Andre asked as he plated up some food.

"In the head, yeah."

"I've been wondering that for years," Andre joked.

Ash sneered at him. He hadn't told him what happened with Caden, knowing that he'd want to hop in the car and head down to the jail so he could bribe a police officer to let him jump Caden in the damn cell.

He took a bite. It tasted like nothing

"Hey, wait. Where's Tayshia?" Andre asked.

Elijah and Ash spoke at the same time.

"She's with her teacher."

"She went to a meeting with her teacher."

Ash felt a violent, possessive rage washing over him, nearly melting him into a puddle of fury right there on the bench. He would have bent his spoon if he didn't care about drawing more attention to himself.

He was done.

"I've fucking had it with you, Elijah," he snarled. "What the fuck do you want with my girlfriend? You know she's mine, right? Did she tell you about the fact that we're practically fucking together?"

Andre dropped his jaw, as did several of the nearby students.

"Not from what she told me," Elijah snarled right back, his bruised, swollen face contorting into an expression of ire. "According to her, you treat her like shit and yell at her. She spends her nights crying herself to sleep. According to her, you're a selfish jerk who only cares about what he wants, and you'll do whatever you can to make sure she does exactly what you tell her to do. According to *her*, the two of you are through."

There was no way Elijah knew the whole story. There was *no fucking way* he knew the extent of Tayshia's manipulation and her lies. How she used her body to get him to buy binge food. How she *admitted* to manipulating Ash into finding a way to let her purge, to think it wasn't as bad as long as he was there.

"You don't even realize it, do you?" Ash said with an incredulous laugh. "She's *manipulating* you, Elijah. She's making sure you only know one side so you'll be on *hers*."

"If you think she's so manipulative, then *why are you with her*?"

He had no idea why he was with her. He used to, but now he couldn't think of anything other than the fear of her dying. That was the only thing that mattered. Keeping her alive. Not letting her die. Not letting her *leave* him.

Why?

Elijah smirked and Ash knew there was no going back from this.

For any of them.

"She can't wait for the chance to never see you again, Ash. She said the worst mistake she's ever made was thinking you were better than exactly who we all know you are. A felon, a failure, and an abuser."

A bad son.

A failure.

A betrayer.

A monster.

He didn't know what to say. He was so overwhelmed and destroyed by Elijah's words that he felt like he'd forgotten how to breathe. It hurt. It hurt badly. He knew he'd fucked up, but had he really fucked up that badly? He'd been fighting so hard to keep her alive, to make sure she was okay, and he'd rendered himself an *abuser*?

Had she ever really wanted him at all?

Ash couldn't handle this. He felt like his heart was ripping itself to shreds inside of his chest. It was such a visceral pain that it almost felt like the day of his mother's death. Like if he looked down, he'd see his mother's unseeing eyes, glazed over as they stared up at him.

"Exactly," Elijah added, driving the stake deeper, twisting it and watching him bleed with a glee in his eyes that showed him he didn't care they were once lifelong friends. "She's trying to get better, and all you do is make everything about you. She said you disrespected her and broke her trust, and you can't ever seem to put yourself in her shoes for even one moment. You told her you didn't want her, Ash, so don't act surprised that she wants nothing to do with you anymore."

"Whoa, dude," Andre said, holding a hand sideways against Elijah's chest. He frowned at him. "I don't know what's going on between you two, but that's a little outta pocket, don't you think? What are you even *talking* about?"

"I'm only telling him what he needs to hear. He's a piece of shit, and he needs to know we all see it."

"All right, but you ain't know their relationship," Andre said, sounding angry. Ash was grateful for it. "Who is *'we'*? This ain't no *'we.'* You don't know the conversations they be having, or the things they been through. You can't definitively say someone's not good enough for anyone. You're not a god. You don't get to decide."

There was silence, and then Andre hammered the nail in the coffin.

"I think you should sit somewhere else, Elijah."

"Are you serious?"

"As serious as a fuckin' heart attack."

A few moments went by of the two of them bickering back and forth, but Ash felt like there was cotton in his ears. It felt like someone had crushed his chest beneath a boulder. He couldn't lift his gaze from the table.

Elijah was right, and Ash was in denial. Everything was about him. What he wanted. What he felt. His own fears. Even the day Tayshia had called him for help, his first thought had been to get angry at her for lying. From his point of view, he was doing everything he could to protect her. From hers, he was wrapping her in chains so he could lock her in a gilded cage.

But who was the person she ran to? Elijah.

Who was the person she'd been hiding from him for months? Elijah.

Who was the person she seemed able to trust more than Ash? Elijah.

He couldn't be here anymore.

Ash got up, leaving his tray of food and heading out of the cafeteria.

He stopped at the end of the hallway and leaned against the wall, tipping his head back. This was the most exhausting thing. Coping with Tayshia's disorder while trying to cope with his mother's death? Coping with the fear of losing her the same way? Wondering whether or not she was manipulating him, lying, or off with Elijah? Knowing that she cried herself to sleep every night, while also knowing that he wasn't the sole cause for that?

Sometimes, he felt too soft. Sometimes, he wished he could get a little apathy and inject it into his veins. Anything to make this hurt less.

"Ash!"

Ash, who had closed his eyes against his intensifying headache, cracked them open. Elijah was walking down the hall towards him. Andre wasn't with him, so Ash assumed Elijah insisted he talk to him alone.

What the Hell was his problem? Why couldn't he leave him alone?

He'd already slashed him open.

"You can't just walk away from this. You're *abusing* her. You think I'm just gonna look away from that?" Elijah came to a stop in front of him, hands in fists at his sides and a dark look on his face.

"No. I'm not claiming that," Ash said, gesturing angrily with his hand. "I'm not going to let you call me an abuser when you don't know the whole fucking story. Tayshia lives a life of lies, and she'll do anything to make sure she has room to destroy herself."

"She doesn't lie to *me*. She doesn't *manipulate* me. But I'm sure you'd like me to think that. That you'd like everyone to think that."

"I don't care what anyone thinks," Ash said, taking a step toward him. "Least of all you. You don't know our relationship."

"I know everything she's told me." Elijah lifted his bruised chin, looking up at Ash with no fear or trepidation. "And I know you're a horrible person."

"What are you not understanding? Tayshia wants to *die*. She wants to die, and she's going to say whatever she can to get you to believe that because I'm standing in the way of it."

"No. That's not true. The only reason why you want me to think that is to save your own ass."

"The only reason why you think you know what's going on is because she *told* you that. We got into a fight and I said something I didn't mean, and what did she do? She went running right to you--someone who had no idea what was going on--so she could get someone to believe whatever she told them. And *you* were stupid enough to fall for it."

"And she's been running to me for a lot longer than last week, Ash. Don't you get that?" In the wake of Ash's shock at his admission, he came toward him. "Every time you guys have a fight, she comes to *me*. Every time you made her feel worthless, she came to *me*. When you told Kieran what happened to her and she found out, who do you think she texted? *Who's* the stupid one?"

Ash clenched his hand into a fist. "You don't know what you're talking about."

"Did you or did you not scream that she'd been raped where anyone could fucking hear?"

"You were there. You know that I didn't do it intentionally."

"It doesn't matter your intentions. You violated her."

Elijah needed to shut the fuck up. He had no idea what Tayshia had been through. Ash had *been* there. He'd been inside her memory, inside her *nightmare*. He knew what it was like to not be able to breathe. He knew what she looked like when she broke down and sobbed until her heart was no longer in her chest. He'd seen the blood and knew how much the man in Paris had destroyed her, and Elijah was just an outsider.

"Shut your fucking mouth, Elijah," he whispered, blinking tears away. "You don't know the first thing about violation. And you don't know half of what we've been through. You only know only what she's shown you. She's it for me. I'd do absolutely fucking anything for her, and I'd do it without hesitation. Does that not make sense to you? I would *die* for her."

Elijah narrowed his eyes. "There's a lot that makes sense to me, Ash, but I'm not sure this does. How does someone say they'd die for someone, but go out of their way to hurt them?"

"You don't understand. It's not like that."

He'd spent his entire life making the wrong choices. Choices that ended up getting other people hurt. He knew now that he shouldn't have been making choices that hurt the people he wanted to save. If he had to control her food to make sure she *ate*, then he'd do it. If he had to force her to leave the bathroom door open so he could make sure she didn't purge, then so be it.

When she came out on the other side, alive and healthy, she'd thank him.

"Now, you've said what you needed to say to destroy me," Ash said, his voice breaking. "Can you just leave me alone?"

Elijah closed his eyes, his fist shaking at his side like he wanted to hit him. Ash wished he would dare.

"If I find out you're hitting her, I'll—"

"*Don't you fucking say that shit to me!*" Ash roared, shoving him backward so hard that his back hit the lockers. "If you *ever* accuse me of doing that again, I will fucking gouge your eyes out, Elijah."

"Maybe that's because you know I'm right!" Elijah shoved him back. "If you don't want people to think you're an abuser, then *maybe* don't abuse her. Then she won't tell people like me—people she *trusts*—that you *are*!"

He was so mad. He was so mad. He was so *fucking* mad.

"*Hey!*" A teacher was barreling down the hall towards them, an enraged expression on his face. "Robards! Ires! You better back up off each other *now*!"

Ash moved backward, glaring first at the teacher and then down at Elijah. He held his stare as long as he could and then, right as the teacher was skidding to a halt beside them, he turned and walked away. The teacher screamed after him, but he ignored him.

He didn't care if he got in trouble, suspended, or kicked out of the program. Nothing mattered anymore. The lengths Tayshia would go to keep a hold of her disorder were so horrific that he couldn't breathe.

As he reached the doors leading out to the parking lot, he let the tears fall. But in the back of his mind, he felt something nagging him, needling into the core of his brain.

How did Elijah know there was something she needed to get better from?

✫✫✫

Ash turned the TV off. He couldn't watch it for a second more. His head hurt. His eyes were puffy from crying. He'd been beating himself up for nearly four hours, trying to figure out where he went wrong, how he could fix it, and how to deal with his anger.

How could Tayshia do this to him? How could she be so cruel?

If he was an abuser, didn't that mean he was no better than his father? His father, who used to throw him down the stairs, punch him until he bled, and who held a gun to his head to scare him into helping him rob an ice cream shop.

Didn't that mean he deserved to die?

He wasn't an abuser. He wouldn't claim that title for himself.

In fact, he would treat her so well that she had no choice but to admit that *she* was the problem.

The moment she walked in the door, he stood up from the couch.

"What the fuck is wrong with you, Ash?!" she shrieked, dropping her backpack onto the floor without closing the front door. "I had to call your godfather for a ride *again* because you can't get the stick out of your ass *again,* all because you're pissed at me for who the Hell knows. I waited in the fucking library for you, and you never showed up. Everyone said you and Elijah fought in the hallway? What the heck was that about? You—what are you doing? Ash, what are you *doing*?"

He came to a stop in front of her, his gaze as intense as sunlight as he walked her backward. He pushed the front door shut with his left hand and, right when her back hit the front door, he was bending to kiss her.

"What are you doing?" she gasped.

"I'm gonna take care of you," he whispered, his eyes slowly sliding open to lock with hers. The intensity of his gaze caused her to look away from him, but he was uninterested in her random bouts of shyness. He took her by the chin and forced her head back towards him. Their eyes met again and she began to tremble.

"Unless you tell me to stop," he breathed, kissing his way down the side of her neck as his hands sought beneath the hem of her dress. "Tell me to stop."

"And if I—" She swallowed a moan when his tongue licked at her pulse. "—if I don't?"

"Then I'll make sure you feel so good that it makes you cry." His hands squeezed her rear, then slid down to her thighs so he could pick her up.

"And if I do?"

"Then you won't know what it feels like when I don't hold myself back from what I want to do to you."

He held her gaze, knowing by the blush on her cheeks that this was different from the last times they'd slept together. The times when she was able to dissociate and turn it into something bad, negative, or less emotional than he wanted it to be. The times when she convinced and manipulated him into degrading her when he didn't *want* to. When he wanted to worship her body and make her sing praises to the sky.

She slid her hands to the back of his neck, averting her eyes before dipping her head to press a soft kiss to his lips. He kissed her back and kept kissing her, tongues laving against one another's as he carried her up the stairs to his parents' bedroom. By the time they were shut inside of it, she was grinding against him, her body shaking with desire, head turning this way and that to deepen the kiss with her fervor. He set her on her feet.

"Get on the bed and put your hands by the headboard," he said before he walked over to his parents' dresser. He opened his father's drawer and pulled out one of his ties.

"What are you doing?" Tayshia asked in a small voice as he clambered on top of her and sat on her hips. Her hands trembled by the bars of the headboard.

"Hush."

Ash wrapped the tie around her wrists, crossing it over so he could keep them together, and then double knotted it to one of the wooden bars. She immediately tried to move her wrists and twist them, and while there was some give, she was as trapped as he wanted her.

This time, she would not dissociate. He'd make sure of it.

"Ash? What did I do?"

"What makes you think you did something wrong?" he asked, knowing full well she was terrified that Elijah had told him what she said. He slid her dress up, up, up, until he was taking in the sight of her chest heaving.

"Nothing. I mean I didn't do a-a-any*thing*." Her breathing hitched, her voice escaping in a rush when he pressed hot, open-mouthed kisses to the undersides of her breasts beneath the wire of her bra. Her back arched and her hips squirmed. "Ash, Ash, wait."

He stopped, lifting his head as he skimmed her sides. Beneath him, he felt her pressing her thighs together. "Are you telling me to stop?"

"No."

"Then what's the matter?"

"I want to know what I did wrong."

"Why would you ask me that, baby?" he said, his fingers blazing a gentle path along her ribcage so as to not exacerbate the remnants of her bruising. They slid up, beneath her bra.

He covered her breasts fully with his hands, caressing them with reverence and sensuality. She closed her eyes, gasping and arching into them. He dropped his head, running his tongue along the soft skin between them.

"Why would you ask me anything when you taste so sweet?" His gaze snapped up to meet hers as he crawled up her body. "Have you ever thought that maybe, I just want to eat my meal in peace?"

There was the smallest flicker of confusion in her eyes, before he kissed her yet again, silencing any word that might have thought to break forth. He tilted his head and devoured her, his hips rolling against hers as his hands slid up the backs of her arms. He felt her pulling against the headboard, and his stomach twisted with the sheer power he felt.

When he brought his right hand down to slip it between her legs, massaging her core outside her underwear, she whimpered into their kiss. Her hips writhed and she tried to break the kiss to groan, but he followed her. No matter how many times she tried, he swallowed every sound she made. He consumed each one like they were made of sugar. Like her tongue was the anathema to the pain she'd caused him, and her cries were the antidote to her poison.

"Ash," she mumbled against his lips, the headboard rattling as she pulled against her bonds. "Ash, please. Inside."

He ignored her, continuing his slow, torturous assault on her from outside the fabric. She widened her thighs, trying to push up into his fingers, but he pulled back infinitesimal amounts until she stopped trying.

"God," she gasped, her head tilting back to get a breath. She sounded distraught. "Oh, what did I do? What did I do?"

She knew what she did.

Ash peppered her throat with light kisses that made her sensitive skin pebble and her arms struggle against the tie yet again. Her fingers curled and her feet pressed flat to the mattress, giving her purchase so she could grind her hips more firmly against his hand.

"Do you need more?" he asked innocently, licking her collarbone, nipping it with his teeth.

"*Yes*," she cried. "Yes, please. I need more."

"Ask me nicely. Use your words."

"Please, Ash. *Please*. I need you inside."

"What do you need inside you?"

"Your fingers."

"Complete sentences, please."

She stammered the words out. "I-I need your f-fingers, p-please."

He obliged, slipping his fore and middle fingers past the barrier of her panties and into the depths of her heat. She keened like she was lamenting the loss of her emptiness. Her fingers splayed out, wrists twisting almost violently within the circle of the satin tie. Her head fell back as her chest arched high enough to touch his.

"Such a good girl," he purred, ignoring the hair that had fallen into his eyes as he gazed down at her. "I'm so proud of you. You're doing so good."

He twisted his hand and pressed against the back of her pubic bone, stroking the spot over and over, enjoying the feeling of her hips twitching and thighs squeezing his sides. Her eyes opened wide.

"Oh, my God. Oh, that feels so good." Her chest spasmed as she choked on air. "You're gonna make me come, Ash."

"Am I?"

She nodded frantically. "I'm like, right there. *Oh, God, I'm—*"

He slid his fingers out of her body immediately, right when she went rigid, and she whimpered at the return of the emptiness. He watched her with an almost blank expression, bringing his fingers to his lips to suck her arousal off of them while he looked into her eyes. In the lines of her brow, he could see her confusion increasing.

"Why did you stop?" she panted, her expression pitiful. "I was right there."

"Because I'm hungry."

Ash slid down her body, his hands pressing her thighs open as he settled on his stomach between them. He tasted her gently, almost hesitantly. Like an hors d'oeuvre he'd never had before. And she tasted divine.

Or perhaps it was her helplessness that tasted the sweetest.

Her breaths became staccato, like they always did before she came. He pulled back, looking up at her and catching her gaze. His tone was commanding.

"Hold it."

"Boy, have you lost your damn *mind*?"

"Don't disappoint me, sweet girl."

"I don't know if I can, Ash, *please*. Please don't make—" She let out a soft scream when he ran his tongue upward through her center, dipping it inside to taste her, and then he moved it up to circle her clit. Her hips jerked against his mouth and the headboard once again rattled. "I can't. I really can't."

He stopped.

"*Hold it.*"

Her thighs shook and she whined. "Ash, I *can't*."

"If you come, I'll punish you," he said, and then, without taking his eyes off of her, he pressed the flat of his tongue against her.

Tayshia's eyes rolled up into her head and her brows came together. "Ash, please. Please. I'm begging you. Don't do that again."

He did it again. Her thighs flexed beneath his hands, trying to push together. She let out a series of panting moans, insisting that she couldn't hold it any longer, and he stopped.

"I'm gonna cry."

"Good," he said. "One more time for me."

She sobbed when he tasted her again, consuming every last drop of arousal that was dripping out of her body. The poor headboard held on for dear life as she pulled against it, trying to escape the torture of his tongue. He held her firmly, keeping her pinned to the point of bruising. The pace of her breathing turned to near-hyperventilation and strangled whines. He could feel her quivering.

"Please, God, please," she begged through her tears. "I need to come. I *need* it."

"Please *who*?" He hummed in disapproval, kissing her in a way that made her back lift completely. If it weren't for the bindings around her wrists, she might have sat up. "I don't like that."

"Just *fuck* me already!"

"Please *who*?" he said again, raising his voice in anger.

She let out a sob of frustration. "Please, *Ash*."

"There's a good girl. Ride my tongue now."

He stuck his tongue out and she wasted no time. Her hips rolled, grinding her cunt against his mouth. He devoured her like he was starving for her and only her. Like his sole mission in life was to make her come so hard she passed out.

But then, when she was whimpering and gasping, her body starting to go rigid, he pulled back.

Again.

"Why won't you let me *come*?" she sobbed in desperation, her eyes squeezed shut.

She opened her eyes to see him rising up on his knees, sliding his belt out of the buckle and dropping it onto the bed. He pushed his jeans and boxers down.

"Shh, shh, baby. Be a good girl for me, okay?" He hooked his hands beneath the backs of her knees and pushed them up until they were near her chest. Rising up on his own knees, he ensured that when he slid inside her, no part of his body touched her clit. "Relax. I'm just gonna enjoy you for a while."

The sounds she made when he started thrusting were heavenly.

"You know how perfect you feel? How beautiful you are?"

"Don't say that. It's not true."

"Yes, it is. Look at me. *Yes,* it is."

Heat rose to her cheeks.

"Will you be good for me and make me come? Huh? Will you be good for me and make me come all over that pretty little cunt?"

"I'll do anything for you if you just let me come," she pleaded, her voice cracking with distress.

"God, you're so fucking beautiful. So pretty. So, so fuckin' pretty."

"Stop."

"You want me to stop fucking you?"

She shook her head. "I meant stop saying that."

"What?" He thrust harder, each one taking him to the heights. "Telling you that you're the most beautiful girl in the world? That you're everything to me?"

"Stop it, Ash!" She glared at him, but it didn't last long when he began to pound into her, his fingers digging into her knees. "Stop, stop, stop!"

"Stop fucking you?"

"*No!* That's not what I'm…What I'm…" She sucked in her breath, a shocked expression melting the anger from her face. "I'm gonna come."

He stilled his hips.

"For God's sake, Ash! Why are you doing this to me? Please, *please* keep going."

"Look at me, Tayshia."

She did, and it was like staring into the eyes of someone so deprived of oxygen, so utterly close to death, that he almost wanted to let her come. That he almost forgot what she'd said about him. What she'd been doing to him for months.

The fury returned.

"I own your fucking cunt," he hissed, slamming his hips against hers to punctuate his words. "It's mine. Come on. Let me hear you tell me. Let me hear you say it, and I'll let you come."

"I'm yours. I'm yours. Please. I'm yours."

"What's mine? You can do it. Tell me in the sweetest voice you can."

She squeezed her eyes shut and then opened them, slowly meeting his gaze. "My cunt. It's yours."

"Do you want to come, baby?"

"Yes, yes, yes. Please." Her hips squirmed every time he pounded into her. He felt her body clenching, gripping him tighter as she neared her orgasm without him needing to touch her.

"You know, Tayshia, I thought about it."

She gasped when he angled his hips so that he hit her deep inside, right in the spot that counted. Once again, she strained against her bound wrists. "Thought about w-what?"

"Letting you come."

She froze, her eyes darting up to meet his again with a trepidation that showed him his arrow had hit home.

"I wanted to. Fuck, I wanted to give you everything." He stopped his train of thought as a wave of pleasure assaulted him. He was close. So close. "*Fucking* Hell, you're gonna make me come."

"I want you to," she said, but the edge to her voice showed him that she knew something was up. That she knew he wasn't happy with her.

That she was in trouble.

"But you said you wanted nothing to do with me. And I can't, for the life of me, see why a bad girl like you should get the rewards that a good girl deserves." His head lolled to the side, his spine tingling and his heart racing. He was right on the edge, gripping her knees so hard that it was hurting his fingertips. "And *fuck* if I don't wish you were a good girl."

She closed her eyes, but it could not hide the guilt etched into every part of her face.

"You know why?" he said.

Her head shook slowly from side to side. No, she didn't know. He was going to tell her.

"Because good girls get to come."

Her eyes snapped open.

Ash lost control, pressing his hand flat to the center of her chest to hold her still as he pulled out. He stroked himself as he came, his entire body shaking as the sensation of it overwhelmed him. It painted her stomach and the undersides of her bra, reaching as far as her dress.

And it felt good.

She stared at him in muted shock as he tucked himself back into his jeans and caught his breath, saying nothing. There was nothing she *could* say. She knew he knew. She knew Elijah had told him what she'd said. And the contrite look in her eyes told him all he needed to know.

What an expert little liar.

Ash threaded his belt back through the loops, got off the bed, and grabbed a towel off the floor. He cleaned her up methodically, like a mess on a kitchen counter, and then he walked to the door.

"Ash, what the Hell? Are you just going to *leave* me tied up like this?"

He stopped in the doorway, glancing back at her as though she were the least important thing on his schedule for the day.

"I thought you wanted me to treat you like you were nothing?"

Chapter Twenty Two

Ash woke up on the couch right as the sun dipped below the horizon.

He couldn't remember falling asleep. All he remembered was coming downstairs, packing a bowl, and then laying down to stare at the ceiling.

Shit.

Tayshia.

Guilt riddled him like gunshot wounds as he hurried up the stairs and into his parents' bedroom. She was asleep, her head lolled against her chest, which was still exposed by the way he'd rucked her dress up above her breasts. Her hands were limp in their bonds.

He felt sick.

What the fuck was wrong with him?

He'd just been so hurt and so angry. He'd wanted to show her that he wasn't going to degrade her anymore, and in the process he'd done just that.

Ash rushed over to the bed, putting one knee on the mattress so he could undo the knot on the tie. As her arms fell limp on the pillow beside her head, he sat down and began to massage them, pressing gentle circles into her muscles from the tops of her shoulders down to the tips of her fingers. She stirred, letting out a pained whimper.

"My hands are asleep," she mumbled.

"I know, baby. Shh. Just let me take care of you."

Her eyelids fluttered open and she watched him as he brought her limbs back to life. Neither of them spoke. When she was able to wiggle and curl her fingers sufficiently, he got up and went into his parents' bathroom. By the time the shower was on and the water was hot, she was standing behind him. He pulled the soiled dress up over her head and dropped it to the ceramic tiles beneath their feet in the bathroom.

Taking her by the hand, he helped her step into the shower. But as he started to pull away to shut the curtains, she tugged, lowering her eyes shyly.

She *wanted* him in there with her?

"Please," she whispered, the water soaking through her curls. She didn't seem to care.

He obliged, stepping into the shower fully clothed, much like he had in her dream all those months ago. And just like back then, he washed her. She watched him as he did, remaining silent as he sank to his knees and washed her. Washed her free of him. Scrubbed his scent to replace it with the calming aroma of lavender.

His heart ached.

When he was standing again, his clothes soaked to the skin and his hair flattened against his face, she looked up into his eyes. The tension increased, both of them seeming on the verge of speaking.

They left the shower.

Tayshia wrapped herself in a towel and walked back to the bed while Ash peeled his wet clothes off. He twisted a towel around his waist, scraping his hair back as he headed for the door.

"Don't go," she said softly, her eyes trained on him from where she lay curled up on her side beneath the comforter.

"I was gonna go get some clothes to sleep in."

"Get me a shirt. One of yours."

Ash nodded, and jogged downstairs to where his bag was, full of the clothes he'd brought from the apartment. He pulled his joggers on and then grabbed her a shirt, heading back. She sat up and allowed him to pull the shirt onto her. Once it settled onto her body, she reached for him, her arms curling around his neck as he slipped into the bed. He raised himself up onto his elbow, opening his mouth to finally say something—an apology, an excuse, *anything*—but she had other plans.

He didn't know how it happened, but one minute, they were looking at each other and the next, they were kissing. She was so wanton beneath him that he was powerless to stop the sudden flare of need that raged through his body like an unchecked wildfire. She writhed and rolled like waves, hooking her leg around his hip and using her foot to push his pants down.

"Wait. Are you sure you want to?" he asked amidst heavy kisses to her neck and shoulder. His hands touched her everywhere she would let him, his own hips rolling to meet hers. "I don't want to hurt you again."

"I'm sure," she breathed, and then she angled her hips so that he would slip inside.

It was like sinking into euphoria.

"*Fuck*," he groaned against the curve of her throat, the sound hovering just beneath her almost exalted cry of bliss. He could feel every inch of her, so hot around him that it almost scorched his skin. "Fuck, I'm so sorry."

He hissed when she dragged her nails down his back, and she gasped to the air. The connection from him to her, her to him, was otherworldly. It was like some part of her had opened up, peeling back to reveal her true self, and he was ravenous for it. Consuming it, leaving nothing behind.

"Look at me, baby, please," he whispered.

She did, her eyelids fluttering open. Their eyes met, the connection intensifying, and then he was moving faster. He pinned her hips to the bed to make sure he hit the spot she liked on every thrust, taking in the sight of the way her eyes shone. Her head fell back further and further, until her throat was exposed for him to lick and suck as he left marks all over the skin.

When she started whimpering out pleas, he realized it was more than just a need to come. It was a fear that he wouldn't let her. A fear that he'd take it away from her again. That he'd show her again what happened when she underestimated him.

Ash held back the emotions caused by his guilt and wrapped his arms around her body. He rolled them over until she was on top, and then he grabbed her thighs, holding her hips against his. Her mouth fell upon him in a series of desperate kisses as she began to grind against him, seeking her undoing with the determination of someone who was terrified of deprivation.

"Are you going to let me...?" She trailed off, dropping her forehead to his chest. Her shoulders shook, like she was afraid to even ask the question.

"I'm going to let you," he murmured, tucking her hair behind her ears and bringing her face back up to his. "You've been such a good girl."

"Have I?" The shyness had reached her tone.

"Mm-hm."

He kissed her to swallow her moans as he thrust up from below, sharpening her pleasure and helping her reach the top of that mountain to meet the sky. And each thrust only brought him closer, too, until they were both gasping and his stomach was clenching tight enough to be sore. She slid her hands to his chest, fingers splayed out over the network of colorful tattoos, and pushed herself up.

Her eyes were like stars.

Bracing herself against him, she began to fuck him in earnest, watching the expressions that flitted across his face as she dragged him up to the skies to soar with her. When he tried to close his eyes, he felt her fingers threading through his hair at his forehead, forcing his head back. He watched her as she rose and fell. As she rode him like he belonged to her.

Because he did.

He sat up, sliding his hands to her waist and holding her tight. She brought her hands to his face, cradling his cheeks as she pressed soft kisses to his lips. He pulled back and looked up at her, the rawness of his flayed emotions displayed in his eyes.

"Why, Tayshia? Why did you say that to Elijah?"

She lowered her eyes, fingers still caressing his cheeks. "Because I hated you."

He dug his fingers into her hips, pulling her against him until he was so far inside of her that there was no beginning and no end. "You told him you were through with me."

"You told me you didn't want me."

"It was a lie."

The look in her eyes was that of an exposed wound, ragged at the edges and seeping with blood. "Mine was a lie, too."

"*Are* you through with me?"

"I'm not. I'm not. I swear."

"Do you want this to be over?"

She shook her head, rocking her hips so that he could feel him moving inside of her. "Never."

"I'm so sorry," he groaned, wrapping his arms tightly around her waist. "I'm so fucking sorry."

"I'm sorry, too." Her voice was breathy, pitched high.

"I'm only gonna tell you that you're good, and worthy, and important." He punctuated the words with another grinding upward. She moaned with each movement. "Because you're so good. Tell me. I want to hear it."

"I'm so good."

"You're such a good girl, and you feel so perfect around me." He flipped them around, so she was on her back with her damp hair splayed out along the pillow and her arms wrapped around his neck. He felt her fingers playing in the hair at the back of his head as he slid in and out of her at an unhurried pace. Each movement sent a shock of electricity through his entire system, each second that their gazes remained locked feeling like an eternity of solace. "I can feel you clenching around me. Are you gonna come for me, my good, sweet girl?"

Something seemed to break inside of her, cracking open and spilling paradise into her. She came suddenly and hard, burying her face in the crook of his shoulder to stifle the way she keened. The way she clamped down around him was enough for his own gates to open wide, for him to feel that electricity thundering across the planes of his body. He pulled out before he could finish inside her, being careful to release into his hand so he didn't degrade her the way he had before.

He wanted her to feel respected.

And it was that respect, coupled with the praise he'd showered upon her, that broke her down. The minute he disappeared into the bathroom to wash his hands, she was throwing the covers back, hyperventilating as she stumbled out of the bed.

"I never wanted this," she sobbed, hands trembling as she covered her face. "I never wanted it to get this bad. I only wanted to have something to control."

He knew what she was talking about.

"I know, Tayshia," he said, coming to stand in front of her. He pulled her hands away from her face, his heart wrenching at the sight of the devastation there. "But it did. It *did* get this bad. And now we're both hurting."

"I'm sorry. I'm so, so sorry, Ash." She collapsed to the floor at his feet, her head bowed. "Please forgive me."

Ash sunk to his knees, holding one of her shaking hands while he lifted her chin with the other. "I'll always forgive you."

"I just want to get better."

Ash sat down beside her, wrapping his arms around her waist and pulling her into his lap. She curled up there and continued to weep, unaware that he was holding his whole world in his arms.

☼☼☼

The following day, when the sky was blue and sunny, Ash woke.

Tayshia was in the shower. He could hear the water through the closed bathroom door. He was lying on his stomach in the bed that once belonged to his parents, feeling completely obliterated from the deepest sleep he'd had in days.

It had been quite the evening.

Ash went downstairs to make them both breakfast, pulling up the blinds so they could look out at the garden that he had yet to show her the full effect of. After it was cooked, he placed their plates on either side of the table and sat down. It was nearly noon, indicating that they'd slept through their alarms and were missing school.

She came down the stairs wearing a fluffy pink robe that fell to mid-thigh, with her hair wrapped in a towel on top of her head. Her facial expression was somber, unreadable in the way it flattened her eyes and mouth. Ash's gaze followed her as she pulled out her chair, sank into it, and pulled one knee to her chest.

They ate in silence until their plates were empty, and then she spoke.

"We can't do it again."

Ash set his fork down. "Can't do what again?"

"What we've been doing." She averted her eyes and remained silent. She blinked several times, a tear escaping her lashes to roll down her face. Quick as a flash, she wiped it away and refocused her gaze on him. "Degrading me. We can't do it again."

"Okay," he said. "Of course."

Once again, she gazed out the window, taking in the garden and its new flowers, trellises, and lights. The quiet was broken only by the sounds of birdsong, echoing up towards the clouds. It was clear that her thoughts were deep today.

"I thought I hated myself enough for that," she whispered, another tear falling that this time, she did not clear from her skin. "And I do. But I think the way I hate myself has nothing to do with you."

Ash turned his own gaze onto the flowers. "You wanted me to degrade you because you don't think you deserve to be praised."

Their eyes met across the table.

"I can't handle the way it feels to be loved by you, Ash."

He stared at her, the words taking ages to sink in. Trying to remember when he'd slipped up. When he might have said the wrong thing, or said something that made her feel like he loved her.

The table.

He'd told her when they slept together on the table.

Oh.

Oh.

Fuck.

Tayshia's phone began to ring, the light sound of tinkling bells sounding from Ash's old bedroom upstairs. She got up, wiping her eyes discreetly as she went to answer it. Ash stayed seated at the table, forearms braced against it, wondering what the Hell he was supposed to do now.

"The clinic just called me with my bloodwork results," Tayshia said as she came down the stairs, her voice getting louder the closer she drew near. She stopped near the table, looking at him. "My potassium is low, and I'm anemic. She prescribed me medication."

"Is that bad?"

"If I don't take the medication, yes." She rubbed her fingers across her collarbone. "So can you take me to the pharmacy to pick it up?"

"Sure."

"Thank you."

She disappeared back up the stairs, leaving Ash to clean up the dining room table. He put the dishes into the dishwasher after a good rinse, then headed up the stairs to ask her when she wanted to leave. He hesitated before opening the door but knew that it was probably best he stop running from things.

It was just a room. It couldn't hurt him.

He turned the doorknob and entered.

"Tayshia, when did you want to go to the…"

He staggered backward, a hand slapping over his mouth to protect his mouth and nose.

The *smell*.

His gaze fell upon the bags first. Plastic bags littering the room, tied shut with full contents. Next to them, containers were full to the brim with more of her vomit. One container had spilled over without a lid, the remnants of her sick clearly having been there for a long time.

Then, he saw Tayshia.

She knelt on the floor next to the open drawer and bed, bent over an open plastic bag with her fingers down her throat and watery vomit sliding down her forearm. She had removed the towel from her wet hair and now wore only the robe. Her eyes widened in stages as she realized that he was actually standing in her doorway

Has she been purging this entire time? he thought, his horror and bewilderment forcing his thoughts to move in slow motion. *This is my fucking bedroom.*

Beside her on the floor was one of Ash's dresser drawers. It was empty of his high school clothes. Now, it was full of food. All manner of packaged sweets and savory goods. All the things he'd seen her binge on and things that he hadn't. So much food that she had to have been collecting and hoarding it like treasure to a dragon.

The fucking *smell*.

Ash had never been more simultaneously disgusted and heartbroken in his entire life.

CHAPTER TWENTY THREE

"What are you doing here?" she asked, voice wrestled into a whisper. Then, the panic exploded in her eyes. *"You can't be in here! Get out of here!"*

"Tayshia," he said, his tone drawn-out as he stared at the physical representation of her self-hatred, contained in boxes and bags all over the room. "What the actual fuck is this?"

She scrambled to her feet and started trying to gather the bags up by the handles. She picked one up and it broke on the bottom, spilling its contents out all over the carpet. The already rancid smell in the room intensified, growing acrid. They both stared at it, then at each other as though it were neither of their faults.

This transcended sanity.

Ash stood there, the indecision rooting him to the spot. Should he help her clean? Should he wait and watch while she did it herself? Should he clean it himself to force her to face it?

This was his *childhood bedroom*. The place he'd spent his entire life in, from the moment he was born to the moment he was arrested. This was his past. It was a part of him, no matter how painful it was to be inside of it, and she'd been using it to hide her.

Puzzle pieces were starting to shift in his mind, rearranging themselves to fit together. She'd been purging this entire time. Every time they ate a meal and she was complacent, it was likely because she knew she could just come get rid of it in his fucking *bedroom*.

Is that why she never wanted anyone in her bedroom at the apartment?

"Is your bedroom like this at home?" he asked, his voice barely louder than a whisper as he stared at her.

"No! I cleaned it before we left. I promise."

Ash turned, feeling his stomach lurch with nausea. It was taking everything he had in him not to gag. He didn't know whether to walk back out into the hall or stay right where he was. The fact that he hadn't stepped in anything or knocked anything over was pure good fortune.

He didn't have any experience with this. His mother was messy, but not intentionally. Any time he cleaned up after her, it was the remnants that she had missed. But this—this was confusing. Tayshia had cleaned the room spotless when they first came back to this house. The contrast of the neatly-made bed, clean dresser, and pristine shelves, to the filth that littered the floor?

"I need to explain." She wrung her hands, standing there with a pile of empty chocolate bar wrappers on the floor next to her left foot and the bowl into where she'd vomited them next to her right.

"Tayshia, I'm going to be fucking sick." The air was so thick that he could taste it. "There's nothing you can possibly say that could explain this."

"You don't understand."

"Then *help me*," he hissed. "Help me understand."

"I have to leave it so I won't think it's okay. It reminds me how fucked up I am."

Ash lowered his chin, giving her an incredulous look. "You know it's not okay, so you leave it?"

"I have to face it. If I don't face it, then I'll think it's okay and I'll never..." She took a couple of deep breaths. Her hand trembled as she held it to her mouth. "I'll never get better."

As he stared at her, watching the tears filling her downcast eyes, his mind betrayed him. It presented him with horrifying scenarios, one right after the other like an onslaught of arrows. Tayshia, keeling over in class, dead. Tayshia, passing out in the bathroom with a ruptured stomach. Tayshia, falling asleep beside him in bed and him being unable to wake her the next morning no matter how hard he shook her.

He was *disturbed* and he just—he needed—

Spinning to face the dresser, he slammed his hands down on top of it. His chest heaved as he struggled to keep his breakfast down, suppressing a shudder as the smell started to overwhelm him. This was too much. This was right at the limit for him.

She was going to die if he didn't fix this.

"Explain this to me," he said, his gaze lifting to glare at her through his reflection in the mirror.

"Sometimes, I binge in the middle of the night and I'm too tired to walk. So, I get out of bed, sit on the floor, and do it here. And then

I just leave it. I leave it so I have to look at it, and smell it, and face it — and — and — and —"

"This is literally not happening again," he said, facing her and slicing a hand through the air as he gestured to her entire body. "Isn't *that* enough to make you face it?!"

The words left his mouth and he didn't see anything wrong with them. He really didn't. His vision was clear.

He'd just forgotten that hers wasn't.

Tayshia's face fell further into the Earth than it already had. Her arms wrapped around her stomach, as if it could hide her sins, and she hung her head.

"Why do you have to be so cruel to me? Why can't you have at least a little compassion?"

"Are you stupid?!" he shouted, holding his hands to his temples and then spreading his arms wide. "Do you not see what I'm fucking standing in?! My bedroom is covered in *vomit*, Tayshia! It smells like shit in here! You vomit in bags and containers, and then you leave it here while you sleep among it all. Why do you not see a problem with that?!"

"I told you I *do* see a problem with it!" she cried, a tear slipping down her cheek that she quickly swiped away. "I didn't want you to see it! You shouldn't have come in here without knocking!"

"As if knocking would give you enough time to fix this. You are delusional."

"You don't even want to be *in* here! This room is essentially *mine*."

"This is *my* house. This is *my* room. And I'm the one that's taking care of you. So, you're gonna clean this the fuck up, and you're gonna do it now."

"No one asked you to take care of me!" she shrieked, hands in fists at her sides. "I don't *want* you to!"

"Well that's too damn bad!"

Tayshia let out a cry of frustration and stormed across the room, barely looking below her. It was clear some of these containers and bags had been there for so long that she had the route memorized. She shoved past him and stormed down the stairs. Faintly, he heard the sounds of cupboard doors slamming shut. Then, she came back up the stairs and pushed past him again, carrying the tub of cleaning supplies and several black trash bags. She glared at him, pushing the long sleeves of her bathrobe up to her elbows.

"I don't want to fight anymore. Can you leave, so I can clean?"

"I'm never leaving you in this room alone again. You're disgusting for this."

She glared at him. "There's no need to be unnecessarily rude on top of everything else. This is humiliating for me."

"Then maybe you shouldn't be doing it."

"It's not that simple."

The urge to scream *"Why not?!"* burned so bright and hot inside of him that it felt like the sun was expanding inside of his chest.

He bit his tongue. Hard.

Tayshia began to move about the room, picking up bags by the handles and carrying them away from her body to one of the black bags. There was a sour expression on her face, which he had no sympathy for. Why would she be revolted by something *she'd* done? If she could let it get this bad, then she needed to clean it. After all, she'd said she wanted to face it.

Wait.

The puzzle pieces finally clicked into place and suddenly, Ash saw the whole picture. He lifted his gaze from the floor, locking eyes with her as she dropped a container in with the others.

"This is why you put those wrappers into the couch. And why you left the dirty dishes out. Isn't it?"

She didn't look at him, stuffing more containers into the trash bag. "I don't know how to explain it."

"Try," he said, holding his hands palm side down with fingers splayed. "Because I need to understand this, all right? I need to understand it, or I'm gonna go fucking insane."

She took a deep breath, like she was pulling all of the emotions to the surface where they could start to churn. Then, she let it out, pulling those emotions back down inside of her where they couldn't take her under. So she wouldn't drown.

"The reason why I put the wrappers into the couch was so that every time we sat down on the cushions, I would be ashamed to know they were there. The reason why I left the dirty dishes everywhere is because it made you so angry that you treated me badly, just like I deserved. The reason why I left all of this in this room and my room back home is because no matter where you or I are, I'll know it's here. I knew it would absolutely mortify me if you ever caught me, and that's why I did it. I leave it so that no matter how sick I get, I'll always have something to remind me that I don't want to be."

In a weird way, it made perfect sense. It was a reminder. A failsafe. Something to keep her aware of the fact that what she was doing wasn't right. That it was dangerous and that at its core, she was ashamed of it. And while he wanted to think that it was in some way a good thing that she wanted to have that last barrier to protect her from herself, he didn't want to feel anything positive towards her. Not for this.

"Okay," he said, placing his hands on the front edge of the dresser by his hips, his elbows bent from the way he was leaning against it. "Finish up."

She nodded, her face blank as she continued to clean up the remnants of her shame. She sank to her knees before the spilled vomit, gathering it up with her hands and dropping it into the bag. He had to swallow as hard as he could to keep from gagging. It was hard for him to watch her picking it up, getting tired from the effort, and stopping to catch her breath. She looked *and* sounded like she was about to fall apart, but he wasn't going to let her. Whether it was because he cared or because he was angry, he wasn't sure.

When the floor was finally clean and she'd finished scrubbing at the carpet, the smell finally starting to fade as it was hidden away in the trash bag, he knelt down in front of her.

"This is never happening again. You hear me?"

"Yes."

"You're leaving this door open at all times."

"Okay."

"I mean it."

"I understand. Are you angry with me?"

"Very."

"I'm so ashamed."

She needed to feel this, this shame. She needed to feel it so that she could really understand what was wrong with her actions. However, somewhere beneath the anger he felt, he could feel something else. Something that ran deeper.

"Tayshia. Look at me."

She looked up at him again.

"I'm proud of you," he said. "I'm proud that you recognize you don't want to be sick. I thought that—"

"That I enjoyed this?" Her voice was as bitter as the air in the room had felt not ten minutes ago. "No. I don't enjoy this. If I could go back to the girl I was before everything got so bad, then I would. The girl I was before Paris. But I just don't know how."

Ash took a step closer, lifting a hesitant hand. Then, he brushed the backs of his forefingers across her cheekbone, sinking them into the depths of her hair, ignoring the feel of her braid tracks beneath his touch. Her eyelids fluttered, like it was painful or filled her with an ache that nothing could satisfy.

"That girl doesn't exist anymore. Stop trying to get her back. You've gotta learn how to be okay with the person you are now, and the person you're gonna be."

"What's the point? I don't want to mourn myself. I'm not dead."

"Maybe you have to learn how to accept it."

She didn't say anything, but it wasn't necessary.

His mother had left a mess behind, with her dishes and her own mistakes. He'd thought it was because she just wanted some stress relief. He'd even thought she'd somehow figured out that he was the one cleaning it up. Now, he wondered if maybe his mother had trouble accepting her lot in life, too. The hardest part was knowing that he would never receive an answer to that question, no matter how badly he wanted it.

Ash knew what Tayshia was terrified of. He knew what the dirty dishes and the bags full of vomit and the wrappers in the couch all represented. He knew they were the only reminder she had that it wasn't good to feel so empty. He knew that if she accepted herself now, that would mean giving up the only barrier she had protecting her from the memory of that alleyway. It would mean taking what she knew and ripping it into shreds that she could actually stomach. Small pieces she could eat one-by-one that wouldn't overwhelm her into wanting to get rid of them.

He had to decide if he wanted to stand there and watch her fight to remain empty.

Sometimes, I don't even want to watch.
Sometimes, I just want to walk away.

Chapter Twenty Four

Friday dawned on Ash's surly disposition.

He wasn't sure how to pinpoint the exact reason why he was angry with Tayshia. He knew he had good reason to be revolted by what he'd seen. The gravity of it showed him just how bad she'd gotten—that she was willing to do anything to keep hold of her disordered habits. He'd managed to stay relatively calm during her explanations, but now that he'd had a chance to sleep on it, he couldn't remain that way.

It had been *weeks*. *Weeks* that she'd let it sit in there, rotting and sinking into the soul of that room. Though it was now clean, it would forever have an imprint of the ghost of Tayshia's self-destruction. It had probably witnessed her breaking down again and again and again. Watched her bend over to purge into bags and containers, or to sit down with a snack of some sort and binge until she was in pain.

Is that how far they'd fallen? Him setting rules, taking away her right to leave doors shut, invading her privacy? Yelling at her, giving her things to cry about, plating her meals for her? Watching her. Degrading her. Controlling her.

Like a parent.

He sat up shirtless in bed, hunched over with his head hung between his hands. His stomach roiled with a nausea that he couldn't quite place. A bit of disgust with himself mixed with his overwhelming desire to force her to live. To force her to live to see a life with him where she was happy and healthy, with the memory of Paris far in her past.

It was all about him, wasn't it?

How selfish.

Tayshia was in the bathroom doing her make-up, and he needed to start getting ready. Ash got up and threw on a hooded jumper colored dark grey, black denims with rips in the knees, and his boots. Grabbing his backpack, he went down to the kitchen to wait for Tayshia. His bag hanging off of his left shoulder, he slipped his forefingers into his front pockets, leaning back against the counter with one leg outstretched. The emotional exhaustion pulled him downward, causing his shoulders to slouch.

He cursed under his breath and turned his face to the right, toward the laundry room. How was he supposed to act around her now that he'd seen her at her worst? How was he supposed to talk to her without thinking about the fact that she could exist within the confines of a room for *weeks* – months, if he included the apartment – while her vomit festered around her, rotting into the carpet? Anyone who could do that? Anyone who could simply let that *go*?

Someone like that might be too far gone for help.

Tayshia entered the kitchen five minutes or so later. Ash, who was in the process of rubbing his right eye, looked at her. She'd curled her hair with a curling wand, creating glossy waves that cascaded out of her scalp, with her edges laid and a pearl hair clip. Her body was clad in tights and a cute mini dress, but he felt sad to see that she still wasn't wearing her necklace, and neither was he.

She looked beautiful.

But at the same time, there was something dark and hideous twisting beneath her appearance. It was in the hollowness of her cheeks and the emptiness of her eyes. The slow way she moved that ached of something much deeper than weakness.

"You're already ready?" she said.

He nodded, not trusting himself to speak lest he betray his morbid thoughts. Looking at her, it felt like he could still smell her room.

"Oh," she said. "Well, I'm ready, so we can go."

"You look gorgeous."

"Thanks." She bit her lower lip, her gaze scrutinizing him. "Are you in pain?"

"Wait...What?"

"Your brows look like this." She scrunched her face up like she was angry. It was cute, but Ash felt too conflicted to do much more than let his lips twitch upward. "You're pouting."

"Oh, pouting, huh?" He huffed and lowered his gaze. He hadn't felt this much discomfort creeping under his skin since visiting his father in prison. It didn't feel right, not where Tayshia was concerned. He reached for her hand, tugging her to stand between his legs. "Come here."

Tayshia pressed her hand flat to his chest. Since he was slouched against the counter, her head was slightly above his. Her teeth sunk into her lower lip as she searched his eyes.

Here she was, that beautiful girl from his dreams, standing before him. They weren't dreaming, but every time he looked at her, his heart leapt to the stars. He wished they could go into his dream world—the world where her smile almost reached her eyes—and stay.

Ash tilted his chin up, his lips meeting hers as his hands found her waist. He hardly moved, barely touched her at all as she threw herself into the kiss with a gusto that he hadn't expected from her. She moved one hand up to his shoulder and wrapped the other around his neck. Pulling her body tight to his, he felt her tongue dipping into his mouth. It was neither exploratory nor familiar. She was just tasting him.

Kissing her hurt, like a demon squeezing his lungs with ropes of fire.

He turned his face away, sliding his hand down her arm as he stood up straight. "Why don't we just eat breakfast here? We're already late. By the time we get there, it'll be half over."

"Are you sure?" she asked, patting the side of her head with the heel of her palm. Apparently, her scalp itched. "Do you really want to cook?"

"No, but I'm tired," he said in a monotone. He let his bag fall to the floor and then moved past her to the kitchenette. "I don't feel like being around all those people."

She went to the table and sat down. The silence that stretched between them while he whipped up some scrambled eggs and bacon was almost awkward in the way it seemed as thin as a spider's silver webbing. It would hold strong, provided something didn't destroy it.

He brought their plates to the dining room and took his seat across from her. The vase full of dying roses was still situated between them, a somber reminder. After he was onto his third bite, he realized she hadn't picked up her fork yet.

"Eat," he said without looking up.

"But…"

"But what?"

"You cooked it in butter."

His head pulled back on his shoulders. "Why does that matter?"

Her fingernails tapped on the table. "I prefer olive oil."

"And that's my problem, how?"

"I can't have butter."

Ash could feel it coming—the anger. It was always there now, lurking beneath the surface. This was just another one of her stupid excuses, now that he had taken her privacy away. She couldn't purge, and he couldn't have this battle forever.

"Tayshia. You do *not* want me to come to your side of the table."

She bristled at that. "Or else, what?"

Slamming his fork down, he scooted his chair back, rising to his feet. She glared up at him as he leaned over the table with his hands flat on top of it. He held her gaze, his face calm.

"Eat your breakfast. I'm not going to do this every single day with you. Just like I said before: you're going to eat three meals a day. Breakfast, lunch, dinner. Those are your meals. That's the way it's gonna be. You don't get to walk to class alone. You don't get to have the doors shut. You don't get to purge. That's your life now. *Eat.*"

She pursed her lips, the panic and thoughts swirling together in her eyes. He could tell that she was hunting through her mind for something, anything she could use to get out of this. Any excuse.

He was so fucking tired.

"No."

"*No?*"

Her chin jutted out as she straightened her back. "No. I'll do whatever I want. If you're gonna make it so I can't purge, then I just won't eat."

"All right. I'll do whatever I want, too."

Ash rounded the table, his right hand lashing out and wrapping in the hair at the back of her head. She cried out, looking frightened as he snatched up her fork and speared a large bite of scrambled eggs with it. He could already feel her shaking, trying to escape. Her hands moved up near her shoulders in a defensive pose.

"Wait—wait, I don't—"

Ash cut her off, holding the fork up near her lips.

"Open your fucking mouth."

"No."

"*Open* your *fucking* mouth!"

"No!" she cried, looking simultaneously bewildered and nauseous.

"Open it, or I'm going to tie you to the chair and make you eat until you're so fucking full you can't even breathe." He tightened his hold on her hair to punctuate, his mind completely devoid of rationality.

She kept her mouth firmly sewn shut.

Twisting her hair around his hand until she screamed in pain, he shoved the fork into her mouth. She closed her lips around it on instinct, looking up at him with eyes that implored him to stop. She whimpered. Whether from the pain on her scalp or the feeling of the food on her tongue, he didn't know. Her eyes were sparkling with unshed tears, but how could he care?

She knew how to cry on command.

"Chew," he ordered.

She did, her eyes squeezing shut. A tear escaped.

He slid the fork out of her mouth and grabbed some more.

"Please," she begged. "Ash, please. I'll eat it. Just don't—not again."

He held the fork up to her, his heart cold and done. "Open."

"*Please.*"

"Open."

Trembling as though she were stuck outside in the snow, she opened her mouth with slow reluctance. He slid it into her mouth again and this time, she chewed.

"I can do it myself," she whispered, her head pulling against his hold. "Please. Ash, *please.*"

Her pleas fell upon deaf ears. They had to. He couldn't let her control this anymore. He couldn't let her get away with anything. She'd had her chance to do this her way, and she'd fucked it up. She'd had her chance to prove she could be trustworthy, and she'd *fucked* it *up*.

The fork returned to her mouth.

The tears continued to fall and splash against the table. Her trembling grew more violent, until her legs were shaking. Something about the way she was breathing seemed distant yet familiar.

"I thought you said you didn't want this?" he snapped, holding up the next bite. "Didn't want your disorder? That you wanted to get better. That means you have to *eat.*"

"Why are you doing this to me?" she cried, her hand knuckle-white as it wrapped around his wrist, trying to stop him. "What did I do *wrong*? Ash—"

The fork in her mouth shut her up.

Ash managed to get her to eat two more bites before she tried to turn her face toward him. She gasped out apologies, apologies that chipped away at the ice cage that surrounded him.

"I'm so sorry," she kept saying, her lashes clinging together with tears. "I'll eat. I'll eat. I'm so, so sorry."

He looked into her eyes, seeing a depth of emotion there that he'd only ever seen before in one place.

"Ash, please. I'll do whatever you want." She was crying so hard that she was on the verge of hyperventilation. He'd never felt her shake this badly. "I'll do whatever you want, just please let me do it myself. I'm *begging* you."

Paris.

His heart shattered, the way it should have five minutes ago. The way it always did around her. The way it deserved to now that he'd violated the sanctity of her body just to get her to eat. There was no excuse, but he'd just been so fucking *tired*.

And he hated himself.

He dropped the fork and stumbled back a step. It was more than toxicity. It was wrong. It was dark. She hugged her arms around herself, chin to her chest as she sobbed like a small child. She looked as broken as she did in that hotel room.

Ash stormed back into the kitchen, scrubbing his face violently with his hands. He felt like a shadow. A shell of a monster who didn't deserve to function or breathe. And she was just sitting there, weeping as she picked up the fork and failed thrice to pick eggs up with it.

"I'm sorry," she whispered, cringing away when he took a step closer. "I'm sorry. I'm doing it. I'm trying."

He watched in somber silence while she ate the rest of the eggs and nibbled at the bacon. She was as pale as taupe, her face splotched red from how hard she was crying. Her hands shook hard enough that she looked like she was hypothermic. He'd traumatized her.

These tears weren't fake.

✪✪✪

Ash couldn't focus on any of his classes for the rest of the day.

He couldn't stand himself. He couldn't stand the person he was, nor the person he'd become. He was disgusting. Worse than disgusting.

What he'd done was wrong. Forcing her to eat, shoving it down her throat. Treating her like property, like she had no say over her own body. Taking her autonomy away.

He couldn't understand why he'd let himself lose control like that. Didn't know how to cope with the intense amount of self-hatred that coursed through his veins. It felt like it would never ebb. It was suffocating him.

The sound of her sobs lived in his head.

At lunch, he was forced to see how viscerally he'd affected her. Both unable to maintain happy faces around their friends, they decided to take their lunch elsewhere. They sat in his car while she slowly ate a sandwich with tears rolling down her cheeks.

In his last class of the day, he couldn't make it all the way through. He had to get up to hide in the bathroom for fifteen solid minutes while he broke down in a stall and sobbed into his hands.

This was an unsolvable problem with no clear-cut solution. He was making random stabs in the dark, hitting flesh every time, and turning on the light to find he'd stabbed the ones he cared about over and over and over. He was so overwhelmed.

It was the room. It had to be. Seeing the state of it had forced him to face just how unwell she was. All this time, he'd thought she was getting somewhere. That he was helping her. Instead, she'd just been hiding a graveyard beneath her skirts. It was the reason why she wouldn't let him sweep her around the ballroom.

It would have exposed the truth.

"I can't fucking do this," he whispered to himself in the stall as he rocked back and forth, his fingers deep in his hair and tears leaking off of the tip of his nose. "I can't do this. I can't fucking—"

He broke off into more sobs. Sobs that took a hook and wrenched his gut out through his mouth, leaving him emptier than a dying star. There was nothing left of him. Nothing left of her.

They were both broken.

When he sucked everything back inside of him and went to the mirror, he hunched over one sink with his hands braced along its porcelain edges. Taking several deep, gasping breaths, he looked at himself. When his gaze locked with his reflection, blue eyes rimmed in red from weeping, he couldn't recognize himself.

He saw his tattoos peeking over the collar of his shirt, seeming to creep up his neck like tendrils of shadow. The roses and chains that signified just how trapped he'd felt as she futilely begged him for help with her father. How he felt watching her burn herself alive every time she purged. How he felt watching her do everything in her power to maintain that control.

During the car ride home, he said four words to her.

"We need to talk."

CHAPTER TWENTY FIVE

There was an awkward air about the two of them as they made their way into the house. Tayshia set her purse on the table while Ash dropped his bag onto the floor. They looked at one another before she pulled out her homework, and he sat down to play video games.

Hours of silence later, when the sun had just barely disappeared and Ash kept losing the boss battle, he knew it was time. They had to talk.

She cleared her throat.

"How was your day?"

Horrific. "Fine. Yours?"

"It was all right." Her fingernails drummed on the table as she rested her chin in her hand. Some of her long hair fell forward to the front of her body. "Are you excited for finals?"

"I guess, just to get them over with," he said, feeling somewhat irritated. How could she want to chat like this, like nothing had happened this morning? Like he hadn't absolutely, unequivocally crossed the line? "Are you?"

"Yes. I just hope I get good grades so I can get my two-year degree."

"Yeah." To deal with the anxiety, he placed one hand on the top of his head, feeling his scalp as he sighed. "It'll be nice."

"I think so."

Another tense silence.

Tayshia spoke again. "Have you applied to any universities for transfer?"

"University?" He shot her a scathing look as he walked into the kitchen. "What are you talking about? As if I have the energy or reason to go to a university."

By the way she flinched back, he could tell he'd scared her. He hadn't meant to treat her like she was unintelligent for asking, but he couldn't understand how she could sit there and try to make things normal when there was no going back.

"Well, have you thought about what interests you?" she asked. "You like video games. You could get a software degree. You also are very articulate in your opinions. Maybe public speaking?"

What the fuck? Why does she want to talk about this?

"I don't want to do those things. I don't want to think about my future when you don't have one."

He could feel her eyes on him, but he didn't move. The sole of his right foot was flat against the cupboard door behind him, his toes against the floor. Though his stance was nonchalant, his energy was pulled taut as a wire.

"I'm sorry," she said quietly. "I was just curious."

They existed in more silence. Tayshia glanced out the open window, at the moon hanging low in the dark blue sky on its rise.

"The moon's full tonight. It looks pretty."

"I guess."

"Ash?"

"Hm?"

"Before we talk about whatever it was you wanted to discuss, I have to come clean about something."

His gaze snapped up and narrowed on her. "What did you do?"

"I—wait. What do you mean, *'what did I do?'*"

"You just said you needed to come clean."

"Why are you being so *mean* to me?" She stood up from her chair, one hand on the tabletop and the other on her hip. "I was trying to be honest with you!"

"Just tell me what it is already," he snapped, turning away again.

She said nothing, choosing instead to stomp up the stairs. She didn't come back. In fact, she was gone for so long that he presumed she had decided not to speak to him, and had decided to stay in her room until dinner. But when she returned ten minutes later with her hands at her sides and a wary facial expression, he saw that he was wrong.

"Hold out your hand," she bit out.

Into his palm, she placed his pipe. He hadn't even realized it was missing. As soon as it was in his grasp, he took a second look at her. Her eyes were unfocused, the veins stained red. She was high.

"You stole my weed?"

She gave him a curt nod. "Yes. I took your pipe last night. I went down to the living room and got it. I was stressed out."

He felt confused. Confused, irritated, and angry. It was annoying that she didn't look remorseful. What in the fuck had given her the impression that he'd be okay with her stealing his pipe after the day they'd just had?

"Anything *else* you need to come clean about?" he snarled, setting the pipe on the counter. "Maybe the fact that you're fucking blazed right now?"

"So you can live half your life high, but when I smoke once, it's a problem?"

"The fact that you think you can just take my shit is the problem."

"Well, I deserved it after what you put me through."

"It's *mine*."

"I thought *I* was."

Fury slammed through him, eradicating any traces of guilt he'd been feeling since that morning. If she wanted to go toe-to-toe, then they would.

"Except that Elijah said you said I was your worst mistake, remember? By that logic, everything we've ever done together is a waste of time because if you had the fucking choice, you wouldn't even be here!"

Tayshia opened her mouth, but no sounds came forth. Then, she tossed her hair back and turned away from him, returning to her seat at the table. She sat down heavy on the wood, resting one forearm on the tabletop as she stared across the dark dining room.

"You're right. I wouldn't have chosen this relationship for myself. I would not have chosen you. You are someone that hurts me time and time again. Any hope of redemption that I had for you was eradicated the second you told me you didn't want me. It doesn't matter that you apologized. I already took what you made me feel and put it away where it couldn't hurt me. The fact that you would say that broke my trust in you. If it were up to me? No, I would not be here. I wouldn't choose you."

Then, her gaze sliced across the dim lighting and reached directly through the pain her words were causing. There were tears in her eyes, tears that were difficult to look at because he didn't want to take the time to decipher how genuine they were.

"But it's not going to work. I can't put my feelings for you anywhere. You came into my life at a time when I couldn't fight for myself and you fought so hard for me that it made me want to get better. Ash, I've told you before and I'm telling you again now that you are the only person I want to choose. I don't want you to go anywhere, regardless of whether or not you want me. I'd spend the rest of my life with you if you asked me to."

Ash squeezed his eyes shut as he looked away, out the window once again. Tremors wracked his body as he fought the urge to break down again. Her words were everything he never realized he needed to hear, but how could they mean anything when he didn't trust her?

He couldn't tell if anything she said was true. He couldn't know if she was manipulating him to believe something by tearing him down and building him back up again, or if she truly had feelings like that for him. What if this was all just part of the same tired ruse she'd been seemingly playing since the beginning? How was he supposed to know who she really was?

"How can you say that?" He turned to face her, one hand on the counter and the other thrown into the air. "How can you say that, when your life might not even last as long as next Winter? How can you sit there and tell me with your whole chest that you want to spend the rest of it with me, when the rest of it might only be six months? Two weeks? Three days? I mean, *fuck*, Tayshia."

"Stop it!" she cried, her brows knitting together with her beseeching expression. She got up from the chair and took a step toward him. "Whether the rest of my life is—is two days or—or one hour, or even if it's ten years—it still means the same thing. I still mean what I say. I'm saying that even if I died tomorrow, I'd want to spend my last day with you."

"Don't say that. Don't you fucking say that."

She took another step closer. "I'm trying to tell you the way I feel, and all you care about is *your* fears. You can't live your entire life in fear of something terrible happening, and then expect me to do better than you! If you're scared, then I have every right to be scared, too."

"And what are you scared of, huh?!" he shouted. "What the Hell are you scared of? You're not the one who has to go on after you're gone. I put my head on that pillow every night, *terrified* that you won't be here when I wake up. And there'll be nothing—no amount of—of begging, or pleading, or protecting you, or—or—or *anything* that I can do to keep that from happening. You can say whatever you want, but I don't believe you."

Her face crumpled and one of the tears that had been brewing in her eyes escaped the trap of her lower lashline. "I'm telling you the truth. I want to be with you. I *want* to be here!"

He came toward her, and she shrank back against the table.

"You don't want me. You don't want eternity. You don't want to be anywhere else other than on your fucking knees with your fingers down your throat."

"No." Her head shook from left to right, her denial as palpable as the tension in the air. "You're wrong."

"That's the one thing you want. That's the *only* thing you want."

"No, it's not! No!" Her voice rose to a high octave, her tears coming faster. "*No!*"

"You told me yourself that you didn't want to get better." He pointed at her again, seething in his own insistence. "You want to be sick. You like being sick. You like the attention it gets you, and you like the way it feels to hurt people so that they match the way you feel inside."

She slammed her hands over her temples, plopped down in the chair, placed her elbows on the table, and ducked her head down.

"No, no, no, no, no, no, *no!*" she shrieked, and it was so shrill a noise that it silenced him. Her reddened eyes were wide and ardent as she glared up at him in her desperation. "I don't want to be *sick*! I want to be *happy*!"

Before Ash could say anything, she pressed on, one hand remaining on her temple and the other waving about in her hysteria.

"I want to be happy and Ash, you're the only one who makes me happy. If I died tomorrow or if I died ten years from now, it wouldn't change anything for me." She patted the center of her chest with shaking fingers, frantic as she continued. "I'd still be my happiest if I was with *you*. I can't do it on my own. I *know* I can't. But when I'm with you, I feel like it's easier to try. I can see a future for myself. Being with you gives me a reason *to* get better!"

If she died tomorrow.

Ash had been living every single fucking day of the last five weeks in sheer terror of that exact thing happening. He'd done everything he possibly could within his power to try and fix it all. To take the pieces that she kept ripping off of herself and put them back together. To hold onto them, caring for each one until she was ready to join them again. He'd fallen so hard and so fast for her that he'd end his own life just to give her his last breaths.

He couldn't bear the idea of knowing that he'd shouldered all that pain and all that trauma for her, enduring the brokenness of it, only for her to be using him the entire time. The dreams they shared, the laughter and the kisses, the deep conversations and the breakthroughs. The milestones. The trust she'd given him. If it was all false, then he'd rather walk the Earth for all of eternity as half a man, than a whole one with a liar at his side.

She needed to tell him the truth.

"Then right now, this is your chance. This is your one fucking chance." He slammed his hand flat on the counter. "Which parts were real, and which parts were fake?"

"What?" She looked on in disbelief. "How do you expect me to answer that? It's not like I—"

He raised his voice, cutting her off. "Which parts were *real*, and which parts were *fake*, Tayshia?!"

"Stop yelling at me, please. Please, please stop."

"Tell me now, or that's it. Do you hear? That's *it*."

"It was all real!" she cried, jumping to her feet. "What are you even *talking* about? Everything I have ever said to you has been the *truth*!"

"No, that's not what—"

"No, you can stop right there, Ash Robards! What Elijah told you was true. I did tell him those things. I said them out of anger and the fact that you'd betrayed something I trusted you with. By saying you didn't want me, it made every time I gave you my body mean nothing, and that was devastating for me. I meant it when I said them to him, but I regretted it once I calmed down and had time to think about things."

"You admitted to manipulating me."

Her glare was as vicious and as sharp as the edge of a dagger. "When I told you how I purged, how often I did it, and how easy it was, *that* was manipulation. When I sat on the couch with you before Christmas and let you make those rules, *that* was manipulation. When we were in the dream world and I told you the way I felt about my body, *that* was manipulation. It's manipulation because it is inherently manipulative for me to tell you those things. And then, when I started noticing that words wouldn't work anymore, I used my body."

"Why?"

"Because when I told you those things, even though they were true, it was me trying to make it seem like I was less sick than I really was. I was trying to soften the blow so you wouldn't make me stop. The clearer the image of me someday getting better became, the more scared I got. The more scared I got, the more liberties I took to try and make it seem less bad. I never manipulated you with the intention of doing so, but I knew that when I told you those things, that they would make you think it wasn't that *bad* that I purged. I *never* lied to you about the way I feel for you."

"So, you..." He frowned, searching her eyes. Panic was starting to creep in on the edges of his vision. "I'm confused."

"When someone has an eating disorder," she said, "they should not be telling you the details of how they binge, how they starve, and how they purge. It's inherently manipulative because it tricks you into believing it's not as bad as it really is. I manipulated you into believing I was okay. I didn't manipulate you into believing I liked you. *That* is real."

There was something rushing past his ears, like the sound of a raging river in the middle of the woods.

"Ash," she said, "you are the only person I would ever let take me to the ends of the fucking Earth and bury me alive, and that *terrifies* me. Do you understand me? I'm *terrified* of you."

He felt his stomach start to churn. He lost his breath, sagging back against the counter. He rubbed his jaw with his hand, sliding his fingers together down the line of either side. Everything she said made sense. He could see in her eyes that she was telling the truth.

And that was the problem.

The puzzle pieces that he'd so neatly fit together started to come apart in his mind. They rearranged themselves into an image that told him exactly what her words meant. They meant that he'd overreacted. That he'd chosen to wear himself so thin that one small miscommunication had caused him to do more than degrade her. To hurt her.

They meant that he *was* a monster.

Horror dawned in Tayshia's eyes like the sun rising in the morning, burning eternally in the vastness of space.

"Is that where all this has come from? You thought that I had lied to you about the things I've shared with you? Everything we've been through together — everything I've given of myself? You thought I lied, and your first reaction was to get so angry that you *controlled* me?"

He could feel the heat draining from his face, blood rushing down to the pit of his stomach. "That's not...I was just so *tired*. I didn't—"

"Ash. You *force-fed* me."

"Well, what was I supposed to do?! Everything I've done to be there for you, to try and help you see how much I fucking cared about you, only to find out you were talking to Elijah. And then on top of that, you just. Won't. Eat!"

"You're supposed to talk to me, Ash!" she shouted back, clapping her hands together to punctuate her words and syllables. "You're supposed to *communicate*!"

Ash combed anxious, tremulous fingers backward through his hair. He couldn't handle this. He could not *handle* this.

He paced out into the living room, taking a deep, gasping breath. She followed him.

"Don't walk away from this. You were the one who wanted to talk."

He spun to face her, both hands having found their way into his hair. "I can't deal with this right now."

"You treated me like Kieran did. You treated me *worse* than Kieran."

"No." His hackles rose, his chest swelling with the still-growing panic. "That's not fair."

"No, it is fair! It is! Because at least Kieran's excuse is that he just turned into an awful person. But you…You were a good person. You were genuinely a good person who chose to do your best to take care of me. But the mere thought that I might not be as perfect as you decided I was supposed to be caused you to hurt me."

This was it.

The limit had been reached. Ash had gone hurling over the cliff, into a ravine of sheer anxiety.

He wasn't a good person. He was worse than Kieran. He was a failure. Admitting that he'd been wrong in this situation would mean having to accept that he was all of those things. That he was *worse* than those things.

"I wouldn't have had to do that if you would have just told me what you meant!" he yelled, pacing back and forth in front of the TV. "If you would have just explained right then and there, when we were in that parking lot, none of this would have happened!"

"This is too much!" Tayshia put one hand on her hip and the other over her eyes. "I have a *headache*. Can you *please* stop yelling?!"

"No. No, you—you let me believe that you wanted to be with me, but you never did. How am I supposed to know that any of what you're saying is true? How am I supposed to know if you really do wanna be with me?"

"I *do*." She sounded exhausted, and her face was buried in her hands. When she lifted it, she looked exhausted, too. "I don't know how else to say it. I've told you everything."

"Then why did you say to Elijah that you couldn't wait to be rid of me? Why would you choose those specific words?"

Ash wasn't thinking clearly. His mind had completely splintered, the shards cutting his heart to add insult to injury. He held nothing inside of him.

He'd lost it.

"I was hurt. Therefore, I vented to a friend. But I couldn't get rid of you, Ash. Don't you understand? I fell in lo—"

"Shut up," he snarled. "Stop *lying*!"

"Okay, fine!" she cried, voice strained. She stood in front of the couch, too agitated to move. "I'll admit, there's dark sides to my problems. Really dark sides. Purging in bags, to start. How afraid I am of losing control. How close to death it brings me every time I do it. But I am *not* a liar. I have never even *wanted* to lie to you. If I did, do you really think I would have let you make those rules for me in the first place? If I didn't mean everything I was saying to you right now—if I didn't care about you—do you think I'd be wasting my time in this stupid, toxic, circular argument with you?!"

No. No. No.

She was lying.

She had to be lying.

Because if she wasn't, then he was an abuser. He was a reprehensible, disgusting, piece of shit who didn't deserve to have any part of her. He wouldn't deserve her roots, her leaves, her blooms—nothing.

He wanted to die.

"Ash," she said. "My heart is tired."

Turning to look at her across the room, his dark expression met the exhaustion in hers.

"Then maybe you should get some fucking rest."

The guilt of what he'd done was too much. The yelling, the arguments, the cruelty, the hatred, the control. The despair, splattered against the backdrop of her disorder and adorned with memories of the moments they'd shared that caused him to fall for her. All of it, rolled up into one.

None of this would have happened if it weren't for her. If she would have just let him fix everything, then it never would have gotten to this point. They could have been happy. Things wouldn't have to be so volatile and hateful and maybe then, he wouldn't be so overwhelmed.

The splintered shards of his mind cracked, spiderwebbing outward from the center of his despair.

He couldn't do this anymore.

"I can't fucking take this," he hissed, his fingers tangled in his hair and his vision blurred with tears of pure, unbearable rage. "I can't fucking look at you for another second. You fucking *bitch*. I can't even look at you without smelling vomit. You won't stop until you kill yourself and you know what? I'm just gonna let you."

Tayshia's jaw hung open, her cheeks streaked with tears that fell, fell, fell. But he didn't care. He couldn't. He'd completely broken down. He breathed a laugh as a tear rolled down his cheek.

"I can't bear to look at you. I can't fucking bear to look at you, you selfish little girl. I give up." His eyebrows shot up as he walked backward toward the front door. "I'd rather you died than deal with this for another fucking day. Because I give up."

Tayshia was crying again, but this time, it was different. It was weak, like she was too breathless to get the necessary air into her lungs to get a full sob out. There was fear in her eyes as she watched him turn to the door. A fear that he knew well enough to taste.

"Ash," she said, his name faltering on a whimper. "Please don't give up on me. I'll do anything, just…Don't leave right now. Please don't leave me."

He left.

Chapter Twenty Six

Ash stood immobile on his godfathers' porch, his head down and his fists clenched. The panic moved through his shaking limbs like a slow poison. Every second that crawled by caused it to mount, to increase, to intensify, until he couldn't breathe. And when Ryo finally opened the door, Steven hovering behind him with curiosity and concern, he burst into tears.

"I can't fucking do it anymore," he sobbed, tangling his hands in his hair. "I can't do everything. I can't save her and I have to watch her fucking die because I keep messing everything up. Every choice I make is the wrong one and it just fucking *hurts*. I fucking can't, I can't, I can't—"

"Okay, okay! Ash!" His godparents came towards him, Ryo's voice barking over the sound of Ash's exclamations, and they wrapped him in their arms. "It's all right, son. Come on now. Everything's gonna be okay."

"It's not. She's gonna die and it'll be all my fault."

"Who's gonna die?" Steven asked, tone soft and cajoling. "No one is going to die."

"Yes, she is. She's going to die. You don't understand. You don't understand."

They ushered him forward, towards the entryway. Ash continued to weep, wiping his eyes with the back of his wrist, standing immobile in the living room as they shut the door.

The lamp was on, the TV playing a movie in the background. Steven picked up the remote and turned the volume on mute, and then the three of them sat down on the couch together. Ash tried to take several deep breaths, struggling to control his emotions, but it was like he'd been thrust into the center of flames that Tayshia had lit.

He couldn't breathe, couldn't think. None of his emotions made any sense to him. They felt like a tornado, countless streams of negativity swirling into a destructive funnel that tore through the lands of his heart. It was more than overwhelming. It was not something he felt he could survive.

Blowing up on Tayshia like that was wrong. Whether he wanted to give up on her recovery or not, it was wrong of him to tell her he was going to let her kill herself. He knew it wasn't her fault. He *knew* that her disorder wasn't something she could heal quickly. What wasn't fair was the fact that he'd hurt her just to make the fact that he was a horrible person easier to stomach.

She *was* trying. Deep down, he knew she was. He'd been shoving that knowledge aside for days just to make his failure to fix her easier to stomach.

Because it *was* unforgivable. He didn't deserve forgiveness for what he'd done to her. He certainly didn't deserve it for the awful things he'd said. No amount of apologies were going to erase it.

He was the selfish one. He was. He'd been doing whatever *he* wanted to try and fix her—also something that *he* wanted—and he hadn't been patient and compassionate. He hadn't been understanding enough to get her to a point where she'd even want to think about getting better.

Why couldn't he see past his fear?

"Tell us what happened," Ryo said into the heavy silence. "Tell us, so we can help you."

"It's a lot," he mumbled, misery keeping him mellow and quiet. Ash rested his elbows on his knees, hunched over, and twined his fingers behind his head.

"Did something happen with Tayshia?"

Ash said nothing.

"You remind me so much of your dad sometimes," Ryo said with a sigh, slinging a nonchalant arm around Ash's neck. "He used to keep his emotions close to the cuff, just like you."

"I don't think so. When he was angry, everyone knew it. *Trust* me."

"He's not talking about anger," Steven said, and Ash felt his hand on the center of his back. "He's talking about the darker stuff—the sadness, the self-hatred, the deepest parts of himself. He didn't like to share those things with anyone but your mother."

"Just tell us," Ryo said. "What problem is it you're trying to solve on your own right now? What is it you don't want anyone involved in? What is it you think you can fix?"

"What makes you think there's something I can't fix?" Ash asked, his voice tight. "Just because my dad lived in the shadow of a permanent crisis doesn't mean that I do."

"I don't think he knew that, unfortunately."

All right, fine, Ash thought, gritting his teeth. *I'll bite.*

"And what *did* he know?"

"That he won the award for Most Dramatic Asshole."

The day Ash laughed at a joke that painted his father in a positive light would be his last.

"Let me guess…Like me?"

Steven said, "The first week we met your parents, we weren't friends. He was convinced we were sneaking over in the middle of the night to poison his soil."

"Why would he think that?" Ash asked.

"Oh, it was his first year growing those roses. He was paranoid that it was us."

"How did he find out he was the problem?"

"By his own dramatics," Steven said, chuckling. "He sat in your dining room for three days straight with binoculars, trying to catch us in the act. The only thing that got him to realize it for sure was me marching over and offering to pay for someone to come check the soil. I think he realized that he was being ridiculous after that."

It was hard to hear stories about his father from before the drugs. From a time when Ash was still proud to be his son. After watching his father destroy their family, he didn't want to remember the good times. Especially when Gabriel didn't deserve to be remembered fondly.

Ryo's voice broke through his despairing thoughts, pulling his gaze up from the stone floor where it had fallen.

"He didn't do drugs because he wanted to hurt you, Ash. He did them because he was afraid that he was failing his family. The roses were beautiful and the awards were nice, but he could barely afford the bills. He was too stubborn to get a job because he believed the garden would pull through. He was traditional and he didn't want your mother to work. He sought out Ricky because he thought he had no other choice. And the stress got the best of him. He tried them once, and then he couldn't stop."

The feeling that shot through Ash's body was unexplainable. It was like an epiphany, an answer to the storm of emotions that had pushed him to his limit. Something that brought a sense of reasoning to his disposition.

He and his father were indeed very alike.

"Did my dad tell you guys this?" he asked, brow furrowed as his thoughts raced, whirling into an image that made more sense than the one he had painted in his mind of Gabriel Robards.

"Some of it," Steven said in a thoughtful voice. "Most of it, we could tell."

"How come?"

"He wore it like clothing. The stress and the guilt and the shame. The fear. He carried it everywhere with him. We just knew."

Ryo dropped his arm from Ash's neck and leaned forward on his elbows, too. They turned their heads toward one another, locking eyes. "Sometimes, Ash, you just act so much like him that it's hard to remember who I'm talking to. You both wear your emotions right here." He patted his hand against his own bicep. "And we can tell. Something is *wrong*. And I don't think it's just Tayshia."

There were three things that had always been certain regarding his father.

One of them was that he had a temper. He'd beaten Ash for things that made no sense, like dying his hair or looking at him with an attitude.

Another was that his father was a massive hypocrite with no regard for anyone's emotions other than ones that served him. He didn't care if Ash was screaming at him to stop hitting him, or if his wife was pleading with him to give her a break. Gabriel's sky was heavy with red clouds.

The third?

His father was ruthless.

Gabriel was *ruthless* and he would do whatever it took to protect what belonged to him. Sell roses, sell drugs, hold families at gunpoint in an ice cream shop. He would do absolutely anything to ensure that his family survived. Every choice he'd ever made had been with the intention of protecting his family from the fate of death by the hand of his own mistakes.

And his mother made Gabriel neither better nor worse as a person. She merely brought out parts of him that he'd already been capable of showing. She brought out the pain and the anger, the hatred and the bitterness. She gave him the freedom to punish his family for things he'd done and continued to do. All his wrong choices, leading their small family to ruin.

And now both of his parents were dead.

For Ash, Tayshia took the parts of him that were like his father and drew them out into the light. The things he wanted to hide inside of a cage of denial in his body, and the things about himself that he didn't want to claim. She took those things and made him feel something more than just numbness. Something more than a need to chase feeling underneath the needles that had etched the tattoos of his memories into his skin.

He could be his father's son if he wanted to.

"Son." Ryo looked at him. "What's on your mind?"

"Do you guys think people can change?" he asked, his voice soft. "Or do you think we stay the same forever?"

"This world is full of many, many different kinds of people," Steven said. "I think there's people who make good choices, and people who make bad ones. But I think all of those people have one thing in common: the desire for happiness. We all dream about it—our perfect life, our perfect world, our Heaven. Some of us make the wrong choices to bring ourselves happiness, and those wrong choices cause other people to get hurt. Some of us make the right choices and get to know what it feels like to live in joy. But at our cores, we all have the ability to make choices that have an effect on the world around us."

He stopped, frowning so deep that it drew horizontal lines across his forehead. He cleared his throat.

"Your dad was our dearest friend. Both of your parents were. They were our absolute *dearest* friends. But your dad wasn't perfect. He made *choices*. As long as we have the ability to make a choice, we can always make the right ones. So…Yes. I do think people can change. I think there's always room to make the right choices, even when it feels like it's too late."

"Do you think I can change?" Ash asked.

"I think you already have. And I think you know that." He pressed his lips together and then lifted one hand. After a moment's hesitation, he placed it upon his forearm. He squeezed, just like his mother used to do, and it made his throat ache and his eyes sting as though they were burning. "But I think you need to think about the choices you've made, and decide which ones are worth it."

"What do you mean?"

It was Steven who placed his hand upon him now. "I think you should put some serious thought into your relationship with Tayshia. I think you need to get some help for what you've been through. And I think you should take the first step to your recovery."

"What if she needs help, too?" Ash whispered, his throat aching at the thought of leaving her. *Really* leaving her.

"It's not your job. Your job is to worry about—" Steven touched the center of Ash's chest with his pointer finger. "—*you*. You worry about you, and hope that she'll choose her own recovery, too."

Ryo spoke up. "You can't fix someone who doesn't want to be fixed, and you shouldn't have to destroy yourself to try and convince them life is worth living. You've planted your roses in her soil, but her soil—"

"Is dead," Ash interjected. "Her soil is dead."

"And it's killing you, too. Don't let that happen. Whatever choice you make, make sure it's not the wrong one."

His parents had been a complete disaster, lying and hiding, hurting themselves and others. As much as he loved his mother, she'd stood by while her son was pulled down into the darkness. His father had done worse, dragging them into the fires of Hell.

Not his godparents.

Steven and Ryo were there for him. They wanted the best for him. They loved him.

In that moment, as the time hung suspended between them, Ash considered telling them everything about Tayshia, the crystals, and his mother's disorder. He thought of opening his mouth and making the choice to let it all come tumbling out. But the second he imagined himself doing it, his chest expanded with a panic that made him want to pass out. The fear that things would backfire, or that Tayshia would hate him for leaving her, or that she would never choose life, made him physically ill. He knew there was a chance he couldn't save her.

But he couldn't give up on her.

I can handle this.

Ash knew Tayshia was sick. She was *very* sick. But she was trying and he was willing to put in the effort to see it through. He was willing to take this to the very edge of the Earth just so he could show her that he wasn't gonna bury her. He would much rather show her what it looked like when the roses he'd planted in her soil bloomed.

There was no need to be perfect. No need to be the person who fixed everything. But he didn't need to be the person who gave up on her, either.

He just needed to be the person who stayed.

CHAPTER TWENTY SEVEN

The moonlight glanced off the hardwood floor of the dining room, spilling opalescent onto the living room carpet. With everything else being so dark, it was almost as though it were directing him down a path into the house. He walked forward, the wall of the kitchen to his right, and stopped at the edge.

He couldn't see her, but he could hear her weeping.

Ash was determined. He was going to go in there and start communicating for once — *really* communicating. He wanted to open up to her in a way that wasn't serving himself. He was going to sit down with her, apologize for everything that he'd done wrong, and ask her what she needed from him.

They had problems, yes, but they were problems that were going to take time to work through. His anger and her fear. Her manipulation and his selfishness. Pain. Grief. This was the destruction the dragon had wrought. It was up to him to put out the flames.

"Tell me if your heart is tired."

Tayshia was on the floor, collapsed. The refrigerator door was open, spilling yellow light out across the linoleum. The freezer and oven were, too.

She was surrounded by food.

It was on the floor, most of it having been emptied from within the fridge. Plastic containers with leftovers were open, empty. She'd eaten an entire bag of mini carrots, all of the celery and broccoli, and none of the fruit was left. The pantry door was open and anything inside had been opened and picked through. There were countless other things strewn about the floor. Food she'd nibbled and set aside for later. Food she'd devoured until there was nothing left.

And she wept.

"I can't *breathe*," she was sobbing, like putting the food into her mouth was painful. Like she couldn't stop. Like she had no reason to. "I *can't*."

Firelight in the Dark

This was all his fault.

She had a spoon and an ice cream carton in her hands, her piteous wails sounding between each bite. Her hair was pulled up on top of her head, a few of the ends hanging down to frame her face from the haste with which she had tugged it up.

"I can't, I can't, I can't."

His heart shattered into millions of pieces that went soaring into different, unfindable dimensions. Broken, he fell to his knees beside her. She jolted, looking up at him with a terrified expression on her utterly destroyed face. The tears continued to fall, and fall, and fall.

But Ash didn't hesitate.

He made a grab for the ice cream carton. She shrieked, dropping the spoon as she latched onto the container with both hands. They struggled, and she turned her back to him, forcing his arm around half of her body as he tried to wrench it out of her grasp. Her leg kicked out, hitting the open refrigerator door and sending it inward a bit.

"Stop! Tayshia, *stop!*"

"*No!*" she screamed, practically sitting on him as she kept a tight hold of the ice cream. "*I need it!*"

"No, you *don't!*"

He ripped the ice cream carton out of her hands and tossed it aside. It crashed against the cupboard beneath the sink and toppled to the ground, rolling to the side. Tayshia cried out and pitched forward, starting to crawl toward it. Ash wrapped his arm around her waist and hauled her back. She kicked her feet against the ground, writhing in his arms until she finally turned to face him while half-sitting on the floor.

Her hands slapped at his chest, her tear-streaked face contorted with fury. He batted her right hand to the side and grabbed her left wrist. She bared her teeth. He snatched her other wrist out of the air before she could land another blow. In the chaos of their battle, the empty containers clattered across the floor and the food she hadn't eaten spilled onto the bare linoleum.

"I'm not gonna hurt you, all right?" he said. "Calm down!"

"No. No, you don't—you need to—*let me go!*"

"Calm the fuck down!"

"Let me go! I need it! You don't understand!" Her breathing came in short, hysterical pants. "Let go of me!"

Ash shook her by the wrists, her head whipping back and forth as he tried to put the sense back into her body. All he needed was a few moments. Just a few short moments to walk her back from the ledge.

Tayshia sucked in her breath and it caught in her throat, held abated. Her eyes were wild, rolling about as she tried to decide between looking at him or looking over at the ice cream.

"You don't need it," he said.

"Please, okay?" she whimpered. Her expression turned desperate and she twisted in his grasp. "*Please*. I need it."

"No." He held firm, his expression dark and cold as he growled through his teeth. "You don't fucking need it."

Her eyes searched his and for a second, he thought she was breathing normally. But when he loosened his hold on her, sure that she had calmed down, she scrambled across the kitchen floor and grabbed the ice cream. Ash knelt there, shocked as she reached into the slowly-melting dessert and scooped out a handful of white. She shoved it into her mouth, her brows furrowed together as though she were in pure anguish.

Ash wasn't the only one who had shattered.

He snapped into action, getting to his feet and reaching down to haul her up by the elbows. When they were standing, covered in the remnants of the food on the floor, he loomed over her like a sentinel in the dark. He grabbed her forearm and squeezed until she cried out in pain and loosened her hold. He grabbed the rim of the carton. With a snarl, he tore it away from her and dropped it.

She tried to dive for it, a pitiful sight in her hysterics. He'd never seen anything like this before and he knew he never wanted to again.

This time, he wrapped his arms around her from the side, over her upper arms to trap her. She struggled, using the full weight of her body, and they stumbled back together. He knocked into the refrigerator door, closing it all the way and plunging them into darkness. He felt a throbbing pain shoot down his leg when the side of his thigh hit the counter.

"Stop!" he shouted.

"You need to let me go, Ash! *Let me fucking go!*"

He held her tighter, his eyes adjusting to the dark with the help of the faded moonlight shining in from the kitchen window.

"Stop."

"Just let go of me! Let go of me!" She fought so hard that it strained his muscles to hold on tighter.

He crushed her against his chest, his heart barely able to pump blood through his body from the weight of his sadness and pity. When she turned toward him, trying to get her hands underneath his arms to push against him with the bottoms of her forearms, their eyes met. In that split second, he tried his best to thread every last bit of desperation he had for her into his gaze.

"Stop."

"Why are you even here?!" Her voice had grown weaker, starting to crack. Her hands curled, her fists shoving against him. "You told me you'd rather I just *died. Why did you come back?!"*

He couldn't speak. Didn't need to. Because as the urge he had to break down and dissolve into tears of his own grew, the tidal waves of her wrath had begun to subside. He could feel the sea leaving her body like the moon had pulled it back to the depths.

"Why can't I just be the girl everyone likes?" she whined, the steam of her outburst slowly filtering out through her words. "Why do I have to be the girl that no one understands? Why do people always want to *hurt* me? Why can't I just be the girl that everyone wants to take care of? Why can't I—Why can't I—"

Keeping one arm around her back, his throat aching with unbidden emotion, he grabbed her chin and forced her to look up at him. She tried to sag downward, to remove herself from his grasp as though he were shining too bright to witness. Her facial expression was pained. Desolate.

"I like you," he said through his teeth, willing her to accept his heart and hold it inside of her. "I understand you. I don't want to hurt you. I want to take care of you. And I'm sorry."

Her chin trembled and her eyes squeezed until they were almost shut. Her tears leaked out past her lashes. He could feel her knees losing strength, felt her weight dragging down against the force of his hold. Felt her pain pulling her down into the depths of soil that kept rejecting her and making it harder for her to take root. He wished he could till the soil and force it to accept her, so she could grow and bloom into a girl whose smile reached her eyes.

So he sank down with her.

The moment they hit the floor, his back slamming against the cupboard and the side of her upper body leaning into his, she began to wail. It was different from before, this weeping. It was the kind that he knew felt like a monster had taken its shadowy claws, reached down into the pit of her stomach, and yanked the emotion through her mouth.

She was sobbing the same way she had in that hotel room in Paris.

Right arm still around her shoulder, Ash wrapped his left arm around the front of her, curving it until his hand cupped the side and top of her head. He tucked her underneath his chin and held her close. Lifting his right knee and letting his left leg stretch out along the floor, he became boneless so she would have something soft and welcome to break down against. He held her because she needed to be held. She *deserved* to be held.

Sitting curled up amongst the food, this was a somber, near-grotesque representation of the state of their relationship. Two broken people held captive by food. Food, which should have been harmless and given life. Food, which had destroyed her and through her, him.

"Just let me die," she sobbed, her entire body trembling with a violence that ached in his own. Her weeping didn't sound human. It was almost too much for him to comprehend, yet not enough to push him away. "Just let me die, Ash, *please*."

"No." His vision was blurring. "No, okay? Never."

"Why not? It's what you said you wanted. It's what you said. You always leave."

"I'm sorry."

And then they were both crying.

Ash fell apart, his own sobs hovering just beneath hers, lifting them up as though he wanted to carry them both. He pressed her head even closer, burying his face in her hair as he wept. There had never been another time where he felt like he treasured her more, here with her curled up against him like this. He felt like he'd kill anyone who laid a hand on her. If she threw herself off of a cliff and he couldn't save her, he'd throw himself off right after.

All this time, he'd been worried about being a failure to himself when he should have been worrying about failing her.

"I'm so sorry," he murmured again and again. "Please forgive me. I'm so fucking sorry."

I'm weak.

"I'm trying, Ash. I am. I'm just so scared."

I'm so weak for her.

"It's okay to be scared. I am, too. More than you know. But I'm here. I'm not gonna leave you ever again."

I'm so fucking weak.

"I don't remember who I was before it." She took a deep breath that shuddered like tree branches in the forest and began to sob again. "I don't remember the girl I was before it happened, and I want her back. I just want her *back*."

"God fucking *dammit*," was all he could manage to push out as he crushed her so tight to his body that he feared she'd stop breathing. "It's all right. It's okay. I'm not leaving."

Her hand finally came up, her fingers curving over his bicep and holding it firm against her chest. She turned her face and he felt the wetness of her cheeks against the side of his throat. Her breath brushed his neck.

"I don't want to be sick anymore," she said. "I just want to be happy."

"You will. I promise you that I will make you happy. I'll take you away from all of it, do you hear me?"

She lifted her head, gazing up at him. It was still dark in the kitchen and the backdrop of the moonlight seemed to illuminate everything but her face. Her gorgeous face, which he cupped between tender hands and held as though it were made of spun glass. A face that he would gladly wake up to again and again if only it meant that she was alive.

"I will take you far away from here and take care of you. For the *rest* of my fucking life. I just need you to keep trying. Okay?" He sniffled again, his hands traveling down her upper arms and finding purchase on her waist. "Okay?"

Tayshia reached one hand up, where she swept her ice cream-stained fingers across one of his tear tracks. Her hand trailed down the side of his neck and wrapped around the nape, leaving the cool air in the kitchen to kiss his skin in its wake.

"I will."

He pressed his forehead against hers. Closing his eyes, he tried to imagine a world without her in it and found that the image was too vivid. Painted across the expanse of his mind like the blood of a dying artist upon their last canvas. It wasn't supposed to look this clear.

Why could he see it so well?

"Don't stop trying," he whispered. Begged. *Pleaded*. "Don't ever stop trying."

Her other hand slid up his chest, her fingers tickling the right side of his neck. He felt her lips grazing his, barely present as she whispered back, "I won't stop."

Ash tilted his chin up, causing their lips to meet in a chaste, gentle kiss.

"Yeah?"

"I won't stop." Another soft kiss. "I won't."

He let out a harsh breath and kissed her jawline, to the left of the corner of her mouth. His mind was already starting to twist with smoke. "Yeah?"

"Yeah," she said as his lips moved up her jaw, toward her ear.

He felt her trembling intensify, punctuated with random jolts and hitches in her breathing pattern as he got closer to the tender flesh beneath the lobe. He laid a kiss there, opening his mouth so he could suck and pull a heavier pant from within her.

When his kisses moved ever-so-slowly down towards her shoulder, his left hand rose. He hooked one finger in the collar of her dress and exposed her bare skin so he could taste the length of her collarbone. Her head lolled to the side, against the front of his right shoulder, and he felt her breath on his neck again. His lips once again found her ear and he breathed into it.

"Yeah?"

"*Yes*," she moaned, her chest arching upward. Her fingers curled tight in his hair while her other hand wrapped around the back of his head to keep his face buried in her throat. He knew she could feel the remnants of his tears, and he tasted the salt of them on her skin as his tongue darted out. "Yes. More."

He kissed her neck until she was a puddle on the floor, sighing and tremulous. She grabbed his hand and pulled it lower. At the same time, she adjusted so that she was sitting with her back against his upraised thigh, placing her feet flat on the floor. He kissed her on the lips as he took control, cupping her through her panties without hesitancy. She moaned when his tongue brushed against hers, and his fingers began to move. She gripped his leg—the one that was flat on the floor—and her head fell back against the cupboard.

"Please," she gasped, sounding dazed and faint. Her hips undulated to the massaging motions of his hand. Her thighs fell further apart. "I want—*please*."

Ash couldn't think about anything other than her. Her, this moment, and everything he felt for her. He wanted to make her happy. He wanted to make her feel good so she wouldn't cry anymore. He didn't like it when she cried because of him.

Ignoring the sound of dismay she made when he pulled his hand away, he took her by the shoulders and pushed. Tayshia laid down amongst the food and empty containers that were still strewn about the floor, her hair fanning out from the speed with which they had moved. Ash swung his knee over to the other side of her.

She looked back at him with sadness. "I'm a bad person."

"No," he said, shaking his head. One hand propping himself up, he leaned down to kiss her neck again. Her back rose until their chests were flush together. "You're not."

She lifted her head as he started to move down her body, his fingers slipping beneath the hem of her hoodie. He pushed it up, up, up, and she helped him take it off of her. She laid back again, clad in naught but her underwear.

"I am," she said, her voice small. "I'm bad to you and for you."

"No," he said as he kissed down her right arm and brought her palm to his lips. His gaze bored down into her through the shadows. "You're so good."

"Everything—" She gasped when his lips found the peak of her breast, his saliva soaking her skin as he pulled it into his mouth. "Everything I do is so—so b-bad."

He hummed his disapproval as he touched her abdomen. It was tight, distended by how much she'd eaten. The grunt of pain she made when both of his hands smoothed over it made him feel sad. He kissed it everywhere, from one side to the other, soft brushes of skin on skin.

"You're good," he murmured, looking up at her through his lashes as he slipped his fingers into the waistband of her panties. He began to drag them downward. "You feel good and you taste good. Will you let me see how good you taste again?"

"Yes," she said, her tone reverent.

Ash sat up on his knees and pulled the underwear off of her. He lifted her ankle up near his shoulder with a light hand and nuzzled his nose along the inside of her calf. He kissed her skin and tasted it. Her toes flexed, pressing into his shoulder. She gasped again, the sounds urging his blood downward.

A whimper escaped her lips right as he reached the inside of her knee and he paused. His hands caressed her leg, kneading the muscle.

"Are you all right?"

"I'm sorry," she said, and she started to cry again. "I just don't think I'm good enough for you."

"You are," he said, remaining patient as he resumed his path to her core. He breathed in her scent, his tongue running through her arousal and causing her hips to come off of the floor. He kissed her in the place that made her thighs shake, and then looked up at her. "I want you to tell me how good you are for me, okay?"

She made several attempts to answer, all while his lips sucked at her clit, but all she could manage were whimpers that decorated her weeping.

"Tell me," he breathed, his hands caressing her hips to pull her down against his tongue. "Say you're good to me."

"I'm good to you." Her fingers trembled in his hair.

He pulled back again, one hand flat on the floor and the other searching between her legs for her entrance. When he found it, two fingers surged forward to hit her in the spot he could find ten times over in the dark.

"Tell me you're good with me," he ordered, thrusting his fingers in and out of her body with firm, hard strokes.

Her eyes were closed, her mouth gaping open. Her legs spread wider, her feet using the sturdiness of the floor to push her hips to meet his fingers thrust for thrust. She shook.

"I'm good—*God*." Another whimper. "I'm good with you. We're—*ah*—good together."

"Yes, we are," he purred, watching the outline of his ministrations in the darkness. "Now, tell me you're good for me, and I'll make you come."

He fucked her with his fingers. He ran his tongue over her clit. She let out a sob, one hand slapping flat. She hit a container and sent it clattering across the floor. She inhaled again and again and again, and then groaned.

"Oh, my *God*," came the words, desperate and pitchy. "I'm good for you. I'm being so good for you. I'm gonna come. God, fuck, I'm gonna come."

He moaned against her core, softening the strokes of his tongue and increasing the pace of his fingers. He heard the lewd noises as she grew wetter and it made his stomach coil with that familiar tightness. She tasted so *fucking* good, and she rode his tongue like she was using it. Like she knew exactly what she needed.

He wouldn't mind being used by her.

"Ash...I...G-Gentler— *Yes. Right there!*" she cried, her fingernails curling into the floor by her hips. He felt one of her feet pressing its toes into his thigh. She gave one more gasp, and then she was sobbing as her orgasm shattered her into trembling pieces.

When he kissed his way back up her body and settled between her thighs, she kissed him with an intensity that he hadn't expected. He turned his head to the side, his hands flat on the floor by her head as their tongues battled and fought. She arched her back up into him, her hips rolling in a way that felt like she was trying to pull him as close as she possibly could. Her fingers gripped, pulled, clung. They tugged, refusing to let him go.

They broke apart for a moment, their eyes meeting. The moonlight made her look pale. The tear tracks that glistened on her face were fresh.

"Why are you crying?" he whispered, his gaze bouncing back and forth between her eyes and her lips.

"Because." She held his face with both of her hands. "I feel safe with you."

His brows twitched together, confusion bleeding through the haze of his intense, deep-rooted lust for her. After everything he'd done to her—after every mistake he'd made—she still felt safe with him?

She caressed his jaw, her fingers fluttering to tilt it to the side. His arms shook as she began to kiss his neck. Any sense of control he had maintained dissipated. His eyelids fluttered and he moaned at the softness of the tingling shocks that shot through him. One hand still on the floor, he cupped the back of her head and pushed his throat into the grazing of her teeth.

"Please," she whispered, her lips mouthing at his earlobe. It caused his hips to involuntarily jerk forward, pressing intimately against her. "Please, Ash. I want you."

He shuddered when she bit his earlobe, moving to grab her hair. He dragged her head back, baring his teeth. Their hips rolled together, an absentminded expression of their fervor.

"Do you want me to fuck you right here on the floor?"

The look on her face turned desperate as a fresh set of tears made their way down her cheeks. "Yes. Yes, please."

His mind was like the inside of a crystal in the sunlight, multi-faceted planes of diamond reflecting all the colors of the rainbow.

And inside of each color was another year he could spend with Tayshia. Another year where they were happy, healthy, and together. It was more than a dream. More than a glimpse of eternity.

She was everything he wanted.

He wrapped his hand around the top of her throat, pulling her up into a wild kiss. His hips rolled against hers, the front of his jeans rubbing against her bare, wet core. She broke the kiss to cry out in pleasure, writhing beneath him, wanton as she ground up against him without shame or care.

"Do you really want this?" He breathed into her mouth, squeezing her throat tighter.

"*Please*," she moaned, and it sounded like it was being dragged up out of the depths of her lungs. "I'll do anything. Just *please*. I can't wait anymore."

The last chain wrapped around his neck broke apart, the metaphorical metal shattering like glass.

Ash slammed his lips against hers, swallowing her sobs and tasting the salt of her tears on her lips. She didn't stop weeping, not even for a second, even as she grabbed the hem of his shirt and started to rip it upward. They worked together to get it off of him, and then her hands went to his belt, tugging the tail out of the loops and buckle. He reached over the back of his head to pull his shirt off, and then her hand was inside of his boxers.

The colors in his mind swirled together.

Her fingers were wrapped around him, moving up and down. She pushed his jeans and then his boxers down over the swell of his rear. Her back hit the floor as he felt her guiding his cock to slide along her center. The feeling was overwhelming, compounded by the knowledge that his heart beat for her.

God, did she deserve to be loved. She deserved to be held, kissed, touched, fucked, and *loved*. She deserved everything she ever wanted, no matter what.

She deserved to be *happy*.

"You know what I mean when I say I'm not gonna leave you again?" he whispered into her ear, his arms straining from holding himself up and still. "You know that it means forever?"

"Yes." She smiled through her tears and the darkness of the kitchen. "I know what it means, and I want this with you. I want eternity."

The words alone were enough to make him want to lose his senses. His hips rolled and her hand went slack around him. She sucked in her breath as the head of his cock slipped inside, as if by accident. A shiver ran through his body and he bit his lip.

"You are mine." He gripped her knees and held her legs open, spreading her wider for him as he sunk deeper into her body. "You're mine to kiss." He went deeper. "To hold." Deeper. "To touch." And deeper still. "To *fuck*."

He slammed in the rest of the way, relishing in the sound of her cry. Her cunt was the epitome of a dream, and it threatened to shatter his heart from the sheer bliss of it. Like velvet wrapped around him, scorching hot in the sort of way that made him never want to leave.

"Look at me now, sweet girl," he gasped when he pulled out and slid back in with an agonizingly-slow thrust. She did, and the intensity of it wracked through him. "*Fuck*, you feel so fucking good."

"Please go harder," she whimpered, her hips trying to urge him faster. "I need it harder."

"Not yet," he whispered, continuing the slow ebb and flow of his hips. He wanted to remember this. The moonlight washing over the far side of the floor. The shadows dancing across her face. Her swollen, parted lips. Her hair splayed around her head like a crown.

"I thought you left me," she said.

"I'm here," he murmured, dipping his head down to kiss first her left nipple and then her right. His tongue pressed against them, causing her to shiver. "I'm not going anywhere ever again."

Tayshia moaned, a short, surprised sound as he hit that spot inside of her. They stared at one another as he gave her one more long, slow thrust.

She reached up with one hand, her fingers sliding into the hair at his hairline. Her gaze washed over him, another tear slipping down the side of her cheek and towards her ear. There was affection in her eyes, trust, and something he didn't dare question. He nuzzled his head into her touch, the blissful feeling causing his hips to jerk forward.

"I love you."

He stared at her, all of the colors in his mind momentarily bleaching white.

"What did you just say?"

"*Please*. Please believe me. I'm so sorry I lied to you. I was scared of the way you make me feel. You fight for me. You fight for me every day, even when it's me you have to fight, and it makes me want to get better. It makes me feel like I can see something in myself worth saving. I don't deserve it, but I want it. I want it so badly. I want you. I love you, Ash. I love you and I'm sorry. I want to get better. I mean it."

He didn't care about any of it—their problems, the things that could go wrong, or the hurdles they were currently facing. She loved him. She *loved* him, and he could tell it was real. Her tears were real. Her trust was real.

After everything they'd been through together, after Paris, after their downfall, she *loved* him.

He surged forward to cut her off with a violent kiss, and then he *fucked* her.

Tayshia threw her arms up on the floor by her head, her hands curling into fists as he slammed into her again and again, fucking her exactly like she deserved to be fucked. She took his cock like it belonged to her, the tightness of her channel devouring him. His fingers pressed bruises into her hips as he leaned over her, pinning her down so she could do nothing more than squirm, moan, and beg.

"Say it again. Please say it to me again."

"I love you."

"You're so fucking beautiful to me, Tayshia. Perfect for me. Just perfect."

Her fingers came up to smooth across the tattoos that adorned his chest and abdomen. His muscles flexed, pulling taut as he thrust so hard that he saw stars die. It felt so good. She was so good.

He sucked his fingers into his mouth and reached between their sweating bodies to play with her clit. Her body immediately went limp, contrasting with the desperate, tight strain of her moaning. He thrust hard and stroked slow, dragging her towards a second climax.

"Say it while you come. Please, fucking say it while you *fucking* come."

Her back arched once more, her eyes rolling up into her head as he played the strings of her violin as though he'd been doing it for years. She created a symphony in his heart with her words and climbing moans. *"I love you."* It would forever be his favorite song.

She came, her walls clenching down on him to hold him tight. He heard her whimpering, felt her shuddering and convulsing, and his thrusting stuttered.

Her song crested and he lost control.

The notes harmonized with the tune of his body. It wound tightly around him and inside of him, pulling him to a crescendo from which he couldn't catch his escaping breath. His chest spasmed and he gasped. He pushed her knees towards her chest, until he was fucking down into her like he was searching for something to the tune of her euphoric wailing.

He found it, whatever it was, and the words fell out of him as he hung on the precipice.

"Fuck, I love you so fucking much," he said, his lips frantic against her jaw. He pushed her thighs open, causing him to sink to the absolute deepest he could go inside of her. "I love you. I'll do anything for you. Anything. Just wrap your arms around me. Please, please do it. Do it."

Tayshia groaned, throaty and delirious as she laid there. She burrowed her face into his neck to stifle her moans as he rammed into her again and again and again and—

He came with his tongue against her pulse and his hands gripping her rear. Pulling her closer, holding her against him as he emptied himself into her. The pleasure was immense. So immense that he whimpered into the junction of her neck and shoulder.

They decided to lay there and catch their breath before going to up to the bedroom to lay down. He pillowed his head on her bare chest while she trailed her fingers up and down his back in lazy, circular patterns.

He could feel it, like a thread of magic sewing them together. Indestructible and comforting, it was only visible to him when he looked for it. But he always knew it was there.

They'd never be alone again.

Chapter Twenty Eight

When Tayshia and Ash woke the next morning, nestled in the soft sheets and comforter of the bed, they talked and decided to put their necklaces back on. After everything they'd been through, they both believed it was fitting. It would represent them putting the volatile past behind them, and trying to make a positive decision for their future.

"Can you imagine what our lives would be like if we'd never pulled these out of the wall?" Tayshia asked quietly when they returned to the bed. They had woken early, so they were lying down as long as they could before they needed to get ready for school. They were lying on their sides, facing one another.

"What if we'd never gone into that cave?" Ash said, raising his eyebrows. "I was surprised to see your goody-two-shoes ass there in the first place."

"I wasn't as much of a goody two-shoes as you thought I was. I was barely passing my classes. I was just involved in a lot of extracurriculars."

"Ah, so your good girl persona was just an act. A facade, if you will."

"Shut up." She wrinkled her nose and scooted closer to him. "You like me better as a *good girl* anyway."

"Mm, I like you better as *my* good girl."

She tilted her chin up right as he lowered his, and their lips met. It was like the fire that they'd set alight the night before had flared to life again, eclipsing them as fast as a forest fire. Within seconds, he had her on her back, one of her thighs pulled against his side as their tongues danced and their hips rolled. They exchanged pants and gasps, each seeking to quell the flames with every movement.

"Do we have time?" she breathed through a moan when he ran his tongue along her pulse and nipped the skin.

"We're going to make time. Come here."

Ash grabbed her thighs and pulled, causing her to slide down on the bed until he was hovering over her.

"Look at me. You know I like it when you look at me. There's a good girl."

She looked into his eyes as he slipped his fingers inside her. With each thrust, she inhaled.

"I'm coming," she whispered, her voice strained, eyelids fluttering and fingers digging into his upper arms.

Right as her breaths turned to whines, he lowered his head to kiss her.

"You're so pretty. Anyone ever told you how fucking pretty you are?"

"You."

"I don't tell you enough."

He sank inside her while she was still shuddering. She threw her head back. Ash didn't stop to let her breathe, his hips snapping against hers as he sought out the center of his own galaxy. She was delirious with the feelings he was bringing her, murmuring praises and gratitude as he brought her to another orgasm with his fingers reaching between them.

It was different now. More intense. The way she felt around him. The way his desire tingled through his veins like wildfire. The arch of her body as she molded it to fit his. The soft press of his tongue to hers as he delved deep within her body like light through the atmosphere.

"Fuck, I love you," he gasped before he sucked and licked his way down her throat, to her collarbones. "Do you love me, too?"

"I love you," she replied, and then her moans grew high-pitched. Her thighs tightened around his hips. She was close, dangling on the edge of euphoria. "I love—Oh, God. Oh, God."

Ash pressed his hand to the center of her chest, pinning her flat as he put his other hand on the bed beside her. His strokes were as deep as they were long, dragging up the inside of her pelvis. Her eyes rolled up into her head.

"Come on, pretty girl. Come on and tell me how it feels."

"It feels so good."

"Are you gonna come for me the way I like?"

She nodded, her brows pulling together as she whimpered.

"Use your words, baby girl."

"Yes, I—" Her eyelids snapped open and their eyes met. "I'm going to."

"Ask me nicely."

"*Please*. Please make me come."

He touched her clit, pressing in slick circles that had her thighs spasming and her lips parting. When she came, her body clenching and tightening around him, he didn't have the strength to bask in it. He grabbed her hips and angled them upward, driving down inside of her on the way to bliss. Tayshia cried out with each thrust, her fingers sliding up to curve over the top of his shoulders. He muttered a string of unintelligible curse words and then, with one final thrust, he felt the pleasure sparking electricity through his blood. He wrapped his arms around her waist as he climaxed, burying his face in the crook of her neck. There was no way to be closer to her than he was, and he knew that if there were, he'd find it if he could.

The crystal was no longer heavy around his neck.

✿✿✿

Tayshia didn't show up for lunch.

Ash sat on the bench of his usual table with the window at his back, casting glances toward the door. Where was she? Everything had gone so well this morning. After the emotional night they'd had, and the wonderful morning, would she really do this? Would she try to skip lunch?

Would she take advantage of him again?

No. He had to think the best of her. He loved her. Love was built on trust. He needed to trust her. Maybe a teacher had kept her after class. Maybe she was seeing Nurse Pritchard for some reason. Maybe she was talking to a friend, and got caught up.

But what if she wasn't?

He couldn't shake the anxiety that had dug its claws into his heart, restricting its beating and making it difficult for him to breathe. Something could be wrong. She could be hurt. She could have fainted in class, or something.

Ten minutes into his sandwich, Ji Hyun walked over to the table. She set her tray down and plopped down, lamenting Andre's absence that day. Apparently, he had allergies.

"You know how it gets for him in the spring," she said with a roll of her eyes. "He's a baby. When I get home, he's gonna want me to take care of him, and it's annoying. But I'll do it anyway because he's cute."

"Yeah, she left at the start of lunch."

Ash frowned. "Was she walking?"

"No, she was with Elijah," another of the girls said. "I heard them say they were going home."

Without thanking the girls or saying good-bye, he ran to his car. He could hear nothing but the sound of his own angry heartbeat as he slid his keys out of his pocket and opened the door. He tossed his books and binder onto the passenger's seat and buckled his seatbelt.

If he left now, he might make it home in time to confront them.

✵✵✵

Ash didn't bother to open the garage. His car screeched to a halt in the driveway of his family home. He slammed the door, hoping they heard it from inside.

Something was wrong. It was inside of him — a feeling he couldn't shake. It nagged at the back of his mind, refusing to let him calm down until he got answers. It was like putting his jeans on backward, or holding his phone upside down on a call.

It was either something was wrong, or they were fucking each other.

He didn't know which would be worse.

The second he stepped into the house, it was like a bug to a lightbulb. His gaze zeroed in on the downstairs bathroom. The door was open. The light was on. Tayshia was on her knees in front of the toilet. Elijah was behind her, his hands scraping Tayshia's hair back out of the way. unaware of Ash's presence. There was a single retching noise, followed by a loud gasp and Elijah's voice saying, "*What*? What's wrong?!"

No.

Fuck no.

There was no way that she would skip class just to purge in his childhood home.

But she would. She had. And as he walked across the carpet and past the dining room, he saw that he was too late.

Tayshia fell to the floor, collapsing on her side with her arms thrown haphazardly by her head, one knee fully bent and the other only half-bent. There was vomit in the toilet. It was smeared across Her face and hand, red and orange and green mixed together like a disgusting tribute to the porcelain god she'd been worshiping for one day too long. Elijah stood over her, his face ashen and his hands sunk deep into his hair, his expression horrified.

"Have you seen Tayshia?" Ash asked, completely ignoring everything she'd just said.

"I didn't see her. I thought you always picked her up from her class," Ji Hyun said, popping a fry into her mouth. "I don't know why I thought that."

"No, I never do. I just wait for her here."

Ji Hyun shook her head, her black hair shaking with the movement. "Maybe she skipped class?"

"Yeah. Maybe."

Except that she wouldn't do that. She wasn't the type. There'd been times where they skipped class together, but she was a girl who liked routine. The routine recently had been for him to drop her off at her first class, to eat lunch together, and then for her to wait in the library after her last class for his last class period. Then, they went home. Tayshia didn't break the routine.

So where was she?

Ash didn't make it much longer. Between his leg bouncing under the table with his heavy agitation and the violent way his stomach kept clenching, there was no way that he could stay there. While Ji Hyun was busy complaining about the taste of the fries, he gathered up his tray and drink.

"Wait, where are you going?" she asked, bewildered.

"To find her."

Tossing his trash into the can, he left the cafeteria.

Ash searched the entire school. He walked so fast, his thighs burned. He checked the halls, the stairwells, the bathrooms. He peeked into the classrooms. He searched the massive building from top to bottom, and it took him thirty minutes to figure out that she wasn't inside. And by the time he'd finished checking the outside, he was concerned that she'd wandered into the woods.

But when he walked down the stairs in front of the school, at a loss for what to do next, he spotted a group of girls from the prerequisite program. They'd been sitting on the stone wall and had just finished their lunches. They were headed right toward him and when they saw him, they greeted him.

"Are you looking for Tayshia?" one of the girls asked, a brunette with her hair in a messy bun.

"Yes, actually," he said, crossing his arms over his chest. The sun was high and bright, warming the top of his head. "Have you seen her?"

It had only been a second. Ash had *just* heard her throw up.

What the fuck happened?

"I-I-I was just holding her—her hair back," Elijah said, his voice desperate and panicked. "I was just holding it back and then she just—she just *fell over.*"

"Shut up."

" I—I don't—I don't know what—"

"Shut up," Ash breathed, his hand trembling as he held it in the air for silence, "and move."

"I don't know what happened." There were tears in Elijah's eyes as he moved back, towards the door to the so Ash could enter the room. "I swear to God. She was fine a second ago. I don't know what happened."

"I told you...To shut. The fuck. *Up.*"

Elijah's mouth snapped closed.

Ash did not possess the wherewithal to grasp that he had seen Elijah holding her hair back. Didn't have the mental capacity to focus on the hows and the whys. He didn't care about that right now. He couldn't.

All he saw was Tayshia, lying prone on the floor. Just like his mother, collapsing in the courtroom. Dying in the hospital, her last breath escaping her before he could catch it. It was every nightmare he'd been fighting so hard to stop from coming true. Like a twisted version of his dream world—where the silver stars in the lavender sky had all gone out, the mountains had erupted, the ocean had reared up in a destructive tidal wave, and the flowers had burned away.

Their last dream had been an omen.

"No. No, no, no. You're not. You're fucking not. Come here. Come on," Ash said in a whiny rush of breath, falling to his knees beside Tayshia, gathering her up into his arms. His fingers smeared through the vomit as he wiped it from her face. He was losing it. He was about to fall apart, and he didn't know what to do.

Elijah stepped forward. "I swear I didn't—"

"Shut your fucking mouth!" Ash roared. "Go call an ambulance!"

"But—"

"No! Go call a fucking ambulance, you stupid piece of shit!"

A pained, terrified expression flashed across Elijah's face, and then he ran out of the bathroom.

"Come on," Ash whispered, his voice nearly a whine. Why was her head lolling backward like that? His soiled fingers fluttered down to her pulse, pressing inward. Feeling. Searching. Trying to find a flicker of life. "Don't fucking leave me, Tayshia. Don't you fucking do this right now. Come on. Please, please. Stay, baby. Please stay."

There was nothing. *Nothing.*

Everything in his mind went white. He dropped her body to the ground and started CPR, his hands pressing down so hard on her chest that he feared he might crack the bone. Sweat beaded on his forehead as he said the numbers aloud. Elijah ran back into the room, his silence so profound that Ash's whispered counting sounded like yelling. He didn't acknowledge him. He had to keep trying.

"Come on."

Not yet.

"Come on, Tayshia!"

I'm not ready to lose you.

"Please don't do this. Please don't fucking *do* this!"

I was supposed to save you.

CHAPTER TWENTY NINE

Breathe.

"How long has it been? How long has my daughter been in there?!"

"*Mom*, stop! Please!"

"Don't *yell* at me, Shay. Terrence, are you going to let our daughter talk to me like that?"

"Calm down, Celie."

"Don't *tell* me to calm down when my daughter is — she's — *Oh*."

"Celie, it's all right. The doctors know what they're doing. They'll get her right as rain any moment now."

Come on and breathe.

"Should we be here, Ji?"

"Shut your mouth, Andre. We're staying."

"But—"

"You *do* realize she's like my *only* friend, right? We're *staying*."

"Okay, fine, but we should stay off to the side. This seems like a family-first situation. Can you at least agree to that?"

"No."

"Ji Hyun."

"*No.* I'm staying right here. But you're welcome to stand off to the side if that's what you wanna do."

"...I'll stay. She's my friend, too."

You can do it. Just take a breath for me.

"Has Kieran gotten here yet, Terrence? Oh, he's going to have his heart broken."

"No, honey, he's not—"

"Where is she? Where the Hell is Tayshia Cole's room?! Where — no, Kieran! I'm not going to lower my voice!"

"You're gonna get us kicked out, Quinn!"

"I don't care! Let them all wake the fuck up and get over it! She was my best friend!"

I'm sorry for everything I did wrong.

"What are you doing all the way over here, Elijah?"

"I don't—I don't belong here. I should go, Andre. I really shouldn't—"

"Why do you think that?"

"Because this is m-my fault. She wouldn't be h-here if I had—if I h-hadn't—"

"Elijah, come on. You guys are such close friends. I'm sure whatever happened was an accident."

"No. No, it—I—I just shouldn't be here."

"Then why are you?"

"Just because I shouldn't doesn't mean I don't want to be."

I want to fix it.

I want to fix everything.

Please don't leave me.

Everyone was here for her. Everyone. The people who loved her. The people she thought didn't love her. They were all here, waiting on the edge of the metaphorical cliff to find out the fate of Tayshia Marie Cole.

And Ash was on the floor.

He pulled his knees to his chest and wrapped his arms around them, the back of his skull hitting the wall as he looked up at the ceiling and its fluorescent lights.

Around him, littered impatiently along the empty hall on their feet and in chairs were multiple people. Mr. Cole. Mrs. Cole. Shay. A sleepy Naveah. Andre. Ji Hyun. Kieran. Quinn.

But Ash only had eyes for Elijah.

He was the reason Tayshia was there with doctors who were working to save her life. He was the reason why she had gotten so sick without anyone noticing, without anyone seeing just how deep into the pit she'd fallen. He'd been helping her dig it deeper, and for what reason? There wasn't a single reason on Earth that made sense.

Nothing excused him for helping her dig her own grave.

They'd been in this emergency department hallway for nearly two hours, waiting for someone to come out of the room and tell them Tayshia's fate. The paramedics had been able to revive her, but her heart had stopped again on the way to the hospital. Ash had been internally distraught, not wanting to make anything worse as he rode in the ambulance with them. At the hospital, once they'd wheeled her into an emergency angioplasty, he started sending texts and making calls.

Luckily, the Coles were on a small trip to Eugene when he called, otherwise they wouldn't be here right now—they'd still be on the road. Apparently, Quinn was living with Kieran at his parents' house—that was the reason why she was here with him. Everyone else was in town. Ash had refrained from texting his godparents, not wanting them to be bothered with this yet. He didn't want to give them bad news.

Now, they were all just waiting outside the emergency department doors.

"What happened?" Mrs. Cole blew her nose into a pale blue kerchief, her brown face blotchy and her eyes leaking constant tears. "Who knows what happened to her? You wouldn't tell me anything on the drive up!"

"She's going to be just fine," Mr. Cole said, his arm strong around his wife's shaking shoulders. "Let's not panic until there's something to panic about."

"Does anyone have any idea?" Quinn whirled in the hall, her black hair wild. "Do any of you know why the Hell she's here?!"

Ash turned his glare on Elijah, who stood against the wall beside an unsuspecting Ji Hyun and Andre. He wanted to hurt him. He wanted to hurt him *badly*. He wanted to tear his eyes out and rip his throat from his neck. He wanted Elijah to bleed for every moment that Tayshia had felt safe enough to purge around him.

But he couldn't move. He didn't want to.

What if he moved away from the door and she died?

"I know why we're here." Elijah stepped away from the wall, his fingers fidgeting before his abdomen. He looked like a mess, eyes red from crying and face pale. His wavy hair was limp with sweat, no doubt from nerves and anxiety. "And it's my fault."

The silence reverberated around the area.

Mr. Cole pulled away from Mrs. Cole and stepped closer to Elijah. His brow furrowed and his arms crossed over his shirt. "What's your name?"

"I'm Elijah." He lowered his gaze. "Sir."

"What happened, Elijah? Why do you think this is your fault?"

Ash gritted his teeth. He wanted to jump up and start yelling. He wanted to launch himself across the hallway at his former best friend and throttle him. Maybe slit his throat and watch the blood stain his clothes.

Elijah glanced down at Ash, who glowered up at him with all the rage burning within him that he could muster. Then, Elijah looked up at Mr. Cole, drawing his shoulders back.

"Tayshia and I have been friends since the first year of the program, for a year-and-a-half now. I noticed pretty early on that she was barely eating, but I believed her when she told me it was just an extreme diet. I realized that it wasn't just a diet. But I knew if anyone found out, it would make things worse. I figured if I involved myself, then she wouldn't get more stressed out, and I'd be able to help her if it got out of hand."

"If what got out of hand?" Mr. Cole asked, both looking and sounding perplexed. "Involved yourself in what?"

"The vomiting."

"*What?*" Mrs. Cole burst forward, coming to stand beside her husband. "She was *what?*"

"She was making herself sick," Elijah said, looking more drawn than he had a second ago. "She was throwing up her food. When we talked about it, I thought that she just needed someone who was gonna accept her the way she was. So I helped her."

"You did *what?*" Now Ji Hyun was there, on Mrs. Cole's other side, and her eyes were aflame. "What are you talking about?"

There was a reluctant expression on Elijah's face as he attempted to start his sentence repeatedly. It was clear he didn't want to admit his sin. But more than that, he was ashamed.

"What did you help her do?" Mr. Cole asked.

"I helped her. I went and picked food up for her to eat and throw up. When you guys cut her off from money this school year, I just started buying it for her. And sometimes, when she was feeling tired or weak, I would go in and help her."

"Help her do *what?*"

"Hold her hair back. Or I'd help her stay upright when she bent over. My goal was to make sure I was there just in case she — well, in case she — "

"Died?" Mr. Cole said, a quiet anger layered beneath his tone.

"I'm sorry."

Ash felt his rage growing again. Holding her hair back was bad. But holding her up so she didn't fall over because she was *dying*?

If he didn't calm down, violent things were going to happen.

He pulled his hood up onto the back of his head, tugged his sleeves down over his hands, folded his arms on top of his knees, and buried his face in them. He was shaking. Absolutely shaking. He was so angry that it hurt. He wanted to kill Elijah as badly as he wanted to kill the man from Paris. His leg began to tremble, bouncing in his agitation.

He was about to lose it.

"I figured she'd stop when she got to whatever weight she thought she wanted to be. That's all it was supposed to be about — she just wanted to lose weight. I thought it was okay. But we got caught." Elijah sighed. "We didn't think we'd ever get caught."

"Are you *stupid*?" It was Ji Hyun this time, and her shoes tapped against the linoleum floor as she came close. "What the Hell is wrong with you?!"

"She said *you* knew she purged, Ji Hyun, so I don't know why you're yelling at me!"

"Because you're standing here telling us that you literally *helped her throw up!*" She was screaming, her rage and indignation palpable in the air. "How do you not see how fucked up that is?! I never helped her. I always encouraged her to get help — like *medical* help."

"I *do* see how fucked up it is!" Elijah shouted right back, prompting Andre to push away from the wall with a warning look. He lowered his voice. "I do see how fucked up it is. And that's why I'm fessing up to everything now."

"To clear your conscience."

"Of course to clear my conscience."

"How clear is it now? Is it made of crystal?" Ji Hyun said with a sarcastic sneer. "Or do you need to polish it a little more?"

Elijah looked away, his hands trembling.

"You're a piece of shit, you know that?" Kieran said, the dark circles under his eyes seeming more shadowed by the overhead lights. "I don't know what planet you're living on that would make you think it was okay to help her do — do *whatever* to herself. Now I have to stand here feeling guilty for not being able to help her when I've known her longer than you."

"Well, maybe you should have been a better boyfriend."

"Guys, let's not do this." Andre joined the group. He shook his head. "We're in the middle of a hospital waiting room. There's other people here."

"Well, everyone's jumping down *my* throat when they should all be looking at themselves, too!" Elijah cried, waving his hands about.

"Why should I have to be the one shouldering all the blame when we *all* stood there and watched as she destroyed herself for months?"

Ash had been carrying that guilt for a long time.

Knowing that she was sick while he messed with the chess pieces on the board to ensure that she had a clear path to the other side. Making things easy for her when he really should have just gone to Nurse Pritchard the day he'd walked in on her purging for the first time.

But everyone needed to learn to carry their own share of the burden. Elijah was right—they had all played a passive role in the sad play that was Tayshia's life. She wasn't a fucking punching bag, so he didn't understand why the universe kept using her as one. And every single one of her friends and family members had stepped aside to make way for the stars to take their aim.

The crystals didn't matter. The past didn't matter. Nothing mattered except her disorder. Nothing *should* have mattered except for that. They should have prioritized it, and now, they were *all* paying the price.

Ash now realized that it didn't matter if she was the one with her fingers down her throat. Their complacency might as well have been the hands holding her hair back while she did it.

He stood up.

Everyone's heads swiveled to look at him, appearing simultaneously worried and apprehensive as Ash loomed there. He seethed, resisting his urge to lunge.

"You don't have the right to be defensive," he said to Elijah, his voice a dangerous, dark whisper. He lowered his chin, holding his gaze. "If you would have told someone sooner, then she might not have gotten as sick as she did. It could have been handled. She could be getting better right now."

"She asked me not to tell."

"Doesn't matter."

"But it was *her* body."

"Doesn't matter."

There was a pause as Elijah floundered. All gazes were intent on Elijah, waiting. Like Ash, they all just wanted an explanation. Ji Hyun and Quinn were the only two who seemed to be uncaring of said explanation—they clearly thought he was trash no matter what.

"I'm not supposed to be responsible for everyone else, Ash. I didn't know it was as dangerous as it is! I didn't know you could have a heart attack."

"Then you *do* your fucking *research*!" Ash shouted. "You do your research and you make sure the person you care about isn't hurting themselves. If you had done your research, then you would have known *immediately* that what she was doing was dangerous, and that she needed help. And even if you really were too stupid to do that, you've got two fucking eyes. She hasn't been herself for months."

Kieran was eyeing him, a begrudging, sour pull to his lips as he looked him up and down. Ash didn't care what he thought or wanted. He didn't care that these people were hearing him say more words than they probably had ever heard him say.

He'd be damned if they didn't realize who he was before the end of the night.

"You're a hypocrite!" Elijah yelled. "You're standing there, telling me what to do as if you're perfect. Why didn't *you* do your research?"

"I *did*," Ash hissed, drawing multiple gazes. "I *did* do my research."

"Then why didn't you say anything?!"

Guilt coalesced in the pit of Ash's stomach, making him feel queasy. He felt it oozing through his veins like sludge, reminding him that no matter how much he felt like he'd changed, there were still dark parts of himself that remained. His selfishness. His inability to trust. His close minded outlook on life. The possessive, protective nature that had caused him to try and save someone who couldn't be saved. All the things that had combined to convince him that he was making the right choices.

Her parents. Her friends. Ash's friends. Everyone in her life.

They'd *all* fucked up.

They were *all* to blame.

They were paying for it now.

"Ash," Mrs. Cole said, her voice thick with the remnants of her emotion. "Why didn't you say anything?"

"Because I made the wrong choice. I accept responsibility for that. I didn't take care of her like I'm supposed to. I'm not gonna make excuses, or apologize to make myself feel better, or even go back and try to figure out what I could have done differently. I'm just gonna do the right thing from here on out."

"What happened to my daughter? Why is she in there? Please tell us!"

"Her heart stopped while she was purging."

"It was—" Elijah cleared his throat. "It was class time, but we skipped so she could—"

"So she could binge and purge," Ash supplied, his bluntness causing a few of the assembled to cringe. "Because I wasn't letting her."

"You weren't *letting* her?" Mr. Cole gave him a disturbed look.

"I had rules for her." He knew how fucked up it was, now that he looked back on it. But there was going to be no shirking of responsibilities, nor apologies from him. Only action and honesty. "Rules we agreed to so we could combat this. Every time they stopped working, we discussed and shifted things around. I realize now that I should have told someone instead."

"Yes, you certainly should have," Mrs. Cole said, sounding angry as she blew her nose into the kerchief again. "You should not have been making rules like that for my daughter when she needed help from her family."

"I *am* her family."

"Then if you're her family, act like it," Elijah said. "Protect her, even if it's from herself. Don't come clawing out *my* eyes for what I've done when you can't even see how selfish you are. Don't come at me for—"

"For selfishly enabling her so she could stay sick and keep needing you?" Ash's glare was as hot as the nucleus of a star. "Don't pretend like your actions weren't selfish. Don't pretend like every second that you spent helping her wasn't for your own personal gain."

"No. No, that's not true." Elijah shook his head. "What could I possibly hope to gain from her being sick?"

"You said it yourself you hadn't done any research, dude," Andre said, hands moving to his hips.

"And?"

"That implies you didn't care how sick she was!" Andre said, raising his voice and laughing a bit. "That means that the only reason why you would help her stay sick if you were getting something out of it! If that's not it, then *why* would you help her?"

Elijah glared at him. "You always take his side. You always defend him."

"And you're avoiding the question."

"Because I already told everyone why!" Elijah tangled his hands in his hair, distressed. "Why does no one believe that I really didn't know how dangerous it was?!"

"What you're not grasping," Ash said angrily, "is that it doesn't matter what you knew or didn't know. Take *responsibility* for what you did. Stop trying to pick which parts to accept blame for and which parts to give to someone else to deal with. Accept that what you did was fucked up, *whether you knew it or not.*"

"I didn't want her to be *sick*. I wanted to *fix it.*"

Everyone assembled was deathly quiet, watching the argument with wide eyes. Tayshia's parents and sisters. Kieran and Quinn. Andre and Ji Hyun.

Ash understood. He did. He knew that Elijah was probably feeling overwhelmed, that he felt like taking responsibility and accepting his share of the blame was equal to murdering Tayshia. That if she didn't survive, he'd have to carry that guilt forever.

But he needed to suck it up.

Holding her hair back, buying her binge food, and keeping her upright so she didn't pass out was not fixing it. It was engraving her name on a headstone.

And it was a lie.

"You didn't want to fix it," Ash said. "You wanted her to be sick because it was the only way you could have her, wasn't it? Because you liked her and she didn't like you back, so the only way you could have her was if she needed you. You needed her to need you."

"That's not what it was about," Elijah said, but his voice was meek. Tremulous.

"Yes, it was." Ash moved closer to him. His fingers clenched into a fist at his side. "I've known it since her birthday when you told me she deserved nice things. You have feelings for her. And that's what this is *all* about."

"You wanna tell me I don't have the right to be defensive?" Elijah jabbed his finger against his chest. "You wanna act like I'm the only one to blame? You need to admit exactly what you did was *just* as bad. You made rules for her so she could keep doing it. How is that any different?"

"I didn't have ulterior motives. You did."

"Or *did* you? You had feelings for her, too."

"Not while I was in jail." Ash's lips curled up into the ghost of a smirk. "Not when you first started helping her. And when I found out she was sick, I didn't know *how* I felt. Me helping her was purely to keep her alive. But you? Your help was for your own satisfaction. You thought if you showed her you were the best choice—that you were freedom and I was a cage—that she'd pick you."

"And you're the one with the record," Elijah spat out as though the very thought of Ash made him want to die. "You're just like your piece of trash dad and the more you try to pretend you're not, the more you look just like him."

"Shut up."

"No. You're condescending to me, and I don't like it. It's not fair!"

Colossal red stars burst in front of Ash's eyes as his fury swelled and burst into flames. He couldn't take it anymore. He wanted to kill him. He wanted to fucking kill him..

If Tayshia died, Ash would rather be in prison.

"You want it to be fair?" he hissed, storming toward him with death in his eyes and murder in the point of his finger. "Then start hating yourself. Start hating yourself until you can't stand it, and then control your food so you can control that hate. And when you lose control of both, then stuff yourself so full of that hate until you can't stand it and get rid of it. Get rid of it *over* and *over* and *over*—" He jabbed his finger against Elijah's chest repeatedly, each jab punctuating his words. "—and *over*, until you're empty again. Because then, when you're empty, the hate has room to fill up again."

Elijah's eyes were wide, his jaw slackened. "That's not—"

"Shut *up*. Shut your damn mouth." Tears of anger glittered in Ash's eyes, blurring his vision. He hated Elijah. It felt like he'd always hated him. "Don't tell me it's not fair. I'll tell you what's not fair. What's not fair is knowing that every single time I thought I was helping her—every single time I made progress with her...*You* fucked it up."

"You know what?" Elijah slammed his palms against his shoulders, shoving him backward so that he stumbled into Andre. "Take a look around, Ash. None of these people know the real you. None of them know what an absolute fucking *nightmare* it was to be friends with someone as self-centered as you. You're not good enough for her."

In one fluid movement, Ash lurched forward, clenched his hand into a fist, and arched his arm back. He whipped it forward, slamming it directly into the center of Elijah's face. His nose crunched beneath Ash's knuckles, the cartilage as weak as their fucking friendship.

In the midst of the frozen shock from the assembled friends and family members, Elijah went down as though he'd simply passed away.

Ash crouched over him, grabbing the front of his shirt even as everyone started toward them. His fist reared back a second time.

In Elijah's face, gone was the anger and temper that had urged him to say the horrid things he'd said. Gone was the indignation and the vendetta and the denial. Instead, there was only guilt. There were tears streaming down his face as he let out an almost anguished sob.

"Go ahead," he said. "I deserve it."

And he did. He did deserve it.

But the longer he looked at the pitiful boy beneath him, the more Ash realized that he was doing it again.

Another wrong choice.

As much as he wanted to destroy Elijah, he knew he couldn't do it without destroying the part of himself that connected him to his past. And if he couldn't stay connected to his past — if he severed that connection with a fist to the face — then he'd forget how he came to be the man he was now.

The Ash who loved Tayshia was born of the Ash who once hated her. He needed that version of himself to be able to stay who he was now.

He couldn't heal without accepting his past.

"You do deserve it," he said, and then he lowered his fist. "But I don't. I don't deserve to live my life knowing that I hurt the people that I love more often than I don't. You fucked up, Elijah, and instead of doing everything you can to reject the blame, you should spend more time figuring out how you're going to make it right."

He stood up, watching as Elijah scooted backward, wiping the blood beneath his nose with the back of his hand.

"I won't be leaving this hospital until she's okay," Ash announced. "And if you care about her, neither will any of you. But if you stay, know that I *am* putting my foot down. *I'll* decide what options we take. I'll be the one to make the decisions for *my* girlfriend. And I don't care if you cringe, complain, or hate that. She is *mine* to take care of, like I promised her. And if any of you do anything to disrupt that, I'll ask you to leave. She isn't easy, but she's worth it."

For the first time since they'd arrived, there was silence in the waiting room.

☼☼☼

"Ash?"

Ash looked up, his fingers twirling the crystal back and forth where it hung from his neck. He was sitting on one of the chairs in the Intensive Care unit's waiting room with his elbows on his thighs and his fingers laced between them, his hood up on his head again. Ryo and Steven stood there in their pajamas, their expressions mirroring each other's concern.

"Who called you?" Ash asked, voice hoarse from disuse.

"Ji Hyun," Ryo answered, taking a seat beside him. While Steven was in his pajamas, Ryo was still wearing his work clothes. "What happened?"

Ash glanced around. The Coles were in one corner of the room, holding Shay and Nevaeh in their laps as the girls slept. Mrs. Cole looked puffy-eyed and drained. Mr. Cole appeared stoic and strong. Ji Hyun and Andre were gone, having left to get something to eat. Kieran and Quinn had stayed, miraculously, and they were sitting on the floor against the wall, scrolling through their phones. Elijah was in a corner of his own, staring blankly at the floor, the skin of his mouth and chin stained red from the nosebleed Ash had given him earlier.

"Is she still in surgery?" Steven asked anxiously, sitting down in the cushioned seat across from Ash.

"No, she's in a room now. We're just waiting for her to wake up."

"What happened?" Ryo repeated.

"She had a heart attack," Ash said, and then he took a deep, steadying breath. "While she was purging."

"Purging? What do you mean by *purging*?"

"Tayshia is Bulimic. It means she eats her food and throws it up. And she had hypokalemia—dangerously low potassium—and wasn't aware of it. Or, she was. She got her blood test results back recently, but she didn't tell me everything that they said in detail. If I'd have known, then I-I would h-have…"

"Ash," Ryo said sternly, placing a hand on his shoulder. "Don't start blaming yourself for a damn thing. There was nothing you could have done that was your responsibility."

He was terrified. Terrified that she wouldn't wake up. Terrified that he'd have to live with the knowledge that he hadn't told her he loved her one more time before she closed her eyes.

Terrified to lose her.

He glared in Elijah's direction. "Elijah was helping her. For over a year, he's been helping her. Buying her food, taking her to binge at a buffet on the other side of town, holding her hair back while she threw up. And you know, this January, there was a time where she thought *I* was going to hold her hair back, and I thought it was so fucking weird. I guess now I know why."

"That's awful," Steven said. "That's just *awful*. He should not have been enabling her."

"Oh, don't worry. I was enabling her, too. I let her convince me to buy her binge food, to give her space to purge. I gave her ridiculous rules that made her think it was okay to do it, as long as it was okay. And I believed it was, too. I knew deep down that it wasn't, but I just…I ignored it. And now there's shit I need to say, and I don't get to say it to her, because of my stupid mistakes."

Ryo and Steven exchanged glances.

"Everything's going to be okay," Steven said with a confidence that Ash didn't feel. "She's going to wake up, and then you'll be able to say all that you need to say to her."

"You're just a kid," Ryo added, squeezing his hand. "You are just a *kid*. It's not your responsibility to fix your girlfriend's mental health, and it's not possible for you to be able to do something that people go to school for *years* to learn how to help with. You can be forgiven for your mistakes—"

"Not if she dies," Ash snapped. "If she dies, I'll never forgive myself. Never."

"You listen to me," Steven said, looking Ash directly in the eyes. "She won't die. She knows you have things you need to say to her. She knows, and she'll open her eyes so you can say them."

"We'll see."

"What did they do to get her stable again?" Ryo asked quietly.

"Emergency angioplasty," Ash muttered. "To get the blockages out of her arteries. And they gave her potassium and calcium. I think they're still giving it to her."

"Well, that's good." Ryo patted his hand and sat back in the seat, crossing one leg over the other. "She'll be just fine."

They waited in silence for a while. Ash made eye contact with Mr. Cole, like he'd been doing occasionally all night. It felt like looking upon a pillar of support. He seemed confident. It helped to see it. If her father was confident that she'd be okay, then he had to believe she would be.

"Is anyone here for Tayshia Cole?"

Everyone looked up. A nurse in blue scrubs stood there. Ash's heart skipped a beat.

"We all are," Mr. Cole said, standing up with Shay in his arms so he could turn and set the sleeping nine-year-old gently on his seat. He strolled over to the nurse. "I'm her father. What's the news?"

"She's going to be okay," the nurse said. "She's still asleep, but that could be because these sorts of things are hard on the body. But we're confident that she'll wake up. She'll be in a lot of pain but we'll have her on a drip to manage that."

"When do you think she'll be able to go home?"

"Well, that's what I wanted to talk to you about. Do you know why this could have occurred? Does your family have a history of heart complications or heart disease?"

"No, but she…" Mr. Cole glanced back at Ash, then at the nurse again. "She was purging."

"Okay, okay. Yeah, see, with purging, there are so many things that could go wrong, and hypokalemia is one of them. She had a potassium level of 2.3, so a coronary was highly likely as it was. With electrolytes, even a slight imbalance can cause this to happen. It could take a day, it could take a year. With frequent purging, it's *going* to happen."

Ash stood up, his body on edge and his hands shaking. "She was purging before it happened. It happened during. I walked in on it."

"That isn't unexpected. She'll have to stay in the hospital until she's stable, and then the doctor has some recommendations for the next steps."

"And what are they?" Ash walked over. "We'll do whatever we have to."

Mr. Cole glanced at him, but didn't say anything.

"There's treatment centers in the area, and our hospital has an in-patient program that would be effective for her recovery. The doctor recommends she be admitted until she's in a better place, and then outpatient programs can be considered. For now, we're replenishing those electrolytes, and we've got her on a feeding tube."

Oh, *God.*

"All right," Mr. Cole said. "If you'd give us a list of phone numbers, perhaps some brochures? Any information would be helpful."

"Of course," the nurse said with a sympathetic smile. "Just follow me to the front desk, and—"

"Wait," Ash said. "Can I go into her room and see her?"

"Visiting hours are over until tomorrow morning, unfortunately. And she's not yet awake—"

He cut her off again, threading as much desperation into his voice as he could. "Please. I just need to see that she's breathing, and I'll leave. I swear to God."

The nurse shook her head. "Sir, I'm sorry, but I can't let you in there."

Mr. Cole cleared his throat. "Perhaps, he slipped through the doors while you were printing out the information."

The nurse stared at him.

"And maybe, he slipped back out before you went back to work."

She sighed and, in a low tone, said, "*Before* we come back. She's in the third door on the left."

Ash didn't wait around. He turned and ran through the double doors. There was a group of nurses at the end of the hallway, headed in the opposite direction. It was no trouble for him to slip into the dimly-lit room and close the door behind him.

The virtually colorless room was small with a bed, a table beside it, one window, a door he assumed led to a bathroom, a TV on the wall close to the ceiling, a simple chair beside her bed, and an armchair in the corner. In the bed, Tayshia lay in slumber, a flourish of beautiful brown skin and ethereal curls amongst the hollow emptiness of the room. There was an IV bag hanging from a silver stand beside her bed. It was attached to a clear package that threaded life into her veins. Her eyes were closed.

The atmosphere was quiet. So quiet that he could hear his own thoughts louder than the beeping of the monitors and machines.

She looked peaceful.

Ash went to sit in the chair by the bed, perching on the edge of it so he could be closer to the mattress. Closer to her.

He didn't know what it was. Perhaps seeing her there, with her chest rising and falling. Seeing her alive. Seeing her and remembering what it felt like to beg her to breathe. Realizing that this was the very thing he'd been working so hard to prevent. Facing his failure.

Maybe that was why he started crying.

Ash ran a hand over his mouth, not bothering to wipe his tears as they fell. He watched her, stared at her in this most vulnerable state. He'd seen her in all of her most vulnerable states, from Paris to now, and he loved her.

He reached for her hand, his own trembling. His long fingers wrapped around her slender ones, gentle so as not to squeeze her. He felt like she might shatter upon the mattress if he was too rough.

Her skin felt warm.

In the next second, he saw their entire future laid out before him. Inside of it, she was happy. She was happy and warm and smiling. And when she smiled, it reached her eyes. Inside of it, she was recovered.

He wanted that.

Ash fell into gut-wrenching sobs, holding her hand to his lips. He kissed it several times, until it became too many, and then he allowed himself the freedom to be sad. To sit in his emotions and embrace them. To not let them overwhelm him by giving them the space to exist.

To accept that she might never get better.

He *was* sad. He was sad because even if she did wake up, she was still going to be in pain. She was going to have a battle ahead of her that would be so tough and so strenuous that she might not win. It was a battle he knew nothing about but that he wanted to fight until the end.

Even if it meant giving her up.

Ash cried for so long that he didn't leave the room like he'd promised. He fell asleep with his head on the bed beside her, her hand clutched tight, and a forlorn wish in his heart.

He hoped he didn't wake up until she did.

CHAPTER THIRTY

Paris was dark.

The sky was empty of stars — completely black. It looked like someone had spilled ink across the universe, covering it in shadows and destroying the cosmos. There were no people, the streets devoid of life. The lights burned eerie, no warmth remaining in them. The Eiffel Tower looked like a beacon for the dead, shining light into the nothing to beckon the spirits closer.

Ash was on the ground in the alleyway. Confused, he sat up, glancing around.

Where were all the people? Why was the sky so dark? Why was his skin crawling?

This was Paris. It had always been their nightmare, but it was supposed to be alive. Where were the people? The voices? The laughter?

Now, it felt dead.

Ash stood up, seeing he was in the same clothes that he'd worn in the waking world. He looked behind him, down the alleyway toward the section of the city that he remembered Tayshia having come from the first time.

It faded into pitch darkness.

A shiver rippled up his spine. This was very, very different from the first two times. It felt sinister. Wrong.

He swallowed and turned to face the street. Walking out to the empty sidewalk, he saw the promenade. It was lit up like Christmas just as always, but there were no people milling about outside the shops. In every direction, everything faded into the pitch that lurked behind him. It was almost like the light existed around him. Almost like it was coming from *him.*

Was he the light in this dream?

Another shudder ran through him, urging him onward. He crossed the street, not bothering to look both ways. If there were no people, then there would be no cars.

He turned and headed for the hotel. It loomed high and blue before him, countless black windows stretching up to the black, starless sky. Only one window was lit up.

Inside, the hotel lobby looked strange. The lights were on but the concierge desk was empty. It looked like there had been people there, but something came and erased them all mid-activity.

He headed for the elevator, feeling another chill traveling up each vertebrae of his spine like a tracing hand. When he stepped inside and turned to face the lobby, the ink of the sky had followed him.

He really *was* the light.

The elevator's music was off-tempo, playing a discordant, broken melody. Like the person playing it was missing half of the sheet music, or the notes were incorrect. It made him feel like his ears were bleeding, or like time was bouncing back on itself.

It felt like he was at the event horizon.

As he stepped off the elevator, the shredded pieces of himself seemed to sew themselves back together. He gasped, clutching a hand to his chest. It felt tight, like the air up here was constricted and thin. Glancing behind him, he saw darkness in the elevator when the doors closed, the warped music still playing inside.

And then it was silent.

Ash looked down the hall to the right. The blue carpet and white walls faded into darkness, just like everything else beyond the halo of light that surrounded him. He couldn't look at it too long. It felt like something was going to jump out.

He went to the left, headed for the room he knew to be hers. This time, he didn't knock. He placed his hand on the handle and turned it, pushing it so that he could step inside. Closing it behind him, he looked in and saw that the room was empty. Outside the window, he saw the tower, its light barely making traction against the blackness of the empty night sky. The light of the lamp was on and the curtains were open, just like they had been the first two times.

This version of Paris existed, but only in a place far away from the Paris he knew. All around him, there was nothing for lightyears and lightyears, just like stars. From Earth, they looked like they existed together. In reality, they were far apart, dark matter keeping them lonely.

There was something so cosmically horrific about it that he believed time had dissolved.

The bathroom door was cracked, dim light spilling out from the small opening. He crept closer and the bubble of silence burst.

Someone was crying.

He pushed the door open and stepped into the small room.

The light was dingy, the lightbulb dirty and hazed. It looked like the room was decaying, the paint on the walls peeling away as though it were hundreds of years old. The large mirror was shattered, lines splintering outward like spiderwebs. Beneath his shoes, the tile floor was cracked and moldy. The tub, once pristine and white, was yellowing with bacteria. The toilet was full of vomit, browns and greens pooled in the dirty water and giving off a scent as rancid as rotting flesh.

Tayshia was nude in the bathtub with her back to the door, sitting in bloody water that sloshed over the edge while the shower poured more on top of her head. She shivered, signifying that it was ice-cold, and her arms were wrapped around her knees. The ends of her curls trailed, floating atop the red surface like tendrils.

Ash took a cautious step closer and saw that the washcloth was floating near her, soaked vermillion. He could hear that her sobs were not as wordless as he'd originally thought. They had purpose and meaning. They were a lamentation.

She was counting.

"One, two, three, four, five. One, two, three, four, five. One, two, three, four, five."

Ash stopped beside the tub, his heart beating a painful tattoo in his chest as he put the pieces together. It was why she was covered in blood. It was why the water ran red.

She'd washed herself for so long that she'd scrubbed her flesh raw.

"One, two, three, four, five. One, two, three, four, five. One, two, three, four, five."

Ash's thoughts tripped over themselves as they came together and formed the answers.

Their dream worlds were different.

Ash's world was rolling hills, a lavender sky, silver stars, gardenias that glowed opalescent in the moonlight. The sprawling grass knolls represented a state of being where he could exist in paradise. The mountains were his father. The sea was Tayshia. The flowers were his mother.

His dream world was a place where he felt loved.

Tayshia's was a dark, tiny, dirty place where all she could do was burn. She burned in torment night after night, forced to relive the moment that time had stopped for her. And now that she had died – now that her heart had stopped and she was barely clinging to life – the nightmare had become her purgatory. It was now a place where she could wash, and wash, and wash, and she would never feel clean. She had a bloody shower, a splintered mirror, decaying paint, and a toilet full of vomit.

Her dream world was a cage.

And that was the answer.

Their dreams were not of their minds. They were not figments of their imagination, existing in their heads to bring those imagined things to life.

They were of their hearts.

Ash's dream world was a reflection of his heart. Tayshia's dream world was a reflection of her heart. The crystals drew a path between the two. Before now, he'd only seen her memory of Paris because she was alone. But he was here now. He had the key to her prison.

She'd finally let him in.

"One, two, three, four, five. One, two, three, four – "

"Tayshia."

She went rigid. "Why are you here?"

Ash was calm as he stood there, next to the bath. "I'm here for you."

"Get out."

"No."

"Why can't you just leave me alone? I just wanna be alone."

"I know. But I'm not gonna let you. Not anymore."

"You're not here because you don't want me to be alone," she spat, her voice thick and muffled as her back hunched further. Her words grew slurred, frenetic. "You're not here because you care. You're only here because you want something out of me. You're all the same. You all want things out of me. Everything. Everything I have. You want to take it. To take it and take me and leave nothing behind."

"That's not true." He took a deep breath, trying to steady himself amongst the putrid air in the room. "I don't want anything that you don't want to give me. I just want you, no matter how much you decide to give."

"I thought that's what you wanted," she said before she let out an anguished sob. "I thought you wanted the real me. But I'm not good enough. Who I am – the real me – isn't good enough for you. I'm manipulative and evil. I'm so evil and everything about me is bad. Maybe if I wasn't so evil, then bad things wouldn't happen to me. Maybe he wouldn't have raped me. Maybe Kieran would have liked me better. Maybe you wouldn't have told me you didn't want me."

Tayshia was dissolving, reverting back to the person she was before. He was watching her fall apart.

He knew now what he'd done wrong.

"And now I'm dead," she continued, weeping like a mournful ghost. "I'm dead, I'm dead, I'm dead. And I'm not coming back."

"You're not dead," he said. "And you're not bad. But you have to learn to see that. It's not enough to see yourself through my eyes – you have to see yourself through your own."

"How am I supposed to do that when everything I see makes me want to vomit?!"

"You heal. You work on yourself, you take it slow, and you heal. I can help you with that."

"No. I'm dead."

"You're not dead — you're just sleeping. If you wake up, you can take the step to helping yourself get better — "

"No!"

" — so you can work on healing and you can recover. And then — "

"No. No, no, no!"

" — you can see your worth on your own without needing me to be your eyes."

"No, no, no, no — " She inhaled and started shrieking it. " — no, no, no, no, no!"

He'd thought everything else was the most difficult set of trials he'd ever have to endure. Jail, watching his father go to prison, watching his mother die... But he was wrong.

This was hard, too.

"You can't do this anymore, and neither can I. For both of us, you have to take the first step. You have to look into the mirror and see. I cannot be your eyes, Tayshia."

Her hands slammed over her ears, the bloody water splashing against his clothes. She shook her head, the denial manifesting as inky darkness that spread outward from her body like smoke from flame.

"You don't love me," she crooned, falling into fresh sobs. "No one does."

"That's not true, either. I do."

"No, you don't. If you loved me, you wouldn't take it away from me. It's the only thing I have. Without it, I won't have anything that I can control."

"And with it, you'll die."

She was silent for a long moment, sniffling as she huddled there. Then, she whimpered.

"I can't."

"You can."

"I don't want to."

"And I love you."

"No." She squeezed her eyes shut — he could see it from her profile. "I don't want it."

"I love you."

"Stop."

"I love you."

"Please stop!" she cried, rocking back and forth with her face buried in her knees. She was curled up so tight, like she didn't want to take up space anymore. Like she wanted to disappear and cease existing. "Stop lying!"

Ash sank to his knees on the dirty tile. He lifted his hand and he placed it on her back, over her wet curls. She jolted but did not move away. The water was freezing cold, a cold so icy that it sunk deep into his bones.

"I chose you," he whispered. "And I'll continue to choose you over and over again, no matter how hard it gets. You are so valuable to me and you have worth simply because you exist. I won't stop until you see that. But I can't carry you anymore, okay? I'm tired. I just want to hold your hand while we get through this together. The right way."

He paused to take a breath. He was vulnerable. This was his heart.

"You are it for me."

She lifted her head, slowly turning it toward him, and looked into his eyes.

And then she screamed.

Her eyes popped open. She opened her jaw wide — so wide that it was almost inhuman — and she screamed. She screamed and she screamed and she screamed.

It hurt.

The volume rose to a crescendo so high that he felt his ears begging him for reprieve. He fell back, hitting the cupboard beneath the sink as he covered his ears with his hands. She looked like a monster, her hair hanging in wet strands over her face, blood streaking her brown skin with crimson. The shadows she emitted grew thicker, pervading the light he gave off and trying to stifle it.

She screamed and screamed and screamed and screamed and –
Then, he heard it.
Cracking sounds, like an ice floe breaking into pieces.
Ash looked up.
It was the walls. They were splintering, just like the glass of the mirror. The louder her monstrous screams grew, the faster they cracked. Her eyes squinted shut. Her screaming intensified, rose in volume, and then –
The room shattered.
It completely shattered, glass shards of her nightmare scattering all over into nothing. He was the only source of light for miles and miles as they fell through that dark, starless sky. His stomach lifted clear into his chest to join his pounding heart, fear bringing a horror that he'd never felt before to the forefront of his mind.
Tayshia wasn't screaming anymore.
She was reaching for him. Reaching for him in desperation, as the things he'd said to her these past months echoed all around them.
'Stop trying to hold it together and be perfect all the time. You certainly don't need to do it for me.'
And Ash knew this was it – she was reaching out. She wanted help. She was reaching for him because she was ready to get better.
He just had to take her hand.
'You don't have to do or say or be anything other than yourself.'
He reached for her, his arm straining as they fell through space and time in circles. The tips of their fingers brushed. Her eyes were wide, full of terror and desperation as she scrambled, trying to grasp hold. He curled his fingers, trying to twine them together, to connect the two of them the same way the crystals did.
But he missed.
'I'm scared I'll hurt you.'
He missed, and her hand went to the right. His fingers slipped past.
They both gasped.
"Tayshia," he said, voice frantic as their gazes locked one last time. "When we wake up, I have to tell you something. If you wake up right now, I promise you that I will tell you everything. But you have to wake up."
"I'm trying," she said, squeezing her eyes shut again and again. "I'm trying! I'm – "
'You. Are. Clean.'
She faded into nothing and was gone.
Ash was alone in the darkness. Falling for eternity. Falling and falling and falling. Something clawed at the back of his mind, one sharp nail gouging at the same spot until he thought he might go insane.

'I still want you.'
Something felt broken.
'I will take you far away from here and take care of you. For the *rest* of my fucking life. I just need you to keep trying. Okay?'
Destroyed.
'Don't stop trying. Don't ever stop trying.'
Shattered.

CHAPTER THIRTY ONE

"I'm not surprised."

Ash woke with a jolt to the sight of the nurse from the evening before pulling the curtains on the window open. His lower back ached from sleeping bent over at the waist, and there was a crick in his neck that felt like whiplash. He'd never slept worse.

The nurse crossed her arms over her chest and spun to face him, her cropped black hair bouncing as she did so.

"I knew you were going to stay the night," she went on. "You're lucky my supervisor didn't catch you in here, because I would be in huge trouble right now if she had."

"Sorry," Ash said groggily, rubbing sleep out of his eyes and sitting back in the hard chair. "Should I go now?"

"No, you might as well move in," she said as she grabbed Tayshia's chart from the end of the bed and went to one of the monitors. "Her parents were in earlier, and then they went to get a hotel and breakfast. They said to let you sleep."

"So you woke me up?"

"Yep." Her green eyes glittered as she grinned across the bed at him. "Anyway, you *do* want to be here when she wakes up, don't you?"

"If she wakes up, yeah."

"Oh, stop. She was just on a sedative last night. She'll wake up naturally soon. You have to remember she just had major surgery."

"I know. If she wakes up, I'll be here."

"*When* she wakes up," the nurse said on her way out of the room, "press the alert button right over there, and we'll come in to help her adjust. I imagine the feeding tube is going to be an issue."

"It'll be a thing, yes," Ash muttered. "Yeah, I'll do it."

The nurse left, and Ash was alone with an unconscious girlfriend, a series of beeping machines, and his own thoughts.

He glanced down at Tayshia, wiping the crumbs of sleep out of his eyes. She looked just as peaceful now as she had last night. There was nothing in her face to suggest the dream they'd shared last night.

The nightmare they'd endured.

He remembered the darkness. The cracked, peeling walls. The lifelessness of the city. The unearthly scream from Tayshia that shattered the dream and sent them tumbling down into nothing.

The crystal around her neck looked so nondescript, just like the one he wore around his. A half of an amethyst that sparkled lavender like the skies of his dreams, it looked like it could do no harm. And on its own, it couldn't. But together, around the necks of Ash Robards and Tayshia Cole, the crystals burned with all the power of the sun. The way they fit together was like the way the fringe of the sea fit against the ragged edges of the sandy shore.

What if they had never pulled them out of the wall?

Which was worse? Having her and losing her, or never having had her in the first place?

He remembered the shattering. The shards of the dream dissipating as they fell and fell and fell. The desperate way she tried to open her eyes.

There was an emptiness in his chest now. One that felt like a piece of himself had been erased—one he hadn't noticed before. Like a shadow that had been following him, sewn to the soles of his heart, had had its seams ripped. Like he was still whole, but there was something missing.

He should have told her from the beginning. Maybe it would have made a difference.

When she woke, he was going to tell her about his mother.

Ash dragged his gaze up from the crystal, to her eyes. They were brown and deep, drawing him in like a siren's song. For Tayshia, he would gladly crash against the rocks and drown. Those eyes, like stars.

They were open.

He reined in the sudden wave of emotion that overtook him as he lay a shaking hand over her own on top of the coverlet. It felt like he would shatter like the dream if he moved too quickly.

"Hi, baby," he whispered, voice tremulous.

"Where am I?" Her voice was raspy, cracking on the inhale. Her throat bobbed again and again, her body becoming aware of the feeding tube. "What's in my throat?"

He curled his fingers around hers and brought his other hand up so he could massage soothing circles onto the back of hers. "I'll tell you everything, but why don't you wake up first? Try to breathe and get used to everything."

Tayshia blinked up at him, her gaze tracking all over his face. She looked simultaneously confused and relieved.

"The dream," she croaked out. "Do you remember…?"

"It shattered."

"Are we still…?"

"Connected? I don't know."

"I guess we'll find out tonight when we sleep," she said. "What happened?"

"I need you to stay calm while I tell you, all right?" he said, moving the massaging circles of his thumb up and down her forearm. He was terrified that if her heart beat too fast, it would stop and she would die. He didn't know if that was possible, but he was too terrified to find out. "Can you do that for me?"

"Yes."

"You were purging. Elijah was helping you. I came home. Do you remember that?"

She nodded.

"Elijah called the ambulance while I tried to do CPR. You had no pulse." Her eyes widened, but she let him continue. "The paramedics were able to get you back. When we were in the ambulance, your heart stopped again."

"What?" Her voice came out tiny and twisted, and her eyes began to fill with tears. "I *died*?"

"Twice. But they got you back both times. And when you got here, to the hospital, you went into surgery."

"What kind-of surgery?"

"On your heart," he said, his tone gentle. "Because you had a heart attack."

The beeping of the heart monitor increased, the pace quickening in spite of how softly he massaged her forearm.

"Your potassium was low. *Really* low. I think you knew that."

She averted her eyes. "I knew."

"Why didn't you tell me the details of the blood test results?"

"Because I thought I could fix it with sports drinks and bananas." The tears fell and she let out a sob. "I'm so sorry, Ash. I should have told you."

"Shh, shh," he said, scooting forward on the chair and holding her hand to his chest. He used his other hand to brush a tender thumb along the lines of her forehead, like he was trying to smooth the furrow flat again. "Everything's okay. You're alive—that's what matters."

"What's in my throat?"

"That's the part I need you to stay calm for…"

"Tell me what it is."

"It's a feeding tube."

She fell into sobs that could not be controlled, no matter how much Ash comforted her. Her fingers wrapped around his as tight as they could. He kissed her tears away with futile lips and whispered words.

But she didn't fight. She accepted it. The acceptance was in the way she clutched his hand, the way her heart rate stayed steady, the way she wept. It was an understanding that the battle was lost. The war was over, and she had not won. She'd died. *Twice.* The third time would not be the charm.

It was time to face it.

"I need to tell you something," Ash said when her sobbing ceased, kissing her fingers between words. "And it's really important. Will you listen?"

She sniffled and nodded, too weak emotionally to speak.

"It's about my mom," he said, lowering his eyes to the bedcovers. He was the one clutching her hand like a lifeline now. "It's something I should have told you months ago, but I was ashamed."

"Ashamed of what?"

He hung his head. "That I wasn't strong enough."

"That's not true." She squeezed his hand. "Whatever it was, I'm sure you were the strongest you could be."

"Not this time."

She extracted her hand from his and brought it to his face. He sat there while she stroked her fingers along his cheek and over the top of his head, down the back of his neck, and along his jawbone. When Ash felt like he could, he spoke.

"My mom used to binge and purge. For years. It's the reason why she had a heart attack so young."

He lifted his gaze to Tayshia, his shoulders remaining hunched and face burning with shame. One-by-one, the boxes that encased the colors of his emotions came open. They spilled across the planes of his mind and heart in a rainbow of colors, painting him with something that overpowered any desire he had to hide from her.

And then it all came tumbling out.

"She would do it in the downstairs bathroom. It didn't matter when, as long as my dad wasn't home, or was asleep. At night, she would binge in the kitchen, and then she'd go into the bathroom and purge. I would wait in the hall while she ate, and then sit on the stairs while she was in the bathroom, even though she didn't know I was there. When I heard the toilet flush, I would go back up to my room, and then I would clean it for her so she wouldn't have to. I know she didn't know I was there, but I just wanted to know she wasn't alone."

"Oh, Ash. I'm so sorry," Tayshia said through a fresh round of tears. Her hand wrapped around his again. "I didn't know. I'm so, *so* sorry."

He squeezed his eyes shut, fighting back his own tears. "When she passed out in the courtroom, I was so scared. I knew it deep down that she wasn't going to wake up again. I knew that was it. But it didn't stop the grief when Elijah came and told me."

"And that's why you wanted me to get better. Because you were scared I was going to end up like her."

"I'm terrified of losing you, Tayshia. I love you so much. With all of my heart. I've never loved another person the way I love you. I *need* you to get better. I'm desperate for it." He started to cry, feeling his tears trail down to drip off of his jaw. "Please, please hear me."

"I do," she sobbed, reaching for him. "I hear you. I promise."

Ash was as gentle as he possibly could be as he leaned further over the bed, cupping her face with his hands. He pressed their foreheads together as she braced her hands on either side of his head.

"I thought you left me," he murmured between sobs. "I wanted to die."

"I'm here. I came back to you. I always will. I promise."

Ash pressed his lips against hers. Their kisses were chaste and unhurried, soft as though they ached. And they did ache. Each one ached like another twist to the nail in his heart. The one that drove home how much he loved her.

"Knock, knock, you two."

Ash pulled back and looked over his shoulder. Ji Hyun stood there, a cup of coffee in each hand. She grinned, her eyes sparkling at the sight of Tayshia with her eyes open.

"I'm sorry, Tay," she said. "I didn't bring you one. Forgive me?"

"I have a feeding tube." Tayshia let out a small laugh as Ji Hyun practically shoved the cups against Ash's chest and flung her arms around Tayshia's neck. Tayshia cried out in pain in spite of her smile. "Ah, ah! Sorry! I'm just so glad you're awake."

Tayshia laughed again. "It's okay. They cut me open, girl. Be careful."

"Your parents are gonna be *so* happy. Move that ass, Ash."

Ash stepped out of the way, cups in hand, as Ji Hyun perched on the edge of the mattress. She held Tayshia's hands. "And you're not gonna believe this, but *Quinn* was here. Kieran, too."

"Ew," Tayshia said, wrinkling her nose. "What did she say?"

"A lot. She acted like you guys were still friends."

"Well, we're not. But I guess it's nice she was here. Who else was?"

"Your parents and sisters," Ash said. "Andre and Elijah, too."

"How are they all doing?"

"Well, Andre is at school," Ji Hyun answered. "I took the day off. Elijah's still out there, moping like a huge baby."

"Rightfully so," Ash interjected.

Tayshia looked guilty. "I'm guessing you two threw hands."

"Oh, he only punched him once," Ji Hyun said dismissively.

"Who?!" Tayshia's eyes widened. "Who hit who?"

"I hit Elijah," Ash said, sipping from one of the coffee cups. He didn't care whose it was. Ji Hyun liked her coffee the same as him.

"*To be fair*," Ji Hyun said, "he deserved one good punch. I mean, what he did was pretty fucked up."

"Yeah, well…" Tayshia sighed. "It's my fault for getting him involved and manipulating his feelings for me."

"Let's not talk about that," Ji Hyun said. She reached for one of Tayshia's hands. "I want to talk to you about what happened. Because you, you know, *died*."

"What is it?"

Ji Hyun glanced at him. "Her parents are out there with her sisters. Can you…?"

"I'll go get them." Ash headed for the door. "Can you make sure to press that button by the monitor? It'll call the nurse in."

✲✲✲

Two weeks passed by, bringing the month to a close. Ash hung on the precipice of April, time in one hand and a decision in the palm of his other. People came and went from Tayshia's hospital room, everyone wanting to check on her over and over. The only two people who were there twenty-four-seven were Ash and Elijah.

Elijah was never in Tayshia's room when he was, but he seemed to understand that the only person who got to sleep in her room was Ash. And even though he didn't want him in there at all, Ash understood that he was Tayshia's friend, that Elijah truly felt remorseful, and that the time of controlling how tight he pulled her reins was over. They had things they needed to work out. Ash had said all he needed to say.

It was done.

Tayshia's parents were there during the days, always with Shay and Naveah. Sometimes, Ash watched the kids out in the waiting room, and sometimes, the Coles dropped them off at the hospital daycare. Ash would sit on the floor and color in coloring books with them, sighing when he had to chase after Naveah and carry her back to their makeshift coloring station. Sometimes, he'd hold his phone while the girls sat on either side of him, and they'd watch cartoons until his brain leaked out of his ears.

Ryo and Steven came by a couple of times, wanting to make sure that Tayshia was recovering well. They would relieve him of his babysitting duties so he could go home to shower. He would walk past the downstairs bathroom without looking, and he would leave the house again without looking over his shoulder.

He wasn't ready to go in there yet.

Quinn never came by again, which he was glad for. Tayshia had been hurt by Quinn's betrayal, and the last thing she needed was a reminder of that pain. That was her best friend and, just like Ash's friendship with Elijah, the loss of it was one that needed to be mourned. She needed the space to do that.

The one time Kieran came by, her heart rate got too high for Ash's liking so after he gave a pitiful apology that Tayshia pretended to accept, he ushered the idiot out and told him he wouldn't need to come by again.

He didn't.

A few other people visited, teachers and classmates, and everyone left flowers. There were so many flowers by the end of the first week that she was in the hospital that the entire room smelled like a garden. Sometimes, Ash woke up in the middle of the night because the scent was so strong. But it put a smile on her face, and that was what mattered to him.

There were many days where Ash and Tayshia talked about everything under the sun while he sat in the armchair and she sat up in bed and did her best to forget about the feeding tube. There were days when they didn't say a word, and he laid his head across her lap while he sat in the chair beside the bed, and she combed her fingers through his hair.

It was those days that he mulled over the decision that he knew would change their lives forever.

"When I sleep," she'd said on one of those quiet days, her fingers twirling a lock of his blond hair around one finger, "it's dark. You're never there. I thought that the dream shattering would mean that we wouldn't get trapped in my memory anymore. That I would have a dream world of my own."

"I thought that, too," he'd replied." Are you wearing your crystal to sleep?"

"Yes. Are you?"

"Yes."

They didn't speak again that day.

A few days before she was due to be discharged, Ash was present when the doctor, a nurse, and Tayshia's parents discussed her options with her. They shared multiple brochures with her, answering her parents' questions. Ash sat on the edge of the bed and looked at the brochures with Tayshia, holding her hand so it didn't tremble too much. She looked terrified, but more determined than he'd ever seen her. She was taking this seriously.

A treatment center was chosen by the end of the afternoon.

A few days later, it was time for Tayshia to be discharged. She had a few more tests to go through, so her parents were talking to the nurses about it. Ash was standing in the waiting room, ensuring that Shay and Naveah cleaned up the coloring books and crayons. There was a family of anxious people waiting in a corner for news of their elderly grandfather, and a woman across the room reading a magazine as though her husband wasn't coming out of surgery.

"Did you ever find the treasure map?" Shay asked when she came back from handing the art supplies to a kindly old nurse. "The one you said your dad gave you."

Ash knelt in front of her, giving her a small smile. "You know, I did. But I didn't have to do much digging. The treasure was with me the whole time."

Shay tilted her head, tapping her chin thoughtfully before grinning. "My big sister was the treasure all along, wasn't she?"

"She certainly was."

"I'm happy that she's alive," Shay said, and her smile faded. "I would have been really sad if she died. When Imani died, I cried a lot."

"Now, tell me," Ash said, placing his hands on her shoulders. "Did you open the letter I gave you? The one from my dad."

She shook her head.

"Good. When you get home, don't open it. Take it and bury it somewhere really deep in the ground. When it's buried nice and deep, close your eyes and make a wish."

"What am I supposed to wish?"

"What do you want the most right now?"

She tapped her chin again. "My big sister to get better."

"Then that's what you're gonna wish for. If you bury the letter and make the wish, then she will. *Never* dig it up."

"Hmm...Okay. I can do that."

Mrs. Cole wandered over, holding Naveah on her hip.

"Shay, it's time to go. You've got to be real hungry by now, hm?"

"Okay, mommy," she said, and then she wrapped her arms around Ash's neck. "Thank you for taking care of my big sister, Ash."

Ash hesitated a moment before he embraced her, holding her tight. Shay was Tayshia's sister. She was part of Tayshia. And because he loved Tayshia, he loved Shay, too.

This would hurt.

They let go of each other, and he stood up.

Mrs. Cole studied him for a long moment, the thoughts washing across her face like the coming tide. He was so sure she was going to tell him that all of this was his fault that he braced himself for it.

"Ash..." She sighed and when her eyes met his, there was no animosity within them. "Thank you. You did your best to keep my daughter safe and happy. That's all I could ever hope for her."

Mr. Cole walked up and slipped his arm around his wife. With his other hand, he reached for Shay and held her fingers tight. The smile on his face was warm.

"And now, it's up to Tayshia to figure out the rest," he said. "She'll recover. I know she will. It's in God's hands now, and He doesn't want her to suffer."

"She'll get better," Ash said, his confidence masking the open hole in his heart that reminded him what he might have to do to get her onto the path. "If it's the last thing I do for her, I'll make sure she makes that choice."

"Why don't you take the girls out to the car so we can go get some lunch, Celie?" Mr. Cole said. "I'd like to have a word with Ash here."

Mrs. Cole gave him a kiss on the cheek and then, with Naveah on one hip and Shay's hand in the other, she headed for the door. Before they reached it, Shay turned to grin at Ash over her shoulder.

"Bye, ugly!"

Ash threw his head back and laughed, waving to Shay.

He hoped it wasn't a forever good-bye.

"We're taking her with us when we leave," Mr. Cole said when they were alone. "I hope you understand."

"I take it you got her into the treatment center in Ashland, then?"

"Yes. And we'd like her to have some time with us before she goes. She'll be in there for at least three months, so I think it's best that she starts the healing process with her family."

Ash swallowed, trying not to take that like a punch to the gut. Mr. Cole grimaced, apparently realizing what he'd just insinuated.

"Not that you're not her family, too. I don't doubt you love her, but my daughter needs to be with us right now."

"No, I understand." Ash ran his fingers through his hair. "It's the best place for her."

"Thank you for understanding."

Ash bit his bottom lip, chewing at it as he struggled for the words he wanted to say. This could very well be the last time he spoke to Mr. Cole. He wanted to be sure that he said exactly what he wanted to say.

Just in case.

"Mr. Cole, I never thanked you for what you did. For calling me the day of my dad's funeral." Ash lifted his chin and squared his shoulders. "You talked to me like a man and told me the truth I didn't want to believe. I believe you now. One day, I won't be so empty. One day, I'll be able to forgive my dad for everything because I get it now. It doesn't matter whether or not my dad left me. He made a choice. A choice that hurt. And it's okay to feel the pain of that. But I can't let it consume me."

Mr. Cole's facial expression softened, and then he pulled Ash into a tight hug. He thumped his hand firmly against his back.

"I'm proud of you for coming full circle, Ash," he said after they'd pulled back, his hands on his shoulders. "I want you to remember that forgiveness isn't something that's done for the person who hurt you. Forgiveness is for you. You can't move forward if you don't accept what happened, and forgive the universe for dealing you the hand of cards that it did. Because sometimes, it's not about the cards you pick—it's about the ones you were given."

The corner of Ash's lips twitched up. "Forgive the universe? Not God?"

"Not God." Mr. Cole chuckled. "There are some things you have to deal with yourself. Only we can make the choices we want to make. And for what it's worth—in case you forgot—I forgive you, Ash. I forgive you for what happened in the ice cream shop. I truly, truly hope you find the healing you deserve from your relationship with your father. You deserve happiness just as much as everyone else."

Ash embraced him again so he wouldn't see his eyes filling with tears.

"What are your next steps?" Mr. Cole asked.

"I know what I need to do. What has to happen."

Mr. Cole pressed his lips into a thin line. Looking down, he searched for words and when he found them, they weren't exactly the words he wanted to hear.

They were what he *needed* to hear.

"You are the right person for my daughter, Ash. But it's the wrong time."

Ash closed his eyes against the pain of that truth. The pain that had threatened to eclipse him for the past two weeks. The pain of the decision that he was fooling himself into thinking he could find a way around. The one that all his mistakes had caused.

He already knew what choice he had to make.

"I know."

CHAPTER THIRTY TWO

April 2019

"I guess my parents are taking me home tomorrow."

Ash glanced over at her in the passenger's seat. She looked exhausted, no doubt from being in the hospital for so long. It was the second day of April, and the sunny Tuesday wasn't bright enough to break through the clouds of his somber mood. He tried to offer her a smile, reaching his hand across the center console to grasp hers.

"I guess they are."

They drove the rest of the way in silence that was so heavy that He felt warm. It was his last day with her. After today, he might never see her again. He might not ever get the chance to see her smile reach her eyes.

But that was okay. Knowing that she was finally going to get the help she needed was the most important thing to him. He'd rather dream of her smile than see her lowered into the Earth.

Once they were home, they headed inside.

"It's so clean in here," Tayshia remarked as she walked through the kitchen. "Did you come home and clean?"

"Steven actually came by a few days ago. He told me he cleaned floor-to-ceiling. Nice of him, huh?"

"Yes."

Tayshia had come to a stop in front of the downstairs bathroom door. Her hands were clasped in front of her chest, pressing on the whorls of each fingerprint of her right hand. Back and forth, back and forth. It was as absentminded as it was a deliberate attempt to soothe herself.

Ash joined her, finding that now that he'd seen the worst happen inside that room, he wasn't so scared of it anymore. It was just a bathroom.

"I'm sorry, Ash," she whispered, lowering her head.

"What? You already apologized."

"Not for this." She turned to face him, lifting a mournful look to his eyes. "I'm sorry I used her bathroom. I'm sorry I disrespected you that way. I mean, I disrespected you so many ways. So many that it's overwhelming to think about but this one needs a separate apology."

"You didn't even know about my mom. What's done is done."

"But—"

"What's done is *done*." He placed his hands over hers, prying them apart and bringing them to his lips. "I care about *you*, not some stupid room."

"It means something to you."

"*You* mean something to me."

Ash pulled her against him, folding his arms around her and dropping his face to the crook of her neck. She wrapped her arms around his waist and squeezed him tight, nuzzling against his chest. They stood there in the dining room, right beside his mother's bathroom, and held each other. Breathed each other in.

He would miss this.

"Why don't we watch movies, and I'll make you some lunch?" he said, tone muted. "Tonight, we'll go have dinner."

"And then you'll show me the garden?"

"Yeah. I'll show you the garden."

☼☼☼

Ash's garden was larger than his father's, with more of a recreational design. There were more flowers than he could name there, all the little pieces of a day when Tayshia seemed happier blanketing the ground. Red and pink and yellow and white and blue and purple. So many that it looked like he'd painted the Earth with a rainbow. Lush green grass made way for a cobblestone path that wove through the colorful flowers, the stones a random assortment of red, beige, and brown. Along the sides of the rectangular garden stretched climber arches for the roses that would grow over the course of the year, around which he had twisted lights. The lights were thicker at the top, with random strands dangling down like falling stars. In the darkness of the cloudless night, the garden shone like a beacon.

A piece of the cosmos, just for the two of them to enjoy.

"Ash..." Tayshia said in a quiet voice, frozen at the mouth of the cobblestone path. "This is *stunning*."

He said nothing, slipping his hands into the pockets of his jeans. This was for her. He wanted her to absorb and enjoy it without his interruptions. If this was their last day with one another, he wanted it to be about her.

She stepped onto the path, taking her time to admire the flowers that lay at her feet like offerings. When she reached the middle of the garden, she tilted her face up to the sky and spun slowly, taking in the lights. Her face, brown skin bathed golden, seemed to glow from within. And when she lowered her gaze back to his, her eyes sparkled.

"Can we dance?"

His eyebrows rose. "Dance? Can't say I've ever done that. I might suck at it."

"So?" she said with a shrug of her shoulders. She held both hands out to him. "We can suck at it together. Put some music on your phone and come here."

Ash made a show of sighing and rolling his eyes, but he was already pulling his phone out of his pocket. He picked a slower song and turned the volume all the way up. In the quiet of the night, there was nothing to muffle the sound. As he walked beneath the arches, he could hear the music perfectly.

He slid his hands along her waist and pulled her close, lowering his chin right as she lifted hers. Their eyes locked as she slung her arms over his shoulders and crossed her wrists behind his head. They began to sway as though they knew what they were doing, and they simply looked at one another.

God, did he love her. He would do anything to be able to keep her. To wake up to her every day for the rest of his life.

Ash *had* to make the right choice for once and choose the path that led them both to healing. He would do anything for her.

Now, he needed to do right by her.

Ash rested his forehead against hers. She sighed, and he felt her breath against his lips.

"I wish we had started like this," she whispered, her fingers playing with the hair at the nape of his neck. "Peaceful. Quiet. Simple."

"Me, too," he said.

"How would you have asked me out?"

"Hmm...I'd have asked you out to coffee."

"Oh, really? How domestic."

Tonight was not for reality. Tonight was for her. One last night in their own world, where nothing and no one could hurt her.

"Once, I danced with my little sister."

"Oh?" he asked, tightening his arms around her and dropping his face to her neck and shoulder.

"It was at Rory and Jamal's wedding. My dad danced with baby Shay. My mom was sitting at the table with Imani. She was already sick by then — she had got a cold that never went away. My mother couldn't bear to leave her with a babysitter, so she brought her to the wedding. I wanted to dance with Kieran, but he didn't want to. I mean, we were only thirteen. So I asked my mom if I could hold Imani and dance with her."

"And she let you?"

Tayshia nodded. "I danced with her in my arms for three songs before I gave her back to my mom. I don't have many memories of her that I haven't blocked out. But I've never forgotten that one."

Ash lifted his head and looked up at the lights above them. "Let's see...I remember a lot of things, but it's the good memories that I have the hardest time with. I never danced, but I have this super vivid memory of the day the band Chevelle's third album came out. My dad came home from wherever he'd been that day and like, a couple minutes after I heard the door shut, he put the CD on the stereo and just fucking *blasted* it."

"Oh, really?"

"Yeah," he laughed. "And I came down the stairs to see what was happening, and he was jumping around the room like he was at a concert. I'd never seen him look so happy. I was five, I think."

"That's a good memory to hold onto, I think," she said, pillowing her head on his chest. "Whether you have a lot of good memories of him or not, I think you should keep the ones that matter most."

Ash was quiet for a second before he stopped swaying. He pressed the side of his knuckle beneath her chin, urging her to look up into his eyes.

"I'll keep all my memories of you."

They danced for a couple more songs before she pulled away, asking if they could sit in the grass. The music still playing quietly in the background, they walked further into the yard and sat in the grass, the garden at their backs, and the fence and the Sunamura's house beyond. Mirroring each other's poses, they wrapped their arms around their knees.

They looked up.

Someone had painted the sky onyx and cobalt, the perfect *mise-en-scène* for the theatrical play that was their relationship. Across the darkness, the artist had chosen to speckle it with stars. Stars that shone bright. Stars that shone low. Stars that weren't visible, but that Ash knew were still there. And a moon so full and heavy that it bathed them in soothing opalescence.

"I know what you're planning to do," Tayshia said, the tone of her voice subdued.

Ash didn't tear his eyes off of the sky.

"And I know why you're doing it," she went on. "I know it's the right thing to do, but it doesn't make it hurt any less."

"I know. I'm sorry."

"I believe you."

They sat in silence again, gazing up at the very stars that had watched over them for their entire lives. The stars that had seen their happiest moments, and their saddest. Their successes, and their failures. Their joy and their grief.

They would see him weep when she was gone.

"What will you do?" she asked. "After graduation?"

"Oh, go to university, I suppose," he said. "There's still time to pull my grades up and get in somewhere as a transfer student. Just gotta figure out what I'm passionate about. What about you?"

"I want to recover." Her voice was fortified with strength. Resolution and determination. "And then I think I'll write a book."

"A book, huh? I didn't know you liked to write."

"I always have. I have a lot to say. I just didn't think I was good enough for anyone to read it, and to be honest, I still don't. But I know that when I'm better—when I reach the other side—I'll see my worth. I'll speak up. And people will listen."

Ash studied a group of stars that looked like a constellation, one he had no idea the name of. "I want to help people. Somehow."

"Me, too."

"What I've learned is that you can't fix what isn't broken. Sometimes, people get hurt and when they do, they're sad. They're in pain. They're not broken." Ash looked down at her, and she returned the warmth of his glance. "If I could do anything in the future, it would be to help people understand that you have to stay by their side. You have to accept that the story will end how *they* want it to end, no matter how desperately you want it to end happy. And if you can't? Accept what will happen when you walk away."

Tayshia studied his face.

"Ash, it's not your fault that I'm sick. I want you to remember that."

"I know."

Her eating disorder was not a choice. It was not a punishment.

It was a symptom of her pain.

There was no reprieve without control. Without the solace that came from knowing she could alleviate that pain by filling herself up and purging the acrid poison that trauma had inflicted upon her. The disorder itself was wicked and would do anything it could to grow and worsen, to take over her body and eat away at it until there was nothing left. It fed on misery. It was a demon that thrived on darkness.

Tayshia was not a bad person. A piece of her had died and the hole it left behind *hurt*. She'd just made the wrong choices in pursuit of relief.

But no matter how dark it got, there would always be light to fight the demons.

"I shouldn't have tried so hard to fix you," he said. "I should have been your starlight."

"You were," she whispered, placing her hand against his jaw. Her voice shook. "I think we should take our necklaces off."

"Why?"

"Because it will be too hard if I see you every time I close my eyes. If we're going to break up, then it needs to be final. We need to tie off every thread."

"Fine. I don't need a crystal to tell me that you're it for me, Tayshia. If we're meant to be, we'll find our way back to each other when we're supposed to."

The serious look on her face turned mournful.

"Hey." Ash stroked a comforting hand along her forearm. "You see that up there?"

She gazed up at the sky. "See what?"

"When it gets hard and you feel lonely? Just look up. I'll be there, watching over you."

Her frown turned into a soft, empty smile. It didn't reach her eyes and it wasn't the smile he wanted, but it was the one he got. If it was the only piece of her he had left, he would dream about it for the next ten years.

"The stars brought us together, Ash," she breathed, and they looked at each other again. "It's only fair they're the ones to pull us apart."

They sat there for a while longer, until the spring night chill got to be too much for them to deal with. That was when they went inside.

In the bedroom, he faced her at the foot of the bed. Their gazes fell to the crystals.

"When do we take them off?" she asked.

"Not until tomorrow. I want to be connected to you until the end. Okay?"

Her lips were against his within seconds, and then she was clawing at his shoulders, pulling herself off the floor. He kissed her back, grabbing her thighs and pulling her up against him. Their tongues slid against one another's as he turned and sat down. He laid flat, her fingers fluttering along his face in the dark. When she found his cheeks, she pressed her lips to his neck. His hands went to her waist, slipping beneath her top, pushing the entire thing up over her breasts. He moaned when she sucked on his earlobe. She whimpered when he played with her nipples.

The flames burned between them one last time.

Widening her thighs, Tayshia pressed her knees to the mattress, putting her pelvis flush with his. Rolling her hips, she ground her body against him. As their bodies moved against one another's and her mouth sought his again, Ash found that the pleasure he would obtain from this dance was minimal compared to the allure of committing the feeling of her kiss to memory.

"If you don't slow—" He gasped into her mouth. "—slow down, you're gonna—*fuck*—gonna make me come like this."

Tayshia ignored him, continuing to grind her pelvis downward. It was like she hadn't heard him. The pressure was building in his spine. He couldn't stop grinding upward.

"Please," he said, a breathy whine. "Not like this. I wanna be inside you. Please."

She stopped the movements of her hips. He took the opportunity, flipping her over. He trailed his hands up her sides, moving to cup her breasts. When his thumbs played with the peaks, her hips jerked and her body shuddered. Her lips parted to let out a sigh.

"You're so beautiful," he murmured as he watched her euphoria build. "I wish I could tell you every day."

His lips molded to hers in a ferocious kiss that felt like he was flinging his body into the depths of Hellfire. She threw herself into it, her hands trailing over the divots of his abdominal muscles beneath his shirt. He felt her brushing the curve of his collarbones as he swallowed her sounds with his mouth.

Their kissing intensified as his hand slipped between them to grip her core above layers of fabric. She turned her face away from him to expel a harsh breath. His fingers sought the apex, pressing soft circles around it until she was writhing, trapped beneath him, forced to endure it.

"You want me to fuck you, don't you?" he growled into her ear. "You want me inside of you?"

"Yes."

"Louder."

"Yes," she wailed. "Yes, please!"

"How hard do you want me to fuck you?"

"I don't want to forget you."

Ash began tearing at Tayshia's clothes, ripping her leggings downward and kissing his way up the center of her stomach as he pushed her panties down to join them at her thighs. She gasped when his mouth closed around first one breast, then the other. It wasn't an easy feat, but she was able to assist him in removing her bottoms and her shirt, followed by his clothing, too.

"I'm gonna taste you," he cooed against her sternum, running his tongue up to her throat. "I wanna memorize how sweet you are."

Tayshia didn't seem able to reply as he began to kiss his way down her body again. Ash slid until his mouth was at her core. She cried out when he ran his tongue through her center, committing it to memory. Committing to memory the way she arched her back, the way her hips rocked upward into his mouth, the way she whined.

She spread her legs even wider, using her feet to drive her hips up to meet the cadence of his tongue against her flesh. Her hands slid upward, underneath the pillows, and wrapped around the bars of the headboard that she hadn't even known were there.

Things began to fall from her lips as he drove her closer and closer to the edge, things that she had never thought she'd say. Her chest and thigh muscles spasmed in unison as her orgasm began to build with lightning speed. If it weren't for his fingers pressing her hips so firmly to the mattress, he feared she might have floated away.

"Oh, God," she moaned. "Oh, God, Ash. Gentler, gentler—yes. Yes. Yes. Yes—"

With one final cry, she came on his tongue with a shaking spasm. She sobbed as the release of energy catapulted her into the sky. She threw her head back so far that he only saw the underside of her jaw.

Ash took her by the hips, still shaking, and pulled her downward. He moved up at the same time, the head of his cock sliding through her arousal.

"I want *you*."

He slid inside of her. They moaned in unison, lost in each other's eyes as he sank deep inside of her. Tayshia lifted her lower body to get him to hit where she wanted him to, deep within her body. He stroked that same spot over, over, over, and over. Until she was mindless. Until all he felt was the flames of pure pleasure. He grabbed a large clump of her curls, his fingers sifting deep within them and sliding over the braids beneath.

"Fuck, you feel so good on me," he whispered as he thrust, his tone a mixture between desperate and proud. "I wish we could do this every fucking day. Such a sweet girl for me. Do you know how much I adore you, baby?"

"I do," she whispered back, her fingernails digging into his shoulder blades. "I do, I do."

"I want you to come for me, okay?"

Tayshia moaned, so loud that it sounded like she was crying, and crested. It was intense—more intense and bone-deep than any orgasm she'd ever had with him before—and he could feel it by the way her body milked his cock. He wasn't sure if it was because of him, or if it was because this was their last time. He just knew that it felt good.

Ash leaned forward to press kisses to the side of her throat. His strokes became deep once more, so hard that she was crying out with each one. It didn't matter that it was echoing off the walls. As macabre as it was, he knew she could be as loud as she wanted to.

There was no else here.

"Tell me you love me," he pleaded. "Fuck. Please fucking say it."

"I love you."

"Ah—*fuck*." He was close. "Do you want me to make you come again? Tell me you want me to. Just one more time. I need to feel it."

"I want you to make me come," she said, her eyelashes fluttering against the skin beneath her eyes. "Please. *Please*."

"Spread your legs wider," he ordered. She did, and then he began to play with her clit. "Come with me. I'm close."

Her body stilled, dangling on the edge. Everything seemed to increase pressure inside of him at once, from the tightness of her core to his hand around her neck to their tandem thrusts. It was hard and it was fast and it was good, good, good.

This was it. This was the last time he would be with her like this. The last time he would get to be part of her. She would be gone tomorrow, driving away from him on the way to a future he might not be a part of. He would be alone.

The emotion eclipsed him.

They were both crying, clinging to one another as though the ocean were crashing over them like it had in the dream world. It was too much. Too overwhelming.

"I love you so fucking much, Tayshia. I love you so much."

"I love you, Ash."

The moment her body clamped down around his, he reached the top of the mountain and hurled himself off of it. He fucked her through both of their orgasms, until they were spent and weak from exertion. Until he was no longer sure where he ended and she began.

They collapsed in a tangle of limbs, panting for breath. Ash moved her curls to begin pressing faint, gentle kisses to the back of her neck and shoulders.

He wished she didn't have to go.

"I don't want to lose you," she whispered as they drifted off to sleep, their crystal necklaces twisted together between their chests.

"You won't."

CHAPTER THIRTY THREE

"Ash...Ash...Please wake up."

His dreams were dark, full of smoke and heat. He was burning, and so was Tayshia. Both of them, trapped in a cage made of bars on fire, their flesh melting off and their screams soundless.

"Wake up, Ash..."

In the dream, Tayshia coughed. She coughed, and she coughed, and she coughed, never able to take in air. Her eyes streamed with tears that evaporated the moment they hit her cheeks. She was covered in scars. So was he. Their skin was mottled beneath the flames that licked up their bodies.

"Ash, please! I can't breathe!"

The ground beneath the cage was molten. In the distance, mountains erupted and burned. They spat out rocks that were aflame—rocks which arched up to burn the sky. Ash watched them through melting eyes, clutching burnt fingers to an equally burnt throat.

This was not a wasteland.

This was Hell.

Ash's eyes snapped open. The window beside his parents' bed was glowing, flickering with soft light. The sky was the color of autumn leaves, fading up into black and stars.

Did I leave the garden lights on? His thoughts whirled with confusion. None of this made any sense. He would never have left the lights on. Did he know for certain that he'd turned them all off?

Why was the window glowing?

Behind him, Tayshia was coughing. Her fingers were weak as they curved over his bicep and shook his body back and forth.

"Ash, wake up!" Her voice was desperate and meek, alternated with violent coughs. "There's a fire!"

He opened his mouth to tell her he was awake, receiving a mouthful of smoke. Coughs wracked his body, the smoke searing the flesh inside his throat. His lungs screamed for air.

The house was on fire.

The fucking *house* was on *fire*.

Without thinking, he threw the over-warm blankets off of his body and staggered to the window. Tayshia followed him, only scrambling back when he took his elbow and used it to break the glass. It shattered open a hole. He did it again and again, until the hole was wide enough for him to push Tayshia through. Whatever happened, he had to get her out.

The air outside was hot.

"Come on, baby," he gasped between coughs, turning to look at her through the smoke. "You have to go first."

He helped her climb onto the dresser, keeping hold of her waist as she put her leg through the wide, jagged hole.

She stopped.

"What's wrong?"

"The garden..." She coughed again. "It's on fire, too!"

Ash dragged her backward, peering down to the ground.

The arches of the garden burned like gateways to Hell, pieces of burning wood dropping to the flowers below. The orange and yellow flames incinerated the petals and leaves, scorching the cobblestone path.

He'd left the lights on.

"We have to go through my bedroom window," he said, pulling her up and setting her on the carpet. "It's on the front side of the house."

"But we can't open the door!" she cried. "If the hallway's on fire..."

"Only if the doorknob's hot. Come on."

Coughing and hacking, the two of them rushed across the room through the haze. Ash reached for the doorknob.

It wasn't even warm.

"The fire's downstairs," he said. "Let's go."

He ripped the door open and immediately lost what little air they had left. The smoke was so thick, the atmosphere so dark that he couldn't see down the hallway. Tayshia collapsed against the doorframe with a wheezing gasp. Ash fell to his knees, clutching a hand to his bare chest as he struggled for air that wouldn't come. Every time he tried, there was only smoke.

But when he lifted his head and peered, he could see it. A slight glow, getting steadily brighter.

The fire was climbing the stairs.

He had to get up. He had to get up right now, or they were both gonna die.

Chest screaming and head beginning to spin and ache, Ash reached for the door frame and hauled himself to his feet. He grabbed Tayshia around the waist, pulling her into the darkness and smoke. The heat increased the closer they got to the glow, the dizziness in his head increasing. Tayshia's fingernails digging into his back and the side of his neck were the only anchors that kept him from collapsing again.

The doorknob to his room was hot to the touch.

He hesitated for a second, ultimately deciding he had no other choice. His parent's bathroom had only a small window, and they would never make it back in time.

He had to hope his room wasn't on fire, too.

Turning the knob, he shouldered the door as though it could protect Tayshia from anything that might burst out. He pushed, and it swung open.

No fire.

Ash slammed the door shut behind them, letting go of Tayshia and trying again for another breath. He was going to pass out. There were spots in his vision.

But he could see it. The window, and the darkness beyond. There was still a glow, coming from the house burning, but he had to believe it wasn't the grass. His bedroom window dropped directly to the left of the porch. If he could get Tayshia through and onto the porch's roof—if it wasn't on fire, too—she might be lucky enough to escape with a sprained ankle. All the struggling and fighting they'd been through, and she was right on the edge of healing. It couldn't end in flames.

She clung to his arm as they made their way through the smoke. Unable to see, Ash slammed his knee against the end of his bed frame. The pain rocketed through his body, but he couldn't stop moving. He had to keep going.

He limped along until he practically slammed against the cold glass of the window. He and Tayshia scrambled to unlock and drag the window up. The air was still warm out there, the smoke too thick inside for them to get any reprieve. Past the crackling and roaring of the flames, Ash could hear voices and screaming outside.

Ryo. Steven. The neighbors.

He mustered the last of his strength and threw his arms around Tayshia's waist, lifting her up onto the windowsill.

"Aren't you coming, too?" she said between her coughing, eyes frantic and wide.

"I'll be right behind you," he said, voice strained and twisted with a wheeze. "Try and make it to the roof of the porch, then drop from there."

"Promise you'll be right behind me, Ash! Promise me!" She sucked in the air outside, her deep inhalations punctuating her words. Behind her, the stars and the orange glow of the fire made her look crazed. Fearsome. Her hands gripped the sides of his face.

Could she tell that his vision was going black?

"Promise me right now, Ash Robards!"

"I promise, okay? I love you. *I love you*. Now go!"

He pried her fingers off of him and curled both of her hands around one of his. He couldn't breathe, but he had to do this. He had to get her outside.

"Use…" He gasped. "Your feet… Against the wall…"

She did, propelling herself down until Ash's arm was outstretched. He leaned out the window, the air outside almost futile. It wasn't enough for him. He wasn't going to make it.

But he had to get her out.

Placing his right hand on the windowsill, he swung her. She helped as best she could, and he let go of her hands. Her body arched and, almost too-perfectly, she landed on the roof of the porch. She swayed a bit, arms out for balance, and then turned to glance up at him.

He looked out at the yard. He could see a motley assortment of neighbors, including old Bertha. Ryo and Steven were there, in a complete panic. Steven was running his hands down his face, crying openly. Ryo paced back and forth, yelling, *"That's my son! That's my son in there!"* at one of the neighbors. Another neighbor was trying to tell him that he'd called the fire department, and that there was nothing they could do until they arrived.

When Ryo saw Tayshia standing on the porch roof, he dashed across the lawn.

"Drop down, honey! I'll catch you! Drop down!" he cried, near hysterics.

Tayshia hesitated. "Ash, come on!"

Ash opened his mouth but all that came out was a wheeze. The dizziness and headache was so bad, the screaming of his lungs so loud, that he couldn't muster up the energy to lie.

His eyes rolled, he stumbled backward, and he collapsed on the floor. His chest spasmed as he gasped for air that refused to enter his lungs. The smoke had grown so thick that the open window meant nothing to it.

He could hear Tayshia screaming his name, her voice far away enough to show him that she'd made it to the ground. In the distance, he heard sirens drawing near, saw their lights flashing against the walls. From where he lay on the floor, Ash could see beneath his bedroom door—could see the flames devouring the hallway. Devouring his past.

"Someone get a damn ladder, for Christ's sake! That's my son in there!"

His bedroom door was on fire, the glow filling the room with the colors of Hell.

"Hurry, hurry! Bring it here!"

After this, there would be nothing left of his family.

"Lean it up against the—yeah. Stay at the bottom. I'm gonna drop him out from the window."

His mother, dead. His father, dead. Their memories, scorched and gone.

"Hold on, son! I'm coming up!"

He hoped death was one big dream where he could see them the way he wished they could have stayed.

Ash blinked slowly, a tear evaporating on his temple moments after it slid from the corner of his eyes. The right side of his body was hot, too hot. He felt like he was crawling in his skin. It singed the skin of his shoulder and arm, which he could feel bubbling and burning. The popping of the fire as it consumed his dresser, bedside table, and his bed was so loud.

He was drifting.

"I've got you, son."

Ryo's face entered his limited, darkening sight. His large hands gripped his shoulders and pulled him upright. His voice was soothing despite the coughs that interrupted.

"Up we go."

Ash's head lolled backward. Ryo's arms slid around him and beneath his knees, lifting him into the air as his godfather carried him to the window. He was just as tall as Ash was, so even though he struggled a bit, he was able to get Ash to the sill.

"I'm so sorry, but I have to drop you down."

Ash's eyes cracked open. He managed a nod. He was in so much pain that he could barely register that the air outside was finally helping him to breathe.

"You guys ready with the blanket?!" Ryo called out the window. Several voices responded with their confirmation. "I'm dropping him!"

And then Ash was falling, his gaze fixed upon the stars on the way down. The same stars that had watched him grow up, watched his family fall apart, watched him fall in love with Tayshia. The same stars that now watched his past burn.

When his back hit the soft blanket, his view of the stars was broken by several familiar faces, including Steven's tear-streaked one. They all moved further along the yard, almost to the sidewalk, and set him on the grass just as the police, fire truck, and ambulance came screeching to a halt in the road.

"Ash, you fucking *jerk*!" Tayshia fell to her knees beside him, openly sobbing, her facial expression enraged. She looked beautiful. "You promised me you'd follow me!"

He couldn't speak. He felt like he was still in the house. His arm was covered in burns. As he lifted it to reach for her, he saw the blisters and reddened skin that marred the tattoos on his hand and forearm.

"The garden," she said, her voice hoarse from the smoke. "We left the lights on, didn't we?"

Ash said nothing. He couldn't. His throat was bathed in agony.

"I'm telling the police as soon as I can. But you have to keep your promises, Ash. You *have* to."

The corner of Ash's lips turned up. It was all he could do.

"I love you," she said, and she wept the words. "I can't lose you."

As the paramedics gathered round and the firefighters began to do their job, his blurry gaze slid past her, to the flames that devoured his home. He was lifted into a stretcher and wheeled up the ramp, into the ambulance.

The last thing he saw was the burning colors of the flames as they faded up into the starry black background of the quiet night.

CHAPTER THIRTY FOUR

"Don't forget to pack this."

Tayshia glanced up from stuffing a stack of shirts into her suitcase. "Forget to pack what?"

"This."

She glanced at what Ash held out to her — a stuffed bear that she'd brought from the apartment. "Oh. Thank you."

After she leaned up to press a quick kiss to his lips, she placed the bear inside the suitcase and closed the lid.

"Help me?" she said.

"Sit on it."

She turned and hopped up, sitting atop the overstuffed suitcase. Ash came to stand in front of her, working around her legs as he pulled the zipper shut. Their eyes searched one another's as he did so, the noise of it sliding the backdrop to the otherwise quiet atmosphere.

"I'm glad I left all this stuff here in the apartment," she said. "Since everything else burned away."

Ash placed his hands on the suitcase on either side of her thighs, studying her face. His arm still hurt beneath his gauze from the second-degree burns he'd gotten, but after two weeks in the burn unit, he was doing much better. "I'm just glad we made it out alive."

"Yeah, but you…" She slid her hand up the side of his neck, cupping his cheek. Her expression was soft. "You lost everything."

The smile he gave her was just as soft.

"Not everything."

On the empty dresser, Tayshia's phone buzzed. She finished pulling the hem of her dress back down, and then rushed to pick it up. Silently, she read the screen.

"My parents are in the parking lot," she said, swallowing hard enough to make her throat move. When she looked up at him, her eyes were shimmering with tears. "It's time for me to go."

"All right. Let's get this—"

"Ash, I don't wanna go." She was crying. Sobbing. Like she'd been holding it back for years. "I don't wanna go. I need you. I can't be without you."

The ache in Ash's chest increased tenfold as he crossed the distance to hold her again. He embraced her so tight that even he couldn't breathe, his hand cupping the back of her head. She was shaking.

"It's okay," he murmured. "Remember what we talked about? Remember what I said? I'll always be with you. All you have to do is look up."

She continued to weep, clutching the front of his shirt. "What if it's too hard? What if I can't eat? What if I can't keep it down? What if—what if I never recover and I-I-I-"

"Hush." He pulled back so he could hold her face, wipe her tears, and caress her cheeks. He looked down at her through his lashes, trying to convey his love for her through his gaze. "You're strong. You *can* do this. You will. You'll get better and you'll find a life worth living. But to do that, you have to take the first step." Ash's voice broke. He fought back his own tears. "I can't take that step with you."

"Why not? Why can't you just *try*?"

"I can't, baby. I'm sorry. I have to take my own path."

"But I love you."

He leaned down to kiss her, heedless of her tears wetting his skin.

"I love you," he whispered. "I always will. This has to happen. You *have* to recover."

They'd already discussed this. Many times. Ash didn't care—he'd say it over and over, until he was blue in the face. All that mattered to him was her. She *needed* to heal. He'd rather be apart from her than have her die in his arms.

"What are you going to do after I leave?" she asked with a sigh, extricating herself from his arms.

"Ryo and Steven are gonna help me pack everything at the apartment and take it to storage."

"That'll be nice." She turned to smile up at him. "A fresh start, hm?"

"Yeah," he said, and then he reached for her elbows. He pulled her against him, dropping a slow, languid kiss to her lips. One that he knew he needed to cherish.

Every kiss was precious.

When he pulled back, her eyes remained closed for a second before she opened them. They fell to his throat, to his collarbones, to the part of his chest that the crystal rested against. She reached up to touch it, lifting it and rolling it between her fingers.

"Funny how something so small could have such a big impact on us," she said softly. "It brought us together. It tore us apart. And now, we have to wait for it to decide our fates."

"No." He closed his hand around hers, hiding the crystal from their view. "*We* decide our fates. If we're meant to be together, then we will be. We'll find our way back."

"I sure hope so."

Ash walked away from her, grabbing her heavy suitcase and carrying it out into the hallway. He stepped aside so she could go down the hall first, and then he followed her. Every step felt like a step to the gallows. He wished it didn't, that their discussions and mutual understanding would be enough to soften the blow. But the closer they got to the front door of the apartment that had taken them from enemies to lovers, the more his heart contracted painfully in his chest.

It would be empty without her.

The tears clawed at his eyes, desperate to break free. He held the front door open for her, the two of them casting each other a lingering glance as they exited. It was a nice temperature outside, a sunny spring day that would otherwise have been like any other. School was out for the day, so the sounds of children laughing and screaming on the complex playground could be heard. There was an elderly couple walking their dog across the parking lot, towards the sidewalk. A boy from the prerequisite program was smoking a cigarette at the foot of the stairs the next building over, focused on his phone. Tayshia's parents were waiting outside the still-running car. In the backseat, Shay sat in the center with a game console in her hands and Naveah was sound asleep in her carseat. There was an open seat by the window for Tayshia.

When Ash passed the suitcase into Mr. Cole's grasp, it felt like hammering a nail into the center of his soul.

"Looks like it'll be an easy drive," Ash said to him, putting his hands on his hips. "Four hours, right?"

"Just about." Mr. Cole held his arms out. "Well, come on in."

Ash stepped into the circle of his arms and embraced him. It was a warm hug, solid and steady, but it gave him only a fraction of the strength he needed to keep the tears at bay. When he pulled back, Mrs. Cole was right there to embrace him, too.

"It was nice to spend this time with you," she said, rubbing his upper back and squeezing him tight. "You were a great help with the girls, and you were a wonderful source of support for Tayshia. Thank you so much, Ash."

They separated.

"Why don't you say your good-byes," Mr. Cole said. "Celie, let's get in the car. We'll be seeing you, Ash."

Ash held up one hand by way of farewell, and then the car doors swung shut with her parents seated inside.

Tayshia looked up at him, giving him a bit of a nervous smile. "My parents are right next to us, so we'd better not kiss."

"Yeah, we kissed inside," Ash said with a cracked laugh. He rubbed the back of his neck, his other hand positioned on his hip. "I guess this is it."

"This is it."

The silence between them was awkward. Awkward and heavy and constricted. There were so many things to say, so many things. Yet they had no purpose. No meaning at all.

Anything they said would hurt.

"Everything's gonna be okay, Ash."

"Yeah."

"We'll see each other again someday."

"Yeah."

"Okay, well…We've got a long drive, so I'll go now."

"Okay."

They shared one final glance, both of them hesitating to turn away. Ash wanted to scream to the sky, to beg the stars to change everything. To heal her immediately so he could have her back in his arms.

"Good-bye," she whispered.

"Yeah. Bye, baby."

She opened the car door.

Ash turned and headed to the stairwell. He knew he was going to break down if he didn't get inside. He didn't want to listen to the car drive away. To the humming of the engine. The crunching of the tires over the gravel.

Right as he reached the bottom step, he heard them.

Footsteps, tapping rapidly against the pavement. He whirled around, surprised to see Tayshia running towards him. Her facial expression was desperate. Her hair flew back away from her shoulders with the force of her speed. He had only the time to inhale in shock before she'd thrown herself into his arms, her own arms wrapped around his neck and her feet dangling in the air. He held her tight, one hand on her lower back and the other arm wrapped around her waist, his fingers splayed over her ribs.

Fuck.

It felt good to hold her.

"I'll fight," she whispered into his ear. "I'll fight for myself. I promise."

"So will I. I want to be happy, too."

"Promise me something, Ash." She pulled back and looked down at him with tears in her eyes. "The moment you realize I'm the one, will you put your necklace back on so I know?"

"You'll see me in your dreams. I promise."

"I can't wait to close my eyes."

He couldn't help it. The innocence of the hope in her tone melted through the ice around his heart. He let the tears fall, let them grace his cheeks even as he smiled up at her. And when she lowered her lips to kiss him one last time, sweet and chaste, he knew that when she left, she would take his heart with her.

He hoped she would bring it back.

Ash stood on the bottom step and watched the car move away, driving her on toward the future she deserved. Away from a life with him, and into a life where she was happy and healthy and unburdened by her past.

A life she felt like waking up to. A life where she would look in the mirror and see what he saw in her.

When he went inside, he walked straight back to his bedroom. He moved past the boxes stacked against the wall, to the chest on the dresser. With tears still clinging to his lashes, he took the first step to his own recovery.

He opened the lid and picked out a letter. It was from December. The handwriting was nearly incomprehensible, the lines jagged and the ink smeared. It looked like the shaking of his father's hands hurt so badly that it was difficult to write.

But he'd written it anyway.

Son,

It's almost Christmas.

I don't know if you remember this, but I can't stop thinking about the day you realized Santa wasn't real. I think you were seven. You were so confused. So sad. Angry. And I remember I didn't know how to explain to you that nobody had lied to you to hurt you–that magic was something you got to choose to believe in. That Santa was real if you wanted him to be.

It didn't really work. You were pretty pissed at your mom and I for a while. Just like how you're pissed at me right now.

I don't exactly have anything to leave you with other than these letters, so...Here's some shitty advice from your shitty dad.

Believe in the things that make you happiest, Ash. No matter how weird it might feel. No matter how confused, or sad, or mad you are. Even if someone lies to you. Believe in what you love. There's no life without magic, I guess you could say.

Anyway, who am I to give you any advice? I'm in prison.

You're a good son. Couldn't ask for a better one. Too bad you can't ask Santa for a better me.

Love,

Your Dad

When Ash had finished crying, he went out to his car. Inside, he reached into the glove compartment, into what once held the gun that belonged to his father, and pulled out the piece of paper that had the number on it. The number that Officer Cook had given him.

He pulled his cell phone out of his pocket.

The line rang, and rang, and rang. Ash's heart beat faster with each second his call went unanswered, the phone slick upon a sweaty palm and the speaker hot against his ear. He took deep breaths, in and out, in and out.

"Good afternoon! Thank you for calling Crystal Springs Behavioral Health. How can I help you?"

In and out. In and out.

"I'm Ash," he said. "Are you accepting new patients?"

There were many things that Ash believed about life. Many things he couldn't see, and things he hoped he one day could.

Things he wanted.

Things he couldn't have.

Memories he held cradled in his hands like jewels.

Laughing with friends, dancing at shows, kissing cute girls.

A broken family, a found family, an uncertain future.

Wishing on stars, wandering through dreams, lying in the grass beneath a lavender sky.

His father was right. He was a shitty dad. There was no way to ask for a better one to be placed beneath the tree. No way to get his mother back, or the family that his dad had destroyed. No gifts to open that would grant him a better past.

The stars had seen fit to give Ash another gift.

Tayshia Marie Cole, the girl who danced by the light of the moon as often as she wept beneath it. Who bathed him with firelight and wrapped herself in ice. Who endured pain with the resilience of the sea. Who kissed him with the fury of starlight and the delicate caress of snow against the Earth. Tayshia, a star that burned in the dark.

But Ash's dad was wrong about one thing. There was life without magic. There was a reason to live without needing that reason to be another person. Ash didn't need an epiphany to heal. He didn't need to pretend that it would be easy. He just needed to take the first step. That was more powerful than any magic.

Eternity would not be cold.

EPILOGUE

December 2029

ONE

Ash's hands froze over the keyboard, one scarred and one unblemished. After running his hand backward through his blond hair, Ash pulled out his inhaler and shook it, lost in his thoughts as he took a puff from it and shook it for a second one.

How was he supposed to word this e-mail?

It had been so long since he spoke to her. The years stretched heavy and wide between them, time and memory pushing them far away from one another. Sending this e-mail would feel like reaching out to a stranger.

But who better to help him tell their story?

This seminar would be the highlight of his budding career. How could he present himself as an activist and advocate for eating disorder recovery if he couldn't manage to tell his own experiences without the very person who influenced them by his side?

Hosted by a prestigious activist group called Recovery Warriors, this yearly fundraiser weekend was one of the most highly sought-after seminars for recovery in the country. The fact that Ash had been accepted for a time slot was not only a huge accomplishment but overwhelming at a foundational level. And as much as he enjoyed his current job as prisoner's advocate for the new job center in Crystal Springs, this was his first opportunity to make a real difference.

He needed her for this.

She'd written a book about it two years ago, about their relationship and her struggles. About what happened to her in Paris, about the crystals in the wall, about the fire. She'd written about how she'd fallen in love with him. She'd told their story, and now she was a bestseller.

He'd read that book so many times he could quote lines from memory.

What if the reason why they hadn't spoken wasn't only his fault? What if she hadn't contacted him intentionally? What if she hated him?

A knock came at the door to his office.

"Come in," he said, setting his inhaler on the desk in front of him so he could adjust his tie.

The floor secretary stepped into the room, her red hair pulled back into a tight chignon at the base of her head. Her green eyes sparkled at him, as they always did.

"Mr. Robards? Officer Cook is here for lunch. Did you want me to send him up?"

"Oh, of course, Mary," Ash replied, glancing down at the paperwork he still had to do. He'd forgotten his old probation officer was coming by to catch up and congratulate him on landing the seminar spot. "Can you also reschedule my appointment with the coalition for tomorrow? I can't move it to later today—I've got another appointment after."

"Yes, sir."

Lunch with Officer Cook sped by, as it always did. The two of them had no shortage of things to reminisce about.

Once Ash's probation had completed, their families had spent time together. Ryo and Officer Cook could both win awards for the most hearty laugh in town.

The conversation turned toward Ash's dilemma soon enough, and Officer Cook was full of all sorts of advice. He stressed to him the importance of setting fear aside. He reminded him how afraid he'd been to call the therapist. The fear that had hindered him from getting help when he needed it. If he could overcome this fear, he stood the chance to help a *lot* of people. If e-mailing her was the one thing that stood between him and doing that, then he needed to push through and do it.

By the time the officer left, Ash was ready.

Tayshia,

I know it's been a while since you heard from me. I hope time has treated you kindly, and that things are going well for you. I've read Apricity, and I think your writing is phenomenal. The way you depicted your struggles and our relationship was stunning. You have a way with words that adorns the page in a way that's honest and raw.

I was wondering if you would be interested in attending a seminar with me in Seattle next weekend? I applied and was awarded a time slot to tell our story, and would be honored if you would be on stage with me. I was hoping you'd be open to talk about your book so we could tell our story together.

The seminar is hosted by an organization called Recovery Warriors, which advocates for eating disorder recovery in men and women. It's a seminar, fundraiser, and gala. The speaking event is on Friday at the convention center, and the fundraiser gala is held Saturday evening at the family estate of one of the organization's constituents. While the seminar itself is professional attire required, the gala is black tie.

If you're willing to attend with me, I will take care of transportation, a hotel room from Thursday night until Sunday morning, and your meals. There will be at least fifteen hundred attendees, so if that is an issue, then I will completely understand if you have to decline my invitation.

Hope to hear from you soon.

Ash

✸✸✸

Ash,

I would love to attend. Thank you for your compliments on my writing. I'm glad to know you approve of the way I told our story, even if I did have to change our names.

No need to worry about transportation. I live in Seattle. Tell me when to check-in and at which hotel, and I will be there. Don't pay for my food, either. I'll take care of myself on that, too.

I've attached my phone number below.

Tayshia

✸✸✸

Ash stepped out of the elevator, adjusting the hem of his sweater as he did so. The lobby was crowded with attendees who were staying at the hotel, headed on their way out to dinner or to shop. It was nearing five in the afternoon now, and she'd texted that her rideshare was almost there.

Tayshia would be in front of him in minutes.

Sweat prickled beneath his arms as a nervous flush rose up his body. He was thirty-one years old, but at that moment, he felt like he was right back in 2019, about to turn twenty-one and saying goodbye to the life he'd known. He worried that his clothes looked bad, that his slacks weren't crisp enough, or that his sweater looked too cheap. That his hair was too messy, or that the burn scars on his body would repel her.

At the buzzing of his cell phone, he withdrew it from his pocket.

I'm here. Help me with my suitcase?

Ash's heart dropped into the anxious depths of his stomach. He put his phone back in his pocket and headed through the mild crowd, towards the golden doors. Christmas trees and lights twinkled to guide his way, bringing a strange magic to the feelings he was experiencing.

What would he see in her eyes?

Tayshia's ride-share car had pulled up to the valet podium, where the uniformed boy watched her at the trunk with the driver. He assisted her with pulling out a large suitcase, setting it on the ground next to a smaller carry-on. Ash reached them right as the driver shut the lid.

When he saw her, his fluttering heart stopped.

Tayshia was beautiful, her brown skin glowing golden and her cheeks pink with a healthy flush. Her back was straight, her shoulders back and head held high. She carried herself with grace, like every step meant something to her. Like each breath she took felt cherished. He could see it there, sparkling in her eyes.

She had embraced life.

Clad in a baby pink tailored suit with black lining, she stepped up onto the pavement in a pair of pointed white heels. Her hair was worn in long, fluffy curls that fell to her waist, just like in their last days together.

His gaze dropped to her neck, empty of the crystal that had once adorned it. He'd brought his crystal, safely tucked in the front of his carry-on suitcase.

Had she brought hers?

"It's so nice to see you again, Ash," she said, stretching her arms up for an embrace. Even her voice was changed. Brighter, smoother. "You look great. Did you have a nice trip here?"

"You look fantastic, too. And yes, I did," he said, gathering his wits to mask his nerves. He wrapped one arm respectfully around her waist to return the hug, trying not to focus on the memory of her body in his arms drifting to the forefront of his mind. They pulled apart, and he offered her the same polite smile he'd given Elijah when he saw him for the first time, three years after college. "Did the drive from your apartment go well?"

"Eh, traffic in Seattle is always a nightmare. But I made it."

She waved a dismissive hand and went back to her suitcases. Ash jumped to follow her, reaching for her larger, heavier suitcase while she picked up her carry-on. As they headed inside and towards the elevator, he explained what floor her room was on, that she'd received two keys, and that check-out was eleven in the morning on Sunday. He also told her that the room was in his name, but that he'd given the front desk explicit instructions not to let any men up to see her without his permission. She gave him a warm look at that.

When he dropped her off at her hotel room, he didn't enter.

"Were you hungry at all?" he asked, voice hesitant. "I was gonna head to get something to eat."

"I actually ate before I left my place," she said as she dragged her suitcase inside. "So tonight, I'll probably just go out and get something. But tomorrow after the seminar, I'd love to go get some dinner and catch up."

"Sure," Ash said, offering her another smile. "Then I'll see you tomorrow morning in the lobby around eight. We go on at noon, so I was thinking we could go over everything together."

She crossed her arms over her chest and leaned against the doorframe. Tilting her head to the side, she studied him.

"You look so put-together," she said. "Like a man."

He slipped his hands into the pockets of his slacks. "And you look like a woman. Like you're doing really well."

"I am. I'm doing very well."

He gave her a soft smile. "I'm sincerely glad to hear it."

"But your e-mail was ridiculous, Ash."

"What?" His cheeks burned.

"You typed like you were e-mailing a teacher."

"What was I supposed to say after ten years? '*How the fuck are you?*'"

"Sure!" she said, causing him to laugh, too. "Anything. Just don't be so professional with me. It's *me*. Ten years later, or not."

"All right."

"Let's have fun this weekend. After all, it's a gala tomorrow and I spent a shit ton on my dress."

"And I spent a ton on my tux, so…Yeah. Let's have fun."

"You know what? I have something for you."

Ash waited at the door of the hotel room as she disappeared inside. The door clicked shut briefly, and then came open again. Tayshia held a shoe box out to him. It was faded and a bit beaten-up, but intact.

"This is for me?"

"Yep. Take it."

He did.

"It's from back then," she said, "when I first went to treatment. I wrote you letters that I never sent. I drew you things, made little crafts when we did art. And I feel like since I wrote a book about us and didn't contact you, this should make up for it."

"You make it sound like you had no intention of giving this to me."

"I didn't."

Their gazes locked, the seriousness of the moment settling into his psyche. These letters were important. The things inside this box were so important that he knew he needed to take care of them.

He would read them when the time was right.

"Thank you," he said.

"You're welcome." She put her hand on the back of the door. "See you tomorrow morning?"

"Yeah."

The door swung gently shut.

TWO

"That was phenomenal, Ash," Tayshia said as they stepped onto the elevator together. She smoothed her hands down the front of her grey-and-white pinstripe blazer. "I always knew you had a way with words."

"You were great too," he said, pressing the button for her floor. He also pressed the button for his. He felt on top of the world. He had more phone numbers of constituents than he'd ever thought he would get, invites to future seminars, and someone to work with on a website for himself. "The way you were able to paint a picture with your words…? I think it got through to a lot of people in the audience."

"Same goes for you." She nudged him. "The way you speak, it has a lot of passion. It's very motivational. It was like it was you, but also a completely different person than I remember."

"I think we're both different people than we used to be."

"I like it," she said.

Ding.

"I'll meet you in the lobby in an hour for dinner," she said, exiting the elevator.

He slammed his hand against the door to stop it from closing, grinning down at her.

"Dress nice," he said. "I wouldn't take you to anything less than a four star restaurant."

The doors slid shut to the sight of her lips curling up.

Later, when Ash was waiting in the lobby in a pair of slacks and a dark grey blazer, he heard the elevator open. Tayshia exited it wearing a pair of emerald green platform heels and a short cocktail slip dress made of beige satin. She was in the process of pulling on a forest green fur coat that looked quite expensive. She'd flat ironed her hair so that it hung pin-straight to her hips, and her legs were so much longer than he remembered, and they were as smooth as the dress she wore.

"Fuck," he muttered, the expletive escaping his lips before he could stop it.

"I hope that's a compliment," she said, the dark berry lipstick on her lips making her teeth appear whiter as she gave him a vicious grin.

"Of course it is," he said. "If there's one thing I'll never forget how to do, it's compliment you."

"As you should. Did you look at the weather? It might rain tonight."

"Did you want me to get you an umbrella somehow?"

"No, no. I'm used to the rain here. But I didn't know if you were."

"I'll be fine."

"Okay, Well, I'm starving. Are you ready to go?"

Ash turned, placing his hand on her lower back as he led her out the door. They waited for only a few moments before the rideshare he'd ordered pulled up. He held his hand out to help her step from the curb to the car, and he didn't let go until she was safely inside. Then, he jogged around to his side and buckled himself in.

The restaurant he'd chosen was just as decorated for Christmas as the hotel had been, with gold and silver and twinkling white lights strewn about in strategic places. Tayshia's eyes sparkled with awe as she gazed around at the decorations.

"I'll never stop loving Christmas," she said as they approached the front door. "It's just so beautiful, the different ways that everyone decorates."

Ash resisted the urge to tell her that she was beautiful, too.

Once seated beneath the low lighting of the establishment, he had a bottle of wine brought to their table, they ordered their food, and settled in to sip from their drinks. Around them, there were more Christmas decorations and lights. The holiday music that played over the speakers was quiet but audible above the din of other patrons and the scraping of forks against plates. Above their heads, a mistletoe dangled from each table's central light.

They ignored it.

Tayshia shrugged out of her fur coat, revealing that the straps of her slip dress were little more than strings. There were gardenias tattooed from her shoulder down to her elbow.

"*Wow*," he exclaimed, nearly choking on his wine. "You got more tattoos?"

"Yep," she said, glancing down at them and running her acrylic nails over the lines. "I went back to Diego, actually."

"*Really*? I haven't seen him in years. I had no idea."

"It was a few years back."

"He does such a good job at shading, doesn't he?" Ash's fingers tingled. He wanted to touch her arm, to reach across the table for her like he'd reached for her the night of the fire. "They look sick."

"Thanks." She took a sip of her wine and set it down. "So, catch me up. How's everyone doing?"

"Well, Andre and Ji Hyun just got engaged. Their wedding is next summer, so I'm pretty excited for that."

"What did they end up doing after they graduated from the pre-requisite program?"

"Andre owns his own construction company, building houses. Ji Hyun is a hairstylist. She works on photo shoots, mostly."

"And your godparents? How are Ryo and Steven?"

"They're great, actually. They're discussing adoption now, and they just went on vacation to Europe this last spring. One last hurrah, you know?"

She sipped her wine after a quick laugh. "My parents felt the same, apparently. They went to Africa on a mission trip, came back, and got pregnant. I have a little brother now."

"*What*? That's kind-of awesome. What's his name?"

"Daniel. He's four and yes, he is just as bratty as Shay." Her eyes found his again. "How is Elijah?"

"He's doing well," Ash said, his voice strong. "I talked to him sometime after college. He moved to Indiana a while ago with his wife. Have you kept in contact with him?"

"No, unfortunately. I kind-of…Well, I left my life behind in Crystal Springs that day." A faraway look crossed her face. "Kieran, Quinn, Elijah, any of my friends…You're the first person I've seen since then."

Ash nodded, her words sobering him. He understood the importance of severing contact with individuals who could hinder recovery. That meant she'd taken it seriously. She'd truly made an effort.

It seemed like she'd succeeded.

"What ever happened to Caden?" she asked. "Did you hear anything after the day they arrested him?"

"He went to prison. They got him on drug charges. He won't be out for a while longer. A couple more years."

"Will you leave Crystal Springs before then?"

He shrugged. "We'll see. I doubt he cares about me anymore. The drug charges came because his friends ratted him out to save themselves. I think he'll be more interested in them."

"What if your public speaking takes off? Where would you go if you had the choice?"

He cocked his head to the side, gazing thoughtfully up at the mistletoe. "Southern California. Maybe Texas. I'm not sure. Somewhere warm. I think I'd travel first."

"Same for me. I'm in Seattle for at least until the end of my lease. And then, I think I'll just get a coffee and leave."

"Get a coffee?"

"It's a very Seattle thing to do. It'd be nice to do it one last time before I go on an adventure."

"An adventure sounds nice."

"I almost wore my crystal tonight," she said suddenly. "I thought it would be nice for nostalgia's sake. But I decided against it."

"How come?"

"Reasons." Her smirk was coy, playful. "Did you bring yours?"

"Maybe."

It was in his hotel room.

"Fine. Keep your secrets, white boy."

He took a drink of his wine. "You keep yours, beautiful."

Oh.

Her eyes lingered on him, and then she spoke.

"So, you're a public speaker now?"

"Trying to be," he answered. "I've done a few events, today's being the biggest one. But no, right now I'm actually working with the city to advocate for prisoners. You know, to help them get jobs."

"That's amazing, Ash. Really."

"And you?"

"Full-time author," she said. "I—"

The waiter appeared with their plates. They dug in, expressing their delight at the flavors, before returning to their conversation.

"I've been working on a book series this past year. After *Apricity*, I took a break to tour for a year, did a couple of interviews, and worked with an artist for a special edition version."

He arched an eyebrow. "Did they make him look like me?"

"*No*," she said, rolling her eyes. "I thought you said you read the book?"

"I did. At least four times."

"Then you know what the characters look like."

"I know I do. And I know you know that having carnations tattooed on the back of his hands is *awfully* similar to—"

"Ash," she said with a gasp, her fork halfway to her mouth. Her eyes were on his left hand. "It scarred."

He glanced down at the mottled, misshapen scar that had warped his rose tattoo. "Yeah. Turns out that one and the burn on my arm were a little worse than they thought. My shoulder is fine, though."

"Can I…?"

He held his hand over the table, a shiver in his spine surprising him when her soft fingers brushed over the sensitive skin. She frowned, the downward tilt of her mouth twisting her pretty features.

"It doesn't bother me," he said, pulling his arm back and picking up his fork again. "It's just a fond reminder."

"Of what?"

"That I saved you."

The waiter appeared, unaware of the way Tayshia was looking at him. Even Ash couldn't name the emotion he saw in her eyes. She only tore her attention away from him when the waiter addressed her, and he took the opportunity to excuse himself to the restroom.

When he returned, Tayshia's good mood seemed to have settled into a more serious one. He sat down, noticing that the air had changed.

"Are you all right?" he asked as he pulled his chair in. "Is something wrong with the food?"

"No, no," she said, voice distant. She set her fork down and rested her wrists on the edge of the table, appearing troubled. "I think we should talk about what happened after."

"After?"

"After I went to treatment."

He set his fork down, too. "Okay."

"You deserve an explanation."

"An explanation."

"I didn't succeed my first time in treatment. I checked in in June of 2019, and I was there for six months. That's when I *'graduated.'* I thought I was better. I did really well until the next year. Got into Portland State. I even lived in the dorms. But that was the problem. The stress of classes, money management, and my struggle to make friends caused me to relapse. I started purging again to manage."

"Tayshia…"

"No, let me say this." Her gaze snapped to him, sharp and clear. "Please."

He closed his mouth.

"During the Fall finals week, I went to a house party with some of the girls from my floor in the dorms. I got drunk. *Really* drunk. And I don't know what happened, but…I binged on the things they had in their cupboards, until almost everything was gone. I purged it in the bathroom and someone caught me. They thought it was just me being drunk.

"He tried to pull me up, and I panicked. I felt so overwhelmed, and I didn't want him to touch me. I had a meltdown and I kicked him, punched him, scratched him. I was so belligerent that people thought I had alcohol poisoning. They called the ambulance. After that, I took winter term off and went back to treatment. And when I was there, I saw a psychologist twice a week."

"What did he say?" Ash asked.

"First, he diagnosed me with complex post-traumatic stress disorder—CPTSD. He also diagnosed me with Bipolar 1, rapid-cycling type. And then he put me on medication. Then, when I got out of treatment, he recommended I go to a center to get tested for Autism because of some of my behaviors."

"And…?"

Her eyes finally met his. "I was diagnosed Autistic. The trauma from being undiagnosed, from having manic episodes, from being raped…It was a really, really unfortunate cocktail. There's so many things I had to work through after finding out, especially managing the feeling of loss."

"I'm so sorry," Ash whispered. "I should have noticed that you were struggling, instead of making everything about your eating disorder."

"Don't be sorry. It manifests differently in women, so you couldn't have known," she explained. "That's why no one caught it when I was a kid. Autistic women grow up learning how to mask for survival. We make eye contact because we have to, and we have to ignore the intense anxiety it gives us. Like for me, I have a hard time with eye contact, but to mask it, I force myself to do it. When I do, I clench my teeth to the point of pain, and I squeeze my fingertips to manage the discomfort. Autistic women also have trouble keeping friends, with understanding societal expectations, with sensory issues. We struggle with things in school, but excel in specific things. We fixate and when trauma happens to us, we internalize it."

"So you internalized what happened in Paris," he said.

"Yes. And I used Bulimia to cope. I needed control because I am Autistic, and I didn't understand what had happened to me on a fundamental level. I didn't understand how to process my emotions about it. And with my Bipolar, I was cycling so fast from depressive episode to mania that I barely had a day of reprieve. It was overwhelming. How else was I supposed to deal with it without help? Purging was the only way that made sense. But in the process, I hurt you. I manipulated you. I took advantage of you. And-"

"Don't," he breathed, his gaze hot on her. Throwing aside decorum, he reached across the table for her hand. "Don't apologize again. You've said sorry for enough lifetimes."

Her eyes watered and she blinked as many times as it took to clear the tears from her vision.

"I'm sorry, Ash. I apologize for all the ways I failed you as a person, as a friend, and as a girlfriend. I loved you, and I treated you like you didn't matter. I'm so, so sorry."

"Stop. I forgave you years ago. I forgave you the second you told me you loved me."

They gazed at each other for a long moment before she slid her hand out of his grasp.

"I see a psychologist every week now. He specializes in Autism-related trauma and he's really quite wonderful. If it weren't for him, I think I'd still be sick. If it weren't for him, my book would never have been written. He helped me see that in order to finally recover, I didn't need to choose to stop. I needed to choose to live. I need to keep going, and I need to keep in mind that no matter who hurts me, I decide my worth. I get to decide whether or not I'm going to be toxic."

"But Tayshia," Ash cut in. "Here's the thing: a person can be toxic and still have worth. A person can have toxic traits, and still deserve to be alive."

"I know that now," she replied, the Christmas lights glittering in the rich browns of her irises.

"And nobody gets to decide you're worth, no matter your mistakes. Not even if you hurt or manipulate someone because you're not well. You were sick. You'd been through Hell. You deserve forgiveness, and you deserve to be alive."

Her lips twitched upward, the sadness bleeding away from her eyes as he studied her. He studied the ways she'd changed and the ways she hadn't, and he decided he was happier right now than he'd been in ten years.

It was raining in Seattle, but inside his head, the sun shone.

"Why don't we get going?" he said. "There was a nice fountain in the promenade back down the street."

"But it's raining."

"I thought you were used to it, Miss Seattle?" he retorted with a smirk.

"Oh, fine. I'll take the challenge."

"Even if your hair gets wet?"

"This weave is virgin, honey," she said, and then they both laughed.

After Ash paid, they set out into the rain. It wasn't too heavy, just a bit of a sprinkle. The worst it could do was irritate their eyelashes. They headed down the street in the cold, his hands tucked beneath his arms and her hands deep in her coat pockets. He didn't care how cold he was. He just wanted to spend more time with her. He wanted this night to go on as long as it could.

"There's the fountain," she said, pointing ahead of them. "Where all those people are."

In the center of a nicely-paved cobblestone promenade, he could see an elaborate fountain. The water was lit up red and green. Strewn between the trees that circled the area were Christmas lights. Holly and red velvet ribbons wrapped up the tall street lights that provided them light. There were quite a few people gathered–families taking photographs, couples walking down the path that led away from the fountain, and an old man sitting on a bench beneath an umbrella.

"It's pretty," Tayshia said over the noise of the fountain water. "I'm glad we walked back."

"This is the most normal night I think we've ever had together. I thought it would be the cherry."

"It is."

They stood in silence for a little while longer, enjoying the lights. he couldn't help the fact that his heart was racing. He hadn't felt this way in years. He'd been on dates, he'd had a girlfriend once or twice in the past ten years, but never had he felt the way he felt around her. It was like she'd turned on the stars for him. Like she'd hung the moon in the sky and told him it was okay to wake up in the middle of the night.

Did she feel the same?

"I wonder where we'd be," she said.

"What do you mean?" Neither of them took their eyes off of the fountain and its glowing, bubbling water.

"If I hadn't been sick. If the ice cream shop had never happened. Would we still have been assigned to the same apartment for the program?"

"Maybe," he said. "I think it would have been interesting."

"I think it would have been very special."

"You think so?"

"I do. I think we would have fought until we opened our eyes and saw each other. I think we would still have fallen in love."

"That's pretty confident of you."

"I know how I felt about you." Tayshia turned her body to face him. "I remember how you made me feel."

"How did..." He swallowed, his gaze dropping momentarily to the dark lipstick on her full lips. "How did I make you feel?"

"Alive. When I wanted to be dead."

As they gazed at one another, Ash realized that there was nothing in their way. The space he thought had stretched between them? It didn't exist. They were connected, just as much as they ever were, and the way she made him feel was no different from when they were twenty-one.

There were no barriers.

Tayshia broke the spell, turning her face back to the fountain.

"You know what I've learned, Ash?"

"What have you learned?"

"Recovery is not a place. It's a journey. It's a path that you choose to walk on. Sometimes, you might stray from it, or stop to take a break. But as long as you get back on the path–as long as you keep moving forward–you'll always be healing. If you're healing, it means you're alive. And that's the goal, isn't it?"

"To heal?"

"To live."

If they didn't leave right now, he was going to kiss her.

"Are you ready to head back to the hotel?" he asked, trying not to grit his teeth.

"Yes. You don't have a coat."

He called them a car, and then they left the magic of that fountain behind.

☼☼☼

The promenade, lit up like Christmas.

The Eiffel Tower in the distance, bright as a beacon.

The streets, full of people milling back and forth with their friends and family.

Cars zooming up and down the street.

Someone playing the violin on the corner.

A blue hotel.

Paris.

Ash stood on the sidewalk across the street, staring at the hotel rearing up ahead of him. There was a sick, sinking feeling in his abdomen. Was this a return to the nightmare?

Where was she?

"Hi."

He turned to look behind him, his heart leaping in his chest.

Tayshia walked toward him, her appearance exactly the same as it was in the outside world–a sign that she truly liked who she was. The Parisian air kissed her with a breeze, lifting her curls from her shoulders so that they trailed behind her. She wore a long red dress that draped off of her shoulders in layers of gauze, and her crystal sparkled around her neck. There was an effortlessness to her beauty that arrested him.

"You put it back on, I see," she said as she came to a stop beside him. "Your necklace."

"So did you."

"Maybe I had something I wanted to say."

"This is your memory," he said, his voice shaking with concern and fear.

"No. This is my dream."

He watched as she placed her hands behind her back and peered up at the lit-up windows. He followed her line of sight, wondering which window she was gazing upon. Right as he did, she pointed up to one specific one.

"One day," she said, "I want to stay in that room."

"In your dreams?"

She shook her head. "Remember when I said I'd get a coffee, leave Seattle, and go on an adventure? My first stop would be Paris. I'd ask to rent the same room that Kieran and I did. And then I'd turn the trip into something beautiful."

They stared up at the window in thoughtful silence. Ash knew that the hotel and the room symbolized the aftermath to her, but the notion that she wanted to go back was a sign of how far she'd come. How hard she'd worked *these past ten years to recover. She had every right to go back to Paris. She had every right to erase the bad memory and make a new, better one. To turn the trip into something beautiful.*

"Let's go inside," she said.

He followed her.

When they got to the room, the doorknob opened without the need for a key card. They stepped inside, surrounded by the decor and the memory.

Tayshia walked over to the window, placing her palms flat against it.

"I spent a long time having nightmares about this place," she said softly. "It tormented me for a long time. For years. Even after the nightmare with you shattered, it came back sometimes. I'd fall asleep and open my eyes to a black sky and an empty city. I'd scrub myself until there was blood in the water. Then, I'd wake up in the real world and cry."

"When was the last time you dreamed of Paris?"

"I can't remember the last time I dreamed of Paris," she went on, "but tonight, I chose to come here because I hoped you'd show up."

"Well, I'm here."

"Yes. You are."

He came to join her at the window. They gazed at the Eiffel Tower, its hundreds of lights twinkling.

"We never did figure out how we could do this," he said. "How we could dreamwalk. The legend of the crystals."

"I think I'm okay with that," she replied. "Not every question has to have an answer. Sometimes, beautiful things happen because they're meant to."

"And what about our feelings for one another?" *At the sharp snap of her gaze toward him, he was quick to amend his verbiage.* "The feelings that we had back then."

"Sometimes beautiful things happen because they're meant to."

When she gazed out the window again, he was still looking at her, just like earlier that night at the fountain. Once again, there were no barriers between them. No illness. No toxicity. No depression. No trauma. This was a dream and what happened here, stayed here.

He could kiss her if he wanted to.

"Remember what you said that night about where you'd be?" *she whispered, hands still flat to the glass of the window. He could see her reflection.* "How you told me that you'd always watch over me?"

"Yes."

"I'm recovering for myself. Not for you, not for my parents, not for my sisters. I chose myself for once and it was — well, it was everything. But I never stopped looking up. And you know what?"

"What?" he breathed as she turned to face him

"These crystals never mattered. You were always it for me, Ash Robards. I hope you realize that." She placed one hand against his cheek, her thumb stroking along his cheekbone. As he gazed upon her, he could see that she was fading from the dream. That it was ending, and they were going to wake up. "I chose you that night in the cave, when you gave me my half of the crystal. I realized it on my birthday, when you held me while I cried. I fought it the night of the party, when you told me to look at you. And I accepted it when I woke up in the hospital and realized that I hadn't died."

A tear slipped down his cheek. She was see-through, pieces of her disappearing as the dream darkened around them.

"You'll always be my first love."

He started to reply, to tell her the way he felt, but she was gone.

Ash woke in a cold sweat, tossing his blankets aside and gulping down cool air. The hotel room was dark and the clock said it was seven-thirty in the morning. The sun had yet to rise. The fundraiser didn't start until seven that evening, so he didn't need to be awake right now. He could go back to sleep.

After the sweat had cooled on his skin, he laid down and pulled the covers back over his body. But no matter how hard he tried, the weight of the crystal around his neck kept pulling him back from the brink.

He couldn't stop thinking about the dream, about the things that Tayshia had said to him. What had she meant? Was she saying goodbye? Or was she trying to tell him that she still loved him?

Did he still love her?

Confusion and fear swirled together in his mind. The thought of a healthy life with Tayshia, a loving relationship coming to fruition while they traveled to Paris to find something beautiful? It made his heart race.

Ash's head rolled to the side, where he could see the shoe box she'd given him on the table beneath the hotel room window. Maybe if he opened it and looked at what was inside, he'd get some answers. Maybe then he'd come to the right conclusion.

Sitting down at the table facing the window, he pulled off the lid of the box, revealing the contents inside to the bright moonlight. The first things he saw were a porcelain bowl that she'd painted, a small wooden box upon which she'd glued seashells in intricate designs, and a beaded bracelet that used tiger's eye stones. He pulled the bowl out to admire it, then toyed with the box. After putting the bracelet on, he looked inside again.

There were the letters.

Ash withdrew them, counting there to be ten of them. Remembering how emotionally draining it had been to read his father's letters ten years ago, he felt hesitant about reading hers now. It had taken him weeks to open them all. There were a few times where he had to do it in front of his therapist just to be sure he wasn't going to completely break down and hurt himself in some way.

Did he want to put himself through that again?

These letters were not from the dead. They were from the living. A living, breathing piece of his past that he'd loved once. They were written by the Tayshia that he knew, given to him by the Tayshia he wished he could get to know.

Ash held it together for the first nine letters, but it was the tenth and final letter that gutted him. It was stained with her tears, with smeared ink and a rip at the top that showed she'd come close to ripping it in half. Holding it felt like holding the heart of the girl he'd loved in his hands.

Ash,

*I think I finally understand. I finally understand that this is going to be with me forever. It's going to be like a shadow attached to my back, following me around until the end of my life. But it doesn't have to haunt me. I may have an eating disorder, but I'm not sick. I'm **not** sick.*

Paris will always be with me, and I won't let it decide how my future goes. I have an eating disorder. I hurt people in my life. I was toxic. I was a person who made the wrong choices. But that doesn't mean I deserve to die. I can get better. I can do it. I will do this. For me.

Thank you for being my starlight. When you were shining, it wasn't so dark.

Love,

Tayshia

As the sun rose, he lifted a tear-stained face to greet the light.

THREE

The ballroom was a blur of sparkling dresses and black tuxedos. Everyone was dressed to the nines. Everyone was dancing. The room was completely bedecked from floor to ceiling with Christmas lights, the grand crystal chandeliers above the room the only other source of light. On the stage at the head of the room, flanked by two sets of grand staircases, was a small orchestra. The music they played was soothing and pleasant.

To the left of where he stood waiting for Tayshia to appear, Ash could see extravagant doors leading out to a balcony. The moonlight shone down upon it, sending a blue hue to battle the glow of lights.

He glanced at the clock on his watch. She should be here any moment. He reached up to make sure his hair was brushed back the way he'd styled it to be, then adjusted his black bowtie. His tuxedo was crisp and smooth, his shoes shiny and free of scuffs. This was the best he could do, as he'd never been to a black-tie event before. And judging by the expensive way everyone else was dressed, he'd hit the nail on the head.

Ash looked at his watch again, seeing a text pop up on the screen.

I'm here. Just put my coat in the coatroom. Headed for the stairs.

Ash turned and hurried out of the ballroom, into the massive entryway. His shoes snapped against the marble floor as he headed down the hall, toward the large open double doors at the end. The grand staircase, which was also made of marble and had banisters lined with holly and lights, stretched down for nearly thirty steps to the wall of a hallway that turned left. There was a small group of men in black tuxedos heading right toward him. He stepped aside for them and looked down.

There she was.

There she fucking *was*.

Tayshia wore a floor-length black gown that sparkled like stars had been scattered all over the chiffon. It trailed gently behind her as she ascended the steps, a long slit running up the front and coming to a stop at the lower half of her thigh. The neckline of the dress plunged to her sternum and the thin straps hugged her shoulders as though they were happy to hold the dress up on her body. Her tattoos stood out, almost stark against her brown skin, revealed in all its glory by her curly hair as it trailed down her back. A pair of silver stiletto heels graced her feet. They matched the silver earrings dangling from her earlobes.

She wore her crystal.

Ash descended the steps to meet her, his eyes wide and his throat dry. He was in absolute awe of how beautiful she looked. He'd never seen anyone or anything that shone brighter.

"You look absolutely gorgeous," he breathed, holding his hand out to her.

"Thank you," she said, giving him a small smile. She placed her fingers atop his palm so he could assist her the rest of the way up. "You look gorgeous, yourself. I don't think I've ever seen your hair pushed back."

"Hopefully it's a good look."

"Yes. Very."

They exchanged glances when they got to the landing, and then he reluctantly pulled his hand back.

Ash took her on a few turns about the ballroom, stopping occasionally to talk with people he knew from Recovery Warriors. He wasn't surprised to see Tayshia having a bit of trouble with eye contact and conversation, but he couldn't be bothered to care when his hand was dancing over her lower back.

It was difficult to be near her after reading her letters this morning. They'd taken him right back to the past, dropping him into the version of himself that would have died for her. Being with her here, now, he couldn't say he felt any different. He wanted to hold her hand.

After a conversation with the person who owned the estate house they were currently in, he noticed that she was looking toward the crowded dance floor. There was a curious, almost longing look on her face. With a slight curve to his lips, he lowered his head to her ear.

"Would you like to dance?"

She smiled. "Have you gotten any better at it?"

Memories of their last night together, when they'd danced in the garden, pushed to the front of his mind. As bittersweet as they were, he couldn't help but laugh.

"A little," he said, and he held his hand out to her again, palm facing up. "Why don't you let me show you?"

"I won't get my hopes up."

He pulled her out to the dancefloor, weaving a path through the spinning couples until they found a space. He twisted her around until her body was flush against his. He started to dance, her naturally following his lead as he swayed.

"I'm surprised," she remarked. "You're markedly better than you were that night."

"It's been ten years, Tayshia," he said through a smirk. "I found time to go ballroom dancing a few times over the course of a decade."

Her eyes glittered like her dress. "With girls, no doubt."

"Jealous?" he countered as he twirled her around and around the marble floor.

"Maybe. Do I have the right?"

"Yes. You have every right."

He dipped her, his gaze fixed upon her face. When he pulled her back up, she was panting for breath. Her eyes flitted up and down his face, a surprised expression furrowing her brow. But before she could say anything, he was spinning her again.

The song changed to a slow one, and so Ash adjusted his movements. They swayed back and forth, his hand pressed flat against her back and his other hand wrapped securely around hers. He held her as close as he dared, savoring the feeling of her laying her head against his chest. It was so hard to be this close to her when he could feel every curve on her body and remembered what they felt like beneath his touch. When he could remember what it felt like to kiss her, to taste her, to be one with her.

Fuck.

He hadn't realized how desperately he missed her.

"I think I need a break," she said.

"Okay. Did you want to go out to the entryway?"

She pulled away from him, glancing around. "Why don't we go out on the balcony? There's no one out there."

The balcony overlooked the back of the estate, giving them an unobstructed view of the sprawling grass-covered lawn, a hedge maze in the distance, and a man-made pond with swans floating in the rippling water. There were more lights wrapped around the balcony, and when they walked up to it and placed their hands on the stone, the lights gave off a certain measure of comforting warmth.

"Are you wearing your necklace, too?" Tayshia asked, leaning over the balustrade with her forearms folded atop it. The leg that peeked through the slit of her dress bent to accommodate the lowering of her upper body.

Ash reached beneath the collar of his shirt, dragging the crystal out so it laid on the fabric, visible beneath his bowtie. "I am."

"How come?"

"For nostalgia's sake."

He mirrored her pose, leaning on the balustrade and bending his knee. They gazed out at the estate, the silence stretching between them. It was cold outside, the December night air seeming to bite against their faces as it warred with the heat coming from the crowded, loud ballroom.

"I read your letters," he said after a while.

"Oh, really?"

"Yes. Thank you for the crafts you made for me, too."

She waved one hand before returning her forearm to the stone. "It was just a bowl I painted and a box I decorated."

"And the bracelet." He tapped one cufflink. "I'm wearing it, but it's hidden."

"Is that so?" Her eyes lit up as she glanced at him. "I'm glad you like them. You're welcome." She paused. "You read the letters."

"Yes, I did. And I'm incredibly proud of you. Not just for the realization you came to the day you wrote that letter, but for the work you've put in to become who you are now."

"I'm proud of you, too, Ash. I can see it in your eyes—you're different now. You're more sure of yourself. You look healthy and happy. You look like your life is complete."

It's not complete, he wanted to say. *It feels like there's one piece missing.*

"I think we've both worked so hard to get to this place," she continued, looking out at the estate again. "We should both be proud."

His heart slammed against the wall of his chest. The memories raced past his mind's eye, battling him for control. Reminding him how special she was. How precious. How beautiful, how ferocious, how unique. The memories of the person she used to be. The possibility of learning about who she was now.

And she was going to leave this seminar tomorrow, say goodbye to him, and he'd never see her again. The love of his life would walk away from him, without barriers, without walls. Nothing stood between them. Absolutely nothing.

Unless he let it.

He stood up straight and faced her, one hand on the stone in front of him.

"Tayshia?"

She gazed up at him, still leaning over the balustrade. When he looked into her eyes once again, he could see a spark there that wasn't there before. It was like magic.

He was looking at the girl who'd decided to fight.

Ash cupped her face and lowered his lips to hers, kissing her for the first time in ten years.

Suddenly, it felt as if all of the electricity in the estate had soared into them, creating a magnetic force that willed them together. The pressure of her lips against his increased as she kissed him back. He moved his hands from her face to the side of her neck and into the depths of her hair. Prying her lips apart with his tongue, he elicited a small sigh from her mouth. She wrapped her arms around his neck and held herself close to him, tilting her head to the side.

This was like a dream.

He kissed her with the pent-up fervor that he hadn't realized he'd possessed for her all these years. The longer they kissed, the more she allowed herself to fall into him, completely molding her body to his. The sweeping of his tongue through her mouth grew deeper and longer, hers sliding to meet his with just as much hunger as he felt. He wasn't thinking straight. His skin was on fire, and he never wanted it to stop.

Tayshia's hands found his chest and pushed him back. She stepped away. There was something empty in her eyes–something guarded. The closing of a chapter. The drawing of a set of curtains.

"Thank you for a lovely night. For this weekend. For everything, Ash. I'll always love you."

"Wait, Tayshia–"

She left the balcony.

"*Tayshia!*"

As he watched her walk away for the second time in his life, Ash finally understood the key to helping someone in recovery.

It was accepting what he couldn't change, and knowing when to step back.

If she didn't want to eat, it was holding her hand to support her.

If she cried out in her sleep, it was being there to hold her until she drifted off again.

If she flashed back to the darkness, back to that dark, shattered nightmare, it was standing beside her with a light while she bled.

No longer would he rip her petals off. He would prepare the soil to ground her and bring her peace. He would water her roots so she could hold fast to an Earth that accepted her. He would melt the snow with the sunlight of his heart, so she would bloom in the cold. He would love her, like she once loved him.

She was it for him.

Ash turned away from the balcony, leaving that starlit night behind, and chased her. His scarred lungs burned, begging him to slow down. He ignored it. They were scars that he would gladly carry.

There were a lot of things he would carry for her.

Pushing past the crowd, ignoring anyone who called his name, he made his way out of the ballroom. He ran down the hallway, seeing her disappearing through the double doors and rounding the corner. He didn't have time to call her name.

He ran faster.

Tayshia descended the stairs, her curls bouncing down the length of her back with every click of her heels against the marble. He could hear her soft sobs echoing, could hear the faint sounds of the symphony having followed him, could hear his own heart beating.

"Tayshia!" he called as he ran down the steps. "Tayshia!"

She kept going, ignoring him as she neared the last five steps.

"*Tayshia Marie Cole!* Stop walking away from me!"

She stopped, her back still to him.

"You have *always* been it for me," he said. "You're the only star in the sky that I want to gaze at. I would never forgive myself if I let you walk out of here looking like a fucking angel without telling you that I'm still in love you."

Slowly, Tayshia turned around with wide eyes. Tears were falling down her face, dripping off of her jaw, streaking through her make-up. Ash was crying, too, unable to stop his eyes from welling up and overflowing. His heart ached and for once, it felt good.

"What did you just say?"

"I'm still in love with you, Tayshia. I'll say it as many times as you need me to. I love you. I fucking love you, and I want to get to know you. I want to hold you, and I want to learn what makes you happy. I want to kiss you, and I want to go on an adventure with you. And I was wondering…"

He cracked a grin, moving down the stairs until he was on the same step as her. Another tear slipped down her cheek, and he brushed it away. His chest heaved for air and sweat beaded on his brow. None of it mattered.

Nothing mattered but her.

"Would you like to get a cup of coffee with me?"

When she smiled, it reached her eyes.

"One day, I think you could make me really happy."
"Oh, yeah?"
"Yeah. And not just because of what you make me feel. Because of who you are."

                        "You know I'm going to marry you, right?"
                        "Hm. Tayshia Robards. I don't know if I like it."
                                "I kinda do. Has a nice ring to it."
                              "Nah. Doesn't roll off the tongue."

"What if I put it to you like this…"
"Like what? Ash? Why are you getting on the ground?"
"Say it again. I think you'll find it rolls off the tongue just right."

                                                              "Yes."
                    "What? No, Tayshia. You have to say the name."
                                       "Don't tell me what to do."
           "I'm trying to propose to you, woman. We are literally in Paris."
                          "Shut up and put the ring on my damn finger."

And now, an exclusive excerpt
from Book One in the *Trapped* trilogy:

Jade towered over Naima as they walked across campus. She glanced up at him, craning her neck.

"I always forget how tall you are."

"Sometimes, so do I," he said with a laugh. "How was your weekend?"

"Probably not as fun as yours. You're the one who got drunk as Hell."

"Sure did. And it wasn't just wine. I went back to Amari's and he had Hennessy. So, you *know* we got ripped."

"Shit, I'm just glad you had a good birthday." She adjusted the strap of her bag on her shoulder. "I wish I could have gone with you. It looked like you guys had a lot of fun."

"Yeah," he said, and his voice sounded soft. "Me, too."

Callan didn't look at her like that anymore.

Jade held the door to the building open for her, and she walked underneath his arm to get outside into the heat. The tops of her curls shifted as they brushed his bare arm.

"That outfit is cute," he said from behind her. "So is your make-up. You look like a doll."

Naima stopped to look up at him. Callan never complimented her in a way that felt genuine, so when Jade did, she never knew how to respond to it. She'd spent two hours on her make-up at Callan's that morning so she wouldn't be late for her bus after he brought her home, and his response was that it looked like too much.

"What?" Jade said. "Why are you looking at me like that?"

"Nothing! I just was—Oh, whatever. Just shut up."

"Shut up? I complimented you."

It was just a compliment. It was *literally* just a compliment, so why was she making a fool out of herself by rejecting it?

And it wasn't like she could thank him now. What if he thought she was conceited? Or worse, what if he was lying and by her accepting it, she was playing into the joke?

I need to change the subject immediately, she thought, terror spreading like wildfire in her chest.

As they crossed the courtyard, she inspected the tattoos on his left arm. A few birds on his bicep, a clock on his forearm, and a snake jumped out at her. There were so many other tattoos interwoven throughout the designs that she couldn't tell what the rest were without significant searching.

"What exactly are your tattoos of?"

"A lot of classic shit," he said. "Birds, flowers, stars, whatever. I just got the smoke filler done a few weeks back. My dad despises them, but my mom thinks they're unique."

She watched as he held both arms out. It looked like hours and hours of intricate work.

"And you don't want any color added?"

"Nah," he said. "I like the black and grey. It's more me. You got any tattoos? Well, besides the roses on your shoulder."

"No, but I want some more. And I do wanna get the shading done eventually."

"Shit," he said, grinning. "Let's go get you one, then. You busy tonight?"

"A tattoo? Tonight?"

"Hell yeah. Let's go do it. It'll be fun."

There were so many things that could go wrong with that situation and they had nothing to do with a tattoo.

"But it costs money," she said, and that was at least true. "Money I really don't have. And I have no idea what I'd get."

"I'll pay for it."

"*What*? No, Jaden. That's ridiculous. Plus, Callan put this app—"

"*Callan?*" He pulled a face and stopped walking. They were

nearing the parking lot. "Who the fuck cares what he thinks? Let's just fucking do it. You think I thought any of these through? When I want ink, I go get it."

She let out an incredulous laugh. "You want me to just...*Go* get a tattoo. Just like that."

"Just like that. Fuck my brother. It's your body, and if you want to do something with it, you can."

Bzzt. Bzzt. Bzzt.

Her phone buzzed in her purse, the vibration rattling against her house keys. It was Callan, to her surprise. She answered it.

"Hey," she said. "I thought you had a meeting?"

"No," he said in a strained tone, the sounds of his car zooming down the road in the background. "Tell Jade not to drive you home. I'm coming to get you."

"Why?"

"Just do what the fuck I say. Tell him to go home."

Click. He hung up.

Her hands shook as she lowered her phone. She tried to force a smile on, to pretend the sky wasn't crashing down around her.

"He said he's gonna come get me."

"Oh, okay. Well...Did you want me to wait with you? I ain't got no place to be. It's my day off."

"No," she said, her voice quivering in her trepidation. She ensured that her smile was plastered on firm and tight. "I'm good. I'll just go into the library. I'm gonna start drafting that essay that Miss Frierson assigned us."

"All right," he said, starting to walk backwards. "But I'm rain checking you on that tattoo, yeah?"

🎵🎵🎵

Callan arrived twenty minutes after Jade left.

Outside, was the only text he gave, and it tumbled rocks in the pit of her stomach. One-word text messages from Callan were never indicators of anything pleasant.

Packing up her study materials, she rushed out of the library. She could see him by the curb, wearing a suit and tie to prove he'd just come from work. Climbing into his car, she hoped her smile was disarming enough to eradicate whatever darkness he felt towards her. She planted a kiss on his cheek for good measure.

Buckling her seatbelt, she pulled the seat forward. She never understood why every time she got into the car, it was pushed back.

"Hey, you," she said. "I thought you had a meeting? Did your dad cancel it?"

"He did not," he said, both hands on the wheel as he drove them away from the community college. "Have a good day?"

"I mean, it was just like any other school day. So, why didn't you go to the meeting?"

"Why are you asking? Did I get in the way of something you planned?"

Okay.

He was angry. And he was accusing her of something.

What was it that she'd done *this* time? For the life of her, she was trying to figure it out, but there was nothing within her memories to indicate that she had slipped up.

"And of course, you're dressed like a whore again," she went on. "Why am I not surprised?"

She flinched against the verbal slap.

Glancing down at her skirt and top, at the outfit that Jade had called cute, she tried not to frown. She was glad she hadn't accepted the compliment or thanked him, because now she was worried that he'd been playing a joke on her.

Of course, that didn't *sound* like Jade, but she didn't know what to believe anymore.

"Why the fuck do you insist on wearing those tops, Naima? I've told you time and time again that they're ridiculous. They make you look easy—like you're going to the club, or whatever it is that you people do. Can *none* of you put some *fucking* clothing on? Can *none* of you put on a piece of fabric that isn't longer than six inches? Life is not a fucking rap video."

As always, she hid her anger and fear behind a layer of silence. Whenever he went on these racist, hateful tirades, there was nothing she could do. If she so much as put a toe out of line, he'd beat her. It was that simple.

Pain was all it took for him to gain complete control.

Callan continued to rant at her for the next fifteen minutes, leaving no opening for her to get a single word in. Even as he got onto the freeway to Portland, she couldn't stop him to tell him she wanted to go home. She was forced to sit there while he lashed her with insults until her mind warped.

She closed her eyes against tears that threatened to spill over and finally, when she could take no more, she cut into his tirade.

"I'm not a slut, Callan! Stop talking to me like that! I'm your *girlfriend*!"

His right hand whipped out and slammed into the left side of her chin. Her lower lip stung and throbbed as it cut itself against her teeth. She tasted metal. A whimper escaped her as the pain reverberated from her jawline to her temple.

"Don't interrupt me!" he roared. "Are you fucking dumb? Have you *lost* your *mind*? *Interrupting me*?! You're lucky I don't pull over on the side of the road right now just to beat your ass, Naima. You're fucking lucky. The fact that you think you can just talk back to me like that...?" He shook his head, and she could hear the disgust in his voice. "It's like you don't even respect me. It's like you don't *value* any of the things I've done for you."

Her lip was numb.

"You know, I was actually considering proposing to you. For fuck's sake. Me. Proposing to a girl who can't even wear a regular shirt and jeans. A whore who stays up until *four-fucking-a.m.* on a messaging app *right beside me in my fucking bed!*"

She sensed his anger was swelling, getting hotter. Her panic warred against it.

Marriage?

To *him*?

As they entered the darkness of the tunnel halfway between Beaverton and Portland, her imagination hurtled through time and space, exploding with images of a future as Mrs. Callan Adams. A future filled with fists, tears, yelling, and rules. A future that existed in a cage with chains and misery. Where she'd be beaten into complete submission, to be controlled and stomped into the dirt until nothing remained of her. Where he'd burn her alive, wet the ashes with blood, and mold her into the perfect wife.

She burst out into tears.

"Oh, what the fuck! Now you're going to *cry*? Just shut up, or I'll give you something to cry about. Is that what you want? Something to cry about? You fucking whore. Who were you messaging? Huh? On Friday, who was it you were messaging all night?"

How did he know? He was *asleep*. Naima remembered ensuring that she logged out of the app. Callan hadn't said anything about it all weekend.

How did he *know*?

"I wasn't messaging anyone!" she cried, a lie seeming like the only way to get through this ordeal. She didn't have the mental capacity for anything else. "I literally wasn't!"

His fiery gaze snapped back and forth between her and the road. He looked like he wanted to murder her. He looked like he wanted her to be dying, to die, and then be dead.

"You absolute bitch. You're gonna sit there and lie to me?"

"Callan, I'm *not* lying."

He scoffed, let out an incredulous laugh, and Naima knew she was fucked.

"When I checked SafeWatch," he said slowly, his voice suddenly calm, "it showed me that you were on Exxchat from Friday night until Saturday morning at four. That was, coincidentally, when you were lying in *my* bed next to *me*."

"It was my friends!"

"Nope—*no*—I know your little girlfriends weren't up all night, messaging you that late. The only reason why people go on there all night like that is when they're talking to someone from a dating site, or something equally bullshit." His voice rose in volume again. "So, who the *fuck* were you talking to?"

It clicked in her mind, like the gears of an old clock.

"You added a *parenting app* to my cell phone?!" she shrieked, tears still dripping down her cheeks. "Callan, what the *fuck*?! I'm not your kid! I'm not your fucking daughter! I'm your *girlfriend*! You can't—"

The car swerved to the right on the road. Thankfully, they were already off the freeway. However, to her dismay, they were on a side road near the Providence Park Max station. She could see people walking down the main road, but no one was on the small block they were currently in.

He wielded his fist like a hammer and beat her.

When it was over, when she was done screaming and pleading, it was only because he'd run out of energy. He was red in the face and he'd said, "*I should kill you,*" more times than she could count. She sobbed loudly into the quiet of the car, the only other sounds being that of his heavy, panting breaths.

Inside her heart, she knew.

This was it. This was her limit. She had reached her breaking point. Like pulling out the last block in a teetering Jenga tower, she had crumbled. There was nothing left of her except for one tiny kernel of strength. The one kernel she needed.

To leave.

"On God," she said between sobs, shaking her head. Her hand unbuckled her seatbelt, fingers trembling. "On God, Callan. We are *through*."

Grabbing her bag from the floor by her feet, she opened the car door. She practically fell out onto the sidewalk, her body still wracked with emotion and aching with fresh, budding bruises.

The car sped off before she had even gotten to her feet.

COMING 2022

Subscribe for updates:
www.starlightwriting.com/subscribe

LOVED THE BOOK?

If you enjoyed this novel, if it spoke to you on an emotional level, or if you feel compelled to tell me your thoughts, please don't hesitate to leave me a review when you've completed it. I want to hear your opinions and most of all: I want to hear your stories. Every review means the world to me. I read each and every single one that I get.

To leave a review, you need only go to your Amazon orders, scroll to the purchase of this book, and click: *Write a Product Review.*

Alternatively, you can review on Goodreads.

www.goodreads.com/author/show/20655146.Mariah_L_Stevens

Thank you so much!

Mariah L. Stevens is a half-Black Autistic author and artist who lives in the PNW. She is a survivor of eating disorders, abuse, and sexual assault. She advocates for recovery and a life worth living. Also diagnosed with Bipolar 1 and CPTSD, she supports mental health awareness, as well as eating disorder awareness in Black individuals, and weaves all of these elements into her work with the sole purpose of helping others seek recovery.

Mariah has been writing since she was 13 years old, and she plans to use her passion and life experience to help other survivors through the power of prose. She loves Japanese fashion, *Kingdom Hearts*, Disneyland, and her cat.

Website: **www.starlightwriting.com**
Tiktok**: @theapricityseries**
Instagram: **@starlight.writing**

Amelia Louise Carter (Meialoue) is a full time graphic designer and freelance illustrator from the UK. She's massively inspired by manga and anime, but also has a unique style all of her own. Completely self-taught, she's incredibly passionate about creating artwork and strives to be better one step at a time, every day.

"If you can't see the end of the tunnel right now, or you feel like everything is just hopeless, please don't give up. Get help, keep going, because if you keep trying and fight for your dreams, whether they're small or large I promise you, if you fight, you'll accomplish them."
☼☼☼ Meialoue, ever the imperfectionist.

Website: **www.meialoue.com**
Tiktok: **@meialoue**
Instagram: **@meialoue**
Etsy: **www.etsy.com/uk/shop/Meialoue**

Milton Keynes UK
Ingram Content Group UK Ltd.
UKHW040819161123
432684UK00004B/311